Quintin Jardine was born once upon a time in the West – of Scotland rather than America, but still he grew to manhood as a massive Sergio Leone fan. On the way there he was educated, against his will, in Glasgow, where he ditched a token attempt to study law for more interesting careers in journalism, government propaganda and political spin-doctoring. After a close call with the Brighton Bomb in 1984, he moved into the even riskier world of media relations consultancy, before realising that all along he had been training to become a crime writer. Now, more than forty novels later, he never looks back.

Along the way he has created/acquired an extended family in Scotland and Spain. Everything he does is for them. He can be tracked down through his website: www.quintinjardine.com.

Praise for Quintin Jardine:

'Well constructed, fast-paced, Jardine's narrative has many an ingenious twist and turn' *Observer*

'A triumph. I am first in the queue for the next one' *Scotland on Sunday*

'The perfect mix for a highly charged, fast-moving crime thriller' *Herald*

'Remarkably assured, raw-boned, a *tour de force*' *New York Times*

'"Revenge is a dish best eaten cold," as the old proverb goes. Jardine's dish is chilled to perfection with just the right touch of bitterness' *Globe and Mail*

'[Quintin Jardine] sells more crime fiction in Scotland than John Grisham and people queue around the block to buy his latest book' *Australian*

'Very engaging as well as ingenious, and the unravelling of the mystery is excellently done' Allan Massie, *Scotsman*

'There is a whole world here, the tense narratives all come to the boil at the same time in a spectacular climax' *Shots magazine*

'Engrossing, ... beautifully ... It all add.. ws

Quintin
Jardine
GAME OVER

HEADLINE

First published in 2017 by
HEADLINE PUBLISHING GROUP

First published in paperback in 2017 by
HEADLINE PUBLISHING GROUP

1

Cataloguing in Publication Data is available from the British Library

ISBN 978 1 4722 0572 8

Typeset in Electra by Avon DataSet Ltd, Bidford-on-Avon, Warwickshire

Printed and bound by CPI Group (UK) Ltd, Croydon, CR0 4YY

HEADLINE PUBLISHING GROUP
An Hachette UK Company
Carmelite House
50 Victoria Embankment
London EC4Y 0DZ

www.headline.co.uk
www.hachette.co.uk

This is dedicated to the memory of Mira Kolar Brown,
my friend, who passed away on March 4, 2016.
A lady of great talent, and an even greater heart.

One

'Of all the gin joints, in all the towns, in all the world . . .'

'What?' Detective Sergeant Harold 'Sauce' Haddock exclaimed, cutting across his boss's incongruous murmur.

'Eh? Oh, sorry,' Detective Chief Inspector Sammy Pye replied. 'Don't mind me. *Casablanca*,' he explained. 'My favourite film. Ruth and I watched the DVD last night. It's Bogart's line, and it struck a chord with where we are right now. Of all the crime scenes in all the towns in all the world, you and I have to walk into this one. This is going to be global, mate, and we are right in the spotlight, yet again.'

Haddock's forehead creased in bewilderment beneath the hood of his disposable crime scene onesie. 'It's a murder, gaffer, okay.' He looked at the body on the bed, face purple, dead eyes staring at the ceiling. 'It's not nice, but we've been in situations like this before. Worse situations; think about the last one, that poor kid.'

'I'll never forget that,' the DCI countered, sharply, then continued with barely a pause, 'but . . . Sauce, man, are you a media-free zone? Don't you know who this is?'

The sergeant shrugged. 'Not for certain, but I'm assuming she's the occupant of this apartment.'

'And her name?'

'Fonter, the concierge said; Mrs Annette Fonter. At least that's what I think he said; after finding her, he was in a hell of a state when I spoke to him, high as a kite. The cleaner he let into the flat was even worse; she was having kittens. The paramedics were talking about taking her to hospital.'

'I'm sure they were all like you say. But I'm fairly sure of this too: as soon as they get themselves together, one or the other of them will be on the phone to the tabloids. Man, this is going to splash on every Sunday newspaper in the country . . . and beyond. When we came through the living room, did you notice the photographs? Big ones, framed, on the wall?'

The young DS raised a trademark eyebrow. 'How could I have missed them? A bit showy, I thought.'

'They meant nothing to you?'

'No.'

'Does the name Annette Bordeaux mean anything to you?'

'Should it?'

'Jesus!' Even muffled by a mask, the bark of Arthur Dorward, the head of the forensic investigation team that was hard at work on the crime scene, carried across the room. 'Even I know that,' he exclaimed. 'Annette Bordeaux is a supermodel. Hers is one of the best-known faces on the planet. She's been on the cover of *Vanity Fair*, *Elle*, and most of the other glossy women's mags. And that's her, lying there dead, in front of us.'

Haddock looked at the body anew; he leaned over the bed, peering at the dead face, its skin the colour of coffee, but dull, without pallor, looking into the bulging eyes, their whites mottled with the tiny haemorrhages that he had seen before in other asphyxiation victims. As always, he steeled himself, willing himself to remain dispassionate. It was a skill he had been advised to master from his earliest days in CID, advised by the big man himself, his mentor. Just as Bob Skinner had never quite succeeded, neither had he; the little dead girl in the car park, that had been bad. He had held himself together at the scene, but a few hours later, at home with Cheeky, his partner, he had been wrecked.

He closed his eyes, visualising the framed images in the living area of the penthouse, and feeling himself go cold inside as he compared them mentally with the cover of the current issue of *Cosmopolitan* that Cheeky had left on the coffee table.

'Oh my!' he whispered.

'You get it now?' Pye said.

He nodded. 'So, where does the name Fonter come from?' he asked.

'From her husband: Paco Fonter. He's a Spanish footballer, currently playing for Merrytown, through in South Lanarkshire. You've heard of them, haven't you?'

'Yeah, but football's not my game.' The DS paused, as a question formed in his mind. 'Hold on: how can a Scottish football club afford a foreign player with a supermodel for a wife?'

'Because of its Russian owner,' his boss explained. 'He bought a controlling stake at the end of last year. The club's his personal project. He's promised to get it up there alongside Celtic and Rangers, money no object. He bought in a whole raft of foreign players, and hired a top manager, a guy called Chaz Baker.'

'Now him, I do know. Cheeky and I were guests at an invitation golf event at Archerfield Golf Club. The place was full of football people. He was there too; somebody pointed him out to us.'

'You ask Cheeky who Annette Bordeaux is. She'll know for

sure.' Belatedly, Pye frowned at his sergeant, as an obvious thought reached to him. 'How did you two, a polis and an accountant, get invited to a gig like that?'

The young detective flushed slightly. 'Through Cheeky's grandpa. The invite was his originally, but his new wife's not interested in golf. So, seeing as he and Cheeky both have the same name, Cameron McCullough, and he knows I play, he passed it on. The organiser didn't mind.'

'From everything they say about your partner's grandfather, I imagine the organiser knew better than to mind. I thought you kept Grandpa McCullough at arm's length,' he added.

'I do,' Haddock retorted, quickly. 'I've never met the man, not face to face. Cheeky understands that cops can't associate with gangsters, alleged or otherwise. She's never put pressure on me about it.'

'And when you get married? Will he be absent from the wedding?'

Sauce winked. 'Everybody will. We've agreed that if we ever do, it'll be in Vegas.'

'But what happens in Vegas stays in Vegas,' a female voice pointed out, breaking into their conversation, in a soft New England drawl.

Both detectives turned to face her as she stood in the doorway. 'Then maybe we will too,' Haddock countered. 'It's a damn sight warmer than Edinburgh in September. Good morning, Professor. You're looking . . .'

Sarah Grace smiled at his hesitation. 'Pregnant, Sergeant; I'm looking pregnant. They say that one size fits all with these crime scene clothes, but I feel as if I'm about to prove them wrong. Are your people finished in here?' she asked, switching into a brisk businesslike tone.

4

'The video guy's done,' Pye replied. 'As usual we're still waiting for the forensic team to finish up. I preferred it when they were our people rather than a central service.'

'I'm not one of your people,' she pointed out, 'so why should they be? Move back, please; let me have a look at her.'

The pathologist stepped up to the hotel-sized bed on which the body lay, crosswise. Annette Bordeaux had died in her underwear, simple black bra and pants. Her face and upper torso were smeared with blood from her battered, misshapen nose, and a brown leather belt encircled her neck, with the end pulled through its silver buckle. It hung loose but her neck bore a vicious, collar-like mark.

'It took a lot of force to do that,' Grace murmured. She reached down to the battered face, feeling the nose. 'Broken,' she confirmed.

'Knocked out then strangled?' the DCI queried.

'Hit, certainly, and hit hard, but would she have been rendered unconscious? I doubt that.'

'She could have been doing cocaine,' Haddock volunteered.

Grace looked up at him, quizzically. 'Not really relevant, but what makes you say that?'

'The CSIs found what could be the leavings of a line in the bathroom, in a crevice between two tiles.'

'Point one,' she asked, 'how do you know it's coke? Point two, how can you tell that she was snorting it? Look at the blood smears on her face. It all came from her nose, but I can see no traces of powder there.' She frowned. 'But let's not speculate, boys,' she said, as she turned the dead woman on her side and pulled down her pants.

Pye winced as she took the rectal temperature; Haddock looked away.

'Time of death?' the chief inspector asked quietly, when she was finished and had checked the thermometer.

'Not a precise science, as you know, Sammy, but . . . This room has a maintained temperature of twenty-one degrees Celsius, according to the dial by the door. Then I have to factor in her size. She was a slim, fit woman, and given her profession, her body fat index would be pretty low.'

'You know who she is?' Haddock exclaimed.

She stared at him. 'Are you kidding? There was a feature on Annette Bordeaux in the *Sunday Herald* a couple of weeks ago. The photography was done in this very apartment.'

'I must get out more,' the DS muttered.

'The long and the short of it is,' she continued, glancing at her watch, which showed two minutes before midday, 'applying the conditions here to the rate of cooling, and the fact that rigor mortis is still established, I'd say she's been dead for not less than sixteen hours and not more than twenty. She was killed between four and eight p.m. yesterday.'

Haddock looked at Pye. 'Do we go get the husband?'

The DCI shook his head. 'He's got an alibi. I can think of at least one good reliable witness who'll testify to it.'

'Who's that?'

'Me. Between eight and ten last night Paco Fonter was playing for Spain in Valencia in a friendly against Argentina. It was on Sky Sports. He scored in the first ten minutes then went off injured.' He frowned. 'They have another match next Tuesday, but he'll be missing it now. Sauce, get on to Chaz Baker. Tell him what's happened and ask him how we get word to Fonter. While you're doing that, I'll call the deputy chief.'

'You may have a problem there,' Sarah Grace observed. 'Mario McGuire and his family left for Italy on Thursday, to visit his mother. I know, 'cos Bob and I invited them to dinner tonight.' She patted her bump. 'My last chance for a while to be a hostess.'

'Then there's nothing for it,' Pye sighed, 'but to break into the chief constable's Saturday morning. Wish me luck.'

Two

'Johnny,' Bob Skinner said, patiently, 'you might be my cousin, but I'm not a cop any more, and even if I was, that wouldn't cut you any slack with the prosecutors, not in this case.'

The squat little man looked up from his seat at the conference table in the office of Alexis Skinner, Solicitor Advocate . . . as the still-shiny sign outside proclaimed. His heavy black eyebrows were hunched, like his massive shoulders.

'You cannae just make it go away?' he challenged.

'Not a prayer. You put the guy in Wishaw General Hospital.'

'Aye but . . .'

'No "buts". You split your kitchen table across the man's back; you broke three of his ribs and cracked two vertebrae.' He picked up a photograph from an open folder. 'Look at the bruising on him.'

The flicker of a grin twisted his cousin's mouth and his eyes twinkled. 'It was a big oak table,' he murmured.

'Then maybe you should just have hit him with a chair!' Skinner laughed, in spite of himself.

Johnny Fleming shook his head. 'Naw, they're pretty solid too. Bob, what would you have done? Suppose you'd walked in on him swingin' a milk can at Alex here, like Barney McGlashan did tae our Gretta.'

'I'd have restrained him and called the police.' Skinner winked at his daughter. 'That's if Alex hadn't kicked the legs out from under him first.'

'Oor Gretta's a sturdy wumman,' his cousin sighed, 'but she's sixty-two. We did call the police, and look what happened. I've been charged and McGlashan hasnae.'

'Because he didn't actually hit her,' Alex intervened. 'And,' she added, 'there's no corroborated evidence that he meant to do so. It's his word against Gretta's, for you came in halfway through their argument.'

'What's to do, then?' Fleming asked her.

'I recommend that you plead guilty,' she told him, firmly. 'We do not want this thing to go to trial. The fiscal will have his say, but he has no reason to press for a custodial sentence. McGlashan has previous for violence, and you don't. I'll enter a plea in mitigation, claiming an unprovoked lunge at your sister, and I'll try to persuade the sheriff that you acted instinctively against what you saw as a real threat.'

'Will he buy that?'

'I hope so. Yes,' she decided, 'I expect so. I've never appeared at Lanark Sheriff Court, but I haven't heard any stories about the sheriff there being a hardliner. There will be a fine, and you might even be ordered to pay some victim compensation, but . . .'

'I'm no' havin' that,' Johnny protested. 'Pay compensation to yon animal?'

'Oh yes you are,' Alex snapped. 'You will nod politely at whatever the sheriff says. You'll utter one word and that will be "Guilty". Understood?'

'If you say so.' He looked up at her. 'Was she aye this bossy, Bob?'

'Pretty much,' Skinner replied, cheerfully. He spoke the truth. He had brought his daughter up alone from the age of four, after her mother had died in a mangled car. While she had never been a rebel, she had staked out her own territory from a fairly early stage. He felt a weird kind of pride as he recalled her, aged five, looking him straight in the eye, after he had answered 'No' to her plea that they watch a video that he had seen so often he had it memorised, and saying, 'Why not?' He had been stumped for an answer, and he had watched *Dougal and the Blue Cat* for the tenth time . . . or was it the twentieth?

'I'd better do what she says then.' Fleming stood. 'What happens next?' he asked.

'I'll advise the fiscal that I'm acting for you,' she told him, 'and I'll ask for an early pleading diet. I'll let you know when we have a date for court.'

'Good. Can I go now? I have to get back to the farm. I'm covering McGlashan's work till I get a new labourer in to replace him.'

'Did you dismiss him formally?'

'No.' He stared at her. 'You don't think he'd come back, do ye?'

'No,' she said, 'but you can bet your boots that he'll be on to a personal injury lawyer as soon as he's discharged from hospital. If you agree, I'll write to him advising that his employment has been terminated without notice on grounds of gross misconduct.'

He nodded. 'Do it. I'll tell Gretta tae call you wi' his address. Do ye think he'd have the nerve to sue me?'

'Bet on it. But we won't roll over. We'll threaten a counter-suit by Gretta for emotional distress, and by you for the things he smashed in the kitchen during the argument.'

Cousin Johnny looked at her, smiling. 'You know what?' he chuckled, as he headed for the door. 'You're a Fleming, right enough. I'm beginning to feel sorry for that bastard.'

Alex stared after him. 'What the hell did he mean by that?' she exclaimed once he had gone. 'I'm a Skinner, pure and simple.' She turned and stalked off towards her office.

'No,' her father said, following in her wake, 'you're more than that. You're the sum total of everything that made you. There are some pretty powerful ingredients in your genetic soup; not just from me but from your mother. The Grahams, her branch of the family, included an African missionary, a contemporary of David Livingstone, who was killed by a hippo before he could convert a single native, a soldier who died beside General Gordon at Khartoum, and a woman who was imprisoned for life for smothering her child.'

She dropped into her chair, frowning. 'Jesus, Pops,' she murmured, 'I'm past thirty years old and you're telling me all this now?'

As he took the seat facing her, Bob Skinner was aware, not for the first time, of his failings as a parent. 'I thought your Aunt Jean had fed you all your family history,' he protested, weakly.

'She did mention something once about Duncan Graham, the missionary. I must have been ten; I was researching Livingstone and Stanley for a primary school project and I asked her about Livingstone, since his museum's near where she lives. She never said what had happened to him, though, and she never said a word about the other two ancestors.'

'She probably wanted to spare you the gory parts. William

Graham, the soldier, was hacked to pieces, literally, and as for Margaret Graham . . . well, most families would bury a story like that.'

'But what about your side?' she asked. 'You've never talked about your family. I remember Grandpa Skinner, of course. He was nice and he was kind, and he was always a soft touch for extra pocket money, but he never told me things, like what you were like when you were growing up, or what my grandma was like.'

'Your Grandma Skinner was an alcoholic,' he retorted, a little too sharply perhaps, but memories of his mother were still painful to Skinner. 'As for my childhood, Dad knew sod all about that, for he was never home. If he never spoke about it at all, that may have been because he didn't want to talk about Michael.'

'My uncle? The one who died?' She frowned, slightly. 'He was a drunk too, wasn't he?'

Bob nodded. 'He was a drunk, he was a sadist and he was a coward. He was almost ten years older than me, and he bullied me all the time I was growing up.'

The frown deepened; it became a look of pain.

'Pops,' she murmured, 'you never . . .'

'Told you about it? Of course not. Why share stuff like that with you?'

'And Grandpa never knew?'

'No, he never had a clue; as for Mum, she was half-pissed all the time and Michael was her blue-eyed boy.'

'How did you stop it?' Alex asked.

'I grew up,' he replied. 'I became what I am; by the time I was about fifteen, even then I was strong enough to put the fear of God into him. I never complained to my father though. I dealt with it myself when I was ready. Not long after that Michael lost it completely, and was institutionalised.'

'And I grew up,' she reminded him, quietly, 'with an uncle I knew nothing about.'

'Sorry,' he murmured sheepishly.

'A man who was locked away without trial, from what you're saying.' There was anger in her tone, at a perceived injustice.

Skinner had to check himself; he had never flared up at his daughter, not once in her life, but he came close then. 'You're talking like a defence lawyer,' he said, curtly. 'Trust me, if you knew the full story you'd want to prosecute.'

His reaction took her by surprise; she backed off. 'Okay,' she exclaimed, 'if that's how you feel, it's my turn to be sorry. But you must admit,' she teased him, 'you've been neglectful as a parent. You mentioned my genetic soup earlier . . . a colourful image, by the way . . . and you're right, it is my genetic history, so I need to know about it. Not least,' she added, defusing any tension with a smile, 'so that when a potential client calls me and tells me we're cousins, I'm not left babbling like an idiot on the other end of the phone.'

He nodded. 'Touché,' he agreed. 'Right, as for Johnny: your Grandma Skinner was a Fleming, you knew that . . . ?'

'Yes,' she agreed, 'but that's all I've ever been told, and obviously I never had a chance to ask her about it, her being dead before I was born.'

'You wouldn't have got much out of her anyway,' he grumbled. 'I never did.'

'Christ, Dad,' she sighed, 'you sound bitter.'

He glanced at her, eyes hooded by his heavy eyebrows. 'Do I?' he exclaimed. 'I'm not really; sad, more like it. I can understand now that she had an illness, but you don't know about these things as a child.'

'What about your grandparents?' Alex asked.

'I was getting to that. Grandpa Fleming died when I was six, but I remember him quite well. He was a tall old geezer, with frizzy white hair. He could be quite severe with my mum . . . now I know why . . . but he was great with me. One day . . . I'd have been five at the time; it was the summer and I was just about to start school . . . he took me on a trip, on the bus from Motherwell up through Wishaw and beyond, heading towards Carluke. We got off at a place called Overtown, and walked till we got to a farmhouse. There was a man there, waiting for us, his cousin. His name was David Fleming, and he was Johnny's father.'

'Was Johnny there too?'

'Yes, but he was working on the farm. He'd have been, what, going on twenty at the time. Uncle David . . . that's what I called him . . . put me on a tractor and drove me around the fields. It had been a good summer; they were harvesting, early, for the weather was bound to break. I met Johnny, but only briefly; he was busy. To me he was huge; you've seen the width of him now, aged sixty-nine, so imagine him approaching his prime. Gretta was there too; she'd have been early teens, a strange, shy lassie with bottle-glass specs. I remember, it was hot but she had on this big thick jumper.'

Alex smiled. 'What about the kitchen table?' she asked. 'Was it there?'

'I guess so. I can't say for sure, but from what I can see in the police photographs, that could have been it; it might have been a hundred years old even then, if not more. Anyway, on the tour of the farm, Uncle David drove us up to this big old mansion. He said it was called Waterloo House, and it had belonged to an ancestor of his, that the farm, or most of it, had been its estate. I remember asking him what an ancestor was. He told me it was a relative who's been dead for a long time. I asked him if he lived in the house now. He laughed and said it was too grand for the likes of him. I discovered much later that it had lain derelict for a while, until Grandpa Fleming inherited it from his grandfather, and turned it into four apartments.'

'So your Grandpa Fleming,' Alex exclaimed, 'my great-grandpa, was actually minted!'

'No,' he laughed, 'because he made hardly any money on the conversion. Waterloo House is a listed building and Historic Scotland, or whatever it was called then, imposed all sorts of conditions.'

'What did Grandpa Fleming do?'

'He was a saddler, a leather manufacturer. It was an old family business that had been big at one time, but he inherited it in time to see it through its final years, until he sold the factory on to a competitor for as much as he could get.'

'Where did it all come from, the farm, the mansion, the factory?'

Skinner smiled. 'Well,' he sighed, 'that's where it gets interesting. After we had seen all of the farm, looked in the milking sheds and everything, we went into the farmhouse and had our tea, in the sitting room. Grandpa said that Auntie Jessie, Uncle David's wife, Johnny's mother, was a famous baker. I have a memory of her in the kitchen, making potato scones; they looked like chapattis before she cut them into quarters.'

'Was she as good as he said?' his daughter asked.

'Haven't a clue; it was polite to praise your hostess for her baking in those days. And for her jam; jam-making was a big thing with Auntie Jessie's generation. I've no idea how good they were . . . this is way back, remember, around the time England won the World Cup. But I do have one memory of that room, one that stuck with me for years. There was a portrait over the fireplace, of a man in middle age, a strong-looking fella. Grandpa smiled up at the picture, and kind of touched his forelock, in respect.'

'What was it?'

'Let me finish,' he insisted. 'He'd have been a good-looking bloke, maybe he'd even have looked a bit like me,' he chuckled, 'but for one thing. There was a big vertical scar down the left side of his face, and his left eye was grey and sightless. The sight of it scared me a wee bit, aged five, and I never forgot it. Uncle David drove us back to Motherwell, in an enormous bloody Jaguar that had sacks of spuds in the boot, and after he dropped us off I asked Grandpa who the man in the painting was. He said it was a long story, and he'd tell me another time.'

'But there never was another time, was there,' Alex guessed. 'You said he died when you were six?'

He nodded. 'That's right; he had a massive stroke the following week and died less than a year later. It was the last day out we ever had, and the only time I ever went to the farmhouse. I've seen Johnny a few times since then, always at funerals. His parents', my mother's, my dad's; not at Grandpa Fleming's though, I was too young to go to that.'

'That's strange, because just now it was as if you and he have been close all your lives. When was the last time you saw him?'

'At my father's send-off,' he told her. 'The time before that was at your mother's. I didn't expect Johnny to be there, but he was, him and Gretta, and that moved me.'

'He never married?'

'No, and neither did Gretta. He took over the farm and she took over the kitchen. She'll be the famous baker now, I imagine.'

'Probably shops in Tesco,' Alex laughed, mocking his nostalgia.

'I'll bet she doesn't. She'll be the last of the old-time spinsters. Did you see that pullover Johnny was wearing? I could almost guarantee she knitted that.'

'Typical man,' she snorted, 'you view women as stereotypes. You haven't seen Gretta in a quarter of a century, and you've put her in a box. She's probably a part-time yoga teacher and drinks Bellinis.'

'Trust me on this,' Bob insisted. 'I'm a Lanarkshire boy and they're an old-time Upper Ward family.'

'That's gobbledegook to me. What about the man in the portrait? Get on with it, Father, I'm busy, unlike you.'

She had a point, and he knew it.

Since leaving the police force when his last post as Strathclyde chief constable disappeared into what he saw as the capacious maw of the new unified Scottish National Police, he had been struggling to balance his life. That was not to say that he had been inactive. He had been involved in a couple of what he chose to best describe as 'consultancy situations'.

The first had led to him becoming a part-time executive director of InterMedia, a Spanish media group, owned by his friend Xavi Aislado and his ancient brother Joe. The company's flagship titles included the *Saltire*, a newspaper rescued from obscurity largely by Xavi's work as a young journalist and then from insolvency by his family firm.

The second had ended unfortunately for the person who commissioned him. As Skinner had explained to him afterwards, 'You can buy my time, but you can't buy my integrity.'

He had also been appointed to the board of the Security Industry Authority, a post he had accepted, without any enthusiasm, to please a friend, Amanda Dennis. He had done so on the basis that he saw it as better to please the head of MI5 than to piss her off.

He found that he enjoyed the media job a lot and gave it more time than the contracted one day a week, but in contrast the SIA post was deadly dull, involving the absorption of reams of submissions that stated the obvious, then rubber-stamping them at monthly meetings in London. After only a few months, he knew with certainty that when his three-year term of office expired, he would not seek renewal . . . if he could stand it that long.

Apart from that, though, he had time on his hands. The phone had rung, the non-executive directorships had been offered, and had been turned down, all of them, because their common thread was the fact that every one of the offering businesses was only interested in what his name and reputation would add to their bottom line, not in any new skills that he might bring to the table.

He had told the last one in no uncertain terms that he had no interest in endorsing the security of their double-glazed doors and windows, when he knew half a dozen ways of opening them without tripping even the most sophisticated alarm system.

Some of that time he had given to Alex. She had walked away from a very promising and very lucrative career in corporate law, and struck out on her own as a solicitor advocate, specialising in criminal defence work. He had done a few small investigations for her, but most of his usefulness had been as a sounding board, advising her on the odds for or against an acquittal.

Basically, he had been telling her when she should defend and when she should attack. That was why she had consulted him about Johnny Fleming; that and her curiosity about the family connection.

Six months before, his situation would have worried him, as he had been a serial workaholic, but his life had changed in more than professional terms.

Sarah Grace, his ex-wife, but partner once again, and he were expecting a late and wholly unplanned addition to their family. Alongside that he had another situation with his oldest son, from another relationship. He was in jail, and would be until the end of the year.

'Okay,' he said, briskly, to his firstborn child, 'I'll keep it brief. That portrait, the one in Uncle David's sitting room: the image burned itself into my head. I asked my mother about it once, when I was nine, but she must have been in a haze at the time for she brushed me off.

'After that,' he continued, 'life intervened. I had my troubles with my brother, then when they were sorted I met your mother, went to university, graduated, joined the police . . . disappointing my father by rejecting his law firm, although he never said so . . . then had you, my career and, eventually, another family.'

'Yes,' Alex murmured drily, 'you've had a lot of distractions, haven't you.'

'Hey,' he protested, 'you were never a distraction, kid, you were the light of my life. But it was a very busy life, until a few months ago, when most of it came to a sudden stop.

'When that happened, like it or not I had leisure time. I don't know when I remembered the portrait, but at some point I did, and I remembered my visit to the farm with Grandpa Fleming, how he reacted when he saw it and what he said about it being a long story.'

Skinner grinned. 'I switched into detective mode,' he said, 'and went looking for it. I could have done the obvious, just called Johnny, asked him if he still had the painting and if he knew who the hell it was, but I fancied a challenge, so I bought myself some credits on the Scotland's People website and went to work. I concentrated on the Fleming side of the family and worked my way back. I found Grandpa very quickly: Walter Weir Fleming, born in Saltcoats Road, Carluke, in eighteen ninety. His parents were Matthew Fleming, occupation saddler, and Jane Grey, no occupation given.'

'What about David?'

'David McGill Fleming, born at the same address in nineteen hundred and three, but to a different mother. Her name was Sheila O'Flanagan.'

'So you and Johnny . . .' Alex began. She was hooked, her work schedule forgotten.

'. . . have different great-grandmothers, which makes us half-cousins in whatever degree of cousinship we are. Mine, your great-great-granny, Jane Grey, died of appendicitis in eighteen ninety-six.'

She winced. 'Ouch! That must have been horrible.'

'Indeed: we don't appreciate the age we live in. Anyway, move on: I found great-grandfather's . . . Matthew Fleming's . . . birth date from the detail in his marriage certificate . . . the first one, that is, and worked back from there. That's where it started to get interesting. He was born in eighteen fifty-one in Home Farm, Waterloo, Lanarkshire, and his parents were Marshall Weir Fleming and Jean McGill, thus, my great-great-grandparents.'

'Was he the man in the portrait? Marshall?'

'That's what I wondered,' Bob admitted. 'So I Googled him; but nothing came up. That didn't rule out the possibility, but . . . then I remembered something I should have been on to from the start.

'I have a box of old family mementos, and among them is an envelope that must have come to my mother when Grandpa died. It's full of photographs and the oldest is one that was taken in eighteen ninety-five, of a family group. I know that date because Grandpa had annotated it on the back. There were six people in it. He was there, aged five, and there was another child, Mary Fleming, aged three. "My sister", Grandpa had noted. She was news to me, but there was a note saying that she died of scarlet fever in March eighteen ninety-seven.'

'Maybe that's where Johnny's sister's name came from,' Alex suggested.

'Maybe,' he agreed, 'but that's not relevant. Matthew and Jane were front and centre, obviously, but there was an older couple beside them, white haired and very well dressed, described as "My grandparents, Marshall and Jean Fleming". The image of the man was perfectly clear and there was no scar.'

'Couldn't have been him, then,' she observed.

'Nope,' he agreed, 'so I went in search of his, Marshall's, parents. They weren't so easy to find, as I was relying on old parish records by then, but I made an assumption and con-centrated on Lanarkshire. I got lucky and found them both, born within a few weeks of each other and baptised on the same day by the parish minister in Carluke, one John Barclay.

'The entry was detailed; Marshall's full name was Marshall Weir Fleming, and his parents were listed as Mathew Fleming, spelled with one "t", and Elizabeth Weir. She was listed as "deceased, of childbed fever", in the same register.'

'That means your great-great-great-grandmother died giving birth to your great-great-grandfather.'

'Add on another generation and yours too,' he pointed out, then continued. 'Jean, great-great-granny's parents, were named as David McGill, estate clerk, and Elizabeth Marshall.'

'That's a bit of a coincidence, isn't it? Marshall having the same name as the woman who became his mother-in-law?'

'Yes,' he agreed, 'but it explains Uncle David's middle name.'

'What about Mathew with one t?'

'He's described in the birth record as a factory owner.'

She smiled. 'We do come from wealthy stock.'

'Yes but he didn't.' His eyes were gleaming. 'I dug deeper,' he went on, 'and found his birth registration; he was born in seventeen ninety-three, in Carluke also. His father, Robert Fleming, was a carter and his mother, Hannah Russell, was a seamstress.'

'A self-made man, then.'

'Was he ever. I went looking for the date of his death and found it: eighteen fifty-five, aged sixty-two. On the certificate he was Sir Mathew Fleming, Knight Commander.'

'You're kidding!' Alex gasped.

'Absolutely not,' her father declared. 'The cause of death,' he continued, 'was given as liver failure, with the qualification that it was a consequence of war wounds.'

'War wounds!' she repeated. 'Then he must have been the scarred man in the portrait, surely!' she exclaimed.

'Yes, indeed, and that portrait, it turns out, is a copy of one painted by the artist Alexander Geddes, one of his last works. I traced it; the original's in the collection of the Palace of

Westminster. I viewed it online and it's absolutely the same as I saw when I was five.

'From there I got all sorts,' he chuckled, 'the whole story. When Sir Mathew snuffed it, there were obituaries in the *Scotsman*, the *Glasgow Herald* and *The Times*. They confirmed that he was the son of a carter, and said that he'd been an enlisted man in the Napoleonic War, a sergeant in the Cameron Highlanders; they were a fearsome crew, by reputation. They said he was severely wounded at Waterloo and then again three years later, also in Flanders, when he lost his eye.'

He pressed on. 'His life changed when he came home, after his discharge. He made his first fortune by patenting a lightweight saddle, and even more dough as an iron founder, in the early years of rail travel, making parts for locomotives.' He smiled. 'Then he gave most of it away, to charitable foundations. He was a member of the House of Commons for eight years and a Deputy Lord Lieutenant of Lanarkshire for more than twenty. The man was a bloody legend in his lifetime.'

'Did he remarry?'

'Yes. He married Jean McGill's by then widowed mother, and they had a child together, a girl, Hannah. She married a man called Graham, and believe it or not she's an ancestor of yours through your mother. You've got a double dose of Mathew's blood in your veins.'

'Bloody hell!' She laughed. 'What happened to David McGill? Did Mathew kill him in a duel?'

He grinned. 'I don't know. I haven't gone there yet, but I will. When I'm ready . . . I've spent enough time in the past for the moment.'

His tale told, his daughter resumed her work, and Skinner headed back to his own office in the building owned by the

InterMedia Group, where he settled down to earn some more of the lavish salary that company paid him for his input.

He found a message awaiting his attention: June Crampsey, the managing editor of the *Saltire*, wanted to see him, urgently.

She had a crisis. One of her less experienced reporters, a young man named Shafik Rasul, had been arrested in Aberdeen and charged with offering a bribe to an off-duty prison officer, in return for access to a prisoner, in the guise of a family member. Their conversation had been recorded by undercover police officers who had the warder under surveillance.

'How should I play it, Bob?' she asked. 'The lad's panicking. He says that the man solicited the bribe and suggested the ploy. He agreed to it just to string him along, he says.'

'How did he come to contact the warder in the first place?' Skinner asked.

'That was the story he was after. He'd had a tip from a source that he won't reveal even to me, that the man had been a messenger for the con . . . his name's Harry Brady, a Glasgow gang lord . . . for years. He was suspected of facilitating the murder of one of Brady's enemies, by carrying an order to a hit man.'

Skinner smiled grimly. 'I know Brady,' he said. 'I didn't bang him up myself, but I had to put the fear of God in him fifteen years back, when I'd been told that he was trying to move his drugs and protection rackets into Edinburgh.

'Who are the investigating officers?' he asked.

'I don't know,' the editor replied. 'The fiscal in Aberdeen wouldn't tell me; she wouldn't even listen to me. How should I play this, Bob? Any advice? I don't want to lose this kid. He's really bright.'

'You could threaten to run the story,' he suggested.

She frowned. 'How would that help?'

'The fiscal would shit herself.'

'I'd be bluffing. Shafik's been up in the Sheriff Court already, in private. The case is *sub judice*.'

'So what?' he countered. 'You don't need to name him. Look, this is an undercover operation, and your lad got in the way. He's been charged because he was a nuisance, that's all; it'll never get to court, I promise you. Has the prison officer been arrested?'

'No,' she admitted.

'No,' he repeated firmly. 'He hasn't because the investigation is still open. The story of the Brady hit goes back a year and more; I was aware of it when I was in Strathclyde. The police aren't just after the warden, they want Brady himself, for conspiracy to murder. If we make the slightest wave, the charges against your kid will be dropped, on condition that he shuts up and stays away. Do you want me to have a word?'

'Would you?'

He smiled. 'Sure. I'm having lunch with the new chief constable in half an hour, as it happens. I think she wants to make me an offer I'm going to refuse.'

He left Crampsey calmer than she had been and went back to his own office, two doors along the corridor.

On reflection he decided not to spoil his lunch with the chief constable by asking her for a favour; instead he phoned Woodrow Butcher, the Lord Advocate, and called one in. The two were regular golf partners at Gullane.

'Remember three weeks ago?' he began.

'Anything in particular?' Scotland's senior law officer replied, cautiously.

'The time when I carried you on my shoulders to a win in a dinner match, money involved.'

'Oh. That. Do I sense that it might be payback time?'

'It could be.' He explained Shafik Rasul's predicament.

'You can vouch for the young man?' Butcher asked.

'June Crampsey can,' Skinner assured him.

'That's enough for me. I'll keep the charge open to ensure the laddie's silence, but when the police are ready to move on Brady and his stooge, it'll be dropped.' He laughed. 'You just can't keep your hands off, Bob,' he said. 'Can you?'

'I could, Woodrow,' the reluctant civilian replied, 'but they seem to be magnetic . . . magnetic for trouble.'

Three

'Was it worth it?' Chief Constable Maggie Rose Steele asked the man who had been her mentor, as the waiter left with their lunch orders, leaving them in a quiet corner of the restaurant.

Bob Skinner smiled. 'Expand on each "it", Mags,' he invited.

'You know what I mean. Do you regret your decision to leave the police service, and are you enjoying your new life? You'd have had the position I now hold, beyond question, but you walked away. Sure, I know,' she added. 'You were opposed to a unified Scottish police service, as were most serving cops. But when it was forced upon us by the politicians, most of us decided to stick around.'

'Most of you didn't have a choice,' he countered. 'You had families to support.'

'So have you,' she pointed out. She winked. 'A family that's expanding year by year.'

'I had other opportunities. I was able to make the move without putting them at risk. Mags, if I had stayed, it would have stopped being a calling and become just a job . . . and I'd have been crap at it. My police career didn't prepare me for running a force of any size, let alone the juggernaut that is the Scottish National Police. I was a detective, Maggie, I caught thieves and

27

murderers; but I was never an administrator. You know that; you were a witness.'

'You were a leader, Bob,' she exclaimed. 'We'd have followed you into cannon fire. Okay, you might have been a better delegator on the CID side, but you never turned up at a crime scene just to check on the work of others. You always contributed and you never undermined the senior investigating officer. The other aspects of policing you did leave to people who knew what they were doing and supervised those from a distance.'

'That's most of the job,' he reminded her. 'When I was chief in Edinburgh, my deputies, Brian Mackie and then you, did most of the work. Effectively that's what you're saying.'

'Not at all,' she countered. 'We implemented policy as you directed; that's the truth of it. And this is true as well: your decision to leave the service was emotional, it wasn't rational. There are people . . . in politics and the media, not in the police . . . who are saying you went off in the huff when you didn't get your own way on unification.'

Skinner frowned. 'I can't argue against that, but even if it's true, it wasn't the whole story. I had another reason for withdrawing my application.'

'And I know what it was,' Maggie said. 'Your son was in serious trouble.'

'My son was going to jail, possibly for life.'

'Bob, you never knew of Ignacio's existence until after his crime had been committed. That could never have been held against you.'

He laughed, bitterly. 'Maybe not, but it would, by the very people you've just mentioned, in politics and the media. The product of a one-night stand with Mia Watson, star of local radio and the daughter of an Edinburgh criminal family, who did a runner after she was duped into setting up her brother to be killed? If the whole story had come out at his trial, they'd have had a fucking field day.'

'You've ridden out worse than that.'

'Maybe, but what would the effect have been on Ignacio, and on my other kids, Alex, and James Andrew, and Mark, and Seonaid? The headlines would have followed them for the rest of their lives.'

'Okay,' the chief constable conceded quietly, 'but it's passed over now, and the fact that Ignacio is your son hasn't become public knowledge. When does he get out?'

'In a couple of months . . . round about the time Sarah's due. We can double up on the champagne. But when he does, he won't be a secret any longer. I'd have acknowledged him from the start, if I hadn't thought it might put him at risk inside. Sure, there will be some tabloid coverage, but Mia and I will be in control of the story. It'll be a one-day wonder.'

'Once that happens, the cupboard will be empty. I assume,' she added. 'No more skeletons?'

Skinner laughed. 'With me, who knows?' he said.

'I think I do,' she declared. 'And at that time . . . Bob, we want you back.'

He shook his head firmly. 'No chance. All due respect, Maggie, but I couldn't work for you. I can't remember the last time I followed an order.'

'You wouldn't be working for me, not directly. I'd be kept aware of what you were doing, other than in one exceptional circumstance, but you wouldn't report to me.'

'I don't understand,' he murmured. He thought for a few seconds, then looked her in the eye. 'If this is the Inspector of

Constabulary post, I've turned it down already, in a very loud voice.'

'No,' Steele replied. 'That's a public position; this is anything but. I'm talking about . . .' She stopped in mid-sentence as the waiter arrived with their starters.

He was barely out of earshot, when Skinner asked, 'Is it a job that needs doing?'

'We think so.'

'We?'

'The First Minister and me. We want to set up a semi-formal investigating unit that would be called in on an ad hoc basis, to investigate crimes and other situations that are seen as having special sensitivity.'

'Other than in one situation, you said. What would that be?'

'If you were investigating me,' she said, quietly.

'That blows it out of the water right way. I know you far too well.'

'We can leave that out . . . not that it would arise.'

'Fine; now answer me this. If not me, who?'

'We haven't thought that far ahead,' Steele admitted.

'Andy Martin,' he suggested, knowing that the very mention of her short-lived predecessor in the Scottish National Police command chair was provocative.

'Not a prayer. Andy turned into a megalomaniac in the job. Nobody anticipated that. I haven't cleared up all the mess yet. The communications department, for example; the way he set it up, the thing was practically unmanageable. There were places where the road accident stats improved because the local press officer went on sick leave for six weeks and wasn't covered. Then there was the deputy communications director, a woman called Cant, who bloody well couldn't, but was allowed to think that she had power of command over senior officers.'

Skinner smiled. 'I heard about her. Didn't Sammy Pye slam a door in her face once?'

'No, he left Sauce Haddock to do it. The bugger is, she's just walked out with a fat redundancy cheque. It was the only way I could fire her.'

'Ironic,' he observed. 'Before unification each of the eight forces had its own media relations structure. All the press officers knew all the senior cops and there was no scope for conflict.'

'Come off it!' she retorted. 'You and Alan Royston argued all the time.'

'We had the occasional disagreement,' he chuckled, 'but only when he did something wrong.'

'Maybe you should come back as director of communications . . . now you have special media experience.'

'I'd sooner sweep up horseshit!' he said, between mouthfuls of rocket. 'Mags, this thing that you and Clive Graham are dreaming up: it wouldn't be just a means of bringing me back into the fold, would it?'

Her soup spoon hovered over the bowl. 'Okay, all I'll admit to is that we won't be offering it to anyone else if you refuse. Think about it, please, Bob.'

'I will,' he conceded, 'but only because it's you who's asking. I warn you, my answer is still going to be "no". I'm happy, honestly.'

'But are you content?' she countered. 'That's the . . .' Her ringtone sounded: the theme from Z Cars. 'Bugger!' she hissed, as she took the call.

'Yes, Sammy,' Skinner heard her say. 'That's understood. What's the crisis?' He watched her face, keenly, as she listened, and her expression darkened. 'King Robert Village, you say? Then the first thing you do is to make that entire complex secure. Nobody gets in unless they live there and nobody gets near the scene itself.

'I'm on my way; I'll be with you inside half an hour. Meantime you should find Perry Allsop, the communications director, wherever he's spending his Saturday. Tell him you're in command at the scene, and that I would like him to join you there as soon as possible, with as many of his most experienced staff as he thinks he'll need.'

Skinner raised a hand, attracting her attention. 'Hotels,' he said.

She looked at him, puzzled. 'What?' she asked, a shade impatiently. 'Sammy, I'm putting you on speaker. I'm lunching with Mr Skinner. He has something to contribute.'

'Only an observation,' the former chief constable called out to the phone as she held it in the air. 'I don't know what this thing is and don't tell me right now, but if it's big enough to rattle Mrs Steele and she can be there that quickly, it's in the heart of the capital city and it's going to need an army of press officers, it sounds as if you could be in for a media invasion. In which case, Allsop might want to warn the Edinburgh hotels to prepare for some unexpected business.'

'You're not free yourself, are you, sir?' the voice of DCI Sammy Pye echoed, mournfully. 'Sauce and I could use all the help we can get.'

'Not me, mate,' Skinner laughed. 'Mrs Steele came here in a taxi and I have my car outside, so I'll bring her to the scene. After that I'm off to the *Saltire* office to tell June Crampsey to hold the front page.'

Four

'So this is King Robert Village,' the chief constable murmured.

'Yes, ma'am,' Sauce Haddock exclaimed, unnecessarily, for she was somewhere in a past life, speaking to herself.

She returned to the present. 'Do you remember it as the Royal Infirmary?' she asked him.

'I remember it,' he replied, 'although I was never in it as a patient, or as a cop. It was closed by the time I joined the force.'

They were standing on the decking of the roof terrace belonging to the penthouse apartment that had become a crime scene. Looking out across the Meadows, Haddock chuckled softly.

'I hadn't been on the job for long when old Charlie Johnston and I had a call that took us out there, in a thick fog, a real pea-souper. It was an anonymous tip; we couldn't find a damn thing until I all but walked into it, a guy hanging from a tree.'

'I remember that,' she said. 'Stevie was first CID responder at the scene and he called me in. We were working together then, before . . .'

Her voice tailed off, leaving a silence as thick and tangible as that freezing October fog had been. Stevie: Detective Inspector Stevie Steele, young, charismatic, the most popular man in

33

CID, a future anything he chose, really. He and Maggie Rose had worked together, fallen in love, and married, to the astonished delight of their colleagues. She had been expecting his child when he walked through a booby-trapped door on an investigation in Northumberland, dying instantly.

While still enveloped in grief, she had been diagnosed with ovarian cancer. She had refused surgery until her child could be safely delivered, however. It had been a complete success, and Stephanie Margaret Steele was blooming in the joint care of her mother and her aunt, Maggie's sister, Bet.

Having plunged his foot squarely into the mire, Haddock pulled it back out as gracefully as he could. 'Of course this building wasn't part of the old hospital,' he continued, 'it's new build . . . obviously. The whole King Robert Village development's a mix of commercial and residential. There's a health club in one of the other buildings, but this one's purely residential.'

'I know,' the chief constable said. 'I'm a member of the health club. I don't use it much,' she explained, 'but there are kids' activities that Stephanie likes. Last time I was there,' she added, 'I saw Annette Bordeaux. I confess that I didn't realise it was actually her; she was in a leotard and leggings, knocking ten bells out of a cross-trainer. To tell you the truth, I dismissed her as a wannabe Annette, and thought no more about her until I took DCI Pye's call half an hour ago.'

'Was Mr Skinner serious about telling the *Saltire* editor?'

Steele grinned. 'Probably. He's really committed to his new job. I don't mind; they might get here half an hour quicker than they would have otherwise, that's all.'

'Ma'am.' Sammy Pye called from the patio doorway. 'Sorry, I've just been briefing the director of communications. Allsop's golfing at Gleneagles today, it seems; I caught him on the eighth tee, apparently. He's not best pleased but he's going to cut his round short and get down here.'

She shrugged. 'The world will turn without him. Are the media on to it yet?'

'They've got chapter and verse; the first call came in ten minutes ago.' He glanced at Haddock. 'Somebody's talked, Sauce, and my money's on that concierge, what's his name, Paul Cope. I suspect he's on the payroll of every news desk in Edinburgh. The Fonters are big news, front and back page.'

'Can't be the cleaner,' the DS observed. 'She'll still be a gibbering wreck.'

'What's our response?' the chief constable asked.

'Just holding at this stage, ma'am; all I've authorised the press officer to say is that we're investigating an incident in an apartment in the King Robert Village complex. Nothing more until we can get hold of the husband. I couldn't raise the Merrytown FC manager, but I have spoken to the chief executive, a woman called Angela Renwick. She knows how to contact him, through the head coach of the Spanish football squad.'

'Shouldn't we be doing that?'

'Technically, but I thought it would save time if I left it to her; plus, she speaks fluent Spanish. I don't. She'll need it to speak to the coach.'

'Fair enough. When the Renwick woman does get through to him, what will the message be?'

'To call me, nothing more. She doesn't know the whole story. All I told her was that there had been an incident involving Mrs Fonter and that we need to speak with him immediately. She'll ask him to use Skype or FaceTime, if possible.'

'When you do speak to him, Sammy,' she said, 'break it as gently as you can. Forget fame; this is an ordinary man who's lost his wife in terrible circumstances. He's going to remember every second of the conversation you have for the rest of his life. The memory, the horror, will never leave him, take my word on that.'

Her words had barely faded when Pye's ringtone sounded. 'In fact,' she murmured, 'if that's him, let me take the call.'

The DCI checked the screen, and handed the phone to her. She took it and walked away, into the apartment.

The two detectives remained on the terrace. 'Nice one, boss,' Pye whispered. 'That was a job I didn't fancy.'

The chief constable returned after a few minutes. 'How is he, ma'am?' Haddock asked.

'As you'd expect, in shock,' she replied tersely. 'At some point over the next hour he'll start to believe what I told him. The head coach was there. He speaks enough English to understand that Fonter needs to be flown home at once.' She frowned. 'Where are they? I forgot to ask.'

'Seville,' Pye told her. 'Do you want me to release the name now,' he continued, 'or wait for Allsop?'

'Neither. Have the senior person on the scene set up a full media briefing, one hour from now. I'll take it; you'll be with me. But not here, we'll use the old HQ building at Fettes. You okay with that timescale?'

'Yes, ma'am,' the DCI agreed. 'It gives us time to take a quick look at this building's CCTV. The security officer's setting it up for me. I rang her office and spoke to her briefly, soon as we arrived here.'

'Wasn't she called to the crime scene as soon as the body was found?' the chief constable asked, surprise in her eyes.

'Believe it or not, no. I reckon that Cope, the concierge, was so keen on selling the story that it never occurred to him to tell site security about it.'

'How comprehensive is the system?'

'Not perfect, but not bad. There's a camera in the foyer and in the lift, and one on each floor. But . . . there's a privacy facility.'

Steele frowned. 'How so?'

'There's a video entry system for each apartment. If the owners don't want their visitors recorded, for whatever reason, they have a switch that they can activate. It turns the security cameras off for three minutes, time enough for them to take the lift to wherever they're going.'

'I see. So the chances are that if Annette Bordeaux was entertaining someone in her underwear while her husband was away, she'd have turned off the system?'

'That's my fear, but I won't know until I've looked.'

'Then go to it,' she said. 'You never know, we might get lucky, and have this thing wrapped up before we see the media.'

Five

'Bob,' June Crampsey exclaimed. 'Guess what? Sky News are running a story that Annette Bordeaux has been murdered. And Al bloody Jazeera! All we're running in our online edition is a serious incident in a luxury apartment at the King Robert Village complex.'

'How come they are and you're not?' Skinner asked, framed in the doorway of her office.

'I guess they paid the price. The source said not only that he was a witness, but that he found the body. Then he asked for twenty grand for an exclusive. My news editor didn't even bring it to me, he told him to piss off. No story's worth that much to us. Sky, on the other hand, can sell it on to all its partners and affiliates.'

'What are you going to do? Run with it?'

'Without police confirmation? It could wind up costing us a lot more than that twenty grand.' She paused. 'What is it? What do you want? I'm snowed under here.'

He grinned. 'I just dropped by to tell you to get your best crime reporter up to King Robert Village. I've just dropped Maggie Steele there, lunch at La Garrigue aborted. She had a call from Sammy Pye; he's SIO up there.'

'What?' she gasped, hoarsely. 'You mean it's for real?'

'I'm not saying that. Maggie didn't volunteer the details, and I didn't press her. If she'd told me, there might have been a conflict of interest, given my role here. But the Scottish National Police communications director's been called to the scene, and she wouldn't have done that for a simple burglary.'

'So? Should I run it?'

'Who's your source, the one the news editor told to piss off?' Skinner asked.

'Bob, we protect them, regardless; you know that.'

'Fuck's sake, June,' he protested. 'I'm on the payroll. Anyway, if he claims to have found the body, the police will know who he is.'

'It's the King Robert Village concierge.'

'No surprise there. Are Sky running photographs?'

'No, but they were offered to us.'

'Then what are you waiting for?'

She smiled. 'For someone on the main board to give me the go-ahead.'

He laughed out loud. 'You mean for someone else to blame!'

The phone on her desk broke in with a buzzing tone. She hit a button, to take the call in speaker mode. 'Yes?'

'The police have just called a media briefing, June,' a male voice said. Skinner recognised its owner as Gordon Scott, the *Saltire* news editor.

'Then run it online. Attribute it to media sources; don't dress it up too much, but make sure you say it's unconfirmed.'

'You don't have to tell me that,' Scott complained.

'I bloody do!' the editor shot back. 'I'll watch your back, but I'm looking out for my own as well.'

She disconnected the call and looked up at Skinner. 'Any advice?'

'Check out King Robert Village building security, any way you can. That's what Sammy Pye will be doing right now.'

'And you wish you were there alongside him,' she ventured, 'don't you?'

He shook his head, slowly. 'No,' he murmured. 'In truth, I wish I was him. But that level passed me by twenty years ago.'

'I don't believe you. I can tell just by looking at you. You're itching to be involved.'

'I can't be, though, and I've never lived in the past.' He frowned. 'Trouble is, my well-meaning friends keep trying to drag me back there.'

Six

'What is this place?' Sauce Haddock asked, as they stopped at a ground-floor office beside an open area, identified as Lister Square by a signboard.

'Site security centre,' Pye replied. 'All the buildings are monitored here.'

He pushed a call button, while holding his warrant card close to a video entry camera. 'Come through,' a disembodied voice instructed.

They stepped into a small foyer area; there was a reception desk, but it was unmanned. Beside it, a woman stood, smiling, in a doorway; she was in her thirties, her frame was solid, with more than a hint of strength about it, and her thick dark hair was close cropped.

'Mr Pye, Mr Haddock?'

The DCI nodded.

'Nice combination,' she chuckled.

'They call us the Menu,' the DS said, drily. 'We hate it. Each of us is longing for the day when we don't have to work together, but for the present, we're stuck with it.'

'At least people won't forget you,' she observed.

'Names aside,' Haddock said, with a quiet confidence, 'they remember us.'

'I know. I read the Edinburgh papers. You two have had lots of coverage this year. I'm Christine Hoy, by the way, King Robert Village Security Manager. And yes, before you say it, my name gets attention too. The next comedian who tells me to get on my bike might wind up wearing his teeth as a necklace.'

'Consider us warned,' Pye told her. 'What's your background?'

'Army. I was a captain in logistics support, to give it its official title.'

'Afghanistan?'

'Two tours,' she replied. 'I wasn't front line, though. I flew intel drones from a relatively safe location. Come on through, let me show you what we have.'

The security office appeared to consist of only two rooms, and a toilet. She led them into the second, in which the wall facing the door was covered almost completely with monitor screens, all but one of them active.

'Take a seat,' she said, drawing one up to a table for herself. 'This shouldn't take long. I've looked at the time period you requested, and added a bit more on either side. First thing I should tell you is that all of the residents of the luxury block have underground parking, and often that's how they enter the building. Mr Pye, I know I told you that the top two floors have privacy systems built into their entry monitoring systems, but that does not include the garage. Everybody who comes in there is on camera, there and in the lift.

'For example . . .' she pressed a button on a console on the table, '. . . this from yesterday afternoon. Top left corner shows the time.'

The detectives followed her pointing finger as they seated themselves beside her. The screen indicated that it was fourteen thirty-seven hours when a big black Audi SUV drove into the garage, parking smoothly in a numbered space. Four people left the vehicle, then walked across the camera's field of vision, stopping at two silver doorways. The image paused.

'Lift entrance,' Hoy said.

The quartet were dressed identically, in dark blue training clothing, with a Nike tick and sponsor logo displayed on the chest, with letters above.

'That looks like Merrytown FC gear,' Pye murmured. 'Can you blow it up so we can read those initials?'

She nodded and rewound the video, frame by frame, to a point at which all four of the arrivals were more or less chest on to the camera, then zoomed in on them.

'JP,' Haddock read aloud, 'OF, AM, and . . .' he peered at the fourth figure, smaller than the others, '. . . that looks like AM too, but no, it's AMcD. A woman, I think, although it's tough to tell in that kit. Who the hell are they?'

'Watch,' their guide instructed. The onscreen image changed, became a view of the quartet inside a small lift, shot from the top corner facing the door, so that no faces were visible. The clock ticked off forty seconds, until the door slid open, and the view changed once more, into one of a carpeted corridor. The quartet stepped out, facing the camera. 'AMcD's definitely female,' Haddock observed.

One of the foursome, a brown-skinned male, OF according to the initials on his training top, dug a key from his pocket and opened the door, standing aside for his companions then following them out of sight.

'That's the apartment directly below the Fonters' penthouse,' Hoy told them. 'The lift they took only goes to the top two floors. Both of the properties are leased by Merrytown Football Club. That one is occupied by three players: James Pike, Orlando

Flowers and Art Mustard. Pike's English, Flowers is American and Mustard is Trinidadian.'

'Who's the woman?' Pye asked.

'I have no idea. Maybe they have a women's team. Staying on them for a little,' she continued, 'this was taken just over three and a half hours later, as the clock indicates, eighteen zero six, six minutes past six in old money.' She clicked on a track pad, and the four reappeared, leaving the apartment.

The three men were dressed expensively. Flowers wore a tan-coloured leather jacket and cream slacks, a black man they assumed to be the West Indian Mustard, in a tailored blue suit, and the third, Caucasian, in black jeans and a yellow Paul Smith shirt. AMcD had changed the most dramatically; there was no doubting her gender in a silver trouser suit, and her lipgloss shimmered in the autumn light that flooded the corridor.

'There was no other activity on that floor during that period,' Hoy said.

'Surely you haven't had time to watch it all,' the DCI observed.

'No need. The camera is activated by a movement sensor. Now let's go back. This is the view from outside the block, and it's twelve minutes past three. Watch.'

The detectives did as they were told. After a few seconds a woman stepped into view. She was tall, slim, long muscled, and she carried herself with a grace that told them who she was, even though her face was half hidden by the hood of her sleeveless, one-piece garment. She had a rucksack over one shoulder, from which part of a white towel protruded, and she held a takeaway coffee beaker in her left hand. The footage continued as she keyed a code into a pad, opened the entrance door and crossed the foyer. It saw her summon the lift, again with a code, then it followed her as she rose to the top floor, stopping as she went into the penthouse, the frame freezing as she stepped through the door.

'That is the last footage of Annette Bordeaux alive,' Hoy told them. 'I've traced her back from there. She'd come from the gym and, as you can see, stopped off at the coffee shop on the way home. She left the penthouse about two hours earlier. During the day, apart from what you've seen and what I'm about to show you, the only other activity on the penthouse floor, and on the floor below, was the coming and going of the cleaner.'

'Could she have let someone in using the private setting on the camera system?' Haddock asked.

'She could,' the security manager admitted, 'but she didn't, for interruptions to the system are recorded. Also, to be frank, the privacy isn't one hundred per cent. Any person who walked up to the outside doorway and pressed the video entry button would be caught by the surveillance camera, so that much of a record always exists. That didn't happen. Every visitor to the building during the day was followed to their destination.' Christine Hoy smiled; it was golden. 'Including this chap,' she said. 'Watch.'

She fiddled with the track pad once more, then clicked. The onscreen image changed as the frozen side view of the murder victim was replaced by the external area they had seen before. The time on the corner of the monitor screen showed sixteen forty-nine as a man came into view, walking purposefully. He was dressed in jeans, moccasins . . . and a Merrytown training top. It would have been identical to those worn by the players they had seen earlier, but for the absence of initials.

His face was partially hidden as he looked down, fiddling with something held in his hands, then completely obscured as he turned his back on the camera while keying in the entry code. His head was still down as he crossed the foyer, and tapped more numbers on the pad by the lift, and even as he rode it to the top of the luxury residence.

It was only when he stepped out into the penthouse corridor and walked towards the apartment entrance that the video captured him full face, as he pressed the buzzer, then stood waiting for a response. It captured a look of puzzlement as it developed, then a shrug of his shoulders as he tried the door, and, finding it unlocked, let himself into the Fonter residence.

'Well?' Hoy exclaimed, bursting with self-satisfaction. 'Does that help?'

'It will when we identify him,' Pye replied.

Haddock's chuckle interrupted him. 'We've done that already, gaffer. I may know fuck all about football, but I do not forget a face, and I've seen that one, very recently indeed.'

Seven

'Has the body been formally identified, Chief Constable?' Steph Maxwell of Scottish Television asked.

'To my satisfaction, yes it has,' Steele replied. 'The concierge of the apartment block where Mrs Fonter lived saw her on a daily basis. His identification is good enough for me, and for the Crown Office. But let's be realistic,' she added, 'you know who the victim was.'

'Have you spoken to Paco?' a voice called out. She looked towards it and saw a man of around fifty, with a white moustache and a nose that had known better days. He was a stranger to her.

'Dave Meredith, *Daily News* sports desk,' Malcolm Nopper, her press office aide, whispered in her ear.

She frowned in the scribe's direction. 'Mr Fonter has been informed; I wouldn't be holding this briefing if he hadn't.'

'Is he a suspect?' Meredith ploughed on.

'He's a tragically bereaved husband, who was in Spain when the murder was committed. You're getting a bit ahead of yourself.' She glanced at John Fox, the BBC's senior crime reporter, who was in a front row seat.

The veteran took the hint. 'In your statement, you describe

the death as suspicious, Chief,' he began, 'but can we take it we're dealing with a murder here?'

'Homicide, John; I'll concede that for sure. Murder, almost certainly.'

'I take it there was nobody else found at the scene . . . alive or dead.'

'Nobody.' She paused. 'Look,' she continued, 'DCI Pye is the senior investigating officer. I'm going to hand over to him for any operational questions.'

'Did Annette Bordeaux own the apartment, Chief Inspector?' Harry Wright of the *Herald* asked, from his customary seat in the second row, out of the line of sight of the TV cameras.

'No, it's leased,' Pye replied, 'by Merrytown Football Club. The owner is a company that bought the property from the developer as an investment.'

'Can you name it?'

'Not off the top of my head, but anyway I'm not going to; it's not relevant to this investigation. The football club dealt with its agent when it leased the place.'

'Properties, is it no'?' Dave Meredith was sharper than he looked, Pye realised.

'Yes, that's true,' he admitted. 'The club also rents the apartment directly below the crime scene. It's occupied by three players, all single men.'

'Pike, Flowers and Mustard?'

'That's them.'

'Are they of interest to you?' John Fox asked.

'We'll be interviewing them,' Pye replied, 'as we will be interviewing everyone who may have been in contact with the victim, but it won't be as suspects. I'm not going into too much detail, but I will say that we don't believe they were in the building when Ms Bordeaux died.'

'Chief Inspector,' a woman called out from the centre of the group. 'Rhonda Mortensen, Sky News. Our sources tell us that there were drugs found in the apartment. Had Ms Bordeaux been using before she died? Can you confirm that?'

He took a deep breath, aware that the atmosphere in the room had changed, and that every member of his audience was looking at him a little more intensely. '*Drug-fuelled orgy*' headlines danced before his mind's eye.

'No,' he said firmly, resisting the urge to glance to his right to gauge the chief constable's reaction. 'No, I can't confirm that. Toxicology carried out during the post-mortem examination will tell us what substances were present in the victim's bloodstream. If any of them were illegal, that will be in our report to the procurator fiscal. What I am prepared to tell you is that I saw the body and it bore no obvious signs of drug use.'

'But there were drugs found in the bathroom?' Mortensen persisted. 'That's what our sources say.'

Malcolm Nopper, seated between Pye and Maggie Steele, moved as if he was about to intervene, but the detective placed a hand on his arm. 'In that case they should be a bit more careful,' he replied, firmly but politely. 'Yes, there was a substance found in the apartment, and analysis will tell us whether it's talcum powder, caster sugar, prescribed medication or something else. But what it won't tell us is who put it there, or who supplied it.'

He smiled, and his eyes narrowed. 'If it is what you suggest, then trust me, that is something we will find out. When we do, we'll want to know when it was put there too. "Your sources", you say, Ms Mortensen. You should consider this before you go any further: at the time when you broke the story, only two people that I know of, other than members of my team, had been in the apartment after Ms Fonter died . . . other than whoever was involved in her death, that is. One of those two is being treated for shock in hospital, so that rather narrows the field when it comes to identifying your informant. If it gets to the point where our investigation is being obstructed, I'll know where to look.'

He looked around the room. 'Ladies and gentlemen, if there are no further questions . . .'

Harry Wright raised a hand. 'I have one, Chief Inspector. How confident are you of a speedy solution to your investigation?'

'I never quantify optimism or pessimism, Mr Wright. Do that and it'll only be used against you; that's something I was taught by a master. All I will tell you is that we are working proactively to answer the questions raised by Ms Bordeaux's tragic death. We'll report progress to you whenever we can.'

'Does that mean you have a suspect?' Rhonda Mortensen shouted, as he pushed his chair back from the table.

He stared at her, then leaned back towards the bank of microphones. 'That was neither said, nor implied,' he told her, then he grinned. 'Go and ask your source,' he suggested, 'see what he can tell you.'

Eight

'I just saw your boss on telly,' Cheeky McCullough told her partner, 'on Sky News. I think it was live. Their reporter tried to put one over on him and he melted her. The rest of the press crew laughed at her.'

'He's just melted the building concierge too; that stuff she had came from him and it was pure shite. There was a wee trace of white powder, that was all. Mortensen could have picked a better day to try it on,' Sauce drawled, his voice laden with irony. 'We've been in the firing line before, but never as seriously as this. I had no idea who the victim was when we got there,' he confessed, 'and even afterwards, for a while.'

'You are joking,' Cheeky exclaimed. 'She's one of the most famous faces on the planet. *Vanity Fair* had her in the top five "most glamorous" list last year.'

'She wouldn't have made it today,' he muttered grimly into his phone.

'Ooh, don't, I can't bear to think of that. Poor girl. Was it bad?'

'Being murdered is rarely good. I don't want to say too much but it was not gentle.'

'I suppose this means that tonight's off: dinner at Jack and Lisanne's.'

'Maybe not,' he said. 'You go there, don't wait for me. I'll turn up when I can. McGurk'll understand; he'll be dead chuffed he didn't catch this one himself.'

'Okay,' she agreed. 'Where are you just now?'

'We're at Merrytown's training ground, following . . . a lead.'

'Mmm,' she murmured, hesitating for a few seconds before going on. 'Sauce, I'd better tell you this before you find out for yourself. Grandpa's a significant shareholder in that club.'

'Eh?' Haddock exclaimed. 'I thought it was owned by a Russian, one of those oligarchs, a guy called Dimitri Rogozin.'

'He's the majority shareholder, and his company provides most of the cash, but Grandpa has twenty-five per cent. Rogozin wanted him on board, just in case he had trouble himself in passing the "fit and proper person" test.'

Sauce laughed. 'You're taking the piss. He recruited your grandpa as a fit and proper person?'

'Why not?' Cheeky protested. 'As far as the media are concerned he's a respected Scottish businessman, with an impeccable business record.'

'True, and his murder trial did collapse when the chief witness did a runner.'

'Be that as it may,' she insisted, 'he meets the criteria set by the football authorities.'

'God bless their wee hearts! Listen, honey,' he said, 'if you want to see me at the McGurks tonight I really have to go. Jackie and I have to talk to someone.'

'Okay, go to it. Love you . . . and yes, about Grandpa, truth is I was as surprised as you are.'

Haddock was smiling as he rejoined his colleague, DC Jackie Wright, in what Jock Shaw, their guide to the training complex, had described as 'the boot room'. 'Sorry about that,' he said. 'I was just rearranging my Saturday with my other half; this took us by surprise.'

The veteran escort glowered back at him. 'Lucky you,' he moaned. 'Every Saturday's a work day for me, apart frae international breaks . . . and this is yin.'

'Sorry about that,' Wright retorted. 'But I doubt that Mrs Fonter chose to be murdered on a Friday night.'

He sniffed. 'Aye, Ah suppose.'

'If there's no game, where are the players?' Haddock asked.

'The boss took them away tae Seamill Hydro for the weekend,' Shaw replied. 'Them as is no' away wi' their countries, like Paco.'

'I see. But they trained yesterday, yes?'

'Aye. The bus left frae here this mornin'. They'll a' be back on Monday, for trainin', like.'

'Wouldn't you have been in today anyway, to get their training gear ready? You are the kit man, after all.'

He stared at Wright. 'D'ye think they've only got one set?'

'It's more than boots come through this room,' Haddock observed, pointing to a large wicker hamper in the corner. 'It niffs a bit in here.'

'This isnae a country club, son. Whit's in there'll go tae the laundry on Monday mornin'. Gets done twice a week, Mondays and Thursdays.'

'How about yesterday's kit?'

'That's a' there. Some of the boys went straight aff after trainin' without changin', but they all brought it wi' them the day when they came in tae catch the bus.'

'So everything that was worn yesterday is in that hamper?'

'Yesterday and Thursday, aye. Why dae yis want tae know?'

'I need to be certain, that's all,' the sergeant replied. 'Would you empty it out for us, please?'

'Eh?' the kit man exclaimed. 'All of it?

Haddock nodded.

'There's a' sorts in there, ripped socks, jockstraps, shorts wi' skid marks. Do ye want the lassie tae see a' that?'

'There'll be nothing I haven't seen before, Mr Shaw,' Wright said cheerfully. 'You should have seen what my university hockey team left behind us. So empty it, please, we need to go through it. That's why we're here.'

Nine

'What are you going to do?' Sarah asked, gazing across the dining table as she plunged her fork into a bowl of strawberries.

'What do you want me to do?' Bob countered. 'I'll do whatever makes you the happiest.'

'Don't cop out, copper,' she laughed. 'If I say to you that I'd love you to stick with InterMedia, and the SIA until you can't stand it any more, and do nothing else but stay home and look after your kids, sure, that would be great . . . at first. It would be great for as long as it took you to feel groundhog-ish, that you were living the same day over and over again. Then you'd become irritable, restless, and unhappy, and because you were, so would I be. Bob, we stumbled into a second chance at a life together, more by luck than judgement, and I'm not going to blow it.'

'So?'

'So my question stands. If the First Minister has his way and this hush-hush thing is a real proposition, what are you going to do?'

'I don't know,' he replied bluntly. 'The theory is I'd be a sanctioned state maverick, operating outside but around the official organisations, the national police service and the

National Crime Agency. But the idea that it would be confidential, that's a nonsense. Wee Clive hasn't thought that through, or if he has he's detached from reality, even more so. Confidentiality and me? We don't go together. Like it or not, I have a high profile, and it won't go away.'

'That's true, beyond a doubt,' his partner agreed. Another strawberry paused halfway on its journey to her mouth. 'But leaving the means aside, it's obvious to me that he wants you back in the tent. If he found an acceptable way, would you want to go?'

'I don't know,' he confessed. 'Some days I miss it. This afternoon for example, dropping Maggie off at King Robert Village, then driving away; that was tough, with every fibre of me bursting to go in with her to find out what the hell was going on in there. It was made all the tougher,' he added, 'by seeing your car parked there, and knowing you were inside. That told me it was a homicide. Until then it could have been any serious crime, but you, my love,' he smiled, 'only turn out for the dead.'

'I'll bet you were pissed off,' Sarah chuckled. 'Now you do know, how do you feel about it?'

'Again, ambivalent. Part of me, the reckless, self-indulgent part, wishes I was leading the investigation. But alongside that, the pragmatist says, "Hell no! The pressure on Sammy Pye to get a result will be bloody global. Who in his right mind would want any part of that?" On balance, this one I can leave.'

'Sure, and part of me believes that, but the part that knows you best says you're still bursting to be leading the hunt.'

'Maybe,' Bob admitted, 'but it's time for the young guys to make their names. I have a hunch that they will too, pretty quickly. There was something about Sammy Pye's body language during that press conference; it told me he thought he was on to something.'

'That quickly?'

'Most homicides are cleared up in the first hour.'

'That's because most are domestic; in this case the husband is in another country.'

'I'm not sure I agree with that assumption, but for sure, victim and killer usually know each other, so most investigations begin with a ready-made cast of suspects. Did they give you any hints when you were there?'

'They weren't pleased with the concierge,' Sarah said, 'that was for sure.'

'I picked that much up from the press conference. Have they identified the substance they found in the bathroom?'

'No, and to be honest, from where it was located it could very well turn out to be talcum powder. I'm still waiting for the analysis of Annette Bordeaux's blood, but if it was a drug that they found, I wouldn't have taken her for the user. She was a very fit woman; her last snack, eaten within an hour of her death, was a banana, and something that looked and smelled like an isotonic energy drink. You don't consume that and follow it up by snorting coke.'

'No,' Bob agreed, 'you don't. But whoever it was she was entertaining needn't have been such an aesthete.'

'Why do you assume she was . . . entertaining?'

'Was the door forced?' he asked.

'No.'

'Were there any signs of a struggle?'

'No, other than a blood smear that Dorward thinks came from her nose when she was hit.'

'Then we're back to what we agreed, more or less, before. She knew her killer.'

Sarah's eyes widened. 'And she entertained whoever it was in her underwear. So the supermodel had a piece on the side.'

'Were there any signs of sexual activity before she was killed?'

'No,' she admitted.

'So her visitor . . . her killer . . . could have been a woman.'

'Then she packs a hell of a punch. Annette's nose was badly broken.'

Bob shrugged. 'That doesn't rule it out. I know a couple of women who could do that . . . my elder daughter among them. I taught Alex to take care of herself from an early age.'

'Maybe, but . . .'

She was interrupted by Jimmy Buffett; Bob's ringtone was 'Margaritaville'. He picked up his phone from the table, and peered at the screen. 'Speak of the very devil,' he said, softly. Accepting the call, he put it on speaker and laid it back down.

'Yes, my child?' he said amiably.

'Pops, have you been drinking?'

The urgency in her tone brought him upright in his chair, sitting to attention. 'No,' he replied. 'I've told you, Sarah doesn't, given her condition, so neither do I: not much anyway. Why? Do you have a problem?'

'I have a client, a brand-new client. He's just been arrested and he's being brought to Edinburgh. I've been instructed on his behalf, by his wife, and I've said I'll be there when he arrives.'

'What's the charge?'

'There isn't one yet, but it's likely to be murder.'

'Who's the arresting officer?'

'Sauce Haddock.'

'Sauce?' Skinner exclaimed. 'He works with Sammy Pye and Sammy's . . .' He whistled. 'Jesus, this is the Annette Bordeaux investigation.'

'Yes,' she confirmed. 'It's massive already and it's going to get bigger when the press find out who's been detained. They've arrested Chaz Baker, the Merrytown team manager.'

He looked across the table, eyes gleaming with something not far short of triumph. 'What did I say?' he murmured. 'Known to the victim.' He glanced downwards once more, as if he was on a video call. 'So, Alex, why did you ask about my sobriety?'

'Because I'd like you to meet me at Fettes,' she said, bluntly. 'They're taking him there because it's the least accessible police station in Edinburgh as far as the media are concerned.'

'True enough but, kid, you don't need me. You have to think of him as just another client.'

'Once upon a time,' she retorted, 'somebody probably said much the same to Charlie Manson's lawyer. Pops, I'm new at the criminal bar. I'm not saying I can't handle the brief, but it's a massive step for me.'

'Then why did you accept it?' he asked.

'Good question,' she sighed. 'I'm a solicitor advocate and as such I have a professional obligation. I can't cherry-pick my clients. On this one, I need support. I'd just like you to be there when I see Baker. After that, we'll see how it plays out.'

'One thing puzzles me,' Skinner said. 'Yes, you are new at the criminal bar, and you're still building your reputation. This is going to be a very high-profile case, so why did Baker's wife call you?'

'She said I'd been recommended.'

'By whom?'

'I have no idea, and I didn't think to ask her. Please, Pops.'

'There might be a problem with me getting involved,' he pointed out. 'Sarah did the autopsy on the victim; she'll be a prosecution witness.'

'I don't see that as a difficulty,' Alex countered. 'The Crown will have to disclose the post-mortem findings, so where's the conflict of interest? Besides, she's my stepmother . . . or she will be if you two ever decide to get married again. The court wouldn't expect me to ostracise her for the duration.'

'Sammy Pye might not see it that way. Maggie Steele might not see it that way. Either of them might ban me from the building, and I'd have no complaints if they did.'

'That's hardly likely, is it?'

'If I was in their shoes, it would be highly likely. For sure there's no way they'll let me in the room with you during any formal interview. Baker's entitled to legal representation while he's being questioned, but I'm not a lawyer. Allowing me to sit beside you would be a precedent no responsible officer could set. Call the Lord Advocate if you like; he'll tell you the same.'

'Then don't sit beside me,' she said. 'But be there, please.'

Skinner looked at Sarah, one eyebrow raised in a questioning gesture. She nodded.

'Okay,' he sighed. 'I'll chauffeur you down there. Forty minutes, tops, I'll pick you up. Be waiting for me outside your place.'

Ten

'That was a bolt from the blue, Cameron,' Mia Watson McCullough murmured, coolly, across another dinner table.

'You're a mistress of the understatement, lass,' he replied, sharply. There was something in his eyes that said far more. *Windows to the soul*, she thought, remembering two other people in her turbulent life who had offered her similar, equally disturbing, glimpses

'Sorry,' she exclaimed, quickly. 'I wasn't being flippant, honestly. That poor woman; it's terrible. But Baker? Who'd have imagined it?'

She had never seen him rattled before. Normally the universally nicknamed Grandpa McCullough was distinguished by his calmness. The legend that had been built around him in his home city of Dundee cast him as cold, ruthless and ferocious. She had heard of him before ever meeting him, and that was what she had expected when she did. Instead she had found quiet, thoughtful equanimity, and had experienced nothing but kindness and courtesy from him. That flash of something else: nothing scared her, she had seen too much, but for sure it had startled her.

And yet, when the moment passed, he was contrite. 'No, I'm

sorry, love. Forgive me for being short with you. It just took me . . .' He shook his head. 'Poor woman indeed; and poor Paco. I was being selfish too, I admit, for I couldn't help thinking, poor Merrytown, as well. What happened to Annette would have been a hell of a blow for the club on its own, but this . . . Jeez, I don't know how it'll play out.'

He offered her a grim smile, then glanced around the busy dining room. 'It could have been worse, though,' he chuckled.

'How?'

'He might have been arrested here,' MCullough said. 'I offered him the freedom of Black Shield Lodge for the squad's away weekend, but he wanted to take them to the seaside. He has a theory that running on beaches and in seawater strengthens the legs.'

'He must have seen *Chariots of Fire*.'

'Maybe. Whatever, having a guy lifted for murder from my hotel wouldn't be the sort of publicity I appreciate.'

'Do you think he did it?' Mia asked.

He frowned. 'What do you think? They found the body around midday, and Chaz was lifted early evening. That suggests to me they've got something pretty conclusive on him.'

'What exactly did his wife say? Have they charged him?'

'No,' he replied, 'but they wouldn't do that there and then. He's been cautioned and detained in connection with Annette Bordeaux's suspicious death. That was the wording they used, she told me.'

'Where are they taking him?'

'Edinburgh, Lita thinks. I suppose it would be. That's where she was murdered.'

'Chaz?' she exclaimed. 'What was he doing there? No, it must be a mistake.'

'What do you think he was doing there?' McCullough retorted, laughing lightly.

'Surely not! She seemed like a very nice girl when we met her. She was ordinary; there was none of the celebrity about her. Her English was very good too.'

'That's not unusual in Eastbourne, or wherever she's from.'

'Are you saying she was English? I always thought she was French.'

'You should read those magazines,' he said, 'rather than just looking at the pictures. Her real name was Annette Brody. That agent of hers, that Sirena woman, she Frenchified her at the start of her career.'

'After she plucked her out of the chorus line in a Paris nightclub,' Mia grinned. 'You see, I do read, sometimes.'

'Aye, the wrong papers. I'm sceptical about that Sirena. When we met her she struck me as a complete fucking fruit loop. Nothing's real about her, not even her name; Sirena Burbujas, for fuck's sake. It means Bubbles, in Spanish.'

'I never took you for a linguist,' she chuckled.

He winked. 'I'm not. I picked that up from a bottle of fizzy water in Madrid on our honeymoon.'

She smiled, then glanced at her empty champagne flute. The tiny gesture was spotted by the wine waiter; instantly, he swooped on their table like a diving hawk and refilled it. He looked at McCullough, questioningly. 'Monsieur?'

'I'm fine, Jacques,' he answered. 'You can open the Sancerre though.'

'Going back to Lita Baker,' Mia said as he withdrew. 'I thought Susannah Himes was your regular lawyer: that woman they call the Barracuda.'

'She doesn't have exclusivity. That Frances Birtles, she's best when a case goes to trial, by a mile; it's her strength. Himes is very good all round, but what she's best at is cutting a deal. A few years back, when my stupid daughter Inez got my granddaughter involved in something that was reckless even by her standards, I called her in straightaway. Cameron walked away scot-free, without a stain on her character, and her career intact.'

'You never told me that before.'

'I try to forget it,' he confessed.

'What happened to Inez?'

'She went to jail,' he said.

'I see. And you blame Himes?'

'Hell no! I wasn't bothered about that at all. She deserved every day she got. No, the thing about the Barracuda, she has a high profile, and that might not be what Chaz needs. Himes very rarely goes to trial, you know.'

'Why not?'

'Because most of her clients are fucking guilty,' he laughed. 'Lita might not want to give that impression in this case.'

'I get it, but still . . . Alex?'

'Why not? Look, Chaz was arrested by my granddaughter's partner. Now he might be defended by your son's half-sister. It'll be Lita's choice. All I'm doing is putting her name in the frame.'

'Fine, but is she up to it?'

'Time will tell,' he said. 'She'll be well advised in approaching the brief, and that's the most important thing.'

'Advised? By whom?'

He stared at her. 'Fuck's sake, my darling, who do you think?'

'Of course,' Mia conceded. 'Even if she goes mental and sees herself as a John Grisham heroine, Bob'll keep her feet on the ground. If Chaz is guilty, he'll know and advise her accordingly. But is he guilty?'

'How would I know?' McCullough snorted. 'But one thing's obvious. They must be able to place him at the scene for him to have been arrested so quickly. '

She gazed at her glass for a time, mulling over his assertion. 'Wait a minute,' she countered, eventually. 'He could have been calling in on the guys who live below. You told me that there are three of them, young foreign guys.'

'One of them's English but yes, that's right. However, if Chaz had gone there, and not to the penthouse, they'd know that. The security camera would have shown him there.'

'You know a lot about the place,' Mia remarked.

'I should do. I own it . . . or rather you do.'

'I do?' she spluttered. 'What are you talking about?'

He smiled; there was a little guilt in it. 'We have a pre-nuptial agreement, yes?' he began.

'Yes, it defines our assets . . . yours, since I brought nothing . . . at the time of our marriage, and if you die before me it guarantees me at least fifty per cent of any property acquired after that date. Fair enough.'

'I'm glad you feel that way. As for those defined assets, you know that my granddaughter will get the lot, with you having life rents on the house here in the hotel grounds and on the one in Spain. That will leave her a very wealthy young lady.'

Mia held up a hand. 'Hold on a minute! It could leave her a very wealthy old lady. You're sixty-two and you're as fit as most of the Merrytown first team. Cheeky could be your age by the time she inherits.'

'That's possible,' he agreed, 'but my grip on the planet might be more tenuous than you believe. I didn't do all the things that Bob Skinner and his pals say I did, but I have made a few formidable enemies along the way, nasty guys with long memories. I might be fit, but I'm not bombproof.' He paused, looking almost coy.

'I was keeping this as a surprise,' he continued, 'but you've stumbled across it now. I've started to move stuff in your direction. I bought the top two floors of that block in King Robert Village, but I did it through a property company I set up, in your name. You're the only director.'

'What?' his wife gasped. He had taken her completely by surprise and that pleased him. 'How could you do that without me knowing? Surely I had to sign something to be a company director.'

'You did. That bank account I asked you to sign for a few months ago, that was for the company. It's called Sparkle Holdings Limited, by the way, after your old radio name when you worked on the station in Edinburgh.'

'Bloody hell, I made that name disappear, sharpish. I hope nobody cottons on.'

'There's nobody left that it would bother. And suppose there was . . .'

'Your reputation would keep them at bay?'

He nodded. 'My alleged reputation. You know I'm a pussycat at heart, but if others think I'm a tiger, let them.'

'Does that include your business partner in the football club?'

'Dimitri Rogozin?' he chuckled. 'He and I know exactly what each other is.'

'Is that why he asked you to invest in the football club?' Mia asked.

'He didn't. It was the other way around. I was offered the deal by the consortium that owned the club before, old guys who'd run out of steam and money. I fancied it, but it had to be a serious business proposition. After the Rangers fiasco, I saw a gap in the Scottish football market for a financially sound, properly run team. The only problem was that I couldn't invest the money it would need without attracting attention. So I brought in Rogozin.'

'Why him?'

'Because I own half of his business in Russia.'

He forestalled any follow-up questions by beckoning the sommelier, and tasting the Sancerre that he had ordered. 'Nice,' he murmured. 'Please tell the kitchen we're ready for our starters when they're ready for us. Customers come first, as always,' he added.

'Commendable,' his wife said, with a hint of sarcasm. 'Now, back to your latest bombshell: you are Rogozin's business partner?' Her stare was incredulous.

'Yes, but that stays between us. Not even Cheeky knows that.'

'I thought she knew everything.'

'No. Some stuff she doesn't need to know. It would be bad for her, professionally. She's a big-firm chartered accountant, remember.'

'So it's iffy.'

'Some might see it that way,' McCullough conceded. 'Let's go back ten years, give or take; at that time my "above ground" businesses, construction, property, leisure, were all going very well, and the Inland Revenue did very nicely out of them. But I was also generating profit below the line and offshore, that I saw as outside its remit. I needed somewhere to invest that money, and I just happened to bump into Dimitri when I was looking around. He was a go-ahead guy then, if a bit full of himself, operating in Russia in some of the same sectors as me, and starting to do well. However, he was short of development capital, so he asked me if I was interested in going in with him. I checked him out via some people I knew out there, and got good feedback. He knew the right politicians and he didn't have any enemies of the wrong sort; he seemed like a sound guy. I went with him on a fifty-fifty basis initially, and it's paid off.'

'You laundered money through him,' she said, bluntly.

He drew a deep breath and his eyes seemed to chill a little, but the moment passed. 'Some might say that,' he murmured. 'That's why I've never shared this with my granddaughter.'

'Or her mother?'

'Inez? God no, she's an idiot.'

'Or your sister?'

'Goldie? God no, she's . . . she's . . . No, all I'll say is don't ever get on the wrong side of her. Goldie's been useful to me from time to time, but she's a fucking sociopath. Some of the rumours about me are actually based on things I've covered up for her.'

'Jesus, Cameron! If anything did happen to you, should I be worried about her? Should Cheeky?'

'No, you shouldn't, and that's a promise. If that happens in the near future, a package will be delivered to young Detective Sergeant Haddock; its contents should take Goldie out of play for the rest of her days . . . although they're numbered.'

She stared at him. 'If you'd do that to your sister, should I be worried about me?'

He laughed. 'Not for a second; I hate her, I love you.'

'That's a comfort. Now, back to Dimitri; you brought him into the Merrytown takeover. Why?'

'So that the investment capital the club needed could come from an outside source, and not ostensibly from me. But in practice, Rogozin's seventy-five per cent stake is held by the company that we both own.'

She nodded. 'Therefore,' it began as a whisper, 'although the media describe him as the majority shareholder, with your twenty-five per cent, plus half of his company's stake, you are.'

'Exactly, and my presence was explained by the rumour we circulated about Dimitri being afraid of failing the football authorities' "fit and proper person" test. He's the front man, and I'm very much in the background, as I always prefer it.'

'How much money have you put into the club since you bought it?'

'Personally nothing, but through Rogotron, the company we own, so far there's been a loan of twenty million, plus another ten million more through a three-year shirt sponsorship deal. That's the cash that paid for Paco Fonter, for Chaz Baker, and for the three players in the flat below where Annette was killed. Merrytown isn't funded to the English level, but it's the best resourced club in Scotland, even above the so-called big two.'

'Will you ever get that money back?' Mia asked.

'Not all of it, but the Russian tax authorities will take some of the hit. It's not just a vanity project though. Baker's target was to win the Scottish Premiership this season, or at the very least make sure the club is playing in European competition next year.'

He glowered into his white wine. 'That's why his arrest is seriously bad news. He's hardly going to do that from inside Peterhead Prison, is he?'

Eleven

'CC54RMS,' she recited as she slid into the passenger seat, enjoying the new leather smell. The car's predecessor had been involved in an accident a few months before and had been traded in at the first opportunity. 'Yes, it suits you? I'm pleased with that.'

His car was a Mercedes E Class saloon, a common enough marque in Edinburgh, but Alex's sharp eyes picked it up as soon as the number plate came within sight. As a serving police officer, Bob Skinner had always vetoed the suggestion of a personalised number plate, but she had bought one for him almost as soon as he had left the force.

'You got my age wrong,' her father grumbled, as he had from the day she sprung it on him.

'I've told you, that number wasn't available. Be patient; it'll match soon enough.'

He glanced to his left. 'You've got the power suit on,' he remarked. 'It's Saturday night, FFS.'

'What do you want me to wear? Jeans and a golf shirt like you? I need to impress this man from the start. He doesn't know me from Adam. If I turn up dressed like a disco diva I'll hardly do that.'

'You realise you don't need to be doing this?' Bob asked. 'Sammy and Sauce won't be questioning him until tomorrow morning. They'll hold him overnight, to let him stew on it so that they're fresh and he's not.'

'All the more reason that I do spend time with him,' she countered. 'The man's in a potentially life-changing situation, he's a murder suspect, probably about to be an accused. Innocent or guilty, he is entitled to a defence and to be properly advised from the start, before the cell door closes on him tonight.'

'Was Baker's wife there when he was arrested?'

'Yes. They picked him up at a hotel called the Seamill Hydro. He was there with his team, and since there isn't a game tomorrow, she joined him.'

'What did Sauce tell her?'

'She said he told her nothing beyond the reason for the arrest and where they were taking him. She was flustered, naturally; she didn't ask him about grounds for detention or evidence. He did suggest that she call a lawyer, though.'

'And she chose you,' he said, as he turned right into St Mary's Street.

'That's right.'

'How did she get your number?'

'Maybe Sauce gave it to her,' she suggested.

'Get real. In all my years of arresting people, I don't recall any of them, accused or his missus, asking me if I knew a good brief.'

She smiled. 'Maybe not,' she conceded. 'I imagine that the person who recommended me gave it to her. Or maybe she rang the Law Society. She could have Googled me. Who the hell knows? What does it matter?'

'It doesn't, not a lot. I'm just curious, that's all.'

He pushed a button on his steering wheel, and then said in a slow, clear voice, 'Call Sammy Pye.'

'Please select a number,' a woman instructed him.

He glanced at the screen on his dashboard. 'Mobile.'

He waited as the chosen number was dialled by the Bluetooth link to his phone, and as the tone filled the car.

'Yes, sir?' Pye managed to sound curious, cautious and tired, at one and the same time.

'Where are you, Chief Inspector?' Skinner asked.

'I'm at the Fettes Avenue building, the old HQ. Can I ask why you need to know?'

The DCI's question was ignored. 'Is Sauce there yet?'

'No, but he will be in a few minutes.'

'So will I, Sammy, with my daughter. She's been instructed by your prisoner's wife to meet him there and consult with him. I'm assuming that all you guys will be doing is putting him to bed for the night. Right?'

'That's our plan, boss.'

'Fuck's sake, stop calling me that, Sammy. Be that as it may, Alex still wants to speak to him tonight. The rights are a bit vague in these circumstances, but unless you've got a reason for denying her access, I'll expect you to facilitate that. If you do turn her down, your reasoning had better be watertight, otherwise a very disgruntled judge is going to be dragged away from his port and cigars to grant her an interdict.'

The detective's gentle laughter seemed to envelop them. 'Chief, Alex can do anything she likes, short of taking her client out for a Chinese. I'll set up an interview room with the custody people; I'll even tell them to put an extra chair in there for you.'

'That's what I wanted to hear, son, thanks. We're just clearing St Andrews Square now. Be with you in five.'

Twelve

'Who the hell are you?' Chaz Baker asked, as he took his seat. 'Are you more cops?' His accent came from somewhere around London.

The football manager blinked under the harsh neon light. He was a slim man, aged somewhere in his forties, with conservatively cut hair, as dark as the day-old shadow on his chin. He wore a crested blazer, over a crumpled shirt; the laces had been removed from his black shoes, and he had clutched at the waistband of his grey trousers as he shuffled across to the table.

He frowned, apprehensively at first, then glaring, as he sized up the two people who were seated opposite him.

'No, we're not,' the younger of the two replied, a tall woman in a black suit that showed off the length of her legs, even though she was seated. Her male companion sat a little behind her; large, casually dressed, at least twenty years older than she was, probably more, with close-cropped grey hair and cool blue eyes that offered no clue to what might be going on behind them.

'My name is Alexis Skinner,' she continued, 'solicitor advocate. I was called by your wife and asked to come here to advise you, and take your instruction if you wish.'

Baker nodded towards her associate. 'And him?'

'My associate. He happens to be my father, but he assists me with some of my work. I specialise in criminal defence,' she explained.

'Is that what I'm going to need?' he snapped, curtly. 'A criminal defence?'

'The police haven't given me any information yet. They're not going to do that before your first formal interview. But as I understand it, you've already been cautioned, and advised that you've been detained in connection with the murder of Mrs Annette Fonter, also known as Annette Bordeaux.'

The prisoner nodded, vigorously. 'That's what they said. I dunno what the hell they're on about. I never killed no one, least of all Annie.'

'Annie?' the grey-haired man repeated.

'That's what her friends called her.'

'And you counted yourself among them, yes?'

He nodded.

'When did you see her last?' Skinner asked.

'Hold on a second,' his daughter said, raising a hand. 'Before we start discussing circumstances, Mr Baker has to instruct me formally.' She looked at him, making full eye contact. 'As I told you earlier, I'm here at the request of your wife. She called me after your arrest and asked me to take your case. I'm willing to do that, but I can only be instructed by you, no one else.'

'What will you do for me?'

'I will represent you fully,' she replied, 'through every stage of proceedings. At the beginning I'll be with you through every police interview, advising you of your rights, and, if you wish, on whether you should answer a question or decline.'

'Why shouldn't I answer?' he countered. 'I'm innocent, I swear it.'

'Guilt can be established through circumstantial evidence. If I felt that an answer isn't in your interests I'd advise you against responding.'

'Okay,' he mumbled. 'Go on.'

'If it transpires that you are charged, and served with an indictment, I'll prepare the case for your defence. As a solicitor advocate, I can prepare a case and present it myself from start to finish. I have rights of audience . . . I can represent clients . . . in every court in Scotland, including the High Court, where serious criminal cases are tried. However, although I've been in legal practice for going on ten years, and reached partner level in my previous firm, I am relatively junior as a Supreme Court pleader. If your case goes all the way to trial, I might well advise you to retain Queen's Counsel.'

'A QC?'

'Yes. My first choice would be a man called Easson Middleton. He's the top silk, and I've worked with him before. If he was onside, I'd be his junior in court.'

'Why did Lita call you?' Baker quizzed her. 'Lita's from bloody Croydon; she knows bugger all about Scotland, beyond Harvey Nichols and Charlie Kettles, her hairdresser.'

She shrugged. 'She told me I'd been recommended, but she didn't say by whom. Look,' she added, 'if your football club has a lawyer, or you have a family solicitor, and you'd rather consult them, I will understand completely.'

'I've got an agent,' he told her. 'He does all my stuff; my life is mobile,' he explained. 'I've managed in three different countries in six years. Before I took the Merrytown job, I was head coach of a team in Ligue Un in France, and before that in the Premier League in England. I own a house on the south coast that I bought during my playing days, but moving from job to job, Cisco Serra sorts out everything, my accommodation, nursery schools for Letitia, our little girl, the lot.'

He smiled. 'They took my phone from me, but I can bet you that there will be missed calls and texts from him backed up on it by now. This, though,' he sighed, 'this is way out of his area of expertise.'

He rocked back in his chair. 'There's a club law firm, of course; I suppose I could call him, but it might have been them that told Lita to call you.'

'Do you know who they are?'

He frowned and scratched his head. 'Curly something; that's all I can remember.'

'Curle Anthony and Jarvis?'

'They're the geezers.'

'My old firm,' she told him. 'They don't do criminal work. If you asked them they'd send you to me.'

'In that case, lady . . . what did you say your name was?'

'Alexis Skinner, Alex.'

'Mmm,' he murmured. 'I used to play beside a Brazilian called Alex; big bugger he was. In that case, you'll do. First priority, how soon can you get me out of this damn fortress?'

'I can't make promises without knowing the whole story. When you were arrested, what did the officer say, as closely as you can remember it?'

'That I was being detained in connection with the suspicious death of Annette Brody, also known as Annette Fonter, also known as Annette Bordeaux. Why did he use all those names?'

The grey-haired man smiled, and spoke. 'It's a routine police procedure known in the business as "covering your arse". Since you've been here, what's happened?'

'They've taken my fingerprints and palm prints, and put a

swab inside my cheek. Oh yes, and they scraped the inside of my fingernails as well.'

'But they haven't charged you with anything?' Alex Skinner asked.

'No. Should they have?'

'It's a grey area,' she said. 'It can be argued that they should have, but once they do, they won't be able to question you any further. They'll have to charge you by Monday morning at the latest, and bring you before the Sheriff Court, for a formal remand.'

'Can I get bail in the meantime? Christ, I don't want to stay here overnight.'

'I've asked already, but that was a pure formality. The SIO said no. They don't know you, it's a high-profile crime and they'd have to assume that you'd be a flight risk if they let you leave here.'

'Can we challenge them?' he asked. 'Make them charge me now or let me go?'

'They would, Mr Baker; charge you, that is.'

'But I didn't do it!' he cried out . . . then seemed to sag into his chair. 'Don't say it,' he moaned. 'All of your clients are innocent.'

'Most of them have been, so far,' she said, cheerfully. 'Let's start with the assumption that you are too.' The smile left her face. 'However,' she continued, 'two bright, experienced detective officers have evidence that makes them believe that you're guilty. Plus, people higher up the food chain believe it too, for they didn't arrest you on their own authority alone, I'm sure of that.'

'Then make them put up or shut up; make them charge me right away.'

'If you insist,' she replied, 'I will do just that. I'll call DCI Pye back in and demand it. But . . . I'd rather not. I want them to interview you.'

'So you know what they think they have on me?'

'They'll have to tell me that anyway. No, if this thing goes to trial, I want you on record denying the accusations in a police interview, under caution, so that I can refer to that in court. Juries like to be clear that the man in the dock isn't relying on technicalities to get him off, he's relying on his innocence.'

Baker glanced at the grey-haired man. 'Do you agree?'

'It's not my place to disagree,' he said, 'because I'm not a lawyer. But as it happens, I've seen more juries than my daughter has, and I've got no doubt that she's right.'

'Then I'll go with that. But how soon can it happen? How many nights do I have to stay locked up here?'

'You'll be interviewed at ten o'clock tomorrow morning,' his solicitor said. 'I've already set that up. After that, I expect them to charge you. Then, because these are special circumstances, they'll arrange for the Sheriff Court to sit in closed session at midday, when you'll appear for remand to prison.'

'Prison?'

'It's a murder charge, Mr Baker; that's the norm. But it's not mandatory, not any more. I'll ask the sheriff to grant bail, on whatever conditions she likes. If she refuses, I'll go straight to the High Court and petition there. There's a better than even chance it'll be granted.'

He sighed. 'Let's hope you're as good as they say.'

'I am, trust me. But I need your help. You can begin by telling me all about your relationship with Annette Bordeaux, and where you were yesterday evening, when she was being murdered.'

Thirteen

'Fizzy water for me, mate, that's all,' Sauce Haddock replied.

Jack McGurk, his host, stared at him. 'Eh? After the day you've had?'

'This is only a brief respite,' he explained 'We've booked our prisoner in at Fettes; we took him there rather than St Leonard's, the divisional HQ, because there's more space around it to manage the media if the story leaks and we get besieged. Sammy's plan is to interview him tomorrow morning, then charge him. I need to keep a clear head for that. We can't afford any slip-ups on this one. It's as high-profile as they get.'

'Who is it you've arrested?' Lisanne McGurk asked, eyes wide as she leaned over the supper table. The detritus of three desserts remained; the new arrival's place was as she had set it three hours earlier. 'We've been sitting here speculating all night.'

Sauce frowned. 'I don't know if I can tell you,' he said.

'No way!' she gasped. 'You can't do that.' She looked up at her towering husband. 'Pull rank on him, Jack. Make him.'

'I can't.' The off-duty detective inspector frowned, pursing his lips. 'The suspect has rights; he hasn't been charged yet.'

'See,' Sauce challenged her.

'Come on, this is us,' she insisted. 'I've been married to two cops; I know you guys, you're serial bullshitters. You can't resist bragging about your cases.'

'This one can.'

'Why?' she taunted him, smiling. 'Have you turned into Sammy Pye's poodle?'

'If I had,' her guest moaned, 'I'd still need feeding. I'm faint with hunger here, Lisanne, and the smell of whatever is in that hostess trolley is making it even worse.'

She grinned. 'If that's what it takes.' She rose from her chair and walked round the table. 'It's chicken and asparagus bake,' she announced as she picked up a dinner plate.

'That's appropriate,' Sauce chuckled. 'We've lifted Chaz Baker.'

'What?' Cheeky McCullough exclaimed, the highlights in her blond hair glinting as she swivelled round, staring at him. 'The Merrytown manager? The guy that was pointed out to us at that Archerfield thing? He looked like a pretty smooth guy, not your homicidal type at all.' She winked. 'You can trust me on that. I come from a family of homicidal types.'

'I've been a cop for a fair few years now,' McGurk remarked. 'In my experience very few homicidal types actually look like homicidal types. How did Baker look when you lifted him, Sauce? Foaming at the mouth?'

'Terrified, more than anything else.' He paused, recalling the moment. 'He looked astonished too. I guess he must have thought we'd never see him as a suspect.'

'Is he denying it?'

'Of course he is; but he's not very convincing.'

'He'd hardly convince the Menu, would he?' Lisanne said as she placed his supper before him.

'Not when we know what we do about him.'

'What have you got on him?' Cheeky asked.

'We've got him on security CCTV footage, right up to the door of Annette Bordeaux's apartment, letting himself in, and then leaving again, forty minutes later. The time frame is bang in the middle of Sarah Grace's estimate of when she was killed.'

'That's it?' McGurk asked, his normal detective's caution verging on undisguised scepticism.

'Hell no,' Haddock retorted. 'He was wearing a Merrytown training top. All the players and assistant coaches have their initials on theirs, but Chaz Baker doesn't. It's a vanity thing with him; he reckons if you don't know who the manager is, you shouldn't be at the club. We went to the training ground this afternoon and looked at the kit that was there, waiting to be laundered. In among it we found a training top with no initials. There was blood on the sleeve.'

'Did you match it?' The DI's expression had changed. His eyes were those of a hunter.

'We took it straight to the lab in the Crime Campus at Gartcosh. The victim's samples were there already. Both were O minus; we can't say it was hers without DNA comparison, but it's about twelve to one on. '

'Okay,' the tall detective agreed, 'but without that absolute match can you proceed to a charge?'

Sauce smiled as he picked up his fork. 'Then there's the belt,' he said, softly. 'Annette was strangled with a brown leather Hugo Boss belt. It was covered in prints. As soon as we got Baker to Fettes we printed him, and got an instant match. He's still denying it, loud and long, but the chief's signed off on a charge, and so has the fiscal.'

'So relax,' Cheeky told him. 'Have a drink, love. I've been laying off all night, expecting to drive us home. Go ahead, tomorrow sounds like a formality.'

'Yes, one might assume that,' he concurred. 'But when one gets to Fettes and finds out who Chaz Baker's lawyer is, one rapidly thinks again. She was waiting for us there, demanding to meet with him in private before Sammy and I sat down with him . . . not that we were planning to do that tonight.'

'She being . . .' McGurk asked. 'Susannah Himes, Frances Birtles?'

Haddock took a mouthful of chicken bake. His head moved from side to side, slowly, as he chewed.

'All the way back,' he said, when he was ready, 'I was assuming it would be one of them. Frankie Bristles would have been fine, even the Barracuda, because they're known quantities. But it was neither of them. No, his wife's hired Alex Skinner. She was there, dressed for battle.'

It was his friend's turn to pause for thought. 'Okay . . .' McGurk murmured, '. . . but still no panic, surely. We all know Alex, have done for years.'

'Sure, we know Alex, the boss's daughter. We know Alex, Andy Martin's girlfriend as was. But we don't know Alexis Skinner, solicitor advocate. From what I've heard of her in that role, she's a tough cookie, up there alongside those other two already.'

He sighed and drank half a glass of sparkling water. 'The real worry, though, is that she wasn't there alone. She'd brought an associate with her; big bloke, in his fifties. He said he was only there as her chauffeur. That'll be fucking right!'

McGurk's eyes widened. 'Oh Jesus!' he whispered. 'Every cop's secret nightmare.'

'What?' Lisanne demanded.

'Having Bob Skinner play for the other team; the big man outside the tent, pissing in.'

Fourteen

*T*hinking? Bob Skinner's daughter wondered, looking at his profile as he drove. *Or not wanting to say what he's decided already?*

The road was clear of moving traffic, yet he checked both ways before turning into Fettes Avenue, heading towards Comely Bank Road. He was silent as he drove, listening to random music from the iPod he kept plugged into the car's sound system.

They had reached the bridge across the Water of Leith before her patience gave out. 'Come on, Pops,' she demanded. 'Say something.'

'You loved that track when you were wee,' he remarked, as the Communards belted out 'Never Can Say Goodbye'.

'Well, it's getting in the bloody way now!' She pushed a button on the dashboard, killing the music.

'Hey,' he protested, 'I was enjoying that, and thinking of me and your mum watching you bouncing up and down on your bed in your jammies with Jimmy singing in the background . . . and probably your mum singing along with him. Pity she missed the karaoke era,' he mused. 'She'd have loved it. You'd have had to tear the microphone out of her hand.'

On any other night, mention of her mother would have

triggered at least fifteen minutes of reminiscence, but Alex was not to be deflected.

'Don't dodge it,' she said. 'I want to know.'

'What?'

'Your opinion.'

'My professional opinion?'

'Yes.'

'Does that mean I'm on the payroll for this one?'

'If that's what it takes! Now stop stalling. What's your view of our client?'

He turned briefly, to look her in the eye. 'I think he's probably as guilty as sin.'

'Really? What makes you say that?'

'Experience,' Skinner sighed, 'coupled with the fact that they're ready to charge him less than twelve hours after the crime was discovered. He's admitted to us that he had a relationship with her.'

'A friendship, he called it,' Alex pointed out.

'That's his first lie. He told us that he went to the penthouse yesterday evening, at her request, and that he waited for her for about half an hour. She didn't show up so he left.'

'That's right. So why don't you believe it?'

'Maybe I do believe it; part of it. But if she wasn't there, how did he get in? Either he had a key or she left the door unlocked for him. Alex, I know that professional footballers live pretty controlled lives, but I do not imagine that it's routine for the manager to have open access to every player's front door. They were more than friends; trust me on it.'

'If he was there,' she protested, 'if he did kill her, why would he admit to having been there? Surely he'd be denying ever having been near King Robert Village?'

'He's afraid they have him on video. A pound to a pinch of pig shit he's right too. They're bound to have CCTV in a place like that.' He glanced to his left. 'Look, here's the scenario. Husband's away, she's called him 'cos she's lonely. He goes along; whether he lets himself in or she does is neither here nor there. They have an argument about something, a big argument, our client loses it, and she winds up dead.'

'How?' she asked.

'What?'

'How did she die? The police haven't released that information.'

'I know how,' he said, 'but I can't tell you. We have to play this by the book, Alex, for Sarah's sake. We know the woman is dead and it's being treated as homicide. That's enough for now. On the face of it, Chaz kills her, he panics and he runs for it. He admitted to us that he was in the flat because he's smart enough to know he can't deny it; even if he hasn't been caught on camera, he'll have left a trace.'

'I don't go with your version,' she replied, stubbornly. 'I believe him; he says he's innocent, and I accept that.'

'Johnny Fleming came in this morning saying he was innocent,' Bob pointed out. 'You didn't believe him.'

'The evidence, the injuries, the broken table and his admission that he hit the bloke didn't leave any room for doubt,' she countered.

'You haven't seen all the evidence against Baker yet. It will be there, and it will be significant.'

'We'll make that judgement after the interview tomorrow. Will you come?' she asked.

'No,' he declared firmly. He frowned, sighing. 'What would be the point?' he murmured. 'They wouldn't offer me a seat in the room, and I wouldn't try to force myself in there. It wouldn't be . . . appropriate. Wouldn't be right for you either. This is your turf now; you have to show that without me backing you up.'

'I know that, Pops,' she said. 'I didn't mean for you to be in there with me, but watching outside on video would be good, if they'll allow it, which I'm sure they will. Sammy and Sauce will have to show their hand in the interview. If you could see how Baker reacts to it, your opinion might help me decide how to advise him and how to frame his defence.'

He glanced at her, grinning. 'If I say yes, will you put the music back on?'

Fifteen

'*It's your Goddamn phone...*' a synthesised voice chirped noisily on her bedside table.

Scowling, Alex snatched up her iPhone and peered at the screen, focusing as she tried to read the incoming number; 'Unavailable' was calling her at twenty past fucking eight on a Sunday morning.

'If this is an automated offer of a Green assessment,' she growled as she took the call.

Throughout her life, one attribute ... she saw it as a virtue ... had always sustained Alexis Skinner. Regardless of her situation, whether she was under pressure at school, then college, then work, whether her private life was serene or she was in an emotional tangle ... as she had been on more occasions than she cared to recall ... she had always been able to sleep.

Her alarm had sounded at 8 a.m., but she was still dozing fifteen minutes later, as her ringtone forced his insistent way into her consciousness. She had downloaded it a month before; already she was coming to loathe it. *Time for a change*, she thought, as she picked up her phone and took the call.

'Mizz Skinner?'

The voice was male, and the accent was heavy, guttural. She swung herself round, to sit on the edge of the bed.

'This is Alex,' she responded. 'And you are?'

'My name is Dimitri Rogozin. I understand that you are the lawyer for my employee, Mr Baker.'

'Yes, that's correct.'

'How much trouble izz he in?' the caller asked.

'I can't tell you that,' she replied, 'for two reasons. One I don't know, and two, for all I do know you could be some joker from a red-top newspaper.'

'I am not one of such people, I ensure you.'

'Well, I'm not about to take your word for it . . . Mr Rogozin. Even if I did, I wouldn't be at liberty to discuss my client's case with you.'

'Mizz Skinner,' the voice growled, 'you would do well to listen to me. I am someone to be taken seriously.'

She felt a small chill of apprehension in the pit of her stomach, and reacted instinctively against it. 'So am I,' she snapped. 'I'm an officer of the Scottish Supreme Court and a member of the Law Society. As such I'm bound by its rules, and they forbid me from discussing my client's business without his express permission. So please don't call me with clumsy half-threats. They won't have any effect.'

'Mizz Skinner, I assure you . . .'

His tone was a little more conciliatory, but she wanted nothing more than to be rid of him. 'And I assure you, I will only take my client's instructions, not yours.'

She ended the call, laid down the phone and walked into her bathroom. As she turned on the shower, she was surprised to notice that her hand was trembling slightly.

She was still thinking about her caller, although a little more calmly, as she ate breakfast. 'Chaz Baker's employer,' she pondered. 'How would that be?'

Rather than taking the time to switch on her computer, she used her phone to run an Internet search for Dimitri Rogozin, making two incorrect guesses at the spelling of his surname, before getting it right. A photo came up, of a moderately handsome man, aged forty-three according to the Wikipedia profile that followed it.

'A self-made multimillionaire,' she read, her lips moving soundlessly, 'Rogozin created his fortune through his company Rogotron, building it over the last fifteen years into one of Russia's leading brands in leisure, travel and property. A potential move into the British market was signalled by his purchase of Merrytown Football Club, a side based in South Lanarkshire, and usually to be found around the middle of the Scottish Professional Football League. A substantial injection of cash funded the acquisition of several star players including Spanish international striker Paco Fonter from Italian club Pugliese, and manager Chaz Baker, whose appointment came as a surprise after his acrimonious departure from FC DuPain, a Ligue Un side in France.'

She closed the page and turned back to her cereal. 'So that's who you are, Dimitri,' she said. 'A wannabe with not quite enough cash to dine at the top table in the English Premier League, but enough to ape the big boys.'

When her father called her from the road to say that he was on his way, Alex's mind had moved on from the encounter. She was focused entirely on preparation for her client's forthcoming interview. She had forgotten about Rogozin entirely when she climbed into his car.

'Ready for battle?' Skinner asked.

She noted that he was dressed more formally than on the previous evening, in a black leather jacket, with grey trousers, a white shirt and pale blue tie. 'Not for battle,' she replied. 'This is about coaxing the police case out of Pye and Haddock.'

'And seeing how your client performs,' he suggested. 'Try to read his body language as he responds to their questions. See if he makes eye contact or avoids it.'

She glared at him. 'Are you trying to teach me my job?'

He smiled, affably. 'Too right I am; this part of it at any rate. I have a little experience in these circumstances. I've been questioning and observing suspects for as long as you've been alive. It's all about eye contact in there.'

'I'll bear that in mind,' she said, archly.

The roads were virtually traffic-free as he drove through the city centre. When they arrived in Fettes Avenue, he saw that the vehicle gates to the police building were closed, but there were very few cars parked in the street. He chose an empty space, and pulled in.

He failed to notice the man in the dark suit until he was almost upon Alex, blocking her way as she closed the car door and stepped on to the pavement.

'Mizz Skinner!' he heard him snap as he closed on her.

What the . . . he thought, springing from his seat, only to find his own movement obstructed by another well-tailored man, younger, leaner, clean shaven, with a tan that he knew instinctively had not been acquired within a thousand miles of Edinburgh.

'You will talk to me,' the one on the pavement barked, as Skinner closed his door. As he straightened, he smiled at the guy who was confronting him, stamping hard on his left foot in the same instant and slamming his right forearm into his crotch.

'Sorry,' he murmured, shoving him away as he folded up, then reaching Alex on the other side of the car in four strides, interposing himself between her and the potential threat.

'Her bodyguard's better than yours, chum,' he said. 'Now . . . explain.'

He edged towards the man, forcing him to step back, his eyes looking past Skinner as he weighed up the unexpected turn of events.

'I am Rogozin,' he announced. 'I am the owner of Merrytown Football Club. This woman is representing a valuable asset of mine and I wish to give her clear notice of my expectations.'

'This lady is my daughter,' Skinner told him. 'If you want to speak to her, you make an appointment and go to her office.'

The Russian glanced past him again. 'You have hurt my driver,' he said.

'I hope so,' he agreed. 'I wouldn't like to think I was losing my touch. I've heard of you, Mr Rogozin. I read the sports pages.' With two fingers he took a card from the breast pocket of his jacket and slipped it into the same place in the other man's mohair suit. 'Take that,' he said. 'Later on you can Google me. Now you're going to tell me who told you we'd be here.'

Alex tapped him on the shoulder. 'This guy's getting up and he doesn't look pleased.'

'Neither would I if my balls were suddenly the size of grapefruits,' her father murmured. 'Tell him to get back in your car,' he ordered.

The Russian nodded, and called out in his own language. From behind him Skinner heard a response. Even in a tongue he could not understand it sounded pained.

'He says he see you again,' Rogozin warned.

'If he does, he won't enjoy it any more than today. Now, talk to me.'

'It was Lita, Chaz's wife. She tell me the lady, your daughter, will be here.'

'So why did you feel the need to talk to her?'

'I have lot of money tied up in that man. I want,' he paused, 'I need him out of prison.'

Skinner glared at him. 'And you thought that bullying his lawyer would speed the process? What were you going to threaten her with?'

'Nothing!' Rogozin protested. 'I just need her to understand how important is to me.' He sighed, then added, quietly, 'And I want to know too; Lita says Chaz did not do this, but is that right? Or did he kill Anya, Annette?'

'The court determines that, not us,' Alex replied. 'My job is to prepare his defence against any charges. Do you hear what I'm saying? He hasn't been charged yet.'

'But you think he will be?'

'Yes,' Skinner admitted. 'That's pretty much certain, or they wouldn't have detained him overnight. We'll know for sure in a couple of hours. Meantime, my best advice to you, friend, is to get back in your box, stop behaving like a Mafioso hoodlum and leave my daughter to do the best she can for her client.'

'I will give her a bonus if she can prove he did not do this.'

'I'm not paid on the basis of results,' Alex retorted. 'Nor is it my job to prove his innocence. All I have to do is prevent the Crown from proving his guilt.'

'The latter not being dependent on the former,' her father added.

The Russian looked at him, puzzled.

'The issue isn't whether he killed her or he didn't,' Skinner explained. 'It's whether the prosecution can persuade eight out of fifteen people on a jury that he did.'

Alex opened her case and took out a business card. 'You have my father's,' she said. 'That's mine. If you feel the need to speak to me again, call me . . . during office hours.'

'We shall see,' he murmured, but he accepted the card.

They watched him as he walked to a black saloon and slid into the back seat. As they moved off, the driver eyed Skinner, who smiled and waved.

'You love that, don't you?' his daughter murmured. 'You can't resist any sort of a challenge, mental or physical.'

'He was trying to stop me from getting to you,' he insisted. 'I couldn't have that.'

'Pops, that . . . that . . . gorilla is half your age!'

'So?'

'What if there had been two of them?' she persisted.

He shrugged. 'It might have taken me a few seconds longer.'

'Pops!' she exclaimed. 'Seriously, you have to be more careful. You're not getting any younger.'

'I'm still young enough; anyway, experience counts for more than youth.'

'You have responsibilities!' She stared at him, scolding.

'And you're one of them.'

'You're not a cop any more.'

'I have a right to defend myself.'

'Using proportionate force.'

'He got up, didn't he?'

'You realise he could accuse you of assaulting him?'

He laughed. 'You'd get me off. Come on, it's over, and you're free of a pest. Time to go to work.'

They walked the few yards to the gateway then up the curving roadway that led to the front entrance of the police offices. As they approached, Skinner's eyes were on the windows of the office that had been his, as assistant chief constable and then as deputy. He had preferred it to the one he had inherited as chief constable. It allowed him to see all of the building's comings and goings, whereas the other had made him remote, removed from the action, the one aspect of top-level command against which he had always rebelled.

Pye and Haddock, both halves of the Menu, were waiting to greet them as they stepped into the entrance pod.

'What happened out in the street?' the detective chief inspector asked. 'Who was that bloke you were eyeballing, Chief?'

'Chap from out of town,' Skinner replied lightly. 'He was lost, but I've put him on the right direction.'

'Oh aye,' Haddock ventured, 'and was the other one just tying his shoelaces, or had he tripped over something?'

'I didn't notice him at all. To business, gentlemen; are you ready to proceed with your interview, or have you decided to release my daughter's client without further delay?' His eyes gleamed as he gazed at the pair.

'We're ready for you,' Pye replied. 'That's to say we're ready for Ms Skinner. Chief, I've discussed this with the chief,' he paused, embarrassed at his clumsiness, 'and neither of us feel that . . .'

Skinner raised a hand, palm outwards. 'Stop right there,' he said. 'I have no wish to sit in with you. It wouldn't be proper, given our past history, and it wouldn't be fair to Alex to have me looking over her shoulder. Anyway, my presence would need her client's approval, and neither she nor I are going to propose it to him.'

The DCI smiled. 'That's a load off my mind,' he admitted. 'Now it's sorted, would . . .'

He anticipated the question. 'Yes,' he nodded, 'I would like to see it through a video link.'

'I guessed you would. It's set up. You'll have company; the chief decided she wants to sit in too.'

The two detectives led them past the reception desk and along a corridor that Skinner knew well. He had spent several years of his career in that wing of what had been the headquarters of the old force before it was swallowed by unification and the Scottish National Police, its bastard offspring. He had used that phrase in what he had been told would be a private after-dinner speech to the Glasgow Bar Association, only to be reminded of the speed and the reach of social media. His words had left the room via Twitter before he had sat down, and had become online headlines before he had left the Hilton Hotel.

There was an unsubtle difference about the atmosphere in the building. Throughout his service there, which had encompassed most of his career, it had been alive, with a constant buzz of activity, seven days a week. That had gone, and he knew that there would be no difference on a weekday. The place was as good as dead; it was just another ugly office block, half of its rooms were unoccupied, and the highest-ranking officer there was a chief inspector. It gave him the creeps, but who was he to complain? He had walked away. Perhaps, if he had stayed, perhaps if he had become its first chief rather than the ill-fated Andy Martin, who had been destroyed by the job in only a few months, he might have been able to impose himself upon the bastard creation and thwart the politicians as best he could.

They stopped at a doorway halfway along a corridor, close to what had been the Special Branch suite in Skinner's time in the command corridor. He wondered what had become of its last occupants, George Regan and Lisa McDermid.

'We've set you up in here, sir,' Haddock said, as he opened the door. 'The chief constable's waiting for you, and coffee will be on the way.'

'And chocolate digestive biscuits, I hope. If unification's done away with them as well, we really are stuffed.'

Maggie Steele occupied one of two seats, at a table on which a TV monitor stood. She rose as he entered, hand outstretched in greeting. 'Morning, Bob,' she exclaimed. 'Welcome to the Chateau d'If. We meet two days on the trot. Maybe we'll get to finish lunch once this is done.'

He nodded. 'Let's try to do that.'

'Have you given any more thought to what we discussed yesterday?' she asked.

'I confess that I have,' he admitted. 'I'm still not won over, but while I'm still officially undecided, maybe I could use that status to seek a favour.'

'Of course you can, without strings attached. What is it?'

'I'd like to know everything that you can find out about a man called Dimitri Rogozin.'

'Consider it done. Am I allowed to ask why?'

'He owns Chaz Baker's club, and he's stepped very close to the line with Alex. If he crosses it, I'd like to be able to hit him where it'll hurt the most.'

Sixteen

'If you don't mind, gentlemen, I'd like a private word with my client.'

Neither Pye nor Haddock was naive, but both were taken aback by the transformation of Alex, the chief's daughter and their friend, into Alexis Skinner, solicitor advocate, in the instant that she stepped into the interview room and saw Chaz Baker, seated, wearing the previous day's shirt, frowning, unshaven, bleary eyed and nervous.

They paused, thrown off balance. Misreading their silence she smiled, with mischief in her eyes.

'If you do mind,' she added, 'I insist. And please kill the video feed.'

'Of course,' the DCI replied, his tone formal, his composure restored. He stepped across to the camera, on its tripod, and switched it off. 'Just open the door when you're ready. We'll be outside.'

'Thank you, Chief Inspector. My client would like his jacket, and his tie. We'd be grateful if someone could bring them.'

'Are they not your favourite people?' her client asked as soon as they were alone.

She grinned, relaxed once again. 'Actually, they're among

them. I've known them for years. I was just marking out my territory, that's all.' She opened her case and took out a toilet bag, opening it to reveal a portable electric shaver, a comb, and some facial wipes. 'Tidy yourself up,' she instructed. 'We want you looking your best on camera.'

He looked, curiously, at the Philishave as he took it from her. 'Do you always carry one of these?'

'On occasions like this I do.'

'Will your other half be looking for it?'

'I don't have another half; I'm one hundred per cent myself. I bought that as a business expense, and I keep it charged. It's quite possible that the recording made this morning will be shown to a jury. I want them to see a man who's neat, alert and assured of his innocence, not some blinking, unshaven slob in a crumpled shirt.'

She stayed silent as he went to work on his stubble, but he read a tension in her eyes, a question waiting to be asked. 'What?' he asked.

'Your boss has been asking after you,' she told him.

'My boss?'

'Dimitri Rogozin. Russian. Good looking, well dressed, gold tooth in the middle of the bottom row. That's how close he got when he waylaid me in the street outside.'

'Rogozin's here?'

'He's anxious about you, he says. He wants to offer you his full support.' She smiled. 'He offered me a win bonus; he must think I'm a footballer.'

'Fuck him!' Baker hissed. 'Pardon my Russian. Whatever your fee is, Alex, I'll cover it. I won't be any more in hock to that bastard than I am already.'

'In hock?' she repeated. 'What do you mean by that?'

'I owe him money. I was in a legal dispute with my French club after I left. Its chairman broke a couple of verbal promises, I quit and he sued me for breach of contract. I'd have taken it all the way, but Rogozin bought me out. He paid the Frenchman off, without my knowledge, and then told me it was a down payment on a contract at Merrytown.'

'You didn't have to sign it,' his solicitor pointed out.

'That wasn't how he saw it,' Baker said. 'Threats were made.'

She nodded. 'Having met him, I can imagine that.'

'He leaned on you?' her client exclaimed.

'Yes, but my father was there, and he leaned back.'

'What about Grigor, his minder?'

'He was having an identity crisis at the time. My dad can have that effect on people who get in his way.'

'Your old man decked Grigor?' Baker was incredulous.

'I don't know what happened. My back was to them at the time. All I heard was a thud followed by the sound of a man in pain.'

Baker grinned. 'You've made my morning.'

'Good,' Alex said. 'Let's carry that into the interview. This is how it will go. They will put questions to you, about your relationship with the victim, and about your presence in the apartment. Say what you like about the first, but my advice to you is to decline to answer the second. You don't need to explain yourself at this stage. Are you okay with that?'

'You're the boss,' he murmured, combing his hair.

'No, you are. Never forget that. Beyond those two questions, we'll be fishing, waiting to see what they put to you.'

'What do you think that could be?'

'I have no idea,' she admitted, 'but my expectation is that it will be significant. You might not like what you hear, but don't react with any sort of surprise, or show apprehension. Whatever they put to you, be as open as possible unless I intervene. Don't deviate from that. The only unprompted statement you should make while the camera and the audio tape are running is to declare your innocence of the death of Annette Bordeaux.'

Baker nodded, then continued to massage his face with a cleansing wipe.

'You're clear on everything, Mr Baker?'

'Crystal.'

'Then let's have them back in.'

She repacked the toilet bag, returned it to her case, then moved across to open the door.

'My client is ready to be interviewed,' she announced to the two detectives, who were waiting in the corridor.

They stepped into the room. As Pye switched on the camera and audio recorder, Haddock handed their prisoner the clothing that his lawyer had requested. He fashioned a double Windsor knot, slipped on his jacket, squared the lapels and took his seat at the table.

The DCI eyed him with a faint, narrow smile, understanding the scenario that had been created.

'I am Detective Chief Inspector Samuel Pye,' he began in a clear voice, 'accompanied by Detective Sergeant Harold Haddock. Also present is Charles Lofthouse Baker and his legal adviser, Ms Alexis Myra Skinner. Mr Baker has been detained in connection with the murder,' a fractional pause in his delivery emphasised the word, 'of Annette Brody or Fonter, also known as Annette Bordeaux, and he has been cautioned. Do you understand the terms of the caution, Mr Baker?'

'Yes.'

'Do you understand why you are here?'

'Yes.'

'Before we go any further do you wish to make a statement?'

Baker looked into the camera lens and frowned. 'Yes,' he replied. 'I did not kill Annie and I have no knowledge of her death.' His gaze switched back to Pye. 'Now you can carry on.'

'Thank you,' the detective replied, without a trace of sarcasm. 'Mr Baker,' he continued, 'you've denied something of which you haven't yet been accused, but do you deny visiting her apartment on Friday evening?'

'No, I don't. I was there, but she wasn't.'

'Why did you go there?' Haddock asked.

'She sent me a text, asking me to come and see her. About something important, a secret, she said.'

'We've seen that text,' the DS confirmed. 'Did she give you any indication at any other time of what that secret might have been?'

The prisoner shook his head. 'No, not a clue.'

'Did you consider any possibilities?'

He shrugged. 'I imagined it must have been something to do with Paco; I've got no idea what. Footballers, they can be a wild crew, but he isn't; he's one of the best pros I've ever worked with in fact. Crackin' player though; way too good for the Scottish League . . . not that he was bought to play there. Europe's the goal for Merrytown, and that is,' he stressed, 'his level.'

Pye tapped the table. 'If Mrs Fonter wasn't there when you arrived, Mr Baker, how did you get in?'

'Who says I did?' Baker challenged. 'All I said was that I went there.'

'We do,' the DCI replied, abruptly. 'Mr Baker, what would you say if I told you we have a video recording that shows you opening the unlocked door of the victim's apartment?'

'I'd say I never saw no camera, mate.'

'Nonetheless there was one. What do you have to say?'

'Nothing,' the prisoner murmured.

'Speak up, please, for the recording.'

His solicitor leaned across and whispered in his ear. 'No comment from now on; we want to see where they're going with this.'

'Nothing!' he repeated. 'No comment.'

Pye intervened. 'Very good; that's your right. Have you been there before, Mr Baker?'

'No comment.'

'What would you say if I told you that we've found your fingerprints in nearly every room in that penthouse, including Mrs Fonter's en suite bathroom?' he asked.

'I would say nothing, nothing at all.'

'What would you say if I told you that we found your prints on the table beside Mrs Fonter's bed?'

'Same answer; no comment.'

'Do you own a brown leather Hugo Boss belt, Mr Baker?' Haddock fired across the table.

The prisoner glanced to his left; his lawyer nodded. 'I own three Hugo Boss belts,' he retorted, 'one brown, two black.'

'When did you last wear the brown one?'

'I can't be certain. A few days ago, maybe.'

'How would you respond if I told you that Annette Fonter was strangled with a brown Hugo Boss belt?'

'I'd be appalled, whatever she was strangled with.'

'How do you respond to the fact that your fingerprints are all over it?'

Alex Skinner put a hand on his shoulder. He drew a long breath, exhaled, then continued. 'No comment.'

'Also noted,' Pye said. 'What were you wearing when you visited Mrs Fonter's apartment, sir?'

'If you've got me on camera you will know.'

'For the tape, please tell us.'

'I was wearing chinos and a Merrytown training top.'

'Were there any distinguishing marks on it?'

Baker shrugged. 'It carries the club's shirt sponsor's logo, and the maker's name.'

'No initials?'

He shook his head. 'No. Mine don't have any. It's my little joke; I say that I don't have any so that when a club sacks me they don't have to get new gear for the next manager.'

'When you left the Fonter apartment where did you go?'

The prisoner frowned. 'I went back to the training ground in Larkhall. I'd come from there, in a bit of a hurry, 'cos of Annie's message, and I went back to change into my suit.'

The DCI nodded. 'DS Haddock and I visited the training complex yesterday,' he said. 'Among the kit waiting to go to the laundry we found a top exactly as you've described it. There were marks on it, on the right sleeve. Laboratory analysis has shown them to be blood, and it's now confirmed that it came from Mrs Fonter. How do you respond to that?'

Baker gazed at the detectives across the table, silently, for several seconds.

'Sir?' Pye murmured.

'No comment,' whispered at first, and then repeated, loudly, with a glance at the tape.

'And as I've said before, sir, that is your right. However, I have to tell you that it leads us to a pretty inescapable conclusion, that on Friday evening you went to Mrs Fonter's apartment at her invitation to discuss something that was concerning her.

Whatever that something was, it led to an argument, in the course of which you struck Mrs Fonter, breaking her nose. You then removed your belt and strangled her with it.'

'I deny that, absolutely. Yes, I was there, but Annie wasn't. I looked for her, all through the apartment. I waited for a while, and then I gave up on her and left. I repeat that I did not see her there and I did not kill he.'

'The evidence says otherwise,' Pye told him. He looked at his solicitor. 'Ms Skinner, we see no reason to delay any further. Your client will be charged formally with the murder of Annette Fonter, and will be taken straight to the Sheriff Court, where we'll ask that he be remanded in custody.'

'Thank you, Chief Inspector,' she replied. 'I'll appear for my client at that hearing. We will,' she emphasised, 'be asking for bail.'

Sauce Haddock smiled. 'Good luck with that one, Alex.'

The look in her eyes wiped the grin from his face. 'I don't rely on luck, Detective Sergeant,' she snapped. 'But be advised,' she continued, 'your remarkable run of good fortune is about to run out.'

Seventeen

'Well?' Maggie Steele asked as the video link ended. 'Do we have a case?'

'You have him there on camera,' Skinner responded. He raised an eyebrow. 'Going in and leaving, yes?'

'Absolutely, and looking flustered as he leaves.'

'What's flustered, Mags? He could just have been pissed off at being stood up. Does the bloodstain show on camera?'

'No, but it wouldn't. The training top was dark blue, almost black, and there isn't a clear shot of his right sleeve. We've got his belt, round her neck, we've got his prints beside the body, we've got his presence in the apartment at time of death.'

'Okay but do you have her presence coinciding with his?' he countered.

'Yes, Bob, we do. She came in from the gym before he got there and she never left.'

'Motive?'

She laughed softly. 'You know even better than I do that we don't need a motive. All we need to do is prove beyond reasonable doubt that he killed her. The law doesn't ask us to establish why. If you want me to speculate, I suggest that they

105

were having an affair and she threatened to go public on it.'

'And he silenced her with Hugo Boss?'

'For whatever reason, he did. Honestly, are you going to tell me you wouldn't charge him with what we've got?'

He sighed. 'No, I'm not. Is that all of it, or is there stuff that you're holding back?'

'We have no more direct forensic evidence as yet, but . . . we have his phone. The text is there, sent from her less than ten minutes after she returned from the health club. "Must see U ASAP. Can't keep secret any longer. Come to apartment. Building entry code is 7585." Secret? Theirs, it looks like.'

'Did he text back?'

'There's a reply, sent immediately. "On my way." He got there seventy-eight minutes later.'

'I see. Pretty solid, I'll grant you. Yet he was vehement in his denial,' Skinner pointed out.

'Is that unusual?' Steele asked. 'The man's a practised liar. He was in a legal dispute with his former club in France, centred on an oral promise he made to the chairman that he would see out his contract there come what may. When he walked out, the man used that promise as the basis for a restraining order preventing him from being employed elsewhere. Before a French judge, Baker denied ever making the promise, then a tape was played. The conversation had been recorded.'

'Is that admissible in the High Court?'

'It doesn't have to be. It's public knowledge. Sammy Pye got it from a sports writer he knows.'

'So what you're saying to me, Maggie,' Skinner stood, 'is that my kid's going down in flames if she takes this case to court.'

'In a nutshell.'

'And what I'm saying to you is that there's no way in hell I'll allow that to happen.'

'Then persuade her to plead him guilty, Bob. It's the only way to avoid it.'

He smiled as he looked down at her. 'How many years was it, Maggie? You know there's another way.'

Eighteen

'**I**'m having lunch there with the chief constable after this is done,' Skinner remarked, glancing at the Royal Scottish Museum. 'Yesterday's was aborted before she really had a chance to go to work on me about some sort of a comeback.'

For all that it was Sunday, Chambers Street had the bustle of a weekday, but he had found a parking place at the South Bridge end, opposite the Richer Sounds Hi-fi store, where he was a regular customer.

'What does Sarah think?' Alex asked.

He grinned. 'About the comeback idea or about me having lunch with Maggie?'

'Both,' she laughed, 'if it comes to it.'

'She's happy about the latter. About the former she's reserving her judgement. How do you feel about it?' he asked.

'I'm reserving mine too. It would depend on what she's offering. Can you tell me?'

'In theory no, I can't.' He smiled again. 'In practice, there being nothing I can't tell you, and since we'll be bound by lawyer–client privilege . . . reading between the lines of what Maggie said yesterday before we were interrupted by the inconvenient murder of the unfortunate Annette Bordeaux, it seems

108

to me that the First Minister isn't completely happy with the powers that have been devolved to him, and wants to add to them by setting up his own little security service, without anyone knowing.'

'Bloody hell, Pops,' she murmured. 'Is that legal?'

'That's a question I'll be asking you if I give any thought to accepting. Hypothetically, if I was to be set up in *de facto* opposition to MI5, I'd want to be very sure of my legal ground. At the moment, I'm inclined to say "No thanks". I don't want to be Clive Graham's fixer; I had a taste of something similar earlier in my career, as adviser to the Secretary of State before the Holyrood Parliament existed, and it didn't end well, for either of us.'

'I'm glad you're being so cautious,' Alex said. 'You've been more relaxed over the last twelve months than you were in the previous twelve years. There is life for you, post-police. For example,' she continued, 'there's Chaz Baker's predicament. You spent all of your career in pursuit of the guilty. This is a chance for you to do it the other way round, by defending the innocent.'

'The problem with that, my dear,' he countered, 'is that all the evidence says your client is guilty. The only thing the Crown doesn't have is CCTV footage of him strangling the poor woman.'

'I know,' she admitted, 'but he says he didn't do it and I believe him. Fight for him; help me prove it.'

'You're wasting your time, kid,' he sighed. 'The police know stuff about him that you don't.'

'Please, Pops.'

'Stop giving me the big eyes,' he chuckled. 'You know I'm a sucker for that look. Okay,' he said. 'When the Crown gives you the police report, let me see it and I'll go through it. If anything in it strikes me as out of place, I might . . . just might, mind . . . look into it.'

She beamed. 'You're a darlin' man.'

'I know that. Now, you'd better get into court or your client will be there before you. It's a private session, so I can't come in with you.'

She nodded agreement and walked through the ornate iron gateway into the court precinct. The entrance door was guarded by a uniformed security officer; she offered her driving licence as identification. He inspected it, checked her name against a list on a clipboard and nodded her through.

'The clerk of the court's there already,' he said, gruffly, visibly annoyed by the disturbance to his peaceful Sunday. 'So's Miss Benedict.'

'Miss Benedict?' she repeated.

'Paula Benedict; she's the advocate depute.' He frowned. 'All we need now's the sheriff.'

'Not quite,' Alex countered. 'We need my client as well.'

She left the disgruntled guardian at his post and moved into the building, heading straight for the main courtroom. She was still relatively new as a criminal lawyer, but already she knew her way around all of the court buildings in Edinburgh and in Glasgow.

As she entered the chamber she saw two people, a man and a woman, in conversation. Alan Milroy, the clerk of the Sheriff Court, was well known to her. He smiled and waved as she approached.

Paula Benedict was not. She was dressed for battle, in a black robe over dark trousers and white blouse, formal court dress. Alex had heard of her from other defence lawyers and not all of their reviews had been positive. A member of the Faculty of Advocates, she had been at the bar for only four years, but saw herself on a fast track to senior counsel status and, beyond that, to the Supreme Court judiciary. A stint as a prosecutor in the Crown Office was an essential prerequisite for both.

'Ms Benedict; Alex Skinner,' she introduced herself, hand outstretched.

Her counterpart, a good four inches shorter than her five feet eight, gave her a look of appraisal that lasted a couple of seconds too long, before offering the briefest of handshakes.

'Ah yes,' she murmured. 'I've heard of you; you obviously know who I am.'

Alex smiled, but not with her eyes. 'You're the only woman in the room and Sheriff Wisdom isn't here yet, so yes, it was rather obvious. The Crown's sending in the heavy artillery early, isn't it, fielding an AD at a first hearing? A fiscal could have handled this, surely.'

Benedict sniffed. 'Could have, yes. But the Solicitor General called me personally and asked me to appear. He's determined there will be no laxity in any aspect of the prosecution of this case. My being here is a statement of sorts.'

'Oh yes?' Alan Milroy laughed. 'Who's noting it down, Paula? This is a private hearing, and it goes from here to the High Court.'

'The Sol Gen's briefing the media at two o'clock. He'll make the point in his statement, once Baker's safely tucked up in the remand unit in Saughton Prison.'

Alex felt her eyes narrow; she held back a retort, but with difficulty.

The official picked up her involuntary signals, but before he could react, a door opened, behind the bench, and Sheriff Lesley

Wisdom appeared. Like Alex, she wore no formal court clothing, only a suit.

She moved straight to her chair, looking down into the well of the court. 'Good morning,' she began then glanced up at the clock on the wall as the two lawyers took their positions facing her. 'No, it's afternoon. Are you ready to proceed, Alan?' The clerk nodded. 'Are you doing the record of the hearing?' He nodded for a second time. 'Counsel?' she continued.

'Yes, M' Lady. Paula Benedict, advocate depute for the Crown.'

'I know who you are, Paula,' the judge said. 'You too, Alex. Do you need any time with your client before I bring him in? If you do, I can give you a few minutes.'

She shook her head. 'No thank you, My Lady. I'm fully instructed.'

'Very good. We're short handed today, no court officer present, so Alan, if you don't mind.'

Milroy stood and walked across the chamber to a door at the rear. He opened it, spoke briefly and returned to his position below the sheriff. As he did so, two custody officers led Chaz Baker into the court and into the dock, where all three remained standing.

'This court is in session, before Sheriff Lesley Wisdom, QC,' the clerk announced. 'The prisoner Charles Lofthouse Baker is charged with the murder of Annette Brody or Fonter, also known as Annette Bordeaux, on Friday evening at a time to be determined, in her home at King Robert Village, Edinburgh. Mr Baker, you are not required to enter a plea at this diet, but do you understand the charges against you?'

The prisoner looked at his solicitor. She nodded, briefly, and he answered, in a clear voice, 'Yes.'

The advocate depute rose to her feet. 'My Lady, the Crown makes application that the accused be remanded in custody pending an appearance for full committal.'

Sheriff Wisdom peered down at Alex over the rim of her spectacles. Her question was unspoken.

She rose. 'Alexis Skinner, solicitor advocate; I appear for Mr Baker, and I move that he be granted bail pending service of the full indictment.'

Her opponent launched herself from her seat. 'My Lady, the Crown strenuously opposes bail in this case. Mr Baker is charged with murder, he is a man of considerable resources, and must be regarded as a possible absconder. I submit that if this court grants him his liberty pending trial it will be sending out entirely the wrong signal.'

The sheriff frowned. 'Noted. Ms Skinner, do you wish to offer reasons why I should bail your client?'

'My Lady,' she replied, 'I would be struggling to offer a reason why you should not. It's well established by recent precedent that the gravity of the charge is not an automatic bar to the grant of bail. Any refusal must be based on objective evidence that the accused is likely to abscond, that he is likely to obstruct the course of justice or that he is a threat to witnesses.'

'Thank you for advising me of the law, Ms Skinner,' Sheriff Wisdom murmured.

'I was advising my learned friend, My Lady,' Alex countered, quietly, 'since her motion seemed to indicate that she might be unaware of those aspects. My client is indeed a well-off individual, and he gives the court an assurance that he would not do anything to put that status at risk. He is prepared to abide by any conditions that you attach to a grant of bail, and to appear at all subsequent hearings in this matter, through to trial.'

She sensed Paula Benedict bristling in her seat, and carried on before she could intervene. 'As for the safety of witnesses, although the Crown has yet to make full disclosure of its case against my client, it is my understanding that there are none. My information is, the evidence that has led the Crown to charge my client is entirely scientific and circumstantial, and that it cannot and will not bring forward any person who claims to have seen Mr Baker murder Mrs Fonter. In all those circumstances I can see no bar to your granting bail, and I respectfully request that you do.'

Benedict made to rise, but the white-haired sheriff waved her back down. Alex suspected that her age was greater than those of both advocates combined. 'You've made your submission, Advocate Depute.' She looked across at Baker, who had remained standing in the dock.

'I know who your client is, Ms Skinner, and what he does for a living. I share your view that there's no serious chance of him absconding, even less if he doesn't have his passport, which will be surrendered in the event I grant him bail. Nor do I believe that he'd be a danger to witnesses even if there were any. But . . . when it comes to obstructing the course of justice, then I can see where he might be a danger, to himself.'

Her gaze switched back to the accused. 'Mr Baker,' she addressed him, 'do you know what *sub judice* means?'

'I've heard the term, My Lady,' he acknowledged calmly, 'but I'm not a hundred per cent sure.'

'Then let me fill you in. It means that the judicial process is under way and that its detail may not be reported or discussed in the media. Any breach is regarded as contempt of court and the breacher is liable to pretty much any sanction that the court may prescribe, including imprisonment. With me?'

'Yes, My Lady,' Baker said, meekly.

'Very good. Now, advise me if I'm correct in this. I understand that in the course of your duties as a football manager you are obliged to appear before the media, at press conferences, before and after games. Is that the case?'

'Yes, My Lady, the league top brass at Hampden, they insist on it. It's the same in England and in France. You can get into real bother over there if you don't speak the language too well. Ironic, innit? They make us speak to the press then they fine us if they don't like the answers we give.'

'Have you ever been fined, Mr Baker?' the sheriff asked.

His smile hinted at both guilt and pride. 'Three times, My Lady; twice in England, once in France.'

'In other words you have a record of intemperance of speech in a media environment.' She looked down at Alex. 'You see my concern, Ms Skinner? I can't make an order granting your client anonymity. In a few hours this will be all over the media, and if your client goes back to work, I can only imagine the chaos at his next press conference.'

'Yes, My Lady,' Alex replied. Out of a corner of her right eye she saw her learned opponent smile, but ignored it, knowing that the sheriff was considering her decision and would brook no interruption.

'Okay,' the judge declared. 'I'll grant bail, on three conditions, one being passport surrender, obviously, the second being that he makes himself available to the police for further interview at any time they require it, and third that from the moment he steps out of this building to the time this case is disposed of, or his bail is revoked by another court, he does not speak to a single journalist, in any circumstances, about any subject under the sun. You can go back to work, Mr Baker, pending your trial, but no more press conferences. If the top brass in the league have a problem with that, they can talk to me, because I'm forbidding it. This case is adjourned, for trial in the High Court at a date to be determined.'

She started to rise, then paused. 'Ms Benedict,' she said, 'I've made my decision, but the Crown does have the right of appeal. Is that your intention?'

'I'll need to take advice, My Lady,' the advocate depute replied. 'I wasn't instructed on that.'

Sheriff Wisdom smiled. 'The Solicitor General was that confident of a remand, was he? Well, you go ahead and take your advice, but I'm pretty sure I know what that will be. Mr Rocco de Matteo knows as well as I do that an appeal wouldn't stand a chance.'

Paula Benedict gathered up her papers. 'See you in the High Court,' she snapped at Alex as her client left the dock and came towards her.

She shrugged. 'You may, you may not. I may instruct a silk.'

'Great game so far, Ms Skinner,' Baker exclaimed, cheerily.

She stared at him. 'That wasn't the game,' she countered, frowning back at him. 'It wasn't even the warm-up. You're still charged with murder, Mr Baker, and if you're convicted you'll be lucky if you get out of prison before you're seventy.'

His smile vanished, and was replaced by a look of naked terror. 'I told you,' he moaned, 'I didn't do it.'

'I'm inclined to believe that, but that counts for nothing. On the basis of what we heard this morning, it'll be difficult to mount a successful defence. They can demonstrate that you were there, in the place where she died, around the time she died. In the absence of anything else, that alone would be tough to overcome, but the blood on your training kit and your belt round her neck . . .'

She sighed, out of sheer exasperation. 'If I was sitting on your jury and the advocate depute asked me where's the reasonable doubt, as it stands I couldn't find it. My job will be to dig it out and plant it in the minds of the people who will be trying you.'

'And if you can't?'

'Then you know what'll happen.'

The fear that had been in his eyes at their first meeting reappeared; his lips moved, but no sound escaped.

'But I will!' she declared, firmly. 'Unless you're lying to me, and you did throttle the woman, in which case I'd slam the cell door on you myself, I will raise that doubt, and I will exploit it. We're not without hope. The evidence they have could work in your favour.'

'How?'

'It may help us in a perverse sort of way. Since you didn't kill Annie, it follows that someone's trying to frame you and it has to be someone with a degree of knowledge of you, and not just a disgruntled Celtic supporter. That's our starting point. And by the way,' she added, 'there's someone else you've got on your side, maybe your biggest asset.'

'Who?'

'My father,' Alex replied.

'He thinks I'm guilty,' Baker protested. 'I could see it in his eyes yesterday.'

'But you're not, and I'll make him believe it. Once he does, he'll see the things I see and, trust me, there's nobody better at digging out what lies beneath them. Now,' she continued briskly, 'about these bloody press conferences that worried the sheriff. They won't become a problem, will they?'

'No,' he assured her. 'I know that judge wasn't kidding. I'll get Tank to take them.'

'Tank?'

'Tank Bridges, my assistant manager. He's not the best with the press, but he's so fuckin' scary they never push it with him. Nobody ever pushes it with Tank, not even Artie.'

'Who's he?'

'Art Mustard, club captain. He's a big West Indian boy, hard as nails. He's one of the toughest guys in the league, they reckon, but even he's respectful around Tank. Paco, now, he might not take any shit, but he's too good to ever have any chucked at him.'

'How does Mr Bridges get on with the owner?' she asked.

'Mr Rogozin? He hardly ever sees him; their paths don't cross as a rule. Tank's at the training ground mostly, and Dimitri doesn't go there.'

'How do you get on with Rogozin? On a day-to-day basis; you've told me your back story with him.'

Momentarily, tension showed on Baker's face, lips tightening, eyes narrowing; then it was gone. 'He's a hard taskmaster, a bit of a bully; not physically, but Grigor's always around, glowering at you. He's given me performance targets and he keeps on top of me all the time.'

'How will he react to your situation?'

'God knows. It's not one you envisage, is it? I'll find out soon enough.'

'That could happen the moment you step out of here. He knew where you were this morning because your wife told him.

I advised her that you'd be appearing here, so . . .'

'Dozy cow,' he snarled. 'For a doctor, she can be dumb sometimes.'

'She's a doctor?'

He nodded. 'Yes. She's the football club doctor, in fact. They didn't have one when I arrived, so I brought her on board.'

'She knows Rogozin professionally as well as personally? I didn't realise that.'

'No reason why you should have.'

'Can I ask you, Mr Baker, how is your relationship with your wife?'

'Fine,' he exclaimed, his face lighting up. 'We've always got on, Lita and me, even better since we had Letitia, our nipper. She's a gem.'

'I'll have to interview your wife in preparing your defence,' Alex said. 'I may want to call her as a witness to your state of mind.'

'Can I be there when you talk to her?'

'No way,' she retorted. 'Now, do you want to avoid Rogozin, assuming he's out there?'

'I'd rather.'

'Then we'll leave by the back entrance and get you into a taxi. The Crown will be briefing the media soon, and you should make yourself scarce. Ideally you should take your family away, somewhere private, and stay there until this is over.'

'But I need to work,' he insisted. 'I need to get to the training complex, and to the ground on match days.'

'We'll cover that, but first let's get your family out of reach of the media. Do you have somewhere you can go?'

'No,' he replied, 'but I know somebody who might help.'

'Then contact him. I'll text my dad to let him know what

we're doing. He's waiting for us outside in Chambers Street, maybe having a rematch with Grigor.'

'I'd pay money to see that,' Baker chuckled.

'You wouldn't get value for it,' Alex retorted. 'It would be all over in seconds. Come on, let's get the paperwork done and get you out of here, and be grateful that you're not leaving in a prison van.'

Nineteen

'Who was that?' Mia McCullough asked as her husband pocketed his mobile. 'Or don't I want to know?'

'If you didn't I wouldn't tell you,' her husband said. 'It was Lita Baker, again.'

'What did the good doctor want?'

'Two things; she wanted to thank me for fixing her up with a good lawyer. Chaz has been charged but he's out on bail.'

'On a murder charge?'

'It happens.' He smiled, grimly. 'I was.'

'Ignacio didn't get bail,' she complained.

'He was a foreign national,' McCullough pointed out, 'and he had to be extradited. It would have been difficult in his case. Mind you,' he added, 'his father could probably have fixed it.'

'If he'd stood up in court and admitted to being his father,' Mia said, 'but neither he nor I fancied the idea of Bob Skinner's son being known to be among the prison population. What else did Baker's wife want?'

'She's looking for a hideaway for the three of them, somewhere Chaz can avoid the media when he's not at work.'

She stared at him across the living room. 'Eh? He can't carry on managing the team, can he?'

'He thinks he can, and Rogozin's backing him up. In fact Dimitri's insisting on it. He flew in from Russia over the weekend, on his executive toy. He called me earlier on when you were in the gym. He was effing and blinding about Bob Skinner. From what he told me, the silly bugger tried to waylay Alex outside the police station where they were holding Chaz: "to incentivise her", he said. Bob was there, and it got a bit unfortunate for Dimitri, and that fucking goon of his. He was going to try again, after Chaz's court appearance, but I marked his card, ordered him not to.'

'You ordered him? I thought Rogozin was the club chairman.'

'He is,' McCullough acknowledged, 'but he understands our relationship.'

'What about the minder? Does he understand it?'

'He'd better. That Grigor, he thinks he can have a go at people in the street in Edinburgh? I hope big Bob's taught him a lesson. If not . . .'

'Don't get involved,' Mia said.

'I never get involved,' her husband countered. 'But it might be best for Grigor if he stays in Russia from now on, and that might have to be explained forcefully, if Dimitri doesn't agree.'

'I don't know if I like the sound of that. Who'll do the explaining?'

'My granddaughter's partner, young Haddock: if it comes to it, I'm sure he will. Grigor has form in Russia, under another name, the sort that would have seen him turned down for a visa if his boss hadn't bought him a new identity and new passport. If I pass the details to Sauce through young Cheeky, the clown's feet won't touch the ground.'

'Maybe you should. He sounds like a potential embarrassment, and Merrytown FC is exposed enough at the moment.'

'Dimitri wouldn't like it.'

'Bugger him!' she snorted. 'Would that bother you?' she asked. 'What he thinks?'

'To be frank, no: this whole bloody mess is down to him. It was him that brought Baker in as manager, and it was him that insisted on signing Paco Fonter. He claims to be an expert, with a database of thousands of footballers and managers, but apart from Chaz and Paco I've seen no evidence of it.'

'Then go ahead. Get rid of Grigor and tell Rogozin to behave himself. What about the Bakers?' she added. 'Can we help?'

'I can give them one of the lodge houses,' he suggested, 'here in the hotel grounds.'

'What if the media find out and stake the place out?'

'We can keep them at the entrance, but I reckon they'd get bored pretty quick. If they did become a nuisance, I could instruct a lawyer to go to court to interdict them.'

Mia shrugged. 'Your hotel, your football club; if it helps them, go for it. But it won't be your biggest problem.'

'Oh no?'

'No. If Baker does go back to work, how's he going to take training sessions when he's accused of killing the wife of his star player?'

Her husband laughed. 'Good point,' he conceded. 'Rogozin can deal with that. After all, he saddled us with the pair of them.'

Twenty

'I wasn't sure we'd even start this lunch date,' Skinner admitted, as he took his seat on the Royal Scottish Museum's Tower Restaurant, on the opposite side of Chambers Street from Edinburgh Sheriff Court. 'I expected you to be hauled into another press briefing, given what's just happened.'

'What has happened?' Chief Constable Maggie Steele asked. 'I know the plan was to get Baker into court at midday, but nobody's told me whether they managed it.'

'My clever daughter got him bailed . . .' he said, '. . . to the fury of the Crown Office, I imagine. I had a text from her saying she was whipping him out of the back entrance, to avoid anyone waiting outside.'

'There wasn't anyone, was there? I had a grandstand view from the terrace and I didn't see anyone but you. Not that any media were expected; they don't know about Baker yet.'

'You can't keep it under wraps any longer. When are you going to make an announcement?'

'We're not; the Solicitor General's doing it himself,' Steele said. 'His press people decreed that he doesn't need any police presence, since constitutionally we act on behalf of his office in investigating crime. Bloody politicians,' she grumbled. 'That de

Matteo's an ambitious boy; he's an MSP as well as a law officer, as you know, and he has his eyes on being the next Justice Secretary.'

'In his dreams,' Skinner laughed. 'Somebody should take the spade off him before he digs himself a hole he can't climb out of. He'll bugger it up, as soon as it gets to questions.'

'He's not taking any. The plan was that he'll make a simple statement, on camera, then he'll get up and walk out, no press questions: two thirty, across the road there in the Crown Office, next to the Sheriff Court. The assumption was that Baker would be locked up in Saughton before they called the briefing. That's knocked on the head now he's got bail.'

All at once, her companion's eyes shone; he beamed. He took out his mobile, checked the time, and called June Crampsey. 'Have you just been called to a briefing in the Crown Office this afternoon?' he asked her.

'As it happens we have,' she admitted. 'News desk's assuming that it has to do with the Annette Bordeaux investigation, but that's unconfirmed.'

'Well,' he chuckled, 'this is a little bird . . . or a bloody great shite-hawk, you choose . . . whispering in your ear. About half an hour ago Chaz Baker, the manager of Merrytown Football Club, appeared in Edinburgh Sheriff Court charged with her murder. He was granted bail on the application of his defence counsel, Ms Alexis Skinner, and his next appearance will be in the High Court.'

He heard her gasp as he spoke. 'Is this for real?' she whispered.

'Check the date; it's September, not April the first. It's legit, and you can use it right away. You're free to get it out in the *Saltire* online version and on your social media platforms, and to pass it on to all InterMedia group outlets. You have Alex's mobile number; if you tell Lennox Webster, the crime reporter, to call her, she'll give her as much of a quote as she's able to.'

'If you were here, Bob,' the editor exclaimed, 'I'd hug you.'

'No you wouldn't, because it wouldn't be seemly and we'd both be embarrassed. Get on with it.'

Steele frowned at him as he ended the call, but her eyes were smiling. 'You are wicked,' she said. 'Every reporter in the room will have gone in there knowing what the story is.'

'That's right,' he agreed. 'Let's see now if the boy de Matteo gets away without taking questions. As you said, bloody politicians. They get on my tits.'

'Is Baker guilty, Bob?' she asked, quietly.

He looked back at her blandly. 'You saw the same interview that I did. You're an experienced police officer. What do you think?'

'As such, I don't think. As I told you, I look at the evidence and it tells me he did it.'

He tapped the spectacles that he had put on to read the lunch menu. 'Never mind that. What did your eyes tell you, looking at him on camera?'

'The same, that he's an impulsive murderer. Now answer my question. What do you think?'

'No different from you, but I'm not going to admit that to my daughter. She's sticking to the presumption of innocence and I'm not going to do or say anything that'll undermine her belief in him.'

He smiled. 'Let's see,' he said, peering at the menu as the waiter approached. 'Sweetcorn soup and fish for me,' he declared.

'And I'll have the salmon starter and the veggie tagliatelli . . . in honour of our friend Mr de Matteo,' she chuckled.

With their selections, Skinner ordered a bottle of sparkling water, and a glass of wine for his friend. 'So,' he said, as the waiter left, 'do we pick up where we left off yesterday?'

Steele nodded. 'We might as well. Have you given it any thought?

'About two seconds' worth,' he replied. 'Mags, I voted for independence but my side of the debate didn't get the result we wanted. I didn't like it, but I lived with it. The First Minister has to live with it too, and with its consequences. He can't set up the equivalent of his own private security service, off the books, unless he has the devolved power to do so. I do not see anything in the Police Scotland Act, or any other piece of legislation, that says he can.'

'His advice is that he can.'

'Who gave him that advice?'

'The Solicitor General,' she said.

'Indeed?' Skinner murmured, with a light smile on his face. 'Suppose I was interested in Clive's proposition, I'd want to hear that advice from the Lord Advocate himself, and I'd want it confirmed by the Lord President of the Court, before I'd take it on.'

He sighed. 'But I'm not interested. I wouldn't touch it with a bargepole because I don't believe that any head of government should have his own private personal heavy. So, Mags, please tell the First Minister that he should have had the balls to approach me personally about this because I'd rather have looked him in the eye as I shot him down than have to do it through you.'

'Word for word,' she promised.

'You think it's rubbish too?' he asked.

'Yes and no,' she responded. 'I've already got a counterterrorism and serious organised crime division under my command. I wouldn't want anyone riding roughshod over them, or bringing my authority into question. But if Clive Graham persuaded the Prime Minister that the Security Service needs to be strengthened in Scotland and given its own command structure, answerable to him as well as Westminster, I'd be happy with that.'

'Then make that case to him,' Skinner suggested. 'If he can swing that, maybe this conversation can happen again; but,' he laughed, 'with him buying the lunch next time.'

Twenty-One

'Jesus, gaffer, what is this?' Sauce Haddock murmured as he and Pye walked towards the suite in the Norton House Hotel, where they had arranged to meet Paco Fonter. 'A minder at the door?' He looked more closely at the man in the grey suit. 'Here, isn't that the guy that the boss . . . Mr Skinner . . . had a problem with in Fettes Avenue?'

'Could be,' the DCI murmured. 'You had a better view of him than I did. If it is him, there's maybe no harm in his being here, for all there are no reporters in sight.'

The hotel had been recommended to the Merrytown chief executive by the police family support officer who had been assigned to Fonter, standard practice following a homicide. It had been chosen for two reasons: its proximity to Edinburgh's general air terminal, where the footballer's private jet had landed, and the fact that no journalists had booked in there after the Annette Bordeaux story had broken.

Pye produced his warrant card and held it up as they reached their destination, and its guardian, Haddock following suit. The man nodded, but said nothing; he simply rapped on the door, then opened it and stepped aside.

DS's eyes widened as he stepped into the suite, and he

struggled to contain a gasp. There were five people crowded into the small sitting room; a buzz of conversation stopped as five heads turned to stare at the detectives. At first glance, Haddock recognised none of them, not until his gaze settled on a man, tall, dark, wearing a suit that would have cost him at least two months of a detective sergeant's salary: the man who had been nose to nose with Bob Skinner in Fettes Avenue, while the heavy in the corridor outside had been picking himself up.

There were two women among the quintet; one of them, slim, platinum haired, early forties, stepped towards Pye, hand outstretched. 'Chief Inspector?' she began, then continued without waiting for an answer. 'Angela Renwick, chief executive; we spoke.'

He nodded. 'We did, Ms Renwick,' he agreed. 'And we arranged that we would interview Mr Fonter here, privately.' He leaned on the word. 'I didn't expect to find . . .' He stopped himself, but only just, from adding, '. . . half the first team squad.'

'The whole Merrytown community is stunned by what's happened,' Ms Renwick said, filling the void. 'Each of us felt we had to be here for Paco. Let me introduce you. This is Sirena Burbujas, who was Annette's agent.'

A short, chubby woman with large brown eyes and dark hair in a curly perm nodded a greeting.

'Cisco Serra, Paco's agent.'

A Latino man peered at them through white-framed spectacles.

'Tank Bridges, assistant manager and first team coach.'

A massive, glowering figure eyed them, making no effort to hide his hostility.

'And I am Rogozin,' the third man in the room declared, forestalling any introduction.

'Mr Dimitri Rogozin is our owner,' the chief executive added, not seeing the flash of anger in the Russian's eyes, that she should believe any explanation was necessary.

'Thank you.' The senior detective looked around the five. 'I'm DCI Pye and this is my colleague Detective Sergeant Haddock. And Mr Fonter?' he continued.

'Paco, he is in seclusion,' Rogozin replied. 'He is in bedroom, resting.'

'I'll tell him you're here,' Renwick volunteered.

'Please do,' Pye murmured. 'We'd be grateful if the rest of you could go somewhere else while we speak to him.'

'I no leave,' Cisco Serra protested, as the chief executive moved towards a door to their right.

'Not I,' Rogozin added.

'I'm afraid we're going to insist that you do,' the DCI told them. 'Mr Fonter has suffered a tragic loss, and we'll treat him as gently as we can, but this is a police investigation.'

'But you have arrested the man you say killed Anya!' the Russian exclaimed. 'You have arrested Chaz. He is in jail.'

'Oh no he isn't,' Haddock countered. 'Mr Baker was granted bail.'

'Bail?' the Russian repeated. 'What is this bail?'

'He's been released,' the DS explained, 'pending his next court appearance and trial. The sheriff must have been satisfied that he wouldn't do a runner.' As he spoke he glanced at Tank Bridges and saw not a flicker of surprise in his eyes. He guessed that he had received a call or a text from his boss.

'Will he come here?'

'He'll have been told not to,' Pye replied. 'He wouldn't be allowed to interfere with witnesses.'

Renwick had reappeared; she was standing in the door of the

suite's bedroom, concern on her face. 'Are you saying Chaz is out?' she exclaimed. 'Does that mean he can come back to work?' she asked.

'That might be a matter for you to decide,' the DCI suggested. 'In theory, if it didn't conflict with any bail conditions, he could.'

She frowned. 'But how could he run a squad when he's accused of killing the leading scorer's wife?'

'No bother.' Tank Bridges' quiet Liverpudlian voice was at odds with his granite-hewn features. 'I take most of the training anyway. Chaz'll pick the team, and give the orders on match day.'

'You say that he will,' Cisco Serra challenged, 'but what if Paco refuses to play?'

'Paco do what he's told,' Rogozin growled.

'Paco is my client,' the agent snapped back at him. 'If I advise him that he no' play, he no' play.'

'That's academic,' the assistant manager told them both. 'Paco's come back from Spain with a buggered hamstring. Our Alice McDade hasn't seen him yet, but the Spanish international physio reckons he's out for at least six weeks, probably two months.'

'Oh shit,' Rogozin sighed. 'How we get to Champions League now?'

'Fucking typical,' Pye whispered to Haddock. 'We're here investigating a murder and they're talking about football.' He stepped forward. 'Enough, gentlemen,' he said, firmly. 'Take it somewhere else, please, and leave us to speak with Mr Fonter.'

'I stay,' the Russian hissed. 'He's my man; I be here when you talk to him.' He stepped forward to within a yard of the senior detective, his handsome face distorted by a frown.

Suddenly Haddock was filling the space between them. 'You

be downstairs when we talk to him,' he murmured, 'or out in the corridor with your other man. That was not a request my boss just made.'

'You Scottish people,' Rogozin whispered, 'you need to learn respect.'

'You're not the man to teach us,' the young sergeant replied, quietly. 'If I construed that as a threat to a police officer, sir, I'd have you in a police van before you could say Pyotr Ilyich Tchaikovsky. If you don't leave us alone with Mr Fonter, I might just do that.'

Pye frowned as he stared at the back his colleague's head. It was an aspect of Sauce Haddock that he had not seen before.

Tank Bridges broke the impasse. 'Boss,' he said to the Russian, 'these are the cops and they're not kidding. The club doesn't need any more trouble than it has already.' He stepped in and ushered the reluctant Rogozin and Serra towards the exit, leaving Sirena Burbujas, who had observed the exchanges in silence, and Renwick to follow. It was only as they left that the bedroom door opened once more, and a slim young man appeared.

Paco Fonter was taller than Pye had expected, around six feet three inches. He had the hollow-eyed look of a man in need of sleep, but he managed nonetheless to convey an air of bronzed athleticism as he moved gracefully, if a little carefully, towards them. He was dressed in black, jeans and a polo shirt, and his long dark hair was tied back in a ponytail.

'Guys,' he murmured. 'Sorry I keep you waiting. And sorry it took me so long to get back from Spain. Dimitri insisted on sending his plane for me, but first he had to have the crew file a flight plan and have it cleared. Where is Annie?' he asked, a hitch in his voice. 'When can I see her?'

'Your wife's body's in the city mortuary,' the DCI answered.

'We can make arrangements any time you like. In fact we can take you there when we're finished talking.'

'Thank you, you do that, please.' He frowned. 'Ms Renwick said your name is Pye, yes?'

'Yes, I'm the SIO, senior investigating officer.' He glanced to his left. 'This is Detective Sergeant Haddock.'

'What's this crazy thing that Angela tell me? You arrest Chaz? The boss?'

'He was charged this morning,' Haddock replied.

'I don't believe it. Chaz is good guy. A tough boss, sure, but good guy. Not like Bridges, who's a gilipollas all the way through.'

'A what?' Pye murmured.

'Arsehole,' his sergeant volunteered, quietly.

'Nevertheless,' the DCI continued, impressed by his sergeant's fluency in street Spanish, 'we know what we know about Mr Baker, and that's enough for us to have charged him. There are still questions to be answered, though, things he won't tell us.'

'Let me talk to him, if you are sure he did it,' the big footballer whispered. 'That might change.'

'You don't go near him, Paco,' Haddock warned.

'Were you and Mr Baker friendly away from the ground?' Pye asked.

'We got on okay.'

'But you didn't socialise?'

Fonter peered at the detective, puzzled. 'What?'

'You didn't visit each other's houses, or go out together with your wives, as couples?'

'No, nothing like that.'

'So it would come as a surprise to you if I told you that there appears to have been a relationship between your wife and Mr Baker.'

'Of course it would,' the player gasped. 'What sort of relationship?'

'Let's just call it a friendship,' Pye said. 'We know that on Friday, Annette sent him a text, asking him to come and see her at your apartment. It mentioned a secret . . . her word . . . but we don't know what that meant. Do you have any idea?'

Fonter shook his head, the ponytail rippling with the movement. 'No, none at all.' The pain that had been evident in his expression seemed to intensify. 'Maybe I don' know my wife as well as I think.'

'How did you meet?' Haddock asked him, quietly.

'It was an accident,' he replied. Both detectives were struck by his fluency in English. 'It was in Madrid, three years ago, when I play for Getafe in La Liga. I had a film shoot for a TV ad for a video game, and Annie was in the same studio. She was doing some stills for an underwear client.' His eyes misted at the memory. 'I had on the suit of lights they make you wear for these things and she was in a dressing robe, 'cos she had hardly anything else on.'

He smiled, transported back to the past. 'She looked at me, and she laughed, and said something I did not understand about *El Senor de los Anillos*, the Lord of the Rings, the movie. I knew who she was, of course; she was famous even then. I felt like an idiot, and started to explain that when they make the ad the graphic guys would put clothes on us. She laugh again, and she said "Ah, you are really naked just now?" I said, "I suppose. How about you?" And . . .'

He paused. 'She stop smiling and she went pink. I thought she thought I was making a move on her, so I said, "Sorry. We're both at work after all." And then she laughed again and say, "You're telling me we both take off our clothes for a living?"

'Then I find myself say, "In a way I suppose we do. My name is Paco Fonter. You are a famous model and I am a crap footballer, but would you like to meet up later when we have both got our clothes on?" She said yes, and that was it. We went to dinner in a restaurant where nobody knew either of us, and we were together from then on. She live in London then, but she came to Madrid whenever she could. A year and we got married.'

'I'm not being funny here,' Pye ventured, 'but did it have an effect on your career, being married to Annette?'

Fonter shrugged and gave an open-handed 'Who can say?' gesture. 'Is possible, but in which way? Good or bad? Sure, still I play for España, my country, but here I am in Scotland, playing for a lot of money but in a very poor league. When I was a young guy with Getafe they talked of me going to Real. Then I was with Annie and my face was in the magazines, and I began to get modelling jobs too, without even looking for them.'

He smiled, but there was sadness in it. 'One day I asked a journalist why he wasn't writing about me and Real any more. He said that their president was afraid I was too much outside the game. Never that was true; I always trained as hard as anyone, harder than most, but the big clubs, they did not come. But Rogozin, he did; at that time he owned a piece of a club in Italy, in the bottom half of Serie A. They signed me and I was the top scorer but still the biggest teams never came. Then Rogozin, he bought Merrytown, and Cisco took me here, where to be honest I hate it and where . . .' his voice faltered, '. . . and where this happened.'

He grimaced. 'And that *puta* of an agent, he brought Chaz Baker too, his other client; we have to talk about that, Cisco and me.'

'Serra's his agent too?' Haddock exclaimed.

'Sure, didn't you know that?'

'No, it's news to us. Which of you was with him first?'

'I was. Cisco took Chaz on as a client when he was with the French club and having trouble. When I sign for Merrytown, it was part of the deal that Rogozin hire him as manager.'

'Is that usual in football?' the DS asked. 'Agents placing managers in jobs?'

Fonter shook his head. 'No, most of the top managers have top agents. And when one of them comes to a club, it's normal for him to bring players with him, players he likes because they suit the way he sets up his team. But what is not usual is for a player to bring a manager, and that is what happened with me, *mas o menos*.'

'Why did Rogozin agree to it?'

The young Spaniard frowned. 'Hey, I'm a good player.' He paused. 'But I know, not that good. Guys like me, we can get a manager fired; that happens all the time. But I never hear of any who get a manager hired. I asked Cisco about it, 'cos I wasn't comfortable with it. He told me, and I quote, to mind my fucking business and let him mind his.'

'Did your wife know about the deal with Baker?'

He looked scornfully at Pye, as if he was in a media conference and the DCI was the dumbest reporter in the room.

'Of course not,' he retorted. 'Why the hell should she? She's . . .' He stopped in mid-sentence and heaved a huge sigh as reality hit him once again. 'She was a model, I'm a footballer. We never got involved in each other's business. She'd no more tell me how to deal with Cisco than I'd interfere between her and Sirena.'

'You never talked to her about your work, your career, your

moves? Where you play must have had an effect on her.'

'Maybe,' Fonter conceded. 'Sometimes I would talk things through with her, to make sure she was okay with them. But not then, not about the move to Scotland, or anything to do with it.'

'Why not?'

'Because Rogozin was involved, and because Cisco was putting it to him about Chaz Baker. I didn't want to be mixed up in it and I didn't want Annie to be dragged in. That Russian, he's not a good man. I don't like him.'

He seemed embarrassed. 'I'm not a guy who scares easily, Senor Pye. I play against some very tough men and they don't take chances with me. That man Bridges, he yells at the rest of the squad but he is respectful of me. But Rogozin: no, I am cautious of him. I am in Scotland and I am at that fucking club for only one reason; because I didn't want to tell him no.'

Twenty-Two

'You're not seriously going to plead your client not guilty, are you?' Paula Benedict drawled. She was on the other end of a phone line, but Alex Skinner could picture the sarcasm in her smile.

'No, I'm not,' she replied, cheerfully.

'Ah!' the young advocate depute exclaimed. 'You've had a night to think about it and common sense has finally drilled its way through your skull. I see it all the time with you newbies.'

'I'm not going to plead anything, Paula,' Alex continued. 'My client is, loud and clear. He maintains his innocence, whatever evidence you may have.'

'They all do! Jesus, you're naive. You were a hotshot in corporate practice, Skinner. You should have bloody stayed there.'

'Hah!' she laughed, abandoning her resolve to tolerate Benedict's patronising tone. 'Thanks for that advice. Feel free to shove it up your arse.'

Her shocked gasp turned into a hiss over the phone. 'You won't be so cocky in court,' she snapped. 'You'll lead for the defence, I suppose.'

'I don't know yet. I'll discuss instructing senior counsel with my client.'

'Who?'

'That would be none of your business,' Alex said, 'not at this stage.'

'Nobody worth his salt will take you on if you persist in this "not guilty" crap.'

'In that event,' she insisted, 'I'll lead myself. I believe in Chaz. He didn't do it.' She hoped that she sounded more positive than actually she felt.

'I don't imagine I'd be facing you across the court,' she added. 'If it's that much of a high-profile pushover, the Solicitor General will be bound to grab it for himself rather than hand it to a junior AD who's only just through the door and who's never led a successful prosecution, or been on the winning side as defence counsel. If that upsets you, Paula, you threw my previous career at me, so don't be surprised by me throwing yours right back.'

'I'll be quite happy to act as Rocco's junior,' Benedict retorted, defensively. 'But it needn't come to that. The fact is, Rocco doesn't want to tie any of us into what would be a very costly trial that can only have one outcome. When I told him about the line you were taking he authorised me to offer you a deal. We'll accept a plea of guilty to culpable homicide, and you can portray it as a tragic loss of control in the heat of a lovers' quarrel. Baker will probably serve five years, max.'

Alex allowed silence to speak for her.

'Well?' her adversary demanded, after almost half a minute. 'Deal?'

'You're that unsure of your case?' she murmured.

'We're dead certain of our case,' Benedict insisted, then seemed to hesitate. 'Look,' she murmured, 'I'll trust you not to repeat this, but Rocco's had a nudge from the Lord Advocate . . . and I think that he's had a nudge from the new Lord Justice

General. Neither of them want the attention of the world's media focused on our High Court for any longer than necessary, hence the offer of a plea deal. The court might even go easy on the sentence, maybe six years with parole after three. Will you put it to your client, Alex?'

'Of course,' she replied. 'I'm obliged to put it to my client. I warn you, though, "I didn't kill her", which is what he's saying, sounds pretty unequivocal to me, and three years in the slammer with no career when he gets out might not sound too attractive to an innocent man.'

'It will if he has any sense,' Benedict retorted.

'Oh yes? There are other parties involved, something that you and the Sol Gen seem to have overlooked: Paco Fonter, the bereaved husband, and Dr Lita Baker, my client's wife. If Chaz accepts your deal, it means that he's admitting that he and Annette Bordeaux were having it away, something that he also denies.'

She paused to let her observation sink in.

'I'll put it to Chaz,' she continued, 'but with no suggestion that he should accept. While I'm doing that you can take my counter-proposal back to the Solicitor General.'

'And what would that be?' Paula Benedict asked, drily.

'Drop the charges, without proceeding to indictment. Let an innocent man go free rather than sending him to prison. But while you're chewing that over, I require full disclosure of the Crown case against Mr Baker, so that I can begin to frame a successful defence.'

Twenty-Three

'It arrived at half past nine,' Alex told her father, nodding towards a thick envelope on her desk, with the Crown Office crest displayed beside the word 'Confidential', and her name and address, handwritten. 'I had a look through it, and didn't see any surprises.'

'Then you haven't looked closely enough,' he replied. 'It's a classic domestic homicide. The evidence says that Chaz Baker is guilty.'

'He says he's innocent.'

'So fucking what? Correct me if I'm wrong, but . . . they've got her on CCTV, going into the apartment, letting herself in with a key. A wee while afterwards, they've got him arriving.'

'Yes,' she agreed.

'How did he get in?'

'The door was unlocked.'

'She summoned him with a text.?'

'Again, yes. Pops, stop cross-examining me.'

'A text sent from her phone?'

'Yes!'

Skinner's eyes narrowed. 'And where's that phone now?'

'I . . .' She paused, took a quick breath. 'I assume it was in the penthouse.'

'No. It wasn't.'

Alex stared at him, angrily. 'How do you know that? Have you been talking to the police behind my back? Do you think you're protecting me from a guilty client?'

'Hey, hey,' he chuckled, 'get off your high horse. I haven't been talking to anybody. They've been talking to me. Specifically, Rocco de Matteo, at the behest, he claimed, of his gaffer, my friend Woodrow Butcher, the Lord Advocate. He called me this morning to tell me he was making you an offer, and to ask me to persuade you to accept.'

'He did what!' she exploded. 'The bastard! He thinks I can be . . . What did you tell him?' she demanded.

'I told him that I couldn't even persuade you to switch from Coco Pops to Corn Flakes when you were six. But I did ask him whether they'd confirmed the origin of the text that Baker received. They have, but it took a while. The victim's phone wasn't in the apartment. It was traced, by its signal, to a waste bin in the motorway service area halfway between Edinburgh and Glasgow. That's on the route between King Robert Village and the Merrytown training complex.'

'Bugger!' she growled.

'That's the bad news. Now would you like the really bad news?'

'Let me take a guess,' she sighed. 'Chaz's fingerprints are on it.'

'Right first time.'

'Oh dear, that is not good.'

'Do you still fancy defending him?'

'Less than I did five minutes ago.'

'Have you put de Matteo's plea bargain to him?' Skinner asked.

'Last night,' Alex replied. 'He turned it down flat, with my encouragement.'

'In the circumstances it seems to me like a bloody good offer. Maybe you should go back to him.'

'I won't have to go far,' she said. 'I'm seeing him for lunch. He's meeting Rogozin and the Merrytown chief executive this morning, then me, all at his hideaway.'

'Where's that?'

'It's a cottage on a place in Perthshire, called Black Shield Lodge.'

'You're kidding me,' her father gasped. 'I know that place. It belongs to Cameron McCullough: Sauce Haddock's girlfriend's grandfather, the guy the serious organised crime people have been trying to nail for years; your half-brother Ignacio's new stepfather.'

'I didn't know that it was his,' she confessed. 'But it doesn't surprise me. I learned yesterday that he's a minority shareholder in Merrytown.'

'Is he indeed? Mmm,' he murmured. 'If you're still wondering who recommended to Baker's wife that she call you, you may have your answer.'

'Why would he do that?' she asked.

'I could think of a couple of reasons,' Skinner answered, 'but the one that appeals to me most is that he knows how good you are.'

'From what you've just told me I'm going to have trouble proving it.' She looked him in the eye. 'Pops,' she said, earnestly, 'I need your help on this, I really do.'

'It may be that the best way I can help you is by persuading your client to take the plea bargain.'

Her eyes stayed on him. 'If it comes to that . . . but before we get there,' she took the police report from her desk and held it out to him, 'take this please, and go through it. De Matteo thinks his case is watertight but if anyone can find dampness in it, it's you. Will you, please?'

He smiled and reached out a hand. 'When have I ever said no?'

Twenty-Four

'Are you sure the media have no idea that you're here?' Alex asked.

'Not so far,' Chaz Baker said. 'The phone lines at the club went crazy yesterday, after that guy de Matteo, the General Solicitor or whatever the hell you call him, made his announcement, but by that time I was holed up here with Lita and Letitia.' He glanced around the lavishly equipped dining kitchen; the Venetian blinds were set at a slant, but narrow shafts of sunlight reflected from the polished black marble work surfaces. 'Not bad, eh? Better than ours at home.'

'And a damn sight better than the remand unit at Saughton,' his lawyer murmured.

'Yeah,' he conceded, 'thanks again for that.'

He pushed the salad bowl across the table towards her. 'More?'

'No, I'm fine.'

He looked at her, frowning. 'Will the press catch on to this place, d' you think?'

'I don't know,' she admitted. 'It depends on how determined they are. The Solicitor General . . . that's what you call him, by the way . . . did warn them against harassing you in the pre-trial period, but it was a bit of an empty threat.'

'There's no chance you were followed, is there?'

'No. I did keep an eye in my rear-view just in case, but when I turned into the Lodge driveway there wasn't another car in sight. Besides, nobody knows I'm representing you yet. As you asked, the football club is referring all press calls to Mr Serra, your agent, and he's saying nothing . . . assuming he sticks to the instruction we agreed you'd give him. I have to say I'm not happy with that, Chaz. We can trust him, can we?'

'We can only hope,' Baker admitted. 'Agreed, Cisco's stuck between the proverbial rock and hard place in this situation, representing both Paco and me. I swore to him that I'm innocent, and I think he believed me. He said he'd make no decision about whether to carry on with me until he'd spoken to Paco. I haven't heard from him since.'

'I don't suppose you've heard from Paco?'

'Are you kidding? You warned me against trying to contact him, but you didn't need to. He's a lovely lad, most of the time, but he's fearsome if somebody has a go at him on the pitch, as Tank Bridges found out, early doors. If he thinks I killed Annie, and that's what he's being told, I don't want to be in the same county as him, let alone the same room.'

'That's wise,' Alex agreed. 'The police will have told him not to approach you, but who knows how a man might react in his situation.' She paused. 'Look, given your agent's conflict of interests, I think you should let him off the hook, and tell the club to refer the press to my office. I'll have to break cover sooner or later.'

Baker showed her a sly grin. 'That'll do you a bit of good professionally, won't it? Get your name in the papers.'

She pushed her plate away and leaned forward, forearms on

the table. 'Do you think I've taken this instruction because it's high profile?' she asked, quietly. 'I don't need my name in the papers, as you put it. Since I turned to criminal work, I've been doing very well, better than I'd hoped. I don't actually need to be seen going down in flames beside a client who appears, at first sight, to the police and to every other expert who's looked at the evidence, including my father, the most expert of them all, to be as guilty as fucking sin. Be in no doubt; if the bookies were offering odds on the outcome, that's the way they'd be leaning.'

'Sorry, sorry, sorry!' he protested. 'I didn't mean to rile you. Alex, I'm grateful just to be sitting here having lunch with you, when I could be on a diet of porridge.' He laid down his fork and looked her in the eye. 'Do you agree with them?' he asked quietly. 'I mean . . . your dad, Christ. Look, if you want to back out, I'll understand. I'll find somebody else.'

'I agree with them, Chaz,' she murmured, 'that you look guilty. The evidence says you are. But you say you're not. I've had considerable bitter experience of being lied to by men; with that to inform me, I'm inclined to believe you. I'll stay the course, but be in no doubt, I'm in it for you as much as for me. Okay?'

He smiled, and reached out a hand; they shook.

'Do you still intend to carry on working?' she asked.

'I did,' he replied, 'but the club's knocked that on the head. Rogozin suspended me this morning. He was bloody brutal; he's got no doubt that I did it. Angela Renwick, the CEO, she didn't say anything but I could see she was relieved to have me off the pitch. Lita too, she's been stood down. Paco Fonter's on the injured list, and as club doctor she'd have had to treat him.'

'Where is she?'

'She's taken Letitia to the seaside. We thought it was best to get her away from here, in case the reptiles did show up.'

Alex nodded agreement.

Baker straightened in his chair, flexing his shoulders to relieve tension. 'Where do we go from here? What do you do?'

'I find an investigator; someone who'll look at the defence case forensically and help me counter it, piece by piece, so that I can plant that seed of reasonable doubt.'

'Anyone in mind?'

'Oh yes, but I'm not saying.'

'Will he be pricey?'

She smiled. 'I shouldn't think so.'

'Then what's stopping you hiring him right now?'

'He has to believe in your innocence as strongly as I do.'

'Does he?' Baker challenged. 'Isn't it just a professional engagement?'

'No,' she replied. 'He has to be satisfied that he wouldn't be getting in the way of justice.'

'Justice is what the jury decides, isn't it?'

'Not to him.' She drew a contemplative breath. 'Chaz,' she continued, 'this isn't just a matter of whether you did it or you didn't. Since you're innocent, that means someone's trying to frame you. In a way that makes it better for us.'

'How, for God's sake?'

'It means that as well as just trying to counter evidence, we can be proactive, look for an individual who has a reason for fitting you up.' She paused. 'But before we go there, I have to ask you about one piece of the Crown case that they didn't let slip during the interview yesterday. The police didn't just find that bloodstained training top at the complex. They found Annette's phone, with solid proof that you had handled it. Of all the bricks in their wall, that's the one that worries me the most. Help me here, please.'

He leaned back, closed his eyes, puffed out his cheeks, then exhaled. A frown was carved into his forehead: then, quite suddenly, it vanished.

'Yes,' he whispered, opening his eyes and looking at her. 'I know. The day Paco left to join up with the Spanish international squad, Annette drove him to Glasgow Airport. On the way back, she called me, and asked me if I was free for lunch. I was. We met in Glasgow, at One Devonshire Gardens. Towards the end, Annie went to the toilet. She left her mobile on the table, and while she was away it rang. I picked it up and looked at the caller ID. It was Sirena, her agent, and at that point Annie was coming back, so I pressed the green button and handed it to her.'

Alex smiled. 'Thank you, God, for that: the call will show on the phone record. Did you speak?'

'Yes, I did. When I gave her the thing I said, "It's for you." Annie said, "It would be, wouldn't it, since it's my phone," and she laughed.'

She nodded. 'So Sirena would know that you had handled the phone?'

'She would,' Baker agreed, 'and I see where you're going, but don't even think about her as a suspect. Annie was Sirena's meal ticket. You could say that they made each other, but without Annie, Sirena would be just another hustler. Plus, Annie was a tall, fit woman, and strong, for all she was model thin. Sirena's mid-forties, five feet and a couple of inches and she smokes like a chimney. No way could she have handled Annie physically.'

'But she might have known someone who could,' Alex declared. 'It's a starting point and at the very least she has to be eliminated as a potential suspect. How do you get on with her?'

'I can't stand the bloody woman; neither could Paco. She bullies Annie, treats her like shit. From the day she moved to

Edinburgh she's been going on about it being the pits, and how she should get Cisco to move Paco to London, or go herself and leave him here.'

'Then she does need looking at. You have a point though,' she conceded. 'She seems to have zero motive.' She sighed. 'Maybe we shouldn't be diverted by you picking up her call: your prints on the phone may just have been a bonus to whoever set you up. After all, it was dumped; there was no certainty the police would ever find it.'

'That's most likely. I just don't buy Sirena for this.'

'Is there anyone you think would like to see you put away for life?'

Baker grinned. 'Quite a few of the footballers I've coached, I reckon; and then there's Claude Chaplin, the chairman of FC DuPain. He and I definitely did not get on.'

'Did he ever threaten you?' Alex asked.

'Oh yes, but only with legal action. Chaplin's a dry stick. He's an accountant by training, but he made his money in the telecoms business. He isn't mega-rich though, like the Arabs who own City, or even just super-rich like Rogozin. I thought he was when I took the job at DuPain. He promised me a fifty million euro transfer budget, but he only ever came up with five. I took his club to sixth in the league even with that, and he used my success as an excuse to renege on his word about the budget. He also welched on a performance bonus that he'd promised me verbally. So I quit.'

'He didn't like it?'

'Not a bit: he went to court and got a French injunction against me working elsewhere, then he sued me for breach of contract. He even froze my assets . . . or as many as he could get his hands on, which wasn't actually all that much. It dragged on for almost a year. I was told I had a winning case, but it was nasty, very nasty . . . until Dimitri turned up out of the blue and bought me out of my contract with him. I've got to thank Cisco for that; he brokered the deal as part of Paco's transfer to Merrytown.'

'And Chaplin's action against you?'

'It was dropped and my assets unfrozen. Chaplin still holds a grudge though. After I left, DuPain went on the skids; they were relegated last season and he blamed me, not the tosser he got in to replace me. He was pretty vocal about it in the French press.' He scratched his chin. 'Mmm,' he mused. 'I suppose. You never know.'

'I don't think so,' Alex countered. 'Whoever did this is part of your circle at Merrytown. Do you leave clothes at the club?' she asked.

'Sure. I always keep a spare suit there and at the training ground, in case I need one in a hurry.'

'And a belt?'

'A couple of those too.'

'Good. That tells us that whoever framed you must have access to the club to get hold of your belt, and then to dump the top in the laundry at the training complex. That narrows it down.'

'Sure,' Baker retorted, glumly, 'to more than fifty people: everybody's in and out of the place, from the chairman to the tea lady.'

'Let's rule her out, shall we,' she grinned. 'This has to be somebody you know, somebody who's familiar with you and your movements. And it has to be somebody who's aware of your relationship with Annette, whatever its nature.'

'What do you mean by that?'

'What do you think I mean?' she snorted. 'Come clean, Mr Baker: were you and she lovers?'

'Honest to God, no!' he protested. 'We were friends, that's it. We were discreet about it, for obvious reasons, but . . .'

'Those reasons aren't obvious to me,' Alex observed.

'She was a player's wife, simple as that. A football manager has to stand at a distance from all his players. He can't be seen to be playing favourites or he'll alienate the rest of the team. The wives are a group too, not all of them, but enough for problems to arise. Annie wasn't one of them, she was an outsider, so if they'd found out, the tongues would have wagged all the way to the tabloids.'

'What about your wife?'

He shook his head. 'Lita didn't know either. Mostly we were fine, but we had been having one or two issues. The French thing got to her, but she reckoned that Chaplin would back down eventually, as the legal advice was in our favour. The thought of me moving to Scotland bothered her more than that. When Rogozin stepped in and offered me Merrytown, she'd only go along with it if she was part of the deal, so she could keep an eye on me. When Annie and I started meeting, I wasn't sure how she'd react, so I kept it to myself.'

'How did it begin, your friendship with Annette? And when?'

Baker pushed his chair away from the table and stood, walking across to lean against the work surface, his back to the kitchen window.

'We all came to Scotland at the beginning of January,' he began, 'during the transfer window, Paco and Annie, me and Lita. The other guys, Artie, Jimmy Pike, Orlando, they came a couple of weeks later, brought in by me, with Cisco's help.'

Alex frowned. 'Were they all his clients?'

'Hell no, I'm not so daft I'd let him palm guys off on me, but he helped with the negotiations.'

'And your own staff?'

'Tank Bridges, my assistant, and I come as a package. Lita was an add-on, because I wanted a doctor I could trust. Alice McDade joined in March.'

'What's she?'

'Physio and fitness coach: she knows eff all about football, but she was an Olympic marathon runner and she's got a degree in sports science.'

'Did Annette move with Paco from the start?'

Baker nodded. 'Yeah. The club put them up in a hotel at first, for longer than we'd anticipated, right through to the end of the February. I told Angela Renwick it wasn't ideal and she came up with the penthouse for the Fonters, and the flat below for some of the other lads. Well, to be exact, it was one of the directors that came up with them, Mr McCullough, the guy that owns this place.'

Alex's curiosity was pricked, but she reined it in, leaving her client to continue his tale.

'They were still in the hotel when Annie called me,' he said. 'Must have been the middle of February. We'd met once before, when Paco signed and we did a photo call, but that was all. She asked if she could see me, in private, to talk through some things. Private suited me, because in truth I was a bit leery about it. Last thing you want as a manager is to get involved in the squad's domestics, but with Paco being the star man, and he and I being connected through our agent, I said okay.'

He pulled himself up on to the work surface and sat there, kicking his heels gently against the drawers below. 'We met in the café at Chatelherault Country Park, an old pile just outside

Hamilton. Figured it was as discreet as we were going to get. As I'd guessed, Annie was having trouble settling down, she'd that fucking . . . excuse my French . . . Sirena in her ear, and living in the hotel wasn't helping. She told me that the location was making travel difficult for her, with a work schedule that could take her anywhere in the world, sometimes at short notice. I promised her I'd sort it as soon as I could, and that was fine, but the longer we were there the more obvious it was that really, the lass just wanted to talk. There she was, her a supermodel, internationally famous, and she was lonely.

'And then,' he smiled, 'I dunno, I just sensed a connection between us. You know when you meet someone for the first time and you know how it's going to be between you?' He paused. 'Or maybe you don't, I'm sorry.'

Alex grinned back at him. 'Let's say that I do.'

'Right, okay, well . . . that's how it was with Annie. But not in a sexual way,' he added, quickly. 'I just realised that she was special and that I liked her very, very much. More than that, I reckoned that she felt the same way about me. Dunno why, to this day, but I did. When we were done, she told me that talking to me had made her feel better than at any time since she'd come to Scotland. I said we could do it again, any time she liked, and we did. From then on we tried to meet for lunch at least once a month, always somewhere we'd never be seen.'

'Did she confide in you again? Did she say anything that might give a clue to the secret she mentioned in her text?'

'Not that I ever . . .'

He broke off as a loud chime sounded. 'Bugger! Who the hell?' His expression darkened. 'Please, not the bloody media,' he sighed.

'I doubt that,' Alex said. 'They wouldn't have got past the

gatehouse. But I'll go, just in case.' She rose quickly and walked through the hall to the front door. It had a large central panel of opaque glass; the shadow of a figure was cast upon it by the midday sun. She opened it, and felt her eyes widen involuntarily.

A woman stood on the step. She was of medium height, slim with close-cut brown hair through which a few silver threads were sewn. Her eyes were brown also, with a few lines in their corners, but fewer than would have been expected of someone in her forties. She was casually dressed, in a T-shirt and white cotton trousers. *Spooky*, Alex thought. The first time they had met she had been clad in exactly the same way.

'Mia,' she exclaimed.

'Alex,' Mia Watson McCullough replied. 'I'd be surprised to see you here if I didn't know from Cameron that you're acting for our guest. I'm assuming that he's in. I thought I'd call in to make sure they were settled.'

'And to size him up?' she murmured.

The other woman smiled. 'That too, I admit. I've met some dangerous men in my time; I'd like to see how he compares.'

'Most of them were in your own family,' she said, drily, 'from what I've been told.'

She chuckled, softly, a throaty sound that took Alex back twenty years, to her adolescence. 'True. Most were, but one of them's yours. He's not with you, is he?'

'My dad? No. Why should he be?'

'Protection? Your client is accused of killing a woman, isn't he?' She beamed. 'Well, can I come in?'

Alex shrugged. 'Of course, sorry.' She stepped aside to allow the visitor to enter.

Chaz Baker stood in the kitchen doorway. 'Mrs McCullough,' he said, as she approached.

'You know me?' she exclaimed; her surprise sounded genuine.

'I've seen you at Merrytown; on the other side of a very crowded boardroom, after a game. Your husband's a director of the club, after all.'

'That's right,' she agreed, 'officially confirmed as a fit and proper person by the powers that be.'

'That's more than I am at the moment,' Baker grunted. 'Your husband's Russian associate told me not to come within a mile of the training base or the ground. He suspended me from all activity and forbade me to contact anyone in the club.'

Mia stared at him. 'Did he now? Cameron wasn't consulted about that.' She hesitated. 'All the same, if he had been, he'd probably have agreed with the decision. He was accused of murder once, you know,' she added.

'I didn't, but obviously he got off.'

'Now, now, Mr Baker,' she chided, 'he didn't "get off". He was acquitted, because he was innocent . . . as you are, I take it. Yes?'

'Yes,' he declared. 'Whatever the police believe, I am. We're going to prove it too.'

'Good for you; at least Alex got you bail. More than she could do for her half-brother, but we'll let that pass. Okay,' she said briskly, 'I'll let you get on with your planning. I just wanted to make sure you're comfortable here.'

'Very, thanks.'

'You're welcome for as long as you need. I'll be off then.' She turned on her heel and headed for the door, Alex following.

'He didn't do it,' she whispered, as she opened it. 'He's a softie. Wouldn't have lasted five minutes where I grew up. Tell your dad I want to see him, by the way. He's making assumptions about Ignacio and his future; I need to make sure they're in line with mine.'

'What the hell was that about?' Baker said, as soon as Alex stepped back into the kitchen. 'Your half-brother? Bail?'

'It's a long story,' she replied. 'The respectable Mrs McCullough was born into one of Edinburgh's most notorious criminal families of the late twentieth century. She moved upmarket but never quite shook it off. When I was a kid, she was a presenter on an Edinburgh radio station and I was part of her devoted teenage audience. She met up with my father during his investigation into her brother's death, and he brought her home to meet me, thinking I'd be impressed.'

'And were you?'

Alex nodded. 'Yes, I admit it, I was. Mia had charisma, no question; there's still plenty of it in her. She still works in radio, on her husband's station; the man owns most of Dundee. My father was impressed by her too. My mum had been dead for almost ten years by then, and he and Mia had a very brief fling. Then she left, vanished, disappeared. She resurfaced last year, and Dad discovered that he had a son he'd never known about. He found out too late to help him out of some very bad trouble.'

'Is he inside?'

'For another couple of months, yes, he is.'

'Mr McCullough: what about him?' Baker asked. 'It's not so much that I've heard whispers, but when we played Dundee last season, and his name was mentioned, more than one person gave me a knowing look.'

'Like Mia said, he was accused of murder but the case against him collapsed. He's never been convicted of anything and he has a substantial portfolio of entirely legitimate businesses.'

'But?'

'But nothing,' she said sharply. 'Forget about Cameron McCullough. It's you who has the problem, and if you're going to have the same outcome he did, we have to work at it. Before Mia called in I was asking you about Annette's secret.'

'That's right, and I still can't think what it might have been.'

'What do you know about her, her background, her early life?'

'Not a hell of a lot, but I do know that she's never been in a Paris nightclub in her life, far less been in the chorus line. All that stuff about her being discovered by Sirena in the Crazy Horse, that was bullshit, pure PR fiction that the tabloids and the glossies just ate up.

'The truth is that she was spotted when she worked in a café in London; she was seventeen at the time. Sirena had a panic on; she was a low-end operator then, and she'd been let down by a girl she'd booked for a photo shoot for a home shopping catalogue that morning. She saw Annette when she brought her a coffee and asked if she fancied making a few quid. It all started there. She went along to the job, the catalogue editor loved her; instead of using her on the kitchen products she'd been hired to display, he put her into the fashion section, straightaway.'

'Did she tell you any more about her early years?' Alex asked.

'Not much; her mum was Sri Lankan, she told me that much, but I think she was adopted. She mentioned being brought up in Worthing, and she said that her dad was a vicar, but when I asked how he met her mother, she just shrugged and looked away. There was a door between us at that point and I let it stay closed.' Baker glanced at his lawyer. 'Annie had a lot of secrets,' he said, 'but I doubt we'll uncover any of them now.'

'We're going to have to,' she retorted. 'Your whole life might depend on it.'

Twenty-Five

'How is our Chaz?' Cameron McCullough asked his wife. 'Is he optimistic or is he just going through the motions of putting up a defence?'

She considered the question for a few seconds. 'They're doing more than that,' she replied, 'but as you'd expect, he's petrified beneath it all; there's no disguising that. Alex is going to have to work hard to keep him on an even keel, especially now that he's barred from any contact with the football club and its staff.'

'By the court? Was that a bail condition?'

'No, that was all Rogozin's doing.'

He frowned. 'It was? Dimitri never told me about that.'

'Does he have to?'

McCullough's eyes narrowed. 'He's the chairman, and in theory, sure, he has the executive power to sack or suspend the manager. In practice, I brought Rogotron into the deal, and in the corporate ownership of the club I'm the real majority shareholder. He seems to have forgotten that.'

'Are you going to remind him?'

'No,' he grunted, 'I'm going to give him a little more rope.'

'If he had asked you, Cameron, would you have disagreed

with him? The press are going crazy over this; they're crawl-
ing all over Edinburgh trying to get background on Annette
Bordeaux and her relationship with Baker. Surely you'd want to
keep him as far away from the club as possible till it all calms
down.'

'We could keep him away from the club but still have his
input,' he countered. 'He's been charged, for Christ's sake. The
media aren't allowed to badger him. Yes, yes, yes, I know we
have to keep him and Paco Fonter apart, but Paco's on
compassionate leave, plus, Angela Renwick tells me he's got a
hamstring tear that'll keep him out of action until Baker's trial
comes up. The way it is, Merrytown FC is denied the services of
its two costliest assets, and yet they're still on our payroll.'

He sighed. 'All that said, Mia, the chances are we'll lose him
permanently in a couple of months.'

'He and Alex Skinner don't agree with you.'

'Are you sure about Alex? Did you get her on her own and ask
her what she thinks?'

'I didn't have to. It's obvious.'

'I should be happy to hear that,' he said, 'but what I get from
the other camp is that the police case is rock solid.'

'Where did you get that from? Your granddaughter, through
her boyfriend?'

'Hell no, I wouldn't put her on the spot by asking her. I have
other contacts, in the legal fraternity . . . although that should be
sorority these days, the number of women in practice. There's a
girl called Benedict in the prosecution team. Her father's one of
our members. I saw him this morning in the changing room. I
was going to the gym and he was getting ready for a round of
golf. He reckons that Chaz Baker will make his daughter's
name.'

'I can think of another father who might tell you the same about his.'

'Can you really? Bob Skinner's a realist; his judgement will be based purely on the evidence.'

Mia's laugh rang out like the chime of a bell. 'Oh my dear, you really don't know him at all, do you?'

Twenty-Six

'How is Alex?' Sarah asked.

'She's okay,' Skinner assured her, his phone pressed to his ear. 'One hundred per cent focused on the man Baker.'

'And will you help her with the preparation?'

'Of course I will. And I'll try to keep her feet on the ground while I'm at it. Her certainty about his innocence is infectious, but I've just read through the police report to the fiscal, and it's pretty bleak. The way I see it the only defence she's going to be able to offer will be along the lines of "A bad boy did it and ran away", and I've never known a jury to buy that one.'

'Reasonable doubt?' she ventured.

'I don't see any. You're the pathologist on the case. Is there any doubt about how she died?'

'None at all: she was battered then manually strangled.'

'Or doubt about the time of death?'

'No, that's accurate to within a couple of hours.'

'And during that time Chaz Baker was on the premises. Reversing down shit creek without a paddle might not be impossible, but that's where Baker is right now.'

Looking out from his office, Bob frowned. 'My worry isn't just for the effect of a loss on her; it's for the impact of this very big case on the rest of her practice. She talks of taking on an associate, but it hasn't happened yet. She has other clients, my kinsman Johnny Fleming for one. He's going to be a guilty plea for sure, and while a custodial sentence is unlikely, it isn't impossible. She'll have to put in a good plea in mitigation to make certain that doesn't happen.'

'Could you speak in court on his behalf?'

'And say what?' he exclaimed. 'That he's my distant cousin, but not much else. I hardly know the man, and the sheriff would want to know the strength of our connection.'

He stood, and stepped across the room to the glass wall, looking north across the city skyline. 'It's not just Johnny, it's all of them; the woman accused of stealing from the Co-op, the seventeen-year-old lad who got drunk on Buckfast and smashed a window that could cost him the career in the RAF that he had his heart set on, the fellow solicitor who's under investigation for misusing his firm's client account. They all deserve as much commitment as she's giving to Baker, and I don't see how she can deliver, not on her own.'

'Then it's too bad you never did a law degree as your father wanted.'

'He hoped,' Skinner corrected her. 'What Dad wanted was what was best for me; he hoped it would be the law, that's all. He'd have been very proud of his granddaughter, that's for sure.'

'Do you know anyone who could help her?'

'I could make a couple of phone calls and put somebody in the empty office next to hers, but would that person be any good? The best thing I could do for her would be to find the thread that would unravel the Crown case against Baker, but I don't see it anywhere in the report I've just read.'

'Bring it home with you and we'll look at it together,' Sarah offered.

'Wouldn't that be professional misconduct, since you're going to be a prosecution witness?'

'Good point,' she chuckled, 'but one, no one will ever know, and two, if you were to cross-examine me as if I was in the box, that would probably be ethical.'

'Okay,' he said, smiling, 'let's do it that way.' He reached across to a coat stand and took his jacket from a hook. 'I think I'll head home now, in fact. I've nothing left to do here. See you later.'

He slipped the phone back into its socket, picked up his document case, and headed for the door. Six floors below, in the street outside the *Saltire* building, his movement was mirrored.

Leaving his office, he headed for the lift, pausing only to wave to June Crampsey, who was at her desk. She waved back, beckoning him into her office.

'Do you know where Paco Fonter and Chaz Baker are?' she asked, as he stuck his head through her doorway. 'My people are having no joy in tracing either of them.'

'No to the first,' he replied, 'to the second, no comment.'

'Oh, come on, Bob,' the editor protested. 'Give us a break.'

'I would if I could, June, but I've got a conflict of interest.'

'What sort of conflict could you have?' she retorted, but as she spoke, her expression changed. 'Wait a minute,' she exclaimed, 'I get it. Your Alex is representing Baker, isn't she? Tell me I'm right!'

'I'll tell you, no comment. I don't discuss her professional life with anyone, not even you, unless I've got her express permission. In this instance, I don't.'

Crampsey beamed. 'I'll take that as a yes. How's he going to plead?'

'June, the case is *sub judice*. You can't report anything until the next court appearance, and de Matteo's warned you all off Baker.'

'As they say in the newsroom, fuck the Solicitor General, and the interdict he rode in on. I know more about media law than he does; I know what's contempt of court and I know what isn't.'

'I'm sure you do, but I'm still saying nothing.'

'Fair enough,' Crampsey conceded, 'but you should mark her card about this. Cisco Serra's hawking exclusive rights to his client's story, once the case is over. I had a call this morning, as did everyone else. Just a courtesy, though, in my case; he knows that the *Saltire* won't be bidding against the London tabloids.'

'Which client?' Skinner asked.

'Paco Fonter, of course.' Her eyes widened as the weight of his question hit her. 'Hold on, are you saying that Serra represents Baker too?'

'As I understand it, yes, he does.'

'I didn't know that,' she said, 'and I don't think our sports guys do either, or one of them would have been bound to mention it. There's a story in that, never mind anything else.'

'Then good luck with it; but . . . and you can regard this as a board level request . . . make sure if you run it that Alex's name doesn't appear in it, anywhere. I want no implication that it came from her.'

'Fair enough,' Crampsey conceded. 'Thanks, Bob.'

'*De nada*,' he chuckled, as she reached for her phone.

He was still smiling as the lift door opened and he stepped inside.

Unusually the ride to the basement car park was uninterrupted, with no stops at the editorial floors, from which there were countless comings and goings during the day. The park was empty of people also, although more than half of the bays were full.

He approached his Mercedes and felt in his pocket for the key, pressing the unlock button as his thumb found it, seeing the lights flash and hearing the horn give one brief 'beep'. Reaching it he gripped the door handle . . . and then his head seemed to explode.

There was no sensation, only a sound from somewhere followed by a time of . . . nothing. It passed, after how long he had no clue, and he was vaguely aware that he had hit the ground, hard. His mind was fuzzy, his thoughts confused as all the possibilities hit him in the same second. 'What? Why? Heart attack? Pacemaker failure? Oww!!' Finally a blast of pain hit him, behind his right ear, in the same moment that he felt a trickle of something that had to be blood flow round his jawline.

He stirred. Less than two seconds later fire swept through his body as a foot slammed into his kidney. His back arched, helping him absorb, partially, a second kick when it thudded into the centre of his spine. A third would surely be aimed at his head.

Pure animal instinct took over. Skinner rolled backwards and over, wrapping an arm around the black-shod foot as it came towards him, then rolled again, putting his full body weight on his attacker's knee and sending him tumbling backwards. Before the other man had a chance to gather himself, he attacked, keeping him pinned down as he heaved himself forward, covering his face with his large right hand and slamming the back of his head into the hard concrete of the garage floor.

He pushed himself to one knee; his rival moaned, but moved,

until Skinner extinguished the last of his resistance by punching him, just once, but very hard, in the middle of the forehead.

'Will you never fucking learn, Grigor?' he gasped.

He unfastened the unconscious Russian's tie, rolled him on to his side, and used it to lash his wrists together, then removed his belt, looped it around his ankles and used it to hog-tie him. Grigor came back to semi-awareness just as the process was complete. He struggled, and yelled, in his own language, what the Scot assumed was a curse.

Spotting a black extendable baton lying nearby, Skinner picked it up, and pressed its tip against the back of Grigor's neck. 'Now here's what's going to happen,' he barked. 'You're going to lie there very quietly and you're going to do it of your own accord, or by the time the police get here you will be anyway, and you'll be crying salty tears.'

As he spoke he heard a movement behind him; he glanced over his shoulder and saw a woman. She was staring at the scene fearfully, over the tip of a mobile phone she held out before her. He recognised her: Lennox Webster, the *Saltire* crime reporter.

'Are you filming this?' he barked, incredulous.

'I thought,' she mumbled as she approached, lowering the phone, 'I just thought, evidence, you know.'

'How much did you see?'

'All of it.'

Skinner pressed the baton into the Russian's neck once more, harder. 'Your lucky day, mister,' he murmured, and then looked back at the reporter. 'Did it occur to you to give me a shout, Lennox, to warn me?' he asked. 'Or were you too busy covering the story?'

'I only saw him just as he hit you, and you went down,' she protested. 'I should have shouted, I know, but to be honest I was afraid he'd come for me. So I videoed it; it was all I could think to do.'

He sighed, showing her a half-smile. 'Journalist first, citizen second,' he said. 'As a director of InterMedia I suppose I should be impressed. If you reckon you've got enough footage and you don't want a close-up, do you think you could spare me some battery time. I fear my phone may have come off badly in that ruckus.'

'Of course,' the reporter agreed. 'What would you like me to do?'

'Jesus!' he exclaimed. 'Calling the police would be a good start. Use my name and tell them to put you through to Chief Superintendent Mary Chambers, the area commander. I want this bastard to feel the full weight of the righteous anger of my former colleagues . . . at least those that aren't pleased to see me get a kicking,' he added.

'I will, right away. But after that, don't you think I should call for an ambulance? You really are bleeding very badly.'

Twenty-Seven

'How many stitches did they put in?' Sammy Pye asked.

'It's staples these days,' the man in the hospital bed replied. 'I stopped counting after six. How did you get involved in this?' he continued. 'Or did you just happen to be passing?'

'No, I'm involved; through the high heid yins.'

The vernacular explanation was enough. He had been sent, by those on high. Skinner nodded understanding.

'CS Chambers called the chief to tell her you'd been attacked. When she said that we have a Russian in custody, well, she knew about the incident in Fettes Avenue on Sunday and made the connection to the Bordeaux case. She phoned me and told me to get along to the Royal to check that you're okay, then to take charge of the investigation into the attack on you.'

'What's to investigate?' the patient grunted, shifting awkwardly in his hospital gown. 'Your man Grigor and I had a run-in; he finished second and he isn't the type to leave it at that. There's only the most tenuous connection to the King Robert Village murder, in that the guy minds the Merrytown owner. When I told Ms Webster to speak to Mary, I didn't expect CID involvement.'

'I know,' the detective agreed. He grinned. 'We like to show we care, that's all.'

'All I wanted was to be sure that the bastard is on the first plane back to Moscow. If he came after me he might have had it in mind to visit Alex as well.'

'As it happens, I'm taking it a lot more seriously than that,' Pye countered. 'Sauce is with him now charging him with attempted murder.'

'Hey, Sammy,' Skinner protested, 'that's over the top, is it not?'

The DCI shook his head, emphatically. 'I've seen Lennox Webster's video, sir, you haven't. If you had, and it was someone else involved, you'd take exactly the same view as us. The man hit you on the head, twice, with a prohibited weapon, a German-made hardened steel expanding baton.'

'Twice?'

'Yes, once to knock you down, then he hit you again when you were on the deck. You were obviously unconscious the second time you were struck. That's what makes it attempted murder, for me and for the fiscal. Then he put the boot in for luck.' Pye grinned, impishly. 'Only it wasn't so lucky for him.'

'Where are you holding him?'

'He's still here, in another part of A and E. They did a head CT scan, just as they did with you, to make sure there was no unseen damage. There isn't, but they want to keep him in overnight.'

'Does he have a lawyer?' Skinner asked. 'If I press charges, he's going to need one.'

'One of the senior people from the Russian Consulate General in Melville Street is with him. But what's this "if" about? He has to be charged, Chief. If you don't, we will.'

'I keep telling you guys, stop calling me Chief. It unsettles me, plus it's disrespectful to Maggie Steele. Sammy, I don't want to be involved personally in a high-profile case. If the guy's deported and put on a watch list so he can never get back into Britain, that'll be enough for me.'

A laugh rang out; the curtain that closed off the cubicle parted and Sauce Haddock stepped inside. 'You are involved personally, sir, like it or not,' he chuckled. 'The *Saltire* posted Lennox Webster's video in its online edition two hours ago. It's been picked up by all the TV channels for their news bulletins, and it's trending on YouTube. I saw one comment suggesting that you'll be getting an offer to fight in the UFC.'

Skinner put a hand to the back of his head, fingering the thick dressing, gently. 'Bloody hell,' he moaned. 'Why did June Crampsey do that?' He sighed, then answered his own question. 'Because she's the best damn journalist I know, that's why.'

'She was also extremely upset,' Pye volunteered, 'and only authorised publication when she was sure you were okay. '

'Everyone else is desperate to catch up,' Haddock continued. 'There's a small army of press outside, looking to talk to you when you leave. The hospital put out a statement saying that you're being kept in overnight, but they're still there.'

'The hospital can stick that one,' the patient grunted. 'I'm going home, as soon as Sarah gets here. She's a doctor, so I'm covered. Cuts, bruises and mild concussion, that's all I've got. I'll stay for four hours as the consultant asked, but then I'm gone.'

'We'll smuggle you out the back way,' the DCI volunteered.

'You'll smuggle me nowhere. I'll speak to the press as I leave, get it over with. If I don't they'll turn up at Gullane and I'm damned if I'm having that. Mind you,' he added, 'I'm not going anywhere until I get some new clothes. My shirt's soaked in blood and my jacket's not much better. They're bound for the hospital incinerator.' He tugged at the gown. 'I'm not walking out in this thing.'

'How many staples did they put in, sir?' Haddock asked.

'Plenty. I didn't count, just lay back and thought about Scotland.' He grinned. 'I have to tell you, guys, it's a walk in the park compared to being shot, or stabbed. Just another scar, and this one's above the hairline. My one small regret is that the Russian bastard was carted away without a mark on him.'

'He's got a seriously sore head though,' the DS observed.

'Oh, me too,' he admitted. 'In fact I feel another Tramadol coming on. I can only hope Grigor feels the same.'

Haddock smiled. 'He does. He's still badly concussed. There's a lump on the back of his head, and one the size of a golf ball in the middle of his forehead. But those are the least of his worries. The Russian vice-consul has a gleam in his eye. He just told me that his name isn't Grigor Yashin at all. His passport is phoney.'

'Forged?'

'No, not forged, but phoney. I gave the consul access to his fingerprints, at his request. He sent them to the database in Moscow, and got an instant hit. His real name is Valentin Afonin, and he's the subject of half a dozen arrest warrants in Russia, all for violent crimes, including murder. He was convicted of shooting a banker in St Petersburg, four years ago. While he was being transported east to begin a life sentence he was sprung, by a gang of specialists. He's been on the run ever since, only he hasn't been, it seems. He shaved off his beard, had a few tattoos removed, got blue contact lenses to disguise his brown eyes, and with his new look he's been gainfully employed as Dimitri Rogozin's bodyguard.'

Skinner glanced at Pye. 'You see, Sammy? What's a wee attempted murder charge in Scotland compared with the stuff his own people have on him? You know what's going to happen now, don't you? The Crown Office will keep the charge against him open, but we'll send him back home and let the Russians feed him for the next thirty years.'

'There's no extradition treaty between us and Russia,' the DCI pointed out.

'We don't need one. Sauce says he's in the country under false pretences, so he can be put on a plane and sent back home. And he will be. Isn't that right, Rocco?'

The detectives turned, eyes focused on a man who had entered the cubicle unnoticed: early forties, sleek black hair, dark eyes . . . *could be Dimitri Rogozin's brother*, Skinner's sluggish mind told him.

'Have you met the Solicitor General, lads?' he asked. 'What's up, Rocco? Did you drop by hoping that the rumours of my survival were false? Or are you thinking of charging me with assault?'

'Come on, Bob,' the law officer protested, with a grin. 'We've had our differences in the past, but I wouldn't wish either of those outcomes.'

'Rocco's an old stablemate of my ex-wife, politically and nationally,' he explained. 'De Matteo, de Marco, they almost sound related. How is the dear Aileen?' he asked. 'Now she's on the Labour front bench at Westminster I see a lot of her in the media, but I haven't heard from her in months.'

'She's very well, thanks. In fact, she called me as soon as she'd heard you'd been attacked, wanting reassurance that you're all right.'

'Thank her and tell her I am.' He picked up on a look of caution in de Matteo's eyes. 'It's okay, I mean it: I don't hold any grudges. She may have been part of the gang in the Holyrood

Parliament that ended my police career by forcing the fucking awful national force on us, but she wasn't the prime mover.'

He pointed at a flat device that the Solicitor General was clutching. 'Can you get YouTube on that tablet? I'd like to see the video that Sauce says is making me a star.'

'Sure.' De Matteo nodded. He tapped the screen of his iPad several times, until he was satisfied, then handed it over.

Skinner hit the play button and watched intently. He winced as he saw himself struck down and again as he was hit while on the floor, but as the movie progressed a thin smile of satisfaction appeared on his face.

'Yes,' he whispered when it was over. 'I can see how that might make good TV.'

'I don't know how you did that,' Sauce Haddock said, quietly.

'I did it because I fucking had to, son. The alternative wasn't acceptable.'

He played the video again, then handed the tablet back to its owner. 'Very interesting, Rocco, thanks. Educational, too.'

'What did it teach you?'

'That Lennox Webster's a liar. She told me she didn't have time to yell and warn me, but she did. The video starts with Grigor, or Afonin if you want to call him that, moving in on me. She had time to set it up, select video, hold it steady and start to film.'

The Solicitor General frowned. 'You're right. I could almost make a case for that being criminal conduct, given that she's benefited from it. Should I?'

'Hell no,' Skinner replied, firmly. 'Leave it with me. Once Xavi Aislado, the *Saltire*'s big boss, sees that, he's going to realise the same as me. When he does, his instant reaction will be to fire her. I'll need to have a conversation with her editor; it might take both of us to save her job, that's if June wants to.'

'And you do?'

'Fuck yes! We're in the age of online newspapers, mate. This is the biggest boost the *Saltire*'s ever had. You can make a case for charging the woman; I can make a case for giving her a bonus.'

'You've changed, Bob,' de Matteo observed. 'The man I used to know would have thrown the book at her.'

'The guy you used to know sees a wider world now . . . and maybe he knows himself a bit better too.'

'In that case,' the lawyer ventured, tentatively, 'would the new man consider talking to his daughter about . . .'

Skinner held up a hand. 'Stop!' he barked. 'Go no further, Rocco. You'd be well out of order if you were to suggest that I try to influence Alex's advice to her client.' He winked at Pye, sending a wave of pain washing round his skull. 'You'd also embarrass Sammy as the SIO in the case, by suggesting that you might not think it's winnable.'

'Oh, we're going to get a conviction,' de Matteo retorted. 'Be in no doubt about that. DCI Pye's case is rock solid, as you must know by now. I assume you've read the report.'

'Assume nothing, presume nothing. You can't raise this with me, you just can't. Thanks for the visit and for your concern, but I think you should go now. You need to get on with the process of removing the man Afonin from the country.'

'True.'

'You might also ask them how he was able to import a prohibited weapon, since I'm assuming that he didn't buy it here. By the way, that was the old Bob Skinner talking.'

The Solicitor General nodded, smiled sheepishly and left the cubicle.

Skinner waited for a few seconds until he was sure de Matteo was out of earshot, then laughed. 'What a fucking plonker that man is. He's a political appointment, unlike his boss, the Lord Advocate, who can't stand him. He used to be Labour, but he jumped ship to the Nationalists for the sake of his career. Be very wary of him, lads, and keep a record of everything you tell him and of every instruction he gives you. If the Baker prosecution does go south, he'll be looking for someone to carry the can.'

'Do you think it will, sir?' Haddock asked, boldly. 'We don't.'

'I'm not going to answer that, Sauce,' Skinner told him. 'Instead I'll ask you a question. You guys, and you in particular, Sammy, have known my Alex for a while. You'll be aware, and I acknowledge, that in her private life, she never gets anything right . . . just like her old man, until recently. But in her professional life, can either of you tell me something that she's ever got wrong?'

Pye smiled. 'I hear what you're saying, boss, but there's a first time for everything. I hate to sound like Mr de Matteo, QC, but a guilty plea to culpable homicide is a pretty good offer.'

'Objectively, I might agree,' he conceded, 'but I'm never going to tell her that. The fact is that neither you nor de Matteo can have any input to how she advises her client in a privileged situation, so don't compromise yourself by trying to influence her through me. She's obliged to put the offer to him, sure, and to advise him as she thinks appropriate, but the decision's his and his alone.'

'And you better believe that,' Alex declared, sweeping the curtain open as Haddock had done and stepping up to the bed. She was not alone; Sarah followed close behind her.

'Time we were off,' Pye said, quickly. 'Personally and professionally, given our respective roles.'

Skinner reached out and caught his arm. 'Agreed, but a suggestion before you go. Before you wrap up the Grigor investigation, you might want to have a word with his employer, if only to rule out the possibility that he might have put him up to it.'

'Do you think he might have?'

'Honestly, no. I'd just like that man's cage rattled, that's all.'

'I'll take the suggestion on board, sir. I'll let you know if anything comes of it.'

'Thanks. See you, gentlemen.'

As the two left, he turned to his daughter and his partner. 'See, I'm all in one piece,' he chuckled.

'I've seen you worse,' Sarah conceded. 'But I've also seen that video. What the hell did that woman Crampsey think she was doing publishing it?'

'It's her job,' Skinner said. 'There's no legal reason why she shouldn't, as charges hadn't been laid when she did.'

'But as soon as they are,' Alex pointed out, 'she should take it down.'

'The punters who uploaded it to YouTube won't, so why should the *Saltire*? The law hasn't caught up with social media; you know that. Anyway, contempt of court isn't going to be an issue.'

He explained the revelations of Grigor's true identity and his past. 'It doesn't matter what the charge is, serious assault or attempt to murder. He won't be here to face it.' He winked at her. 'I don't suppose Chaz Baker has any outstanding warrants that might take precedence.'

'Stop it!' She stifled a laugh.

'Only kidding. How did your meeting go?'

'I saw Mamma Mia; she dropped in on a snooping mission. She wants a meeting, by the way, about Ignacio.'

'I suppose,' he murmured. 'As long as McCullough isn't there.'

'Pops,' Alex warned, 'McCullough is his stepfather. You may not be able to keep him at a distance.'

'Maybe not, but I'll try. How about the purpose of your trip? How did that play out?'

'Better than I'd feared,' she admitted. 'I know how my client's prints came to be on the victim's phone.'

'You know how he says they came to be there,' he corrected her.

'Bloody cynic!'

'Devil's bloody advocate. You won't simply have to offer it as an explanation. The prints are there; that's evidence. A plausible story doesn't always equate to reasonable doubt, unless it's proved.'

'I'll grant you that, but that may be possible. I'll have to send an investigator to interview the staff at One Devonshire, in Glasgow, but it could be worth it. They might not recall Chaz, but they're bound to remember Annette Bordeaux.' She smiled. 'Would you do it, once you're mobile again?'

'I've told you, you can't afford me.'

'My client can. It needs to be done, Pops.'

'Maybe,' he sighed. 'I'm free tomorrow, so we'll see.'

'No we won't,' Sarah intervened, her tone ruling out any argument. 'You're going nowhere tomorrow, other than home.'

'I'm going there now. Gimme what you brought, there's a love.'

'Certainly.' She smiled, sweetly, reached into her shoulder bag and produced his electric shaver, a pair of pyjamas, a toothbrush and a tube of toothpaste.

'What the hell's this?' he exclaimed.

'Bob, my love,' she said, 'they want you to stay in overnight, as a precaution.'

'But I'll have you as a carer back in Gullane,' he protested.

'Honey, I'm a pathologist, that's my specialty. If you were dead, yes, I'd take you home. But you're not, and since you're not, there is no way that I'm going to countermand the recommendation of an A and E consultant, not least when he tells me that you've got a cracked rib and you're pissing blood. Get used to it, big boy, you are spending the night here.'

He sighed, and admitted defeat. 'Okay, but I want to be gone from here first thing in the morning. Alex, can you pick me up and take me to the office, so I can collect my car?'

'Your car can stay there,' Sarah said. 'You shouldn't drive for a couple of days. I'll collect you in the morning.'

'What about the media crowd I'm told is waiting outside?'

'They have two choices,' Alex declared. 'They can carry on waiting in vain or go home for the night.'

'How about you talk to them for me?' her father suggested. 'Thank them for their concern, but tell them that I've been in worse scrapes with tougher guys than Grigor and walked away from them all.'

'Me? Read badly from a prepared statement?' she said. 'I'm not sure that's me.'

'You'll carry it off,' he insisted.

'When they see me they may be more interested in Chaz Baker than in you,' she pointed out. 'The word is out that I'm acting for him.'

'Mmm,' he murmured. 'I hadn't thought of that. Maybe you shouldn't do it.'

'No, I will. Chaz is being crucified in social media. If this gives me a platform to assert his innocence, I'd be daft not to take it. What information have the police released about the man who attacked you?'

'None. Don't get drawn into that. If you're asked who he is, refer that straight back to Sammy Pye . . . or better still, Rocco de Matteo.'

'Is he involved?'

'He used it as a pretext to get to me, in the hope that I would get to you about the plea bargain. You missed him by a couple of minutes, that's all.'

'Cheeky bastard!' Alex growled. 'That's misconduct. I could complain to the Lord Advocate about that.'

'You could but you won't. Rocco's a wanker, but he isn't your enemy. Don't make him one.'

'Did he get to you, Pops? You think Chaz is guilty, so you must believe he should take the plea on offer.'

'I cut him off at the knees, love; didn't let him get that far. As for my feelings . . . look, it's not a matter of my belief. When I look at the case against Baker and put myself in the shoes of the average jury member I can only be honest, and say that it's a banker conviction. If it goes to trial the best you can hope for is that the judge gives the option of a culpable homicide verdict and they go for that, but don't build your hopes up.'

'Bob,' Sarah pleaded, 'cut her some slack. Don't paint such a black picture.'

'What good would that do?' he countered. 'Black is what it is. Christ, love, you did the autopsy. You saw the state of the body and you'll be a witness for the Crown. Do you see this as anything less than . . .' He stopped abruptly. 'No, don't answer that. I shouldn't be asking.'

'That's okay, it isn't prejudicial to anything. No I don't: Annette Bordeaux was murdered, brutally. Did Chaz Baker murder her? That judgement is outside my remit.'

'And mine. I've promised to study the report carefully and I will, but beyond that . . . Look, I know a good investigator, her name's Carrie McDaniels and she could take on your leg work at a reasonable cost.'

'Is she capable of overturning the police case and proving Chaz's innocence?'

'No,' he admitted. 'No more than I am,' he added. 'I don't believe that anyone is.'

'Pops,' Alex sighed. 'I know that the notion of working against the police runs counter to everything you stand for, but I really need you. I need you to do more than read the paperwork, I need you to close your eyes, take a blind leap of faith and commit to proving Chaz Baker's innocence. If that sounds like emotional blackmail, that's exactly what it is.'

He laughed, then winced as that simple movement strained the staples in his head again. 'In that case, I give up. I will tilt at your windmill, but with as much chance of success as old Quixote. Now go and talk to the media but don't even think of telling them that I'm on the case.'

He watched her leave then reached out to take Sarah's hand. 'Better give me those jammies, love. I've got a confession to make. My head hurts like buggery, my back is sore, I feel very tired, and I need to take another painkiller and sleep it off.'

Twenty-Eight

'Did they believe you?' Mia McCullough heard her husband ask. She gazed at him, standing in their conservatory with his mobile pressed to his ear. She gestured to him and he read her correctly, putting it on speaker mode and holding it up.

'. . . course they believe me, Cameron. These are simple peoples, small-timers.'

'I'm not so bloody sure I would have,' McCullough retorted. 'If I were you I wouldn't be a hundred per cent certain that they did. And do not underestimate these men. Edinburgh might be a small city compared to Moscow, but its CID is better than yours. There's no whiff of corruption about it either. As for those men you're dismissing, they are not simple, they are serious. Trust me on that.'

'They never catch you,' Rogozin said.

'Those two never tried. By the way, watch your mouth on an open phone line, Dimitri,' he added.

'You worries too much.'

'You can never worry too much, pal. For example, I'm still worried that you're lying to the cops and to me. I wouldn't put it past you to have set that fucking baboon on Bob Skinner.'

'Why I do that?'

'To send a message to his daughter, perhaps. To give her an added incentive to get Chaz Baker off.'

The phone in McCullough's hand fell silent; there was no response. Husband and wife exchanged frowns.

'If I thought you had done that,' he continued, 'I would be very displeased. You're in my country now, and I expect you to obey its rules and conventions, one of those being that cops are sacrosanct.'

'What?'

'Off limits, untouchable.'

'This man Skinner, he not cop.'

'He may be off the strength, Dimitri, but that means nothing. He is also not exactly a soft target, as your idiot has just found out. You know what? If that woman hadn't been there filming and if Skinner hadn't seen her when he did, there's a fair chance that Grigor would have wound up in intensive care.'

'You joking with me, Cameron,' Rogozin laughed.

'I'm bloody not. He would have if he'd tried that on me, and that's if he was lucky. Listen, pal, you and I have had a mutually beneficial business relationship up to now. You need to be sensible, to make sure it stays that way. The man Grigor, or whatever his real name is, I told you he was a liability; I told you not to bring him to Scotland. You ignored me and now we're scraping shit off the fan. It's already played out badly, but it could get worse.'

'No!'

'Oh but yes. You're the chairman of Merrytown Football Club. If the Crown decide to prosecute the fella, he will be tied to you. The question of your involvement will be raised in court, and your fit and proper person status might be questioned by the football bosses.'

'What are you saying?' the Russian blustered.

'They might ban you. To tell you the truth I wouldn't be upset if they did. Just lately, Dimitri, your attitude and your manners have been annoying me. I let you import big Paco Fonter, a luxury player who is, frankly, a fish out of water in our league and I let his agent make Baker part of the package. Okay, Chaz knows what he's doing, he's a top manager, but Christ, will you look where we are with him now? Did you know he was shagging Fonter's wife?' McCullough shouted, his usual calm abandoned. 'Was I the only guy in the club who wasn't aware of it?'

'He was not. That not true.'

'So why did he kill her? Oh, never mind! I don't want to know.' He stopped, for breath and to regain his composure.

'As it happens,' he continued, quietly, 'Grigor won't be going to court. The police have discovered his real identity and the Russians want him back. I've reached out to our Solicitor General through an acquaintance. He assures me that the problem will be back in Moscow in a couple of days.'

'So no problem. Why you so excited, Cameron?'

'I was excited, but now I'm calm. So listen to me. From now on, you will come to Scotland alone, on your expensive flying company-owned toy. No more Grigors, no more minders at all. You're under no threat here; in fact very few people have ever heard of you, and to be honest, nobody who has gives a fuck about you.'

'No, no. I bring who I like.'

'No, you don't. Bring your girlfriend, bring your other girlfriend, bring both of them at the same time, no problem. But no more walking disasters.'

'Cameron,' the Russian drawled, 'you don' want make an enemy of Rogozin.'

'Actually, Dimitri,' McCullough replied, 'it's the other way around. But as long as Rogotron carries on paying me my dividends, I don't care about you one way or the other. I'll see you at the Motherwell game next Saturday.'

He ended the call and pocketed his phone, and turned to Mia. 'What do you think of that?'

'Did he really tell that man to go after Bob, do you think?' she asked.

'I don't know, but it wouldn't surprise me. Dimitri's got a hoodlum fixation, that's his problem. He likes to act the Mafioso, but the truth is he's a wimp.'

'Why do you tolerate him? You could buy him out of Rogotron any time you like, and take over as Merrytown chairman yourself.'

He laughed. 'Why would I do that? The deal I have with him includes an arrangement that if either of us dies, his shares pass to the survivor, with the condition that the heirs of the dead one continue to receive their share of the profit. It would be frustrating if I bought him out and then he stepped in front of a bus.'

'Wouldn't it just,' his wife murmured. 'But if he stepped in front of that bus tomorrow . . .'

Twenty-Nine

'That's a definite refusal? Are you absolutely sure?' There was something about Paula Benedict's voice that pushed Alex Skinner's hostility button, every time. The woman could have been reciting the Lord's Prayer and her hackles would still have risen. Add to that her manner, and Alex could not think of anyone she disliked more heartily.

'My client's position is that he denies absolutely being involved in the death of Annette Bordeaux. That's not going to change, Paula, so don't waste your time or mine by pursuing the matter any further.'

'I'll convey that to the Solicitor General,' the advocate purred. 'He'll be disappointed.'

'No, he'll be crapping himself about putting his reputation on the line by leading in such a high-profile trial. If I were you I'd be prepared for him to back out and leave you carrying the can.'

'I hope he does,' Benedict declared. 'It'll be like shooting fish in a barrel.'

'I've often wondered what sort of idiot would try to do that,' Alex murmured, then hung up.

She was in the act of reaching into her laden filing tray when the phone rang again. Impatiently she snatched it from its cradle. 'Yes,' she snapped.

'It's the Lanark procurator fiscal,' her secretary announced, 'about the Fleming assault case. I could tell him you'll call back.'

'No,' she said, 'I'll take it.' She waited, hearing a click as the connection was made. 'Mr Black, what can I do for you?'

'It might be the other way around,' the prosecutor replied. 'I read in this morning's *Herald* that you've been instructed by Chaz Baker. That's going to take up a lot of your time, so I just thought I'd say that I can be flexible in scheduling the Fleming case if it helps you.'

'How flexible?' she asked.

'I can either call it quickly or kick it into the long grass for a while.'

She frowned, mentally assessing her workload. 'Could you schedule it for Thursday morning?' she ventured.

'No problem. Do you simply want to enter a plea or proceed to disposal? I'm not going to press for a custodial sentence. Your client's a popular local man, descended from a Lanarkshire legend, and his record is spotless.'

'Subject to final instruction,' she replied, 'he'll be pleading guilty. You know about the famous ancestor?' she added.

'Oh yes. Legend isn't a word I used lightly, but Sir Mathew Fleming certainly was one. He led a very colourful life. He wasn't a man to mess with either; your client seems to have inherited that quality.'

'He's not the only one,' Alex chuckled. 'Johnny Fleming's a distant cousin of mine, and thus of my father.'

'Fascinating,' Black exclaimed. 'Sir Mathew had a reputation as an investigator too. There's a story involving murder, conspiracy and an innocent man going to the gallows. He uncovered the truth, they say. See you in court on Thursday morning.'

'Yes, I will. Thanks for your help, and thanks for that story too. I'd like to think that history might be about to repeat itself, but without the unfortunate outcome for the innocent man.'

Thirty

'You're a hard woman, Sarah,' Bob Skinner grumbled, as he climbed into the passenger seat of his wife's off-roader in the southern car park of Edinburgh Royal Infirmary, after making his way silently past a group of photographers who had been waiting for his departure. 'I had about two hours' sleep in that place last night. Jesus, but it's noisy.'

'You wouldn't have slept any better at home,' she assured him. 'The kids would have been looking in on you to check that you were all right.'

'How much do they know about this?' he asked, as she drove off.

'The boys know all of it,' she replied. 'One of Mark's friends texted him a link to YouTube. He showed it to James Andrew, but happily he had the good sense to keep it from Seonaid.'

'Are they okay about it?'

'More than that: they've got serious street cred out of it with their pals. They were all impressed by you anyway, but now the legend of Bob Skinner has been cracked up another notch.'

He smiled. 'It's strange that you should use that word. I've just heard it from Alex too, in another context. How's the press coverage this morning? I haven't seen a newspaper.'

'Everyone's catching up on the *Saltire*. June Crampsey released still images from the Webster woman's video and all the other papers are using them.'

'I know. She called me on my mobile . . . it was undamaged, by some miracle . . . just after you left last night, to get my approval. Xavi called too; as I expected, he was out for Lennox Webster's blood, but I calmed him down. I suggested that if she's that fucking ruthless he should ask June to transfer her to the parliamentary staff. He laughed at that and said he would.'

'You're being too magnanimous,' Sarah said. 'I'd have been happy to see her canned. That man could have killed you, yet she kept quiet, with her phone on video.'

'She and I will have a further chat about that,' he promised, 'but let it lie for now. What are the media saying about it? Are they speculating about motive? Have the police named Grigor?'

'Hah,' Sarah chuckled. 'The Solicitor General's taken charge, it seems. He was on the TV news last night. He's all over the story, soaking up the publicity and the glory. He named your attacker all right, but under his real identity, Valentin Afonin. He's even issued arrest photos from Russia, along with details of his convictions there.'

'He hasn't been linked to Dimitri Rogozin?'

'No, not at all.'

'De Matteo must have been asked what it was all about, surely?'

'Yes,' she confirmed, 'he was. He said the assumption was that it was a mugging that went wrong for the mugger.'

Skinner laughed out loud. 'And the media bought that?'

'Are they going to call the Solicitor General a liar?'

'He is a bloody liar! Why shouldn't they?'

'Do you want the truth out there?'

'I don't know what the truth is. The chances are that the guy was trying to get even for our disagreement on Sunday, no more than that. But I meant what I said to Sammy Pye; I would like to be sure that his boss, Rogozin, didn't set him on me to send a warning to Alex.'

'And if he did?' she asked quietly.

'If he did, if I was sure that he did . . . he'd better leave the country too.'

'Don't talk like that, Bob,' she murmured, as she turned left at traffic lights on to the Wisp. 'It makes me nervous.'

'Relax, love, I'm not saying I'd do anything physical to him, but I know that if I put my mind to it I could find ways of making him very unwelcome here. For a start there's his odd relationship with Grandpa McCullough. I suspect that if I shone a light on that, Cameron might not like it. That might make him see Rogozin as the liability that I am sure he is.'

'What makes you sure?'

'I did some Googling on those two last night, during my sleepless hours. The story was that they knew each other through both having interests in the leisure industry, and that when he took over Merrytown, Rogozin brought Grandpa in on the deal, in case the football authorities didn't fancy him as a controlling director of a club. Sounds plausible but there's no reason why they should have. Rogozin has no criminal convictions in Russia or anywhere else. His business success is down to his own foresight and efforts, and didn't involve putting guns to old ladies' heads to force them to sign over shares in oil and gas companies.'

'So why bring in McCullough? Is that what you're asking yourself?'

Skinner shook his head. 'No. I'm wondering whether it

happened the other way around. Did Grandpa bring Rogozin in on the takeover to keep himself out of the spotlight?'

'You could always ask his wife when you meet her,' Sarah suggested.

He sighed. 'Yes, I need to do that. We need to talk about our son.'

'Do you?' she murmured, her eyes set on the road ahead.

'What do you mean?' he asked, quietly.

'For almost twenty years,' she replied, 'Mia made all the decisions about your son's life, because you didn't know that he existed. Okay, now you do, but does that mean you need to be involved? She's a rich woman now, thanks to her marriage. She doesn't need your resources.'

'It's not about resources, is it?' he protested. 'He's my son. It's about blood. Yes, love, you're right, I could stand back from him. I could say to Mia, "You've raised him for all those years without me, so just you carry on." But look what she did on her watch; she let him take a path that led him straight to the Young Offenders Institution. Do you think I should forget about that? Do you think I should abandon him to the influence of his unscrupulous mother and a stepfather who's either the most misunderstood man or the most successful criminal I've ever met?'

'I'm not saying that. I'm not suggesting anything. I'm asking a question, that's all.'

'Would you resent Ignacio becoming part of our family?' he countered.

'Not for one second, I promise you. He'll be welcome any time . . . but that's assuming he wants to be part of it. Bob, what I'm leading up to saying is that you can't suddenly explode into the boy's life and expect your word to be law. If you and Mia are going to be jointly involved in guiding him from now on, you have to be prepared to compromise, both of you. If you can't do that . . . and you don't have a great track record in that respect . . . maybe you should stand back.'

He smiled. 'I hear what you're saying. I have to be diplomatic, I know.' He glanced at her. 'My big hope is that Alex can be my secret weapon. She was involved in organising Ignacio's defence and she's built a relationship with him since he's been inside. If I can make her his role model, that's the best way forward, and that's what I'll say to Mia when we meet.'

'You might want to say it to Alex first,' she suggested.

'Of course I will, but I know she'll be up for it. I may be getting this wrong, but I feel she needs a strong connection in her personal life, but not romantically. She hasn't said as much, but the second break-up with Andy Martin destroyed her confidence in her ability to sustain a relationship. She's past thirty now, resolutely single. Yes, she loves her brothers and her wee sister, and she'll love the new one she's going to have in a couple of months, but she's more of an auntie to them than anything else. Ignacio will be good for her.'

'How will Mia feel about that?' Sarah asked.

'Strangely enough, I think she'll be as enthusiastic as me. She likes Alex and she'll welcome her input.'

'And her husband?'

'When I want his advice,' Bob retorted, 'I'll ask for it. His daughter's in jail, just like my son. It's the one thing he and I have in common.'

He reached out and patted her arm, gently. 'If I ever wrote an autobiography . . . which I won't . . . it wouldn't be honest if I didn't admit within it that I am a complete fuck-up as a parent.'

'No,' she protested. 'I know four kids who would disagree

with that. You haven't been a parent to Ignacio yet, so the jury's still out on him.' She laughed. 'Fuck-up as a husband, yes, but that's not the issue.'

'Fuck-up as a detective too,' he grumbled, with a light grin on his face.

'You're not a detective any more,' she pointed out. 'But what brought that on?'

'I have this nagging feeling that I'm letting my daughter down,' he confessed. 'She's put her professional credibility on the line with this man Baker, because she's convinced herself of his innocence. I want to help her, I'm desperate to help her, but I spent a lot of last night reading and re-reading the police report but I just cannot see the way.'

'Maybe there isn't a way,' Sarah suggested quietly.

'There has to be,' Skinner insisted. 'If her faith is going to be vindicated there has to be.'

'And your faith in her?'

'By extension, yes.'

'That means that you believe in Baker's innocence too.'

'Goddammit yes, it does,' he conceded. 'I've met the man, I've listened to the man, and for all the report says he's guilty, I find myself setting aside all my training and experience and coming down on his side. But,' he sighed, 'when it comes to proving it I'm stuck.'

He shifted in his seat as she turned right at traffic lights.

'The case against him is comprehensive. She was strangled with his belt, her blood was found on his clothing, his prints on her phone and he was at the place she died at the time she died. Rock solid, but in the absence of a witness to the killing it's circumstantial. Now you can undermine a circumstantial case by demonstrating an alternative possibility . . .'

'Such as?' she asked.

'Place another person at the scene; that would be a good start. Trouble is the crime scene team have scoured the place and the only people they can put there apart from Annette and Chaz are Paco Fonter, Sirena Burbujas, Cisco Serra, Cope the concierge and Elsa Golota, the cleaner, who found the body. The husband was out of the country when it happened, and the two agents were in London and Geneva respectively. There isn't a trace of anyone else. Ouch!' he winced, as the car hit a rut and the shock reached his cracked rib.

'You see my frustration,' he went on. 'Our client might be innocent, but it's that rare situation where the Crown doesn't actually have to prove his guilt. All it has to do is satisfy the jury that nobody else could have done it.'

'Yes, I see,' she said, 'but couldn't you go at it from another location, from the training complex?'

'Explain.'

'The bloodstained garment was found there. If Chaz really is innocent they were put there. Could there be a trace, I don't know, CCTV, a register showing who was in the complex at the time?'

He nodded. 'In theory, although I doubt that anyone would put a security camera in the laundry room. As for a register of who's on the premises, that's a health and safety standard these days, but what it's most likely to do is prove that Chaz Baker had the opportunity to dump the stuff himself. Add on the fact that any frame's been put together very effectively. I don't see the perpetrator signing his name to it.'

'Dammit,' she muttered, eyes ahead as she took a roundabout, 'you're right, on all counts. We have a register in the office. When it comes to forgetting to sign it, I'm the worst offender, but nobody ever pulls me up over it.'

She drove on for a while, in silence, until they had joined the A1 and were past the junction with the Edinburgh bypass. 'Wait a minute,' she whispered as a smile spread across her face. 'There might be . . . It's an outside chance but worth pursuing. You know that the SOCOs found powder traces in Annette's en suite. They were near her cosmetics so nobody got too excited, but a sample was sent for analysis. So was the victim's blood.'

Skinner straightened in his seat, eyes brighter than before. 'There was nothing about that in the police report to the fiscal,' he said.

'Sammy probably didn't think it needed including, otherwise he'd have waited for the test results. They came back from the lab yesterday afternoon. The powder wasn't talcum, oh no, it was good quality cocaine. But Annette's blood sample showed no trace of drug use. Do you see where I'm going with this?'

'Yes,' Bob exclaimed, 'I surely do. Did Sammy and Sauce take a sample of Baker's blood for analysis? I saw no record of it in the police file and Alex has never mentioned that being done. How long does cocaine stay in the blood stream?'

'Three days, give or take, that's received wisdom; but when the stuff is metabolised it leaves a by-product, benzoylecgonine. That can stay in the system for a month.'

'Better and better. Alex needs to have a sample of Baker's blood sent for testing soonest. If it's clean, it raises the question, whose was the Colombian marching powder? It wouldn't clear him, not by a long way, but it would be the first step to establishing the reasonable doubt we're going to need.'

'And if it isn't clear?' Sarah ventured.

'Then Chaz may have to get used to the sound of slamming cell doors. But I'm not going to consider that. I just don't see

Baker as a drug user; he's strait-laced, he's a family man and on top of that he's plain fucking boring. This could be a break, a crack in the wall of evidence, and we have to widen it as far as we can.'

Thirty-One

'Are you really telling us, Mr Rogozin,' DCI Pye snapped, 'that you had no idea that your personal bodyguard was a convicted murderer and a fugitive from justice?'

The Russian stared at him across the coffee table in his suite in Glasgow's Grand Central Hotel. 'How many times, Mr Policeman, I have to say it? To me, Grigor Yashin was his name, always. He had papers, he had passport; he do a good job for me. Why should I question that?'

'How did you come to employ him?' Sauce Haddock asked.

'I told my secretary place an ad.'

'Where?'

'In the papers, where else?'

'A specialist employment agency would have been a good start,' the DS suggested.

The Russian snapped his fingers, impatiently. 'So? She place the ad and she got Grigor. Is her fault. When I get back she's fired.'

'When you hired him did he provide references?'

'Don' understand.'

'Letters from former employers recommending him.'

'I don' know. I tell her hire someone, she hire Grigor, okay?'

'What did he do for you?'

'He drive me, he carry my bags, he make sure that everywhere I go I have everything I need and that things are ready for me when I arrive. He make sure the plane is always there at airport. He look after me.'

'And if you have a problem with a person, you send Grigor to fix it?'

Rogozin smiled, reaching out for his coffee cup. 'Please, sir. I no have problem with anybody.'

'You seemed to have a problem on Sunday outside the police building.'

'That was misunderstanding. I need to speak to the lawyer of my worker Mr Baker and that man get in the way.'

'That man was our former chief constable; he believed that you were trying to intimidate his daughter, and he didn't like it.'

'Intimidate? What is?'

'To frighten her.'

'No, no, not frighten, but I want tell her that she must do her very best for Baker, make sure he is released soon. I want to tell her but this man, her father you say, he knock down Grigor and he get between us.'

Haddock stared at him unsmiling. 'You have a habit of getting up close and personal with people, Mr Rogozin. You tried it with my boss in the Edinburgh hotel. We see that as aggressive behaviour.'

The Russian met his gaze. 'I see it as making my point,' he murmured in suddenly improved English.

'What do you do if your point isn't understood? Do you send Grigor to make it more forcefully? That's his real job, isn't it? Did you send him after Mr Skinner with the intention of throwing a scare into his daughter?'

The man's eyes flickered. 'I not send Grigor anywhere. He is my driver, that is all.'

'No, Mr Rogozin,' Pye exclaimed, stepping back in. 'That doesn't cut it with us. You liked to have Grigor around because it makes you look tough, simple as that. And I flat out do not believe your story that you picked him up through a newspaper small ad. Neither, incidentally, does your country's vice-consul in Scotland. He wasn't amused by the news that a convicted killer had open access to Edinburgh in a private jet. The media haven't got that part yet, but if they do, Russia will be seriously embarrassed. As it is, you'll have questions to answer when you get home. The vice-consul called this morning to tell me you're under investigation for sheltering a fugitive. When your plane lands in Moscow, you'll be met at the airport.'

'That will not worry me,' Rogozin said quietly. 'I did not know who he really was. And also,' he added, 'I did not send him to attack your Mr Skinner. That was all his own idea,' he laughed, a short unpleasant laugh, 'and a very bad one, as it can be seen.' He leaned forward. 'But if the lawyer woman sees it as a message from me . . . that will not worry me either. I want her to know that Baker must have what is coming to him, what he deserves.'

Abruptly, he rose to his feet. 'Now, policemen, I have said enough. You are here with my agreement, and now you don't have it no more. Go on, leave me.'

Haddock looked at Pye; he said nothing but his eyes asked a question. *Are we going to take this?*

The DCI nodded and stood. 'We're leaving, Mr Rogozin, but we may be back. Valentin Afonin had nothing to say when we interviewed him yesterday, but as the man who brought him here, your status is still subject to review by the immigration authorities.' He looked around the room. 'Don't get too comfortable here.' He turned and led his sergeant from the room.

The door had barely closed before Haddock exclaimed, 'What did you think of that, gaffer? The arrogant bastard! We should have lifted him, and worried about justifying it later.'

Amused by the younger man's uncharacteristic outrage, Pye shook his head. 'Nah, Sauce, we'll let him alone for now. We've no way of proving he knew who Grigor Yashin really was, or that he sent him after Bob.'

'Would we get away with leaking to the press that Afonin worked for him?' the DS pondered.

'Probably, but we're not going to do that either. I'm more interested in what he said about Baker. His English is a bit confusing at times, but the way I took that, he wants him convicted.'

Thirty-Two

'Are you sure you should be here?' Mia McCullough asked. 'I've seen the video; you got pretty banged about.'

'I did, didn't I,' Bob Skinner agreed. 'But at the end it wasn't me that was trussed up like a chicken, and on the way to Siberia, or wherever the Russians send their lifers these days. I'm fine; I had a night in the Royal then twenty-four hours at home. Sarah gave me the all-clear this morning.' He grinned. 'I'll bet your old man loved seeing me get whacked.'

'You misjudge him,' she insisted. 'Cameron has nothing against you, only against those Tayside cops who hounded him for years. He thought that what happened was appalling. I'm sorry he's not here, by the way. He has a meeting in Dundee.'

'I'm quite happy that he's not here. Did he recognise the guy who hit me?'

'Oh yes,' she said, 'he knew him all right.'

'Is he wondering why he hasn't been charged?'

'We know that too. Cameron and Dimitri have had words about it.'

'I might want a chat with Rogozin as well,' Skinner murmured. 'If it happens, it won't be filmed, that I promise you.'

'I'm sure it won't. But don't do anything drastic, Bob, please.

Cameron has the man under control. He's not worth it.'

'If he was trying to intimidate Ignacio, would he be worth it?'

'But he isn't,' Mia countered. 'As for Alex, he knows now that she's off limits.'

'He'd better.' He paused and glanced around the large drawing room in which she had received him for their hastily arranged meeting. The McCullough residence was a modern villa on the Black Shield Lodge estate, out of sight of the hotel and guest cottages, but within easy reach of all of them. 'You've finally landed on your feet, gal,' he observed. 'Be careful you don't screw this up.'

'Why should you worry if I did?' she shot back, archly. 'You never cared before.'

'I barely had time,' he countered. 'Mia, you were in my life for about a week, then you were gone. But even at that, if I hadn't cared about you . . .' he paused, considering a twenty-year-old memory, '. . . either I'd have locked you up as an accessory to murder, or I'd have left you to your evil cow of a mother.'

'If you'd locked her up instead it would have solved a lot of problems down the road.'

'I'd have loved to, but I'd no excuse,' he sighed. 'It worries me, you know, the fact that she's part of our son's genetic inheritance.'

'Worries you?' she exclaimed. 'It scares the shit out of me. Let's face it, Bob, Ignacio's descended from one of Edinburgh's least likeable families.' She looked up at him. 'Honesty time?'

'Always should be.'

'I'm glad you're his father. If I could live my life again . . . I'd have come back from Spain as soon as I knew I was pregnant, and I'd have told you.'

'I wish you had,' he murmured.

'What would you have done?' she asked. 'You must have asked yourself that question since you found out about him.'

'Oh, I have,' he admitted. 'Over and over again. I still don't have all the answers, but this I do know. I'd have loved our boy from the start and I'd have been as proud of him as I was, still am, of his sister. I'd have wanted to bring them up together, and we'd probably have fought about that . . .'

'Unless we'd become a couple.'

He frowned, opened his mouth to reply then closed it again. 'I was going to say "In your dreams",' he confessed, 'but I can't. I wouldn't have let you go back to your old life, not carrying my child, so yes, you might well have moved in with Alex and me.' Unexpectedly, he grinned. 'She wouldn't have been too happy about sharing our kitchen with another woman, mind you.'

Mia smiled back at him. 'I'd have deferred to her, honest.' She paused and sadness came into her eyes. 'It wouldn't have lasted, would it? You and me?'

'No,' he agreed. 'It wouldn't, and it would have been my fault when it failed, 'cos it always is. It might even have got nasty, with us fighting over custody. But,' he said firmly, 'through it all, there would have been one certainty. I would have kept you safe from your mother and everybody else on your dark side, and none of them would ever have been allowed near Ignacio.'

'Who would probably have been called Robert,' she pointed out.

'More likely William, after my dad.'

She shook her head. 'No way. I'd an uncle called William; he'd never have been called after him.'

'See,' he chuckled, 'we're arguing over him already.'

'But no more,' she insisted. 'This is why I wanted to meet with you, to make that clear. We're talking about him as if he was still a child, but he isn't. He'll be released from that place as a fully functioning adult, entitled to live his life however he chooses. He could tell both of us to fuck off, after giving him such an awful start. But he won't; I know this because he and I have talked about it. He would like to get to know his brothers and sisters, but most of all he'd like to get to know his father. I want that too. He may be descended from brigands on my side, but he comes from a line of law-keepers on yours, and that's the influence he needs now. Do you have room for him in your life?'

Skinner reached out and took his former lover's hand. 'Mia,' he murmured, 'I have room for him in my house, not just my life. Sarah and I have been all over this and she's more than happy to have him with us.'

'Even with the new baby?'

'It's a big house, we have a nanny, and Sarah will be taking maternity leave from next month. I'll find him a college to study for his exams, and he can aim to start university next autumn.'

'Shouldn't he have a job, under his probation terms?'

'He will, if they say he needs one. I can find him something at the *Saltire*, or Alex might be able to keep him busy. She has a spare room, by the way. If Gullane ever gets claustrophobic, or too crowded for him, or even too quiet, he can crash out there.'

She squeezed his arm. 'You're not such a bad bloke, are you? Maybe I should have hung around, twenty years ago.'

He looked around the opulent room once again. 'Maybe,' he murmured, 'but long-term it's worked out okay for you. Now,' he said, glancing at his watch, 'I must be going. You're not the only person I came here to meet.'

He picked up his car coat from the chair where it lay, and moved towards the door.

'Why do you want to see Baker?' she asked.

'I want to see everyone involved in the case. I've promised to help Alex prepare his defence; that means starting from scratch and interviewing all the witnesses, as if I was still a cop.'

'Does that mean you think he's innocent? I do.'

'Let's just say I'm open to the possibility.'

Outside, the steady rain that had followed him from East Lothian had eased to a faint drizzle. Rather than drive the half mile to the cottage where the Bakers were staying he walked, following Mia's directions and taking a pathway that cut the distance in half.

Two cars were parked outside, and a pushchair with a clear waterproof cover stood beside them. Skinner smiled as he saw a small figure sheltered there, crumpled in sleep.

He was still smiling as the front door was opened, by a woman clad in a jogging suit and slipper socks. She had golden blond hair, matching that of the sleeping child, and she looked to be around Alex's age, maybe two or three years older.

'Dr Baker?' he asked, rhetorically.

'Mr Skinner?' she responded, then put a finger to her lips. 'Sshh. Don't want to wake Letty. We should have another half an hour of peace and quiet if we're lucky.' She stood aside to let him into the house. 'I suppose I should really ask you for ID, but you're pretty well known after that video the other day. Besides, you're not a policeman any more, so you won't have any.'

He smiled as he stepped inside. 'I still have my warrant card from my last job. Trouble is, it says "Chief Constable, Strathclyde Police" and that force doesn't exist any longer.'

Lita Baker led him into a living area at the front of the house. 'Would you like a coffee?' she asked.

'No thanks,' he said. 'I'm on a ration, and I've had my one for this morning.' He looked around. 'Mr Baker?'

'Chaz is running,' she told him. 'He's going crazy being bottled up here. He won't be long, I promise.'

'That's all right,' Skinner assured her. 'I want to talk to you too, and it suits me that it's just the two of us.'

'Then fire away,' she said as they sat, each choosing a white leather chair. 'I don't know what I can say that'll help, but try me.'

'Okay but I have to be blunt. Were you aware of your husband's friendship with Annette Bordeaux?'

'No, I wasn't,' she admitted. 'Chaz never mentioned it; he never spoke about her in fact.'

'Never? It must have been an unusual situation for him as a manager to have a player with a supermodel for a wife.'

'That was a first, I'll grant you, but players these days can have pretty exotic partners. Chaz's teams have had pop singers in England, and a politician's daughter in France.' She shot him a quick glance and a faint smile. 'We also had the son of a judge, but that was kept very quiet.'

'What's he told you since the murder?'

'He confessed to me that they had a friendship, instigated by her, on account of what she said was her feeling of isolation in Scotland.'

'You sound as if you're sceptical about that.'

'I am; she has a global schedule. In the last six months she's had shoots in Shanghai, in Cape Town, and in New York . . . and those are the ones I know of. To me that doesn't suggest lonely isolation, but what do I know? I'm a doctor, not a psychologist. Maybe she and Paco were having trouble and she didn't like to admit it.'

'I'll cut to the chase,' Skinner said. 'Now that you do know about it, do you think they were having an affair?'

Lita Baker threw back her head and laughed, 'Absolutely not! Chaz wouldn't know how. He isn't the best conversationalist generally, and with women . . . forget it. His first chat-up line to me was, "Do you come here often?" We were at a sports injury seminar in the FA headquarters in England. That's how gauche he is. So the idea of his sweeping a supermodel off her feet, that's a non-starter.'

He looked at her and held her gaze, his expression blank. 'Suppose it was the other way around. Suppose she did the sweeping? Is Chaz an impressionable man?'

For the first time, there was a hint of hesitancy in her response. 'No, well, not really. Although . . . the pop singer girlfriend at the English club, she turned his head, I think.' She smiled. 'She didn't turn anything else though.'

'Noted,' Skinner chuckled. 'To sum up, you are absolutely convinced of Chaz's innocence, yes?'

'Totally and completely. He might be a prickly guy on the outside, and he might have had a reputation for a quick temper as a player, but I couldn't bring myself to believe he'd kill someone, whatever pressure was put on him.'

'Pressure?' he repeated. 'What did you mean by that?'

'Oh nothing, nothing at all. I wasn't . . .'

She was interrupted by the sound of a door opening at the rear of the cottage. 'That'll be him,' she exclaimed. 'Chaz!' she called out. 'Mr Skinner's here.'

'Gimme a minute,' Baker responded, from the kitchen, then burst into a paroxysm of coughing.

He appeared in less than that time, zipping up a tracksuit jacket as he stepped into the living area. His hair was damp and ruffled and a towel was draped round his neck. 'Sorry, chum,' he wheezed. 'I had to get out of here. Wish I hadn't now. I'd no idea I was so badly out of shape. Don't take training any more, see.'

'I'll leave you guys to it,' his wife declared. 'I need to fix Letty's lunch before she wakes up, demanding attention.'

'Did you two have a good chat?' Baker enquired, as she went out, retracing his steps.

'It was helpful,' Skinner replied. 'Have you two spoken much, about the situation, since it arose?'

'What do you think?' Baker retorted, ripping open a can of an orange drink and dropping into a chair. 'Of course we have,' he sighed. 'Lita wanted to know what the hell I was doing in Annie's apartment, and I couldn't really tell her. I couldn't tell her because I didn't bloody know.'

'Mr Baker,' he continued, 'I know you've been through this with my daughter, but I will ask you this once more. Were you in a sexual relationship with Annette Bordeaux? Look me in the eye when you answer and do not lie to me, because I will know if you do.'

The football manager, the accused, stared back at him. 'No,' he said, quietly. 'No, sir, I was not.'

Skinner held his gaze for a few seconds; and then he nodded. 'Okay,' he replied. 'I believe you. Now, did you kill her?'

'I promise you, I did not.'

'I believe that too. The trick will be proving that you didn't. To do that you're going to have to continue to be honest with Alex and me, all the way.'

'I will. What else do you need to ask me?'

'Are you or have you ever been a recreational drug user?'

Baker blinked. 'You're fucking joking. I was a footballer but I had to work hard at it; I had no time for any of that shit. Now I'm a manager, but more than that, I'm the father of a two-year-old daughter. I couldn't possibly put either of those at risk.' He stopped, then frowned. 'The blood sample that Alex had me give yesterday: test that and it'll prove it.'

'That's why it was taken.'

'How will it help?'

'It might not, Chaz,' Skinner told him, 'but to be frank, at the moment it's all you have in your favour, assuming it doesn't throw up any nasty surprises.'

Thirty-Three

'Why should I talk to you?' Sirena Burbujas said, with a look of disdain in her eyes that Skinner did not like. 'You are working for the man who killed lovely Annette.'

'No,' he corrected her, 'I'm working for my daughter, who has been instructed by Mr Baker to prepare his defence against that accusation.'

'But he did it!' she squealed, drawing glances from other customers in the Palm Court of the Balmoral Hotel. 'Everybody knows.'

'Keep your voice down, please,' he snapped. 'Everybody knows what, exactly?'

'That he killed her. He went to her apartment while Paco was away and he killed her.'

'Mr Baker denies that, Ms Burbujas. He will plead not guilty and the case will go to trial. When it does the Crown will have to prove its allegations. Until it does he's an innocent man, and any stories that are being spread around about him are slanderous and prejudicial.'

'I'm not spreading any stories,' Burbujas protested. She spoke with a slight transatlantic twang that Skinner knew was an affectation.

'No?' he retorted. 'Somebody is. There's a piece in the *Mirror* this morning; "*The secret life of Annette Bordeaux*", it's titled, only it's not really secret at all. It's all about her work and her professional relationships, routine stuff slapped together to sell papers. Nobody's quoted directly but it could only have come from somebody with a detailed knowledge of Annette's diary. Her husband, maybe, but the police have him holed up in a hotel, well away from the press.' He paused.

'That's to say he was until this morning, when reporters and cameramen from the *Sun* and Sky Television turned up in the driveway as he was being taken for a scan on his injured hamstring. Not many people knew he was there, but you were one of them.'

She gazed back at him; for a second he thought she would respond, but she thought better of it, shrugged and picked up her coffee cup.

'I know what you're thinking,' he said. 'Let him believe what he likes, but he'll never prove anything, and suppose he does, so what? And you're right, so what? You're on the make, Ms Burbujas, but I don't care.' He smiled, sipping his mineral water. 'Have you done the book deal yet?' he asked.

The question seemed to push a button; she stiffened in her booth as if a small electric charge had gone through the seat. 'You think I'm so mercenary that I'd look to profit from Annette's death?' she asked, icily.

'Yes,' Skinner replied, evenly, 'I do. You profited from her in life. Why should her death make you altruistic? I know that you approached the editor of the *Saltire* newspaper, offering information on the state of the Fonter marriage.' Her eyes widened, her mouth tightened. 'Surprised I know that? I'm a director of its parent company. But I'm bound by its code of confidentiality, so

213

don't worry,' he added. 'Anyway, as I said, I don't care. We live in the golden age of prurience, shock and scandal, and there's bugger all the likes of me can do about it, other than defend my own privacy . . . and that's something I've failed spectacularly to do in the last few days.'

'So I saw,' she murmured. 'I wish the guy had got another couple of whacks in.'

'Yes, so does he,' Skinner said. 'How was the Fonter marriage?' he continued. 'I'm asking as my daughter's investigator,' he added, 'so any reply will be privileged, until it's raised in court.'

'It was strained by the transfer to Scotland,' the little agent replied, 'but it wasn't under threat. Paco was always Annette's weak point, and to be fair to him, he did love her.'

'Did you ever try to split them up?'

'I might have in the early stages,' she admitted, 'if I'd known about them, but by the time I found out it was too late. So I lived with it . . . until the move to Scotland. I thought that was crazy, and I told them both.'

'And her relationship with Chaz Baker? What did you think of that?'

'I didn't know they had one. Sure, she talked about him, and it was clear that she liked him, but only as Paco's boss, no more.'

'She sent Chaz a text on the day she died. That's why he went to see her. In it she mentioned a secret; she said she couldn't live with it any longer.'

She tilted her head back and looked down her nose, in his general direction. 'He was the secret? He killed her because she was going to expose it? Is that what the police think?'

'Yes, it is. I don't have a problem telling you that because it's unreportable. Anyone who published that in advance of the trial, any way, anywhere, would wind up in jail. But our client denies it. He says that his relationship with Annette was one of friendship and nothing more. So can you think of anything else in her life that might have been troubling her to such an extent?'

Burbujas pursed her lips. 'No,' she replied, without even the briefest pause for thought. 'Nothing. Nothing at all.'

'Nothing from her past life?'

'No.'

'Tell me about her.'

'She was an exceptional young woman, a sensation from the moment she posed for her first photographs, and walked her first catwalk. She had the rarest gift of drawing the eye of those who looked at her to every aspect of her but, most important, always through her to what she was modelling. In fashion shows, she had a way of moving that was unique, a stride that seemed to adapt itself to whatever she was wearing. She was the greatest model of her generation, and I knew she would be from the moment I first saw her on the stage at the Crazy Horse in Paris.'

Skinner held up a hand. 'Please, Ms Burbujas, I am not a *Hello!* magazine reader so please don't treat me like one. I know that story is bullshit, something that you or a PR company made up. I know how you really met, because she told Chaz. Again, I don't care; I'm not going to out you. But I would like to know more about Annette, Annette Brody as she was in the beginning.'

'I don't know very much,' she said. 'She was always reticent about her family and her upbringing, but from the little she did say, it was modest and unexceptional. Her father was a vicar, her mother was a teacher, and she was brought up in Worthing, on the south coast; that's all she ever told me.'

'I see.'

'But,' she continued, 'I'm pretty sure she was adopted. One day, I found a photograph in her bag. I wasn't snooping,' she added, 'she was getting changed and we needed something so she told me to look. The picture was of her and her parents . . . he was wearing a vicar's dog collar so they must have been . . . and the thing that jumped out at me was that they were both white, and Annette, well, she wasn't. As everyone in the world knew, she was mixed race.'

'You met her in London, yes? Come on,' he insisted, seeing her hesitancy, 'I know you did. Did she ever say why she left home?'

'No. She never did and I didn't ask. I'd built the Crazy Horse legend by that time and I didn't want to know about the alternative version.'

'What happened to the photograph?'

'I took it and I tore it up. I didn't want anyone else to see it. Annette must have known I did that, but she never mentioned it. Mr Skinner, that's the only secret Annette had that I know of, and while it might rewrite some of her personal history if it was revealed, it's hardly worth killing her to keep it.'

Thirty-Four

'You found out all of this in one morning?' Alex exclaimed.

'Not quite,' her father admitted. 'I did an Internet search last night for people called Brody in Worthing. It didn't take long to come up with a news item from twelve years ago about the death of a vicar's wife, Mary Brody, in a sailing accident. She was crewing in a race in the Channel when an unpredicted storm blew up. Her boat capsized, and when they righted it she wasn't there. It was reported nationally, but only in any detail in the local paper. She wasn't the only person lost; there were four others lost from three yachts. The Worthing paper went big on it, though.'

'Photographs?'

'Yes. One of her, one of Tristan, the vicar, and a family shot. It was taken when Annette was twelve, so the editor can be forgiven for not knowing that for the last few years he's been sitting on a bigger story: the true identity of Annette Bordeaux.'

'And the rest? Where did that come from?'

'Sussex Police. I called the Worthing station and spoke to an inspector, a woman who's served there for over twenty years. She knew the vicar because she went to his church. She said he never got over his wife's death. He took to the booze, big time, and died of liver failure within a couple of years.'

'Could she give you any family background?'

'She didn't know the family,' Skinner said, 'personally or professionally. Mary Brody wasn't seen in church all that often, only at the big events in the calendar, Christmas, Easter, Harvest Festival, and Annette never went without her. Inspector Donald didn't even know her name.'

'Did you tell her who the daughter became?' Alex asked.

'I didn't see any need to do that. It'll all come out soon enough. A journalist, or a biographer, will look in the right places and ask the right questions, and it'll be revealed that the Crazy Horse dancer was actually an ordinary girl from a seaside town who moved to London after her life was turned upside down by tragedy.'

'When you put it that way,' she observed, 'it's actually a more intriguing story than the one Sirena Burbujas made up.'

'Agreed. She's the one who'll look stupid when the truth does come out, not Annette.'

'I wonder if Paco knows the real story?'

'I'll ask him.'

'Are you going to talk to him?'

He looked at her, surprised by the question. 'Of course I am. Look, love, he's her husband. If she had a secret that she felt she had to get out in the open, he's the person most likely to have known what it was. If so, did he want her to spill it?'

'Are you saying he's a suspect?'

'He's a person of interest. I won't know whether he's a suspect or not until I've been face to face with him. As for him having an alibi: being in another country at the time of the crime doesn't automatically mean you're not involved.' He stood. 'Do you have anything new to tell me?' he asked.

She nodded. 'Baker's blood analysis is complete. I've shared the findings with the police, including a DNA profile which I had done just to be thorough. There wasn't a trace of cocaine in his system.'

'Good. You can put that in the positive column. I'm off to see if I can find any more ticks.'

'Where are you going?'

'King Robert Village,' he said. 'I've read the report, but I haven't seen what Sammy and Sauce have. I need to remedy that.'

Thirty-Five

'Afonin's gone, has he?' Pye asked as his colleague walked into the room.

'Out of our hair for good and all,' Haddock replied. 'The vice-consul and I saw him all the way on to the London shuttle, handcuffed to two of our largest, and into back row seats. His Russian escort officers are meeting him at Heathrow.'

'What happens if he wants to pee?'

'We thought about that: we made him go before he boarded. Nasty bastard,' the DS said. 'I was really glad to be rid of him. Yes, there's an open attempted murder charge hanging over him, to be taken up if he survives the Russian prison system for long enough to be released, but I reckon we'll both be retired by the time that happens. How about Rogozin,' he continued. 'Will there be any action against him?'

The DCI shrugged. 'No idea. I like the guy about as much as you like his minder, but legally, he's none of our business. If the immigration authorities want to pursue him for bringing a felon into the country, that'll be their choice, but if I was in their shoes I'd be leaving it alone. They allowed him entry, so they'd be investigating their own culpability.'

'I suppose so. Like you, I don't care.'

'One thing happened when you were away,' Pye continued. 'Alex Skinner called. She's had an independent blood analysis done on Baker. She commissioned it to determine whether it was him that snorted the cocaine we found in the bathroom.'

'I don't imagine it was,' the DS said, 'or she wouldn't be telling us about it.'

'No, and you're right, it was clear. I imagine that'll be the linchpin of her defence. Annette didn't use it, and nor did he, so she'll float the idea with the jury that a third party must have, and she'll portray that person as the real culprit.'

'Are we worried about that?' Haddock asked.

'I don't see a reasonable doubt there, Sauce, do you?'

'No,' he agreed, 'not even at my most bloody minded. She'll need to do a lot better than that, for there's no doubt at all that Annette was strangled by his belt, with only his prints on it, and that her blood was on his training top. What did Alex want you to do with her analysis?'

'Nothing, other than put it in the record. She emailed it across and I've added it to the file, for the attention of everyone with access.'

'Fair enough. Anything else new since I've been away . . . preferably unconnected to football?'

'Mary Chambers wants us to look into an outbreak of tyre slashing in North Berwick, but apart from that, nothing.'

Haddock stared at him. 'Run that past me again?'

'Three nights on the trot, cars had their tyres done in the same street.'

'Excuse me? Is that CID business?'

'Normally no, but a Member of the Scottish Parliament was one of the victims. The lack of response by uniform is likely to be raised at Holyrood. I've sent Jackie Wright out there to check the locus and interview residents. The chief super will assign officers to do a stake-out tonight if Jackie reckons the layout makes it possible.'

'Let's hope she gets a result,' Haddock muttered, 'otherwise I have a terrible feeling that I'll be out there next.'

'That'll be . . .' Pye broke off as his desk phone rang. He reached out and picked it up. 'Yes?'

'DCI Pye? Arthur Dorward. A word, Sammy,' the forensic scientist said. 'I've just been looking at your update to the Annette Bordeaux file . . . as obviously you haven't, at least not carefully enough.'

'No?'

'Definitely no. We need to talk about this. I'm not saying it knocks your case on the head, but it gives it a whole new dimension.'

Thirty-Six

'I thought you had left the police service, Mr Skinner,' Christine Hoy remarked.

'So did I,' he laughed, 'but the life won't leave me alone.'

'Why are you here? Do the Menu need a second opinion?'

'No, they're pretty sharp. By the way,' he added, 'you should be pleased they told you their nickname. It means they like you. No, I'm here on my daughter's behalf,' he explained. 'She's a criminal lawyer, acting for the accused in the Bordeaux case.'

'Then she's up against it. I've seen the tape.'

'And I've read the summary in the police report,' Skinner said, 'but I'd like to see for myself.'

'Do you need a court order?' the security manager asked.

He smiled. 'I hope not. I'm assuming that you gave the police a copy of the footage they need. Technically they're obliged to share that with the defence, but those lads are busy and I'm busy, so I'm hoping that you'll be as cooperative with me as you were with them.'

'I will if you answer one question,' she replied.

'That will depend on what it is.'

'How old are you? None of the papers said, and usually they're obsessive about people's ages.'

'I'm over fifty but under fifty-five,' he volunteered. 'That's all I'll own up to. Why do you ask?'

'Because like the rest of Scotland I've seen that video, and I'm impressed.'

'Don't be. I'm embarrassed by it, and if I'm truthful, a bit chastened. I have young children, and another on the way. I shouldn't be putting myself in situations like that.'

'You didn't put yourself anywhere. You were attacked.'

'There was more to it than that, but I'm not going into it.'

'Still, the way you took him down: a man of . . .'

'A man of my age?' He chuckled. 'Listen, Ms Hoy, that was experience on my part and carelessness on his. One more whack on the head with that baton and I could have been a cabbage. Now, can I see that tape or not?'

'Of course.'

She led him into the monitoring room; he had been in many similar places before but he was impressed by the array and by the range of CCTV coverage. The King Robert Village seemed to be a secure zone.

'Quite a change,' he murmured.

'From the old Royal Infirmary? Yes, that's what everybody says.'

'I prefer this incarnation,' he admitted. 'The old one had too many bad memories for me.'

Hoy sat at the instrument console and went to work, directing his attention to one of the many screens, as she scrolled through her archived footage. 'This is it,' she said, when she was ready.

He had never met Annette Bordeaux alive, nor had he seen her in death, but he knew her as soon as she walked into shot. He watched as she entered the building then rode the lift up to the penthouse floor.

'Note the time,' Hoy told him. 'She entered the penthouse at quarter past three, and she never left it again.'

'You would have known for sure if she had?'

'We would have known if she'd deactivated the security camera, to cover her leaving or someone else arriving, but she never did.'

'That's an unusual feature,' Skinner observed.

'Yes it is,' the security manager agreed. 'It was added to the system at the request of the owner of the penthouse, and the two apartments on the floor below.'

'Who is the owner?'

'A property company in the Isle of Man.'

'Who owns that?'

'I have no idea. It's none of my business. Let's move on to sixteen forty-nine.'

She clicked on a mouse and a second clip appeared. He watched as Chaz Baker entered the building, dived into the lift just before its doors closed, and pressed the key for the top floor. He was frowning as he stepped out, and as he pressed the door button. Skinner watched him fidget as he waited, saw him press the buzzer again and, finally, try the door handle. His look of preoccupation changed to one of surprise as it opened. He called out, silently, then stepped inside and out of the camera's range of vision.

'How long was he in there?' he asked.

'Twenty-seven minutes.' She pulled up another video clip, and ran it, showing his departure. His face was in profile as he left, but Skinner could see that he looked even more agitated than he had before. Then he turned, turning his back to the camera as he left and as he waited for the lift. There was no clear view of his training top, nor was one offered by the cameras in the lift and the lobby, as he made his way swiftly out of the building.

'Can you roll it back?' he asked. 'I'd like a proper look at his hands.'

Hoy reversed the footage frame by frame until she found an image that showed what he wanted to see. 'How's that?'

'Good enough. He wasn't carrying anything when he left. It was a long shot, but I needed to confirm that he wasn't holding the victim's phone.'

'Would that have helped?'

'Definitely not,' he said. 'Can I see the rest of the footage you showed the police?' he continued.

'If you need to, of course, but is it relevant?'

'I'm just being thorough,' he told her. 'I want to see for myself who was in the vicinity when Annette was killed. The police will have interviewed them all, but I need to do the same.'

'No problem. I copied that section as well; just let me cue it up.' She turned back to her console and set to work. 'You'll see four of them,' she murmured. 'Three men, one woman; they arrived just after half two and left just after six, on foot, heading for a restaurant, pub, whatever.'

She started the clip; he watched it to its conclusion, in silence, seeing it unfold as she had described. 'The three men are players,' she volunteered. 'I don't know who the woman is, though.'

'I can guess,' Skinner responded. 'I have a list of the Merrytown staff; it includes a woman called Alice McDade, the club physio. Those were the initials on her training top. I can only guess at what she was doing there.'

'Was one of them injured?' Hoy asked. 'Could she have been treating him?'

'Possibly, but I doubt that it would have been in the sense that you mean. Orlando Flowers was massaging her bum gently on the way down in the lift.'

She smiled. 'Ah! I didn't notice that. It is a big apartment,' she murmured. 'Three bedrooms, all en suite.'

'I see. What about the other apartment on that floor? Is it occupied?'

'No,' she answered. 'The football club lease the top two floors, but that one's left vacant, for use by the occasional visitor. A man called Serra stayed there a couple of times, when the transfer window was open; he's Mr Fonter's agent, I believe. The owner, Mr Rogozin, he has used it as well, but only on occasion. I believe he stays in a hotel in Glasgow on most of his visits.'

Skinner felt a prickling sensation on the back of his neck, but he did not allow his surprise to register on his face. 'When was the last time he used it?' The question was as casual as he could make it sound, but inwardly he was buzzing.

'The week before last; on a Thursday, as I recall. I remember thinking it was unusual. Merrytown had a Europa League tie that night; the players were all away in Finland and yet the owner was here.'

'You don't happen to have the security tapes for that night, do you?'

'No, sorry. We erase them after a week. The owners wouldn't like it if we kept them for longer than was necessary.'

He nodded. 'Sure, I understand that,' he conceded. 'How secure is the building, Ms Hoy?' he asked. 'Can the upper floors be accessed by any means other than by the lift? There must be stairs, surely.'

'The stairway goes to the sixth floor but no higher,' she

explained. 'The floors below can't access the top two levels at the back of the block. Those have their own internal fire escape stair. There are doors at the back of the penthouse and in the apartments below.'

'Where's the exit at ground level?'

'At the back of the building; it opens on to a lane and cycleway that goes down to the Meadows.'

'Is there CCTV coverage there?'

'No need; it's secure.'

'So in theory someone could use that back stairway to go all the way up to the penthouse?'

'In theory,' she agreed, 'but they'd need a machine to force the door; a hand-held ram wouldn't do it. Suppose they did, once they got up there they wouldn't be able to get in. The apartment fire doors are steel as well, with multi-point security and they can only be opened from the inside. I'm sorry, Mr Skinner, I can see where you're going with your questioning, but believe me, that apartment is intruder proof. I promise you, the person who killed poor Annette got in through the front door, and by no other way.'

Thirty-Seven

'Of course we knew Annette,' Jimmy Pike replied. 'She was Paco's missus, so she came along to our nights out.'

'Did you see much of her as a neighbour?' Skinner continued.

The footballer leaned back in his chair as he considered the question, gazing through the window of the Merrytown training complex cafeteria at the three pitches outside. Two were deserted, but on the third a six-a-side game was under way, one team wearing yellow bibs, the other purple. 'No, not a hell of a lot,' he admitted. 'It's an unusual situation, living so close to a teammate; the three of us gave Paco and Annette their own space. Mind you, she was away quite often,' he added, 'on 'er modelling jobs.'

'Even then,' Art Mustard chipped in, 'we didn't go ringing Paco's doorbell. He wasn't, well . . .'

'One of the lads?' Skinner asked.

'No, not really. He missed Annette when she was on a trip, but, I dunno, I think he sort of enjoyed it too, the absences being part of her being famous. Know what I mean? He worshipped her, man. I tell you, if he ever gets his hands on the boss, he'll fucking kill him. Paco's a lovely fella, but if there's one guy in the world I wouldn't want getting mad at me, it's him.'

Pike and Orlando Flowers nodded agreement. 'Hardest man in the squad,' the Englishman volunteered.

Skinner smiled. 'You don't hear that said about a striker very often,' he suggested.

Mustard laughed. 'You're not a football man, mate, or you'd know better. Trust me, I've been a centre back all my career and I've come up against some seriously hard men. They have to be if they're going to make it to the top, with guys like me knocking fuck out of them every Saturday. Did you ever play the game?'

'Not seriously,' he conceded 'but I still do, most weeks. A bunch of us have a five-a-side group, every Thursday in North Berwick Sports Centre; we've been going for over twenty-five years now.'

Pike eyed him up. 'You might be well 'ard too,' he suggested. 'What position you play?'

'Any position I fucking like, mate.' He drained his soft drink, then looked round his companions. 'Okay, back to last Friday; you all got back to Edinburgh around two thirty and went straight up to your apartment.'

'That's right,' Orlando Flowers agreed, 'but there were four of us. Alice was there too.'

'Yes,' Skinner said, 'I was aware of that. She was with you, am I right?'

The American nodded. 'You are; we're an item.'

'Okay. So you were there for about four hours. Did you pass the time together or individually?'

'We all went to our rooms,' Mustard replied. 'We had no game last weekend but Tank Bridges didn't go easy on the training. In fact, it was tougher than usual.'

'He's a fuckin' sadist, that bastard,' Pike growled. 'He was just the same in France, with DuPain. I hope they bring in the boss's replacement soon, so we get rid of fuckin' Bridges.'

'Don't be a pussy, Jimmy,' the club captain chuckled. 'What else would you do with that surplus energy? You don't have a steady woman to burn it off you, not like Olly here. I do,' he added, glancing at Skinner, 'but she back in Trinidad having our second baby. Anyway,' he drawled on, 'we all in our rooms, restin' for the evening. Alice wanted to see *Mamma Mia*, the stage show, so we all got tickets. The game plan was go for a meal then the show, and back home not too late 'cos we had to meet the squad next morning for the bus to the hotel.'

'In all that time,' Skinner asked, 'did any of you hear anything from the penthouse?'

'I heard Annette come in,' Flowers volunteered. 'I was in the hall at the time and I heard the lift going up.'

'How did you know which way it was going?'

'Heard it stop and the door open. It's not the quietest.'

He looked around the group. 'Did anyone else hear it again?' Each of the trio shook his head.

'Okay, other than that, was there any noise from above, any sound at all?'

'I thought I heard a door bang one time,' Mustard said. 'But it could have been from the apartment below. Gen'rally, the sound insulation in the building is good. We hear very little from outside, only that noisy lift.'

'So if the neighbours had an argument, you wouldn't hear it?'

The West Indian smiled. 'How would I know that if they never did?' he countered. 'Paco and Annette, I can't imagine they ever fought. Any time I saw them together they was always smiling at each other. Ain't that true, boys?' he asked the others.

'Absolutely,' Pike agreed. 'They never did. Lucky bastards. When I was married we fought all the time. We got threatened with the local equivalent of an ASBO once when we lived in France. That's when I was big time,' he added in explanation, 'and playing for a proper team in a proper league.'

Skinner felt his Scottish hackles rise. 'That's what you think of Merrytown, is it?' he murmured.

'No, no,' the English footballer exclaimed, quickly, 'I didn't mean to be disrespectful. Merrytown pays my wages, it's just that . . .' He paused, putting his feelings into words. 'Five years ago, I never thought I'd be playing outside the Premier League at this stage of my career. I knew it would finish up eventually, early thirties, the age I am now, but I assumed the next stage would be a step down to the Championship and that I'd have another few years, maybe all of them at that level. As it happens I went to France instead, and now I'm 'ere. But the trouble is . . .' He looked at the club captain, helplessly. 'What am I tryin' to say here, Art?'

'You're trying to say,' Mustard told him, 'that we are none of us in control of our own destiny these days. We all have agents, and they play a big part in our lives. You thought Championship, Jimmy, but the agent, he thinks, where can I make the most money, for my player, and for me? So when we get to this stage, to the second half of our playing career, the offer that is put to us, it's the offer that the agent decides we'll see. When we're younger, maybe clubs get into bidding wars over us, but step over the thirty threshold and that don't happen.'

'Who's your agent, Jimmy?' Skinner asked.

'Cisco Serra,' Pike replied.

'You too? He's had a big influence on Merrytown.'

'He sure has,' Flowers agreed. 'He's not my agent, but he approached my guy on behalf of Merrytown, and brokered the deal. Both of them would pick up a fee on the back of my deal.'

'Same here,' Mustard volunteered. 'I was playing in Belgium; I didn't have an agent, havin' just fired my last one, and Cisco approached me, on behalf of Merrytown. He told me that the owner had ambition for the club and he was prepared to back it with cash. He even threw in the apartment as part of the deal.' He grinned. 'Didn't tell me about these guys at the time, but it's worked out okay, with us all being on our own . . . unless you count Alice, but she's only an occasional visitor.'

'How about Chaz Baker?' Skinner asked. 'Have you ever seen him here?'

All three men looked at him; none of them was smiling. The captain assumed the role of spokesman. 'Absolutely not. Never. This is where we live; the boss don't come where we live. It ain't his place. I know, I know,' he continued, his tone agitated. 'There's talk about him and Annette havin' an affair. Me, I don' believe it, but if they was, they wouldn't be having it in Paco's place.'

'Is there?' he exclaimed. 'Is there talk about Chaz and Annette? I haven't seen that suggestion in any newspaper.'

Mustard seemed taken aback by the question. 'It's the talk on the training ground,' he offered in reply. 'Ain't that right, Jimmy? You heard the story, didn't you? It was you told me.'

'And who told you, Jimmy?'

The Englishman pursed his lips. 'A Partick Thistle player, I think,' he murmured, 'but I can't remember his name.'

'Do you believe it, Art?'

'Last week I'd have laughed at the idea,' Mustard said. 'But that was before Annette was murdered and the boss was arrested for killing her. After that, I wouldn't cross out anything.'

'Well, I don't believe it,' Jimmy Pike declared. 'Not Chaz, no way.'

'He'll be pleased to hear that,' Skinner said. 'He's maintaining his innocence.'

'And it's your job to prove it, yes?' Flowers suggested. 'That's got to be why you're here, yes?'

'I'm here on behalf of his lawyer, yes, and that's her job.'

'Then she better be damn good at it. That guy I saw on television on Sunday, the prosecutor, he seemed damn sure of himself.'

'Of course, and that's his job too. But what you have to remember about lawyers involved in a criminal case is that by definition fifty per cent of them are wrong. Don't base your judgement on confidence alone.'

'We'll see,' Mustard said. 'Is that all, sir, or do you have anything else to ask us?'

'Only one thing, about the apartment next to yours. Is it occupied often?'

'Not very often. The owner, Mr Rogozin, he was there a couple of weeks back. And Lita, the doc, the boss's wife; she's used it a couple of times when she's been shopping in Edinburgh.' He grinned. 'She likes Harvey Nichols, and she goes to a hairdresser just down the hill from there. She's never stayed over though, far as I know.'

'Between the four of us, what do you make of him? Rogozin?'

The Trinidadian looked at his teammates; it seemed that they were having a conversation without words. 'Owners are owners,' he replied, when a consensus had been reached. 'They're the same as lambs are to a farmer; you can like them, or not, as the case may be, but not too much; you don't get close to them. Rogozin pays our wages, and that's it.'

Skinner might have pressed him further had his phone not played its tune. He excused himself and took the call.

'Pops,' his daughter said, 'where are you?'

'Merrytown, talking to some people, but I'm done now. Why?'

'I've just had a call from Sammy Pye. He wouldn't go into detail but he wants to see me as soon as possible, and he said you should be there too, if possible. He's coming here at five thirty.'

He checked his watch. 'I can make that,' he told her. 'Is it good news or bad, do you think?'

'I don't know. All I can say for sure is that it's got him excited.'

'That's a rare occurrence with DCI Pye,' Skinner declared. 'I'm on my way.'

Thirty-Eight

'How much is all this going to cost our client?' Alex Skinner asked her father as she handed him a bottle of mineral water. 'You've covered a lot of territory in the last couple of days.'

'I don't have a clue,' he answered cheerfully. 'It'll probably depend on the outcome. What's the going Legal Aid rate?'

'Don't make me laugh,' she said. 'How did it go today?'

'To be honest, I haven't learned anything new, other than the fact that the apartment next to the players' place has been used by Rogozin. I'd be interested to know why he was there a couple of Thursdays ago, but I'll have to wait to ask him. I'm planning to invite myself to the Merrytown home game on Saturday; I should bump into him there.'

'How are you going to pull that off? I'd have thought that the club would want to keep you at a distance, all things considered.'

'The chief executive might, Rogozin might, but if I'm there as the guest of a director there won't be a hell of a lot they can do about it.'

'A director?' she repeated 'You mean . . .'

'That's right, Cameron McCullough. I might need a long spoon for the soup course, but it's a price I'm ready to pay if it helps Baker. I called Mia on the way here to ask if she could fix it up. She didn't pick up, but I left a message.'

His daughter frowned. 'Pops, you don't want to be getting too close to that woman.'

'Don't worry, there's no danger of that, but we're singing from the same song sheet as far as Ignacio's concerned, so I thought I'd cash in on her spirit of cooperation.'

'Mmm.' She looked doubtful, but let it drop. 'How about the rest of it? Did you meet the four who were on the tape?'

'Only the players. We were right about Alice the physio, she's with Flowers, but she couldn't join us this afternoon. None of them are going to be any use as witnesses. Flowers heard the lift go up, but apart from that, none of them had anything to say.'

'Did you ask them about drug use?'

'Why the hell would I do that? I wanted their cooperation, not to antagonise them by quizzing them about footballers' nose candy habits. Besides, they gave me the distinct impression that I'd have been wasting my time. The three of them are mature men, serious professionals; there's nothing laddish about any of them. The only thing I picked up from them concerned Serra, the agent. I didn't realise he was as deeply into the club as he is. I knew that Paco and Chaz are both clients, but Pike is too and it seems that he was involved in bringing in Mustard, and Flowers as well. He acts directly for Jimmy, and he found the other two on behalf of the club. He must have cost Rogozin a bundle in fees over the last couple of years.'

'Can you have a foot in both camps like that?' Alex wondered.

'It seems so. I don't know how ethical it is, but to be honest I don't care either. It's a murky world, with its own rules and practices.'

'Maybe,' she said, 'but in corporate terms it's a business like any other. In my former life I did a couple of deals involving football clubs; the law's the same as anywhere else, so are the principles.'

'The law might be, but when personal vanity is introduced, established principles and rational behaviour go out the window. As a friend of mine said once, when many otherwise successful businessmen walk into the boardroom of a football club, they leave their brains in the car park.'

He checked his watch, with a quick, impatient frown. 'Quarter to six: where are the guys?'

'They said they'd try and make it for half five, but they didn't promise. Do you have to be home soon?'

'If I want to spend the evening with my kids, yes I do.'

'Go on then,' she said. 'I can fill you in later.'

'I think I . . .'

He was heading for the door when there was a knock and it opened. 'Sorry we're late,' Sammy Pye said as he and his sidekick stepped into the room.

'Will it be worth waiting for?' Skinner asked.

Haddock smiled. 'Oh yes, I think it will.'

'There are few people more infuriating than a smug detective,' the former chief constable growled.

Alex ushered the newcomers to chairs at her small conference table. 'So,' she said, 'are you dropping the charges?'

'No way,' Pye replied, 'but we are dropping what we think will be a bombshell, unless you've been withholding from us.'

'Which we have not!' she retorted, indignantly. 'I shared the result of my client's blood analysis, didn't I? That's evidence of good faith.'

'Agreed, Alex. You shared it, but you didn't look at it closely enough. And to be frank, neither did we. It took Arthur Dorward of the Forensic Service to spot what was lurking in there. None of us thought to compare the DNA profiles contained within the report. There were quite a few in there for elimination purposes, but Baker's wasn't. His prints were all over the place so we decided we didn't need to do one. It was only when you did, and it was added to the file, that Dorward, part genius, part pedantic bastard, picked it up: a connection between Baker's profile and one other.'

'Whose?' Skinner asked, looking intently at the DCI.

'The victim's. There are strong similarities between the two, strong enough to suggest . . . a sibling relationship.'

'They were brother and sister?' Alex gasped.

'Half,' Haddock said. 'Given Annette's racial mix obviously they couldn't be full siblings, but the likelihood of a relationship was overwhelming, according to Arthur.'

'But not absolutely conclusive, surely.'

'Not without a comparison with the DNA of a common parent,' Pye agreed, 'but there are other ways of confirming the link. That's why we were late getting here. We've been chasing birth certificates.'

'That couldn't have been simple,' Skinner suggested, 'given that Annette was adopted.'

'You know about that, Chief?'

'Of course I do.' He outlined the discovery he had made in Worthing. 'Not material to your case, but of interest to us.'

'I can see that. We got there eventually. First, though, we looked at Baker's background. He was born in Croydon, forty-two years ago, to Conrad Baker, musician, and Mildred Pearce, nurse. His mother's still alive; as for the father . . . I'll get to that. The marriage was dissolved when Chaz was ten.'

'And Annette? How did you trace her?'

'We did the obvious;' the DCI replied, 'we asked Paco. He

told us about her adoptive parents in Worthing. We went looking for them but we found that they're both deceased. We thought we were stuffed then, with no obvious means of tracing the adoption, and no way of knowing what was on Annette's original birth certificate. We went back to Paco in the hope that he might have it. He didn't, but he did tell us that Annette had a very large indemnity insurance policy arranged through a London brokerage, covering her against any illness or accident that might end her career. When she took it out it required full disclosure.'

Skinner nodded. 'You went to the broker?'

'Yes,' Pye confirmed, 'and after jumping through all sorts of data protection hoops, we were able to obtain the application document and an image of Annette's birth record. She was born Anesha Gunawardena, twenty-eight years ago, in London, to a Sri Lankan mother, Keshini Gunawardena, and an English father . . .'

'Conrad Baker,' Alex exclaimed.

'The one and only,' Haddock chuckled.

'Thing is,' Pye continued, 'Keshini was sixteen years and four months old at the time, and Conrad would have been forty-five. She'd have been under age when Annette was conceived, and he'd have been at risk of prosecution if it had been brought to the attention of the police. There's no record of them ever marrying, nor has there been any trace of Conrad since he renewed his passport seven years ago, from an address in South Africa.'

'What about Keshini?'

'She could be anywhere. She could be dead. We didn't go looking for her, Alex. If we ever needed to confirm a relationship between Annette and Chaz, she'd be no use. We'd need Conrad's DNA for that as the common parent. For the purposes of our investigation, I'm content to rely on the paper trail that we've established.'

'Does it weaken your belief in his guilt?' she asked.

'Why should it? If anything it strengthens it. Baker denies vehemently that they had a sexual relationship. Annette's text can be read as a threat to reveal a secret. If that secret was their kinship and Baker didn't want it revealed, it gives him a motive for killing her.'

'Why would he want to keep it hidden?'

'To prevent his father from being outed as a paedophile?' Haddock suggested.

'His father walked out of his life when he was ten,' Alex countered.

'We hold Chaz's passport,' Pye said quietly. 'There's a stamp on it showing that at the beginning of June, in the football off-season, he took a trip to Durban. Conrad Baker's renewed passport was mailed to a Durban address.'

'Oh,' she murmured.

'Alex,' the DCI continued, 'we want to convict your client because we think he's guilty, but we don't want to railroad him. At the very least, there are questions to be asked. We're here to do you the courtesy of allowing you to ask them first.'

Thirty-Nine

'Ground Control to Detective Sergeant Haddock,' Cheeky McCullough sang out, across the table. 'Come in, please.'

Her partner blinked, and shook his head as if to clear it, like a boxer who had just been caught by a lucky punch. 'Eh? What? Sorry.'

'You were gone,' she said. 'On another planet. In fact, you've been in outer space pretty much since you got in.'

'No I haven't,' he protested. 'I was just contemplating the excellence of that dessert I knocked up out of a couple of bananas, a couple of pears and a scoop of spices.'

She laughed, the gentle, deep-throated molasses laugh that helped make her the most attractive woman he had ever imagined, let alone met. He looked at her and melted yet again into the amazing surprise of realising that he was even happier than he had ever hoped to be.

'Yes, it was wonderful,' she agreed. 'Since you got that smoothie machine, you have been unstoppable. And you know what? Give it a month and it'll be in the back of the cupboard along with the juicer, the toastie maker, the milk frother, the percolator and the electric knife sharpener. Most couples our age move to a bigger house to start a family. We'll do it because we've run out of room for bloody gadgets.'

He grinned, sheepishly, wondering whether he should tell her about the garment steamer and fluff remover that he had just ordered from Amazon.

'But that's not what was on your mind. Come on, big boy, out with it.'

'Nah, it's work, and I don't like to bring that home.'

'Not any old work, though. I can always tell if you've been at a crime scene that's upset you. It shows in your eyes; sometimes I think I can see it myself. This is different, as if you were trying to work something out.'

He stood, picked up the dessert bowls and carried them through to the kitchen, knowing that he would not get off so easily, that she would follow him; as she did, taking two more Cobra beers from the fridge, uncapping them, and handing one to him.

'You're too shrewd for your own good,' he murmured as they settled into the couch, back in the living room. 'Your clients should be glad you're working for them and not for HMRC. No, it's not a new crime scene. It's something that's washed up in the current investigation.'

'I thought that was all done and dusted,' she said. 'The "Tragic Annette Bordeaux" headlines are gone from the tabloids: probably holding their fire till the trial.' She pierced him with a gaze. 'There is going to be a trial, isn't there? Baker's still guilty?'

'Yes he is,' he replied. 'The case against him is as solid as it ever was. Alex Skinner's doing her best, but she hasn't got anything to weaken it.'

'Not even with her dad on her side?'

He frowned. 'How did you know that big Bob was helping her?'

'I'd a phone call from my granny just before you came in.'

'Your granny?' he exclaimed, laughing.

'Mia, my step-granny. She's working very hard at being liked.'

'Is she succeeding?'

'I don't know,' she confessed. 'I can't make up my mind about her. She's got pizzazz, personality, but I can't help wondering if that's just the radio presenter talking to me, and the real Mia's someone else.'

'I think you'll find that she is,' Sauce observed. 'This is a mother who allowed her teenage son to crystallise methamphetamines in an old sherry bodega in Spain, then set up a distribution network in Scotland. She got away with it because the people who could have given evidence against her were all dead. That's your granny. By any measurement she's a dangerous woman. If I was Grandpa I'd be putting my own sugar in my tea.'

She dug him in the ribs. 'He doesn't take sugar,' she laughed. 'This driftwood that's washed into your investigation, what is it?'

He drank some of his beer before replying. When he did, it was with a question. 'Suppose you had a brother,' he asked. 'Or a half-brother. One you didn't know about until you were grown up. If he came into your life, how would you feel about him? Would there be an instant bond between you?'

'I can't say with any certainty that I haven't,' she pointed out. 'My mum got herself knocked up when she was still at school. My dad got out of town, did a runner, disappeared, rather than face Grandpa and Auntie Goldie. I never knew him, so I have no idea what he did after that. I could have half a dozen brothers and sisters, for all I know. It's not something I fantasise over, but the thought does cross my mind on occasion.'

'If you did, and one of them came into your life . . .'

'I'd probably feel the same about him as I do about Mia . . . uncertain. But no, maybe not; he'd have my blood, she doesn't.'

'If he proved a threat to you in some way, would you live with it or would you try to eliminate it?'

'That would depend on the threat, but if it was serious enough I'd want it to go away.'

'Would you take extreme action to get rid of it?'

'What? I don't get you, Sauce. What are you asking me?'

'Nothing,' he murmured, shaking his head. 'I know the answer. You wouldn't because you don't have it in your make-up. Someone would need to have a special kind of ruthlessness to do that, and you don't have any. The question is, does Chaz Baker? I'm not sure that he has.' He looked down at her, smiling at her puzzled expression. 'Forget about it; I have. Tell me, what did your granny want?'

'She rang to invite us to the Merrytown game on Saturday. Posh seats in the directors' box.'

'Football? Me? Did you tell her no thanks?'

'No, I said yes, we'd love to. Lunch in a hospitality suite, then the game.'

'I'm golfing,' Sauce protested. 'It's the monthly medal on Saturday.'

'You can miss one without losing your handicap,' she said. 'I want to, love. Please?'

'I don't know if I should be going near Merrytown in the circumstances. Or being too close to your grandfather in any circumstances, given my job and his reputation.'

'Why not?' Cheeky countered. 'Bob Skinner will be.'

'He's going?'

'So Granny Mia says. She told me he called her to invite himself, and she wants to keep the playing field level.'

'In that case she's on. If the big man's prepared to be in the same room as Grandpa, he's up to something. I have to see what it is.'

Forty

'He asked you rather than me?' Cameron McCullough grumbled. 'So he still doesn't want to get his hands dirty.'

'Don't take it that way,' his wife said. 'He has my mobile number, not yours. And he did ask me to pass on a request to you.'

'One that you felt able to grant yourself.'

'Yes, I did,' she declared, defending herself against the criticism implied by his tone. 'You're as keen as I am to normalise relations with Bob; don't tell me otherwise.'

'I'll grant you,' he admitted, 'that our shared interest in your son makes it desirable that I get on with the guy, but it isn't something I lie awake thinking about.'

'I don't notice you lying awake at all,' she laughed. 'You could sleep through a hurricane. Come to think of it, you did, when we were in Florida. It attracted me to you, truth be told: I took it as the sign of an easy conscience.'

'That's interesting, coming from an insomniac. Okay, Mia, I don't mind you inviting Skinner to the game, but you have to remember that for the best part of my life people like him have hounded me. Because I was incredibly successful in a range of businesses, they assumed I was bent and put me right at the top of their fucking to-do lists. He'd still put me away given half a chance; I don't hold that against him, by the way. It's what he does.'

'Not any more. He's retired.'

He looked at her, then laughed. 'Do you actually believe that? He's still connected in some way or other. When he wound up in A and E on Monday it was a race between the CID and the Solicitor fucking General to be the first at his bedside.'

'How do you know that?'

He tapped the side of his nose with two fingers. 'Sources, like they say on telly. Bob Skinner may be on the non-executive director circuit, and making very nice money out of it, but he's the police equivalent of that old Pope who retired. "The Servant of the Servants of God", they call him. Skinner's the servant of the servants of Mammon; he's still the go-to man. His successor, the guy Martin, he tried to distance himself, and look what happened to him. That bastard,' he muttered, grimly. 'He gave me a hard time when he was deputy chief in Dundee.'

'I remember him from twenty years ago,' Mia remarked. 'The first time I ever met Bob, Andy Martin was with him. He was a raw young detective constable then. You could see he fancied himself with the ladies, and he had the light of the zealot shining out of those weird green eyes.'

'Good riddance to the . . .' McCullough growled, then switched off the scowl that he showed very rarely. 'Why does Bob want to come to the game? Did he tell you?'

'He said he'd like to get a feel for the ambience of the club. He told me he believes that Annette's murder originated there in one way or another. He asked me if Dimitri would be there, and other stuff about him too.'

'Such as?'

'How much time does he spend in Scotland? Why was he here the week before last? Who controls the use of the spare apartment in King Robert Village?'

'Does he know that you own it?'

'I don't think so. I don't think he's interested in who owns it, just in who uses it and when.'

'Not many people,' McCullough said. 'Was Dimitri here the week before last?' he pondered. 'He told me he was missing the game in Finland because he had business in London. I really am going to have to sort that bastard out,' he murmured. 'He can play all the silly games he likes, but I will not have him on my patch without my knowing about it.'

'No,' his wife agreed, 'you shouldn't. Cameron, I don't like the man, and I do not trust him. He's a lecherous, bullying, dangerous creep and I wish we were rid of him.'

He grinned. 'I can think of a way of bringing that about.'

'How?' she asked.

'Drop the word in Bob's ear,' he replied, 'that Dimitri really did send Grigor after him to put the wind up Alex.'

'There's no way of proving that.'

'He wouldn't be worried about proving it. Dimitri's on dodgy ground for bringing that guy into the country. Bob Skinner is owed favours by people in London as well as in Scotland. If he called one of them in, I'll bet you that my fellow director would suddenly find himself *persona non grata* in Britain.'

'Would you drop that word . . . or would you want me to do it?'

'Neither at the moment. Let's see how Saturday goes. Is he bringing his wife?'

'Yes, he is. Technically she's still his ex-wife; they're back together but they haven't remarried.'

He grinned. 'Doesn't she trust him? He has a couple of ex-wives around, doesn't he?'

'Just the one, apart from Sarah; Alex's mum died in a car crash. Whether she trusts him or not, I couldn't tell you. She'd be wise not to. When we had our mini-fling, there was someone else on the scene. Alex made that clear; I think it was her way of warning me off.'

'Was that why it didn't work out between you?'

'No. The truth is, he frightened me. Scary man.'

'And I never have?' he asked.

'No, you never have, but you hide things away. Bob can't do that; everything's out there with him. By the way,' she added, changing the subject, 'you've invited someone else to the game.'

'I have? Do we have any seats left in the directors' box?'

'You have for these guests: your granddaughter and her partner.'

He stared at her, with a wide, incredulous smile. 'What? I'm getting to meet the detective sergeant, officially?'

'In a crowded room.'

'Even that's a step forward.'

She patted him on the shoulder. 'When we married, successful businessman with a shady reputation and top-rated radio presenter with a mysterious past, I promised that I'd make you respectable. This is a step along the way.'

'Very good,' he said. 'What's the next?'

'Getting rid of that Russian wannabe hoodlum. But, one step at a time.'

Forty-One

'How did they find out?' he asked, hoarsely.

Chaz Baker sat on a couch in his temporary home, with his face buried in his hands. Skinner thought that he might be sobbing, but his eyes were dry when he showed them again, sunken, with dark shadows below.

'All it took,' Alex told him, 'was for one smart guy to look at the DNA profiles of you and Annette and to reach an obvious conclusion. The rest was basic police work. The question is, Mr Baker, how did you find out?'

'From Annie,' he replied. 'In February, after we'd all settled in at Merrytown. She told me at that first meeting in the café at Chatelherault. She was edgy all through the meal, but eventually she came out with it. "Chaz," she said, "you're my brother." Just like that.'

'How did you react?'

'You can't imagine.'

'Actually I can, but tell me anyway.'

'I thought she was crazy. I thought she was trying to screw some more money out of me for Paco. I thought there was some sort of a pitch coming. I told her flat out that I didn't believe her. "Look at your skin colour," I said, "and look at mine." She smiled at that, and told me that although her birth mother was from Sri Lanka, her father was English. And then she went into her bag and showed me the paper that proved it. My old man, the stupid old bastard, fathered a child with a fifteen-year-old girl he met in a club where his band was playing. When she told him, you know what he did? He fucked off to South Africa.'

'Where you visited him in June,' Skinner said.

'Too right I did. Then I wished I hadn't. I made the big mistake of telling him who his daughter had grown up to become, and he got all excited. He said he'd come back home to claim her. I told him I'd cut him off at the fucking knees if he did that, and that if I heard from anyone that he'd breathed a word about it I'd go straight to the Metropolitan Police and shop him.'

'A quarter of a century on they might not have been interested.'

'Oh no? What about all them ancient disc jockeys they keep hauling into court.'

'Fair point,' Alex conceded.

'Anyway,' Baker continued, 'when I realised she was telling the truth, all sorts of stuff fell into place.'

'For example?'

'For example, Cisco Serra. The guy's one of the top agents. Players hammer at his door wanting him to take them on, and players are where the money is for agents, not managers. Yet Cisco approached me, and asked if he could work with me. One thing I am is a realist; I don't have a huge ego and I know my place in the pecking order. Plus, I wasn't exactly a hot property at the time. I was locked into a court case with the owner of the French club I managed, with a fair chance that I'd lose it.

Frenchman versus Englishman in a French court? Who would you back?'

'I'd usually back the guy who can afford the best lawyers,' Skinner murmured.

'That wouldn't have been me, mate,' Baker shot back at him. 'Anyway when Cisco pitched himself to me, first thing I said was, "Why?" He said that he thought I was an interesting bloke, and a bit of a challenge, given my circumstances. So I thought, "Why the 'ell not?" and I signed with him. A few weeks later he tells me that this Russian guy Rogozin that I've never heard of, he's paid off the Frenchman and he's giving me a three-year contract at Merrytown.'

He paused, glancing at his interrogators. 'First thing I said to him was, "Where's Merrytown?" Cisco says it's in Scotland, and I said, "Fucking Scotland?" but he pointed out rightly that it got me off a very sharp hook, the money was decent and the Russian was signing good players, with Paco Fonter at the head of the queue. I'd have done it anyway, but Paco was the icing on the cake. He's far and away the best player I've ever worked with: he's not Ronaldo, not Messi, but very, very good.'

Picking up a bottle of water that sat at his feet he took a drink, and then continued. 'What I didn't know then, 'cos Cisco never said, was that Paco had insisted on me going to the club as part of his deal. I didn't know either that Cisco approached me because Paco told him to. And I certainly didn't know Paco did that because Annie asked him. It all went back to her, everything, after she found out about her and me being half-brother and half-sister.'

'She took you under her wing?' Alex said, quietly.

'And then some.'

'What about her birth mother? Keshini? Did she look for her?'

Baker nodded. 'She traced her, then wished she hadn't. Her parents sent her back to Sri Lanka after Annie was born and given up for adoption. She died there, during the civil war against the Tamils. She was working in a hospital that was shelled by government forces; she was killed. Her name's on a list of casualties compiled by Amnesty International.'

He frowned. 'She traced her grandparents too: the Gunawardenas. They're in their seventies and still living in South London.'

'Did she get in touch?'

His expression grew even darker. 'She did in a way,' he said. 'They ran a dry-cleaning business. When she found out what had happened to her mother, Annie bought the shop that they rented and terminated their lease.'

'That's pretty serious payback. Did they know who was doing it?' Skinner asked.

'Not as far as I know. I think she bought it through a pension fund she'd established.'

'Whose idea was it to keep your relationship secret?'

'It was mutual. Annie reckoned that if it came out that the whole Crazy Horse thing was a fantasy made up by her agent, they'd both look foolish and her career would be damaged. As for me, I didn't want to be known as the son of a paedophile.'

'How long have you been in touch with your father?'

'I was never out of touch. He didn't run off and leave Mum and me penniless; he was a session musician, but he had steady work and made good money. Even after he left the country he supported us without having to be chased by the CSA or anything like that. When I was twelve I was offered a place in a football academy, but there was an up-front cost; you had to contribute to your training, and provide most of your own kit. Dad stumped up the cash without a murmur.'

'Do you visit him often in Durban?' Alex asked.

'I try to get out there once a year; more often than not I make it. Dad's well known out there; he's one of the top two or three jazz guitarists in the country.'

'But you were angry when you found out about Annette?'

Baker sighed. 'Yeah, I was hard on him. I'd never have shopped him to the Met though; that was just a threat. It wasn't needed either. As soon as I explained that him showing up out of the blue would be bad for Annie, he got the message and dropped the idea.'

'He must know about her death by now,' Skinner said. 'Has he been in touch?'

'The other way around. I called him on Sunday, and told him what had happened. He was gutted, poor old bloke. He'd just got used to the idea of having a daughter, now she's gone. We had this idea, Annie and me, that I'd take her out to Durban next summer, so they could meet.'

'Does Paco know?' he asked.

'Definitely not,' Baker declared. 'Annie would have told him, but I asked her not to, for footballing reasons rather than personal. I'm Paco's boss; I'd rather not be his brother-in-law as well, not when we've the other connection.'

'And Lita?'

'You got to be fucking joking, mate. I couldn't dump a secret like that on her.'

'So,' Alex interjected, filling a silence as it developed, 'it looks as if your relationship was the secret that was referred to in

Annette's text. Why would she suddenly want to bring it into the open?'

Her client shook his head. 'I've got no idea, honestly, not the faintest, not a Scooby.' He looked at her. 'Is it important?'

'The prosecution may suggest to the jury that you killed her to prevent her from doing that.'

'Why would I want to do that?' he challenged.

'To protect your father from possible prosecution, and from career damage; it might be suggested that you didn't get the Merrytown job on your own merits, but as part of the Paco deal.'

'I wouldn't fancy either of those,' he conceded, 'but I wouldn't kill her over it.'

'There is a way of countering the Crown,' she added. 'It could be damaging if it came out in court, but if we pre-empted that and released the story ourselves before the trial, it wouldn't have any viability as a possible motive.'

'But Dad will be in the shit if we release it.'

'It's going to come out anyway, Chaz. You can't stop that.'

'What about Annie's reputation? Sirena's Crazy Horse legend and all that?'

'That too; it'll be revealed in court.'

'Are you saying to me we should come clean about everything?'

'The more I think about it,' she admitted, 'the more I realise that I am. It wouldn't be simply tactical. It wouldn't only be about taking a weapon away from the Crown. We would be planting a question in the minds of the jury. Is this man such a monster that he would actually kill his own sister? Reasonable doubt, Mr Baker; that's what our defence is all about. And such a doubt, in the minds of the fifteen ordinary people who will make up your jury, will be a very large one indeed.'

He sat silent for a minute and more, shifting in his chair as he wrestled with his dilemma. 'If I agreed,' he murmured, finally, 'how would we do it? I'm not allowed to talk to the media. Would you hold a press conference?'

'Hell no, the Law Society would crucify me for that.'

'But they couldn't touch me,' her father said. 'I have access to the media, at editor level. The information we're talking about here is all in the public domain, birth records and such, and I'm not an officer of the court, so if I give it to my contact, there would be no comeback for you or for Alex.' He paused. 'But if you agree to me doing that, I would want to give, no, I'd insist, that we give advance warning to Paco Fonter.'

'Okay, but why?'

'Because there's every chance the police will tell him, as soon as they've interviewed you. And because morally it's the right thing to do. I'm seeing Paco this afternoon. Do I have your permission to tell him about you and Annette, even without a decision to take the story to the media?'

'I should tell him myself,' Baker said.

'The sheriff would slam you straight inside if you spoke to him. Besides, the way things stand at the moment he might kill you before you got a word out.'

'Okay,' he sighed, 'go ahead.'

'Thanks. This has been a very interesting meeting, Chaz. It's given me a lot to chew over. Not least . . . and I keep coming back to this man . . . the role of Dimitri Rogozin in all this. What you're telling me is that your becoming a client of Cisco Serra and then your move to Merrytown were orchestrated by Annette Bordeaux, so that she could have her husband and her half-brother in one place.'

'It seems that way,' Baker agreed.

'But hold on: part of that plan depended on you being bought out of your legal dispute in France, by Dimitri Rogozin. How much money are we talking about here, Chaz, what was the settlement figure?'

'I don't know the final amount,' the manager replied, 'but the Frenchman was suing me for two million euro plus costs.'

'Two million!' Skinner whistled. 'That's a big bag of cash in any situation. And with respect, Chaz, Merrytown is only Merrytown and you ain't Jose Mourinho.'

Forty-Two

'No,' Paco Fonter said. 'I had no idea of this.' A trickle of sweat ran from his forehead and down a furrow in his cheek. It looked like a tear.

'Did your wife ever talk about her early life?' Skinner asked.

The footballer rose from the large, complicated, exercise machine; he wore cycling shorts and a sleeveless red vest, on which damp patches showed. He had insisted that they meet in the gym of the Norton House Hotel. 'I can't play just now, but I can keep myself fit. I need to hurt myself just now.'

All through Skinner's story of his wife's secret past and her relationship with the man who was accused of killing her he had been pressing weight, an impressive hundred kilos, over and over again.

'Of course,' he replied. 'She told me about her parents in the first month after we met. She loved them, and what happened, it hurt her very badly. I could see it in her eyes when she talked about them; her mother dying and her father no longer believing in God, and killing himself with whisky.'

'She told you she was adopted?'

'Yes, I knew that.'

'Did she ever talk about her birth parents?'

Fonter shook his head as he seated himself at another machine and adjusted the weights, selecting eighty kilos. 'No, she didn't. I asked her if she had ever tried to trace her real mother, but she brushed me off. I saw that it upset her so I left it alone.' He paused. 'She was killed, you said?'

'Yes, in the civil war in Sri Lanka, after her parents sent her home.'

'And she really did that to them, her . . . *abuelos*?' he exclaimed, reverting to Spanish for the lack of the word in English. 'She threw them out of their shop and killed their business?'

'That's what she told Chaz. You'll find it among her assets, I'm sure, when you wind up her estate.'

The footballer pulled on the levers above his head, drawing them down to the level of his shoulders; the weights rose up in their cradle. 'She must have been very angry with them, to do that,' he said, as he lowered them. 'Annie was a kind lady, a very gentle lady. She had no cruelty in her.' He repeated the exercise, smoothly, with no apparent effort, then did it again, and again. Skinner was impressed; of all the machines in the gym he used in Gullane, that was the one he hated most.

'How did she feel about her father?' he asked, resting after ten repetitions.

'I don't know. Chaz didn't say. But he did hope that she would go to South Africa with him, to meet him.'

'I need to talk to him,' Fonter said. 'He knew things about my wife that I did not. Can you help me?'

'I don't think so,' Skinner answered, frankly. 'His bail conditions wouldn't allow it.' He hesitated for a moment, then asked, 'If you did meet him, how would you feel, looking at him, knowing that he's charged with killing your wife?'

'Good question,' the footballer murmured, as he increased

the weight on the machine by five kilos. He launched into another series of exercises; he did fifteen repetitions, straining over the last two or three. 'When the police told me, last Sunday, that the boss was accused, at first I refused to believe. Then when finally I did, I wanted to kill him. Not any more. Now I want to ask him if it is true. If he tells me it is, then maybe I want to kill him again. But right now, no. I am confused, sir, and that is the truth.'

'What do you feel, Paco? What does your gut tell you? Do you think Chaz did it?'

'I ask myself that a thousand times,' he replied, wiping his face with the towel draped round his neck, 'and each time I think I believe it a little less. What you tell me now, that he and Annie have the same father, that makes a difference. Now I say no, I do not believe. But who? Who else?'

'If I knew that,' Skinner said, 'he'd be locked up already. But I don't. Your wife was murdered in an apartment that is pretty much impregnable. Chaz Baker was there at the time, and there's no direct evidence that anyone else was. So . . . Did Annette, Annie, have a problem with anyone, in her business life or personally?'

'No,' Fonter protested, 'for sure no. Annie was lovely, and everybody loved her.'

'Somebody didn't; that's self-evident. How about you, Paco? Is there anyone in the world who'd want to hurt you so badly?'

'There's a crazy man in Spain gave me trouble when I played there. I scored three against his brother's team and because of the way I celebrated, he went loco. He got on Twitter and he sent me bad messages, threats, you know.'

'He was a troll.'

'Exactly, that's the word. Things got so bad with him that he waited outside my house one night with a gun. It only shot little white pellets but to me it looked real, until I realised it wasn't. He scared me, it's true. I took it from him and I gave him a beating. One of my neighbours saw the whole thing and called the cops. They arrived and they gave him a beating too, then took him away. I never heard from him again. There are wild people about football, Mr Skinner, people who are not cool, but usually they are also very dumb.' He shook his head. 'No,' he said, 'I can think of nobody who hates me so much they would kill my Annie.'

'Without implying anything,' he continued, 'how are your relationships with people within the club? I know that Chaz respects you, but how about the rest? I assume that you're the highest earner there, the best paid player.'

Fonter nodded, as he added five more kilos to the weight load, then took hold of the levers.

'How do the other guys feel about that? Is anyone openly jealous?'

He had to wait for an answer, as the man punished himself on the machine, pushing himself to the limit of his strength, snarling as he completed a set of twenty pulls. The last left him red faced, with cord-like veins standing out on his arms. Skinner retrieved the water bottle that lay at his feet and handed it to him.

'Thank you,' he gasped, then took a long drink. 'There are always players within football clubs,' he said, 'who think they should be paid more money, but they blame their agents, not the teammates who are more fortunate than they are.'

'So you get on with all your teammates,' Skinner suggested.

'I did not say that,' the player corrected him. 'I don't like the American, Flowers. He's arrogant, and he's not as good a player as he thinks he is. Also he doesn't pass to me when he should. But what I do not like the most is the way he treats Alice, the physio; she's his girlfriend, but maybe you know that by now.' Skinner nodded. 'He disrespects her.'

'In what way?'

'He talks about her when she is not there, in a bad way. He describes what she does when they are having sex, how she likes it. He and I, we . . .' He stopped.

'Go on,' Skinner said. 'You had a fight?'

'No, no. If Flowers wanted to fight someone it would not be me, it would be someone he knew wouldn't kick his ass. We had an argument. He was talking about Alice in the showers after she had gone; he said she had small tits, as if that was a falta. He's from Miami and he speaks Spanish so I said to him, "*Me pregunto si ella le dice a sus amigas que tiene un pequeño pene.*" It means, "I wonder if she tells her girlfriends that you have a small cock." None of the guys knew what it meant but they could see from his face that he didn't like it.'

'Did he say anything to you?'

'He called me a *hijo de puta*. That means . . .'

'I know what it means.'

'I called him a *concha* . . .'

Skinner smiled. 'I know that one too.'

'Then I said, "*Tú no eres hombre, si usted no sabe cómo respetar a una mujer,*" "You're no man if you don't know how to respect a woman," and I walked out.'

'When did this happen?'

'At the beginning of August.'

'Has he said anything to you since then?'

'No.' Fonter stood, ripped a stretch of paper towel from a container on the wall and wiped down the machine, carefully, removing all traces of sweat. 'He's quiet whenever I'm in the room. He says nothing around me. But Jimmy Pike told me he still talked about Alice after that, until Art Mustard said he didn't want to hear any more.'

'Is Flowers your only problem on the staff.'

'Among the players, yes. But the assistant manager, Bridges, that guy I do not like. Nobody does. He's not a pleasant man; he's a big guy and he will pick on people who fear him. Unfortunately, that means most of the people in the club.'

'But not you?'

'But not me. And not Art. Everyone else though. We arrived in Scotland at the same time, me, the boss and Bridges. We had not been here long when there was a training game; we were short so Bridges played for the B team. The first time the ball came to me, he kicked me from behind. Not to injure me but to hurt. You know?'

'Sure,' Skinner said. 'Old pro stuff.'

'Yes. So I told him that if he ever did it again he would pay for it. He tried, and he did. I stood on his foot as he came on at me, and put my weight against his knee. It damaged a ligament, and put him out of action for a month, but no one ever knew, except Bridges and me, and the boss, of course, who knows everything.'

'Why does Baker tolerate him?'

'Chaz keeps him because he is himself a nice man. In a group of trainers they can't all be nice men; you need a nasty guy, someone who will shout from the touchline and yell at the lazy. That's the job that Tank Bridges does and he is very good at it, too good because he takes it too far. I don't like to see young players in tears, but I have done.'

'What did Annie think of these people, Bridges and Flowers?'

'She hardly knew them. Bridges not at all, and Flowers only because he lives in the apartment below ours.'

'Was that arrangement all right with you? Living so close to teammates? Living above three single men?'

'It was never a problem, because we never saw them and never heard them. The noise does not come through the floor. It is a strong building.'

'Will you go back there?' Skinner asked.

'Never,' Fonter declared. 'I told Angela Renwick to find me another place. And I told Cisco Serra, find me another club in the January window. I never should have come to this country. If I had not come to this country, Annie would still be alive.'

'Will Rogozin let you move?'

The footballer picked up a pair of padded training gloves, slipped them on and walked across to a punchball. He hit it gently, setting it swinging, then again and again and again, first with his right fist, then both, until he had established a steady rhythm and the ball was no more than a blur. 'That's what I think of Rogozin,' he said as he worked. 'And that,' he added, as he finished the sequence with a final savage punch. 'Rogozin will have no say in whether I move or not. I wasn't at Merrytown very long before I learned that if you want anything done there that Chaz cannot fix you don't go to Rogozin. You go to the other director, Mr McCullough. He is the real boss.'

Why does that not surprise me? Skinner asked himself. He had always seen an incongruity in the notion of Cameron McCullough playing second fiddle to a blustering Russian bully. He made a mental note that at some time in the future, when the Annette Bordeaux case and its tragic victim were both laid to rest, he would use his contacts to explore the links between the two men. Too much had been taken for granted.

'I appreciate you seeing me, Paco,' he said. 'You didn't have to, and the news I gave you will probably take some time to sink in. Before I go, there is one more thing I need to tell you about. When they went through your apartment, after Annie's murder, the forensic team found traces of a white powder in the bathroom. It was analysed and it proved to be cocaine.'

'*Mierda!*' Fonter hissed.

'I'm sorry to drop that on you, but I should add that there's no suggestion that your wife was a user. Her blood showed no trace of any prohibited drug, and neither did the sample that was taken from Chaz Baker. Our thinking is that whoever snorted that stuff in your bathroom was the person who killed Annie, and that's the suggestion my daughter will make to the jury.'

The footballer's face darkened. 'I don't know what to do here, sir.' He stared straight ahead. 'Look, if I tell you something, can I trust you?'

'Legally, probably not,' Skinner admitted. 'I'm here on my daughter's instruction, as her agent. If you told me something that was helpful to Chaz Baker's defence, I'd be bound to take it back to her and she'd be obliged to introduce it in court. Personally, if it falls outside that condition, and you're not going to admit to a major crime, yes you can.'

Fonter nodded. 'If I told you something that was harmful to the boss's defence . . .'

'My instinct says that I'd rather not hear it,' he replied, then saw the implication in the other man's hesitancy. 'But if we use the presence of cocaine as part of the defence, it'll be open to exploration by the Crown. You'll be called as a witness in the trial for sure and so . . .'

'It was mine.' Paco glanced at him, then looked away again. 'We all have our weaknesses, Mr Skinner, even you, I'm sure. I drink very little alcohol, only wine at table, I eat only free-range chicken and eggs, and I do not buy farmed fish. And I am faithful to my wife, unlike more than a few of my fellow footballers. But occasionally, very occasionally, I took a little cocaine. I was careful,' he added. 'I didn't use when the season is on, unless I have a full week until the next game and I knew that I wouldn't be tested.'

'How did you know that?'

'Tests are supposed to be random, but I am a top player, and I am tested a lot. Never more than once in a month though, so once I have a test I know there's a little space.'

'When did you use the stuff that was found?'

'At least three months ago. I'm amazed there were traces still there.' He chuckled. 'They should fire the cleaner; she's pretty sloppy.'

'How did Annette feel about it? Did it cause difficulty between you?'

'She was worried that my supplier might use it against me, but otherwise she was fine with it. She knew it would not turn into a major habit; she knew plenty of people in her world who were serious users and she knew that I was not one of them.'

'Could she prove to be right?' Skinner asked. 'Can you trust your supplier?'

'It's not an issue any more. I promised Annie I would quit for good, and I have done. I'm sorry,' he added. 'That was not what you wanted to hear, I know, and it will not help you with the boss's defence. But if there is anything else I can do, you only have to say. After all, it seems that the man is my brother-in-law.'

Forty-Three

'Do you think they put us at the same table deliberately?' Sauce Haddock asked, as he gazed around the crowded dining room of the Merrytown Football Club hospitality suite.

His partner laughed. 'Not they,' Cheeky corrected him. 'He. This has Grandpa's fingerprints all over it.'

'I see. This is the police table, is it? He might as well have put a blue lamp in the middle.'

'Not me, lad,' Bob Skinner chuckled. 'You polis, me civilian. How's work anyway, Sauce?'

'Dominated, Chief,' the young sergeant reminded him, 'as well you know, by something that you and I can't talk about.'

'Of course we can. You're off duty, and there's nothing about your case against my daughter's client that I don't know . . . or there had better not be, otherwise she'll be on to the Solicitor General about failure to disclose.'

'Are we really going to talk shop all through lunch?' Sarah Grace asked. 'If we are, I had the aftermath of a road accident in yesterday, multiple fatalities. I could talk you through the autopsies if you like.'

'And I could talk you through the tax calculation of a major, although nameless, investment management company,' Cheeky

McCullough added. 'Let's talk about football.'

'Okay,' Sauce responded. 'I don't see Paco Fonter here.'

'No,' Skinner confirmed. 'And maybe you never will again.'

'You've seen him, then? We're visiting him again on Monday,'

'I spoke to him yesterday morning. He's a sad and angry man, pounding ten bells out of himself and out of punchbags in the hotel gym. But every time he hits one, it isn't Chaz Baker's face he sees, not any more.'

'You broke the news to him about . . .?' He caught Skinner's glance towards his girlfriend. 'Cheeky knows, it's okay.'

'Yes I did. He was as surprised as you could imagine, and also, although he didn't say so, a little hurt to discover that Annie had kept something so important from him. I know, Chaz wanted it kept out of the dressing room, but I don't think Paco saw it that way.'

'Does that mean he won't be a cooperative witness at the trial?'

'Guys!' Cheeky protested.

Sarah shook her head. 'Too late: it's overflowing and running downhill; unstoppable. Let them flush it out of their system.'

'It means,' Skinner continued, 'that if de Matteo asks him, "Do you believe that Mr Baker killed your wife?" he'll say that he doesn't. That's Paco's conclusion, not one I put into his head. You can ask him yourself on Monday.'

He fell silent as a waiter served their starter, three prawn cocktails and grapefruit for Sarah.

'You and Alex will be happy about that,' Sauce suggested, fork in hand. 'And about the coke that neither Annette nor Baker snorted.'

'Yes to the first and no to the second,' Skinner murmured. 'The defence isn't going to raise that.'

Haddock looked puzzled. 'Why the hell not?'

'You know the first rule of cross-examination? Sure you do; never ask a question unless you know the answer already. Sometimes it works the other way. You don't ask it because you know the answer.'

Sarah leaned forward. 'Are you saying what I think you are?'

He nodded.

Haddock understood. 'It was Paco's?' he asked quietly.

'Yes, and you can tell Sammy. It'll be de Matteo's choice. He can either raise it in direct examination, thereby trashing unnecessarily the reputation of a bereaved and honourable man, or he can ignore it, knowing that we will too.'

'You don't see Paco being involved in any way?'

'If I did, son, I'd have proved it by now. No, he's a victim too; one out of five.'

'Five? How do you work that out, Chief?'

'Simple.' He held up his left hand, as a fist, then extended the thumb. 'One, Annette Bordeaux, murdered.' The index finger. 'Two, Paco Fonter, widowed.' The second finger. 'Three, Chaz Baker, framed as her killer.' The ring finger. 'Four, Sammy Pye, detective chief inspector.' The little finger. 'Five, Sauce Haddock, detective sergeant, the last two having been set up as the instruments by whom an innocent man was to be put away.'

'I don't feel like a victim,' Haddock protested.

'Do you feel the same confidence in your case as you did last Sunday?' Skinner asked. 'Or has the first glimmer of doubt crept into that large detective's brain of yours?'

'Cheeky's right; let's talk about something else,' the young DS said, briskly. 'Who's supposed to win the game this afternoon? There's a woman coming round the tables with betting slips. Who should I back?'

'My sons are Motherwell supporters, like their dad,' Sarah told him. 'I'll have to place bets for them.'

Skinner nodded. 'Me too; no choice, it's in my blood.'

Haddock looked to his right, at his partner. 'Well?'

'There's one rule I've always had,' she confessed, 'ever since I was a wee girl: never bet against Grandpa.'

Each of them took a slip from the uniformed woman when she reached their table, and filled them in as they waited for the main course to be served. Skinner bet on a scoring draw then wrote the name Jimmy Pike in the 'First goal-scorer' section.

'Why him?' Cheeky asked him.

'He'll be taking the penalties with Paco Fonter missing. Motherwell give away more penalties than any other team in the league and their goalie hasn't saved one all season.'

'How do you know all that?'

'It's called research, lass. I never go anywhere unless I'm well prepared for it. That's something I tried to drill into your other half's head, but from the look of him I was wasting my time.'

'No,' she said quietly, as her partner studied the match programme looking for inspiration for his bets. 'Everything stuck; be in no doubt about that. Some people quote Shakespeare, but not Sauce. He quotes Bob Skinner, all the time; you're his bible. When you left the force, he was heartbroken. Grandpa didn't really fix the table plan,' she confessed, 'I did. We were going to be seated with him and that man Rogozin. Sauce would probably have arrested them both just to impress you.'

Forty-Four

'Whose bright idea was it to let Flowers take the penalties?' Skinner grumbled to Grandpa McCullough as he followed him into the boardroom.

'Tank Bridges, I suppose,' his host replied. 'What are you complaining about? Your team won.'

'So did the bookie, thanks to fucking Flowers.' He scowled. 'Aiming a penalty kick at the goalie's belly button on the assumption that he'll dive! Jesus! Looks great if it works, but if the keeper just stands there and gathers it in . . . What a twat!'

'We're agreed on that,' McCullough said. 'Between you and me, Flowers won't be here after January. He's bad news in the dressing room, so I've told Cisco Serra to find him another club.' He sighed. 'I fear we could lose our star striker too. He doesn't want to go back to the penthouse, and I don't blame him. I don't think he wants any more to do with Scotland either.'

He picked up a bottle of sparkling water from a table by the wall on their right and offered it to Skinner. 'I assume you're driving, given your wife's condition.'

'Yes, thank you.' He accepted it and picked up a glass, as the other man poured himself orange juice from a jar.

'Want a pie? Prawn sandwich?'

'I don't think so, not after that lunch.'

'I know,' McCullough agreed, smiling. 'It seems to be a Scottish football tradition; catering in the boardroom at half-time and after the game. I don't understand it, but we keep it going because the other teams expect it. The same with the ladies going back to the hospitality suite rather than coming in here. It's completely non-PC but it still happens; Mia has her eye on it, though. She and Angela Renwick had their heads together after the last game. The board might be under pressure to make a change at the next meeting.'

Skinner looked around. The boardroom was crowded with directors of the visiting club and other guests. 'Young Sauce seems to have gone with them.'

'He's breaking me in gently, I think. Since he and young Cameron got together he's kept me at arm's length. This is actually the first time I've met him face to face. You may have had something to do with that situation, I guess.'

'I may have,' the former chief admitted, 'but Sauce is well smart enough to have figured it out for himself. Just as you're smart enough to know why it had to be. If you have any misgivings about him, lose them. The boy's a diamond. I'm not the only one who thinks that. He's a protégé of the new chief constable as well. She spotted him when he was a probationer; she's raised him from a fledgling, more or less. I made detective superintendent when I was thirty-six; Sauce will match that or beat it.'

'Then I'll make sure that no member of my family does anything that gets in his way,' McCullough promised. 'Just as the boy's been careful around me, young Cameron won't have anything to do with her mother or her aunt. My daughter is a fool, that's all. My sister, though, she's a total psychopath.

However, she won't be a problem for much longer; she has terminal brain cancer. And don't say you're sorry to hear that,' he added, 'for I'm not. I understand,' he went on, 'that you and Mia had a positive conversation about your son.'

'Yes, we did. I'm visiting Ignacio at Polmont on Monday. We can all make plans for him, but he has to agree with them.'

'Too true. If I can help . . . in a positive way, I promise you . . . then I will. Now,' McCullough looked directly at his guest, 'cards on the table, Bob. Why are you here?' he asked quietly.

'Chaz Baker,' Skinner replied. 'I'm helping Alex prepare his defence. I've seen most of the witnesses and I wanted to get a feel for this place.'

'In what way?'

'I don't know; just a sense of it, I think.'

'Is it telling you anything?'

'Nothing so far, I must admit.'

'Have you seen Paco?'

'Yes. Your fear of losing him, it's well founded. Will you try to keep him?'

'No, I wouldn't be that cruel. I'll let Serra find him a new club in the January window . . . he won't have to look far; I could name at least two who were sniffing around in the summer. He can go, Flowers will go, we'll sign three or four decent players with the money they bring in and we'll cut the overall wage bill at the same time.'

'The man Serra: Merrytown seems to have a strong connection with him,' Skinner observed.

McCullough shrugged. 'Nothing to do with me. I didn't know him from fucking Adam when I got involved. He's Dimitri's man, his fixer. I think he's a slimy little toerag, but he can get the deals done. Agents,' he muttered, 'they're a necessary evil, and not just in football. Have you met the clown that looked after Annette Bordeaux?'

'Yes. No comment.'

'Exactly.' He took a breath, then ventured, 'Is your daughter going to get Baker off?'

Skinner smiled, grimly. 'I'd put it another way. She intends to establish his innocence, preferably before the case gets to trial.'

'Is he innocent?'

'I believe so. I took a bit of convincing, but I do now. And so do you,' he added. 'You recommended my kid to his wife, and I don't think you did that as a casual favour.'

'No,' McCullough murmured. 'I recommended her along with two others, each for a different reason, hers being that I guessed you'd come as part of the package.' He paused. 'But they were at it, weren't they? Chaz and Annette, they were doing the business?'

'No. They were close, yes, but there was another reason for it. In a few hours you and the rest of the world will know what it was.'

His eyes narrowed very slightly as he contemplated the shock waves that would be created when the first copies of the Sunday edition of the *Saltire* hit the streets late that evening, and appeared on its website.

'When it does,' he continued, 'maybe that smug little twerp of a Solicitor General will begin to contemplate the possibility of being wrong, and focus on the three key questions. You know what they are, don't you?'

'Who did it and why; I guess they're two of them.'

'Yes, and the third is how. How the hell did he do it?'

'Any candidates for the first one?'

275

'I might have, but I'm stuck on question three. I wouldn't be saying unless I was sure of everything, and then I'd tell Sauce and his boss, nobody else.'

'Not me?' McCullough exclaimed. 'Not even a hint? I have a major interest in this. You wouldn't be here if you weren't looking for the answer within the club. If you're right, it'll have a hell of an impact.'

'That's just one line of inquiry,' Skinner said, then caught his companion's eye. 'One thing I have picked up on today. When you talk about the football club, Cameron, you don't sound like a minority investor. The fans, the press and the public see the Russian as the main man, but it doesn't sound that way to me. Nothing about you is ever as it seems, is it?'

McCullough laid his empty glass on the table. 'Go and check at Companies House,' he replied, evenly. 'It's all on the record there. Rogotron is the majority shareholder and Dimitri Rogozin is its owner.'

'He's a fucking balloon, man; we both know that.'

He glanced across the boardroom to where the Russian stood, deep in conversation with Tank Bridges, to whom Skinner had not been introduced. The assistant head coach's face was flushed, in contrast to the whiteness of his knuckles as he gripped his beer glass. As Skinner looked on, Rogozin turned on his heel and headed in his direction.

'Sir,' he exclaimed as he approached, 'it is a surprise to see you here today. Cameron did not tell me you were coming. Your lovely daughter; is she not with you? I would like to see her again.'

'Why?' Skinner asked, icily.

'Because she is a lovely lady, and because I wish to assure her again of my support for Baker.'

'You've already done that once; she got the message. Another meeting would not be appropriate.'

Rogozin grinned. 'Surely it is for her to decide whether to see me?'

There was a lascivious sneer in the man's expression that made Skinner wish that Rogozin himself had come after him in the car park.

'As I said, you saw her a week ago, when you ambushed us outside the police station in Edinburgh. You don't go near her again. End of discussion.'

The Russian moved closer to him. 'Is that a threat?' he hissed.

'Absolutely. Now back off, you're invading my space.'

'Dimitri,' McCullough said quietly. 'Behave yourself; I'm not having any more of your shit. Be warned, and leave us alone.'

Skinner noted Rogozin's instant deference. 'If you don't mind,' he said, 'now that your colleague understands the situation, there is one thing I'd like to ask him.'

'Then fire away, but do it quietly, Bob, please.'

'In a whisper. A couple of weeks ago, on a Thursday night, when Merrytown had a Europa League tie in Finland, you used the untenanted apartment below the penthouse block in the King Robert Village building. Why?'

Rogozin stared at him for several seconds. Skinner read his thoughts in his eyes; surprise, confusion and possibly a little fear.

'Who says I did?' he murmured, eventually.

'It's a secure building. Invisibility is difficult to pull off there.'

'Then my bizniz is none of your concern.'

'When I'm investigating, as a cop or now, as a civilian, I don't have concerns, I have questions.'

'Then I not answer. My bizniz is private.'

'Your privilege, for now. That may change. Seven days ago,'

Skinner continued, 'at eleven thirty-five in the morning, Annette Bordeaux's body was discovered in her apartment by a cleaner. She had been dead for a maximum of eighteen hours by then. In their investigation the police reviewed the security tapes around that period, looking at the movement into and out of the building around the time of the murder. I went a little further than that; I had a look at the footage that was shot on Saturday morning.'

He paused, his gaze locked once more on to the Russian's eyes, seeing them widen involuntarily. 'At nine a.m.,' he went on, 'the three occupants of the tenanted apartment, Mustard, Flowers and Pike, accompanied by Alice McDade, the club physio, left via the garage to join up with the squad at the Merrytown training complex, for the away weekend at Seamill.

'Just over one hour later, at eleven minutes past ten, you arrived in the underground car park, in a black Lexus, driven by the man who was known then as Grigor Yashin. You left him there and took the lift to the seventh floor, where you let yourself into the untenanted apartment with a key. At ten twenty, a call was made to the landline in the Fonters' penthouse from the phone in the untenanted apartment that you were by that time occupying. Half an hour later a second call was placed to that same number. Not unnaturally, there was no answer to either one. At two minutes past eleven, you left, just before Annette's' body was found.'

'Dimitri.' The low growl made Skinner glance to his right: Cameron McCullough's urbane mask had slipped and what had replaced it was full of menace.

'I haven't shared this with the police yet,' Skinner said, 'but when I'm ready I will. When I do, I'll tell them also that you flew into Scotland, not on that same morning, but twenty-four hours earlier, through Prestwick Airport. You picked up the Lexus there and checked into the Central Hotel in Glasgow, at twelve fifteen. What did you do after that, Mr Rogozin, in the twenty-two missing hours between then and turning up at King Robert Village? And what was between you and Annette Bordeaux?'

'Go fuck yourself!' the Russian hissed.

'You understand the question, then? That's good. Because there's more. As part of their thorough investigation into the murder my former colleagues looked at the victim's mobile phone records, and what they found was included in the report that was disclosed to my daughter. Almost everything there is accounted for, normal business and personal traffic, but there's one item that isn't.

'Several calls are shown as received from a UK number, all incoming; she never called the number back. It's a pay and go phone, one of these untraceable things that you can re-credit over the counter or at an ATM. The last call was registered at fifteen thirty-eight hours on the day Annette died. The one before that was made eight days earlier, when you were in Edinburgh, in the King Robert Village apartment.'

He paused and turned to McCullough. 'Cameron, I know that mobiles are frowned upon in here, but please, indulge me.' He took out his phone, selected a number, and pressed the red icon on the screen. A few seconds later, a ringtone sounded, muffled, from within Rogozin's jacket, until the call was discontinued.

'I could call Detective Sergeant Haddock in here right now,' Skinner said, 'but I won't, because it's his day off and young Cheeky wouldn't appreciate it if I broke into it.

'I'm not saying that you killed Annie,' he added, 'because you made those two calls after she was dead, and I haven't persuaded myself that you're smart enough to have done that as a smokescreen, but there's a lot of mystery surrounding her murder and you are part of it, no mistake.'

The Russian's normally handsome face was twisted into something that was anything but, eyes bulging in fury.

'I reckon you have forty-eight hours, tops,' his tormentor continued, 'to get your story right. Have a pleasant weekend. I'm sorry your team lost.'

Rogozin spat in his face, turned on his heel and stalked from the room. McCullough, enraged, made to pursue him, but Skinner held him back with one hand, reaching for his handkerchief with the other. Several faces in the room had turned towards them; almost as one, they looked away.

'I'm sorry about that wee drama,' he said. 'I hadn't planned to square him up here, but the opportunity was too good to miss.

'I don't know the story between you guys, Cameron,' he continued. 'Whatever it is, you want to distance yourself from him right now. I'm going to call Sammy Pye tonight, and I'm going to suggest that he calls the Russian vice-consul, who owes him one for handing over Grigor slash Afonin without a fuss, and ask him to have a background check done in Moscow on your colleague.'

'That's a hint you didn't need to drop, Bob. I'd run out of patience with him anyway. Dimitri's going to find that he's just resigned as chairman of Merrytown Football Club, and a lot more besides.'

Forty-Five

'What the hell's rattled his cage?' Sauce Haddock exclaimed as Dimitri Rogozin stormed through the hospitality room on his way to the exit.

'I don't know,' Sarah Grace said, 'but from the look he threw you, you won't have many invitations back here.'

'You're welcome any time you like, Sergeant,' Mia McCullough exclaimed. 'Your other half might be a director one day, you never know. Roll on the day, if it ends that misogynist boardroom men-only tradition.'

'No chance,' Cheeky declared. 'If I was on the board my firm would be barred from acting as the company's auditor and tax adviser. So please don't let that thought lodge in Grandpa's busy brain.'

'You think I have that much influence? If he did think about it he probably wouldn't tell me. Suppose he did, once he's made up his mind about something, that's it. Ladies in the boardroom, though, I'm working on that.'

'I wonder what was up with Rogozin?' Haddock murmured, still musing upon the man's furious exit.

'His team lost,' Sarah chuckled.

Mia shook her head. 'Truth is, Dimitri doesn't give a shit

whether Merrytown wins or loses. He's here for the prestige. Owning a football club's a status symbol for men like him in Russia.'

'Do I sense you don't like him?

'The man doesn't have a likeable bone in his body, Professor. You can make money, but you can't make class. You've met him, Sauce. What do you think?'

'I don't think,' Haddock replied. 'I'm a detective; I deal with the facts I see before me, and with the actions of individuals. Personal feelings about people could get in the way of my judgement, so I try not to have any.'

'Bob used to say the same,' Sarah admitted, 'but he never quite managed it. I remember two villains he dealt with in his time, Tony Manson and Jackie Charles: you may have heard of them. Manson was probably the more ruthless of the two, until somebody did him in; Bob had spent half his career pursuing him and yet there was something about the man that he liked . . . although he'd never admit it. Charles, on the other hand, he loathed. He had a party when he was put away.'

'Is he still away?' Cheeky asked.

'Yes. He's due for parole in the next couple of years. He'd better behave, though. If he steps out of line, retired or not, Bob will be after him.'

'He never caught Manson,' Mia said, quietly. 'I know, because my brother worked for him for a while. I imagine he's told you.'

'Yes. Sorry, I forgot.' Sarah fell silent, realising that she had stepped into a part of Mia McCullough's past that she had been unwilling to revisit.

'If you really twist my arm,' Haddock exclaimed, breaking the tension between them, 'I will admit that I don't like Rogozin either. I've met him, and I was watching when he tried to ambush Alex outside our office. Whatever happened in there, I have a fair idea who was involved in it.'

Sarah looked at Mia. 'He wouldn't do anything silly, would he? Like wait for Bob outside?'

'Much as I'd love to see it,' Mia replied, 'that's not going to happen. He may be an arrogant slimeball, but he's not suicidal.'

Forty-Six

'How did your introduction to the football culture go?' Sammy Pye asked his sergeant as he walked into the office. It was eight twenty and the DCI had been at his desk for half an hour. As always, BBC-TV's *Breakfast* was in full red-hued swing on the wall-mounted television: as always, it was drawing little attention.

'The game was a bore,' Haddock said, 'but the social side was fascinating. How about your weekend?'

Pye poured a little milk into his builder-strength tea. 'It was quiet, until Saturday night when I had a call from the big man.'

The DS switched on the kettle and spooned some Colombian instant coffee into the Santa Claus mug that Cheeky had given him nine months before and that he had used ever since, season through season. 'About what? Did he give you a run-through of the game?'

'No, he put me off my dinner.' He grimaced. 'He's been taking a broader look at the Annette Bordeaux case than we did, Sauce. My back's still tender from all the pats it's had over the last week from Rocco de Matteo, Mary Chambers, the chief herself. Mario McGuire even phoned from his holiday in Italy to say "Well done" for wrapping it up so quickly.'

284

'We did,' Haddock pointed out as he stirred his mug.

'Yes, we did, and as things stand I am still reasonably confident that we'll get a conviction, even with the bombshell about Baker and the victim being half-siblings. But Bob's as confident that we won't. Between you and me, he's starting to piss me off.'

The DS stared at him; Pye's unflappability was legendary.

'Maybe it was personal with him,' the DCI went on, 'after his run-in with the Russians and the thing in the car park, but he's come up with stuff that passed us by, because we were so sure of our case against Baker that we went for an early winner.'

'Enough of the football analogies please, Sammy. What did he say?'

Succinctly, Pye related the substance of his call from Skinner and the information he had uncovered about Rogozin's movements, his use of the untenanted apartment and his calls to Annette from the landline and the pay and go mobile.

When he was finished, Haddock grinned. 'That explains why he went storming out of the Merrytown boardroom like his arse was on fire.'

'The big man didn't mention any of this to you?'

'No, or I'd have called you myself on Saturday. We talked about the case, but in broader terms. He thinks that Baker's been set up and that we have too, that we've been shown a line of evidence and reeled it in exactly as we were meant to.'

He sampled his coffee. 'Oh yes, and he said we should all forget about the cocaine, because Alex is going to. It was Paco's, and he's not about to lay any more grief on the guy.'

'He's all for laying it on Rogozin, though.' Pye shook his head, slowly. 'I dunno,' he grumbled 'it's as if he'd never chucked it. He more or less ordered me to ask the Russian consulate to look into the guy's past in his homeland, to see if there's anything interesting in it.'

'Is he saying that Rogozin killed Annette?'

'Not flat out, but he's pointing us at some sort of link between them. I'm not sure it'll help Alex and him, though. If that was the "secret" in Annette's text, it offers a new scenario. She tells Chaz, he's outraged, they have a fight and he throttles her.'

'Maybe.'

'You don't sound convinced.'

'That's because it isn't convincing,' Haddock countered.

His boss eyed him, quizzically. 'Are you losing faith?'

'I don't operate on the basis of faith, gaffer, and with respect, neither should you. Classic definition: faith is based on spiritual conviction rather than proof. The evidence, the proof, of Baker's guilt is still there. But it's so strong that it's closed our minds to anything else. Mine is open again.'

He paused, his eye caught by something on the TV screen. *Breakfast* had reached the Scottish news opt-out section. The presenter faced the camera presenting the day's hot story earnestly and clearly, but the detective sergeant was ignoring her words, concentrating instead on the scene behind her, the usual live backdrop fed from a camera on top of the BBC building, of morning traffic flowing across Glasgow's famous Squinty Bridge.

Something was happening in the river below: two small boats, one with police Day-Glo markings, floated side by side pointing upstream, away from the camera. The figures on board were discernible as they tried to secure something in the water.

Haddock gestured with his cup. 'What's going on there, d'you think?'

'I don't know,' Pye replied, 'but I know what it looks like.'

Forty-Seven

'If I had known about you sooner,' Bob Skinner whispered to an empty room, 'what would I have done?'

Not a day went by without him thinking about his oldest son, conceived in Scotland, born in Spain, to a woman he could have locked up but instead had advised to get out of town for her own safety.

As he had admitted to her, he had asked himself that question many times, but he had been less certain about the answer than he had suggested. If he had been confronted with Mia's pregnancy, questions would have been asked within the police service, and his answers might have been less than convincing, career-threatening even.

Had he told her to leave for her protection, or for his own? Both, possibly. If she had come back, would he have been able to confront the issue? He hoped that he would, but feared that he might not.

It's all academic now, he thought as the tall young man, with his physical frame and some of his facial features, came into the private office that the Governor of the Polmont Institution allowed them to use for their meetings. The prison authorities recognised that if the inmate population discovered that Ignacio

Centelleos was Bob Skinner's son, it might have put him at risk, and so the secret would be kept, until, in a few weeks, he stepped through the gate in the clothes of freedom.

'How are you?' his father asked.

'I am very well,' Ignacio replied. 'You look a little tired, though, Padre.'

He laughed. 'I can't get my head round that. You make me sound like a priest.'

'It comes most naturally to me. Honestly, I'm not sure what to call you.'

'I've told you; call me what you like. Everyone else does.'

'Then Padre it will be . . . Padre. It suits me and it reminds me of what I am: Spanish.'

'That's how you think of yourself, is it? As far as I know you're one hundred per cent British.'

'Not a hundred per cent Scottish?'

'No,' Skinner replied. 'I had an Irish great-grandmother; my mother's middle name was Niamh, after her. On your mother's side . . . I doubt if she knows for sure.'

'Mamma has never talked to me about her family,' Ignacio said. 'I asked her all the time I was growing up, but she never did. I didn't understand until I met my grandmother.'

'I'm not going to talk about the Watsons either, son. But I did meet Mia's father, your grandfather, once. He seemed like a decent man, but the Spreckleys, your granny's side, they drove him out.'

'And your family? All I know is Alexis, and you.'

'That's true,' he conceded, conscious yet again of the fact that he and his son were strangers to each other.

'Okay, quick rundown: your grandfather was a lawyer, a successful one; he fought in the war, in special operations that left their mark on him for the rest of his life. He never spoke of that, but he was decorated for it by the state, given a very important medal. Your grandmother, my mother, was an alcoholic . . .' he paused, and grinned, sadly. 'You didn't have a lot of luck in the granny department, son.'

'It seems not,' Ignacio agreed.

'On the other hand, further back than that you're descended from another war hero. But that's old family history; I'll tell you everything I know when we have more time. We have current matters to talk about. You're due for release soon. When that happens, you'll have some decisions to make. First of those is where you want to live, even if it's only short-term. I'd like it to be with me.'

'I know, because you've said already, but are you sure you have room? How does your wife feel? What will your children think?'

'Sarah is fine with it. If she wasn't, I'd tell you and we'd make another arrangement. The boys? They'll be intrigued; I've told them about you, although not about where you are just now. They're gobsmacked by the idea of a new older brother.

'As for accommodation, here's what I'm thinking: no, it's what I'm going to do regardless of your decision. My garage sits beside the house and it's big enough for three cars. I'm going to build above it and create an apartment. I'll show you the plans if you like, they're pretty neat. It'll have an open-plan living area, an en suite bedroom and a small study. When it's done, that's where you'll live.'

Ignacio looked at him. 'Padre, that is very good of you, but are you sure? You hardly know me. Look where I am, look what I've done. You really want me alongside your children?'

'Everything you've done,' he answered, 'you did for your

mother. You're here because you defended her. The trouble you were in in Spain, you did that for her as well, and she was reckless enough to allow it.'

Skinner sensed a ripple of tension in the young man. 'I know,' he said, quickly 'she's still your mother and you love her. I'm not going to condemn her. I know more than you do about her past and about her childhood, and I'll tell you she's done bloody well to survive it all, let alone wind up as comfortable as she is now. If you want to live with her,' he added, 'that's open to you as well.'

'She says if I want they will give me a place of my own.' He smiled. 'But she said also that I should choose to live with you if I can. She said it is time you put some effort into our relationship.'

'That's bloody rich,' Skinner chuckled, 'given that she concealed it from me for all those years. So,' he continued, 'you'll live in Gullane?'

'Yes,' Ignacio agreed, 'thank you; but I want to work,' he added.

His father frowned. 'We, Mia and I, we'd both like you to go to university. You've shown your flair for chemistry, in very practical if not very legal ways.'

'I don't want to study chemistry;' he said, abruptly. 'Already I've had enough of that in my life.' He hesitated, suddenly concerned. 'Padre, me having done what I've done, me being in this place, does it mean I can never be a cop?'

'You want to be a police officer?' Skinner exclaimed.

'Yes. I think that I do. But I guess that's not possible now.'

'Anything's possible, Ignacio,' he replied, 'if you really want it to happen. The fact is, criminal convictions aren't an automatic bar to you being a policeman. Every applicant is vetted and judgements are made individually. The recruiters look into their background, their education, their beliefs and their past, and they look at close family members as well. Having me in support of your application, that will help, no question, but the selection process is complex. There are written exams, physical tests and interviews.'

'Are you really saying that I can't?'

'No I'm not, but I am saying that my support alone won't get you automatic entrance.'

'But you would support me?'

'Of course,' Skinner said, firmly, 'but my very strong advice is that you go to university and get yourself a degree.'

'What would I study?'

'Whatever you like, mostly. I have an MA, from Glasgow. It's a general degree and you could do the same; you could read economics, philosophy, politics, or you could do the obvious and study Spanish. Do you have any other languages, apart from English?'

'I studied Italian at school; it's pretty easy for Spanish people.'

'There you are then. Degree-level fluency in two European languages would get you big points in the selection process. Did you complete your Spanish school exams?'

'Yes, I have Bachiller in six subjects, with distinction in five, maths, chemistry, English, Italian and Spanish. While I have been in here, I have sat Scottish qualifications in the languages, and I am doing maths this year.'

'Great,' Skinner exclaimed. 'I'll try Edinburgh and Heriot Watt Universities with what you got in Spain. The university term hasn't started yet; we might even squeeze you in this year. Do you have your school certificates?'

He nodded. 'Mamma has them.'

'Then let's have a go. Are you up for it?'

Ignacio beamed. 'Are you serious?'

'You bet I am. And I know people in both universities. If there are vacancies, I'll find them.'

'But Padre, I don't get out of here until November.'

Skinner winked at his son; his enthusiasm was more fired than it had been in months. 'I know people on the Parole Board too. If you have to wear an electronic tag to go to classes for the first few weeks, so what?

'Look,' he said, 'don't let me railroad you into something you don't want to do, whether we can get you into university next session or next year, will you consider it?'

'I still want to be a cop.'

'A degree will give you a better chance of acceptance.'

'Then yes, I will consider university. But,' he continued, 'I still want to have a job. I need to earn my own money. I have done since I was fifteen.'

'I know that only too well.'

Ignacio grinned. 'I admit it, I shouldn't have produced crystal meth; it was wrong. I should have stuck to making poppers; they're legal in most places . . . and much easier to produce.'

'That career is definitely over,' his father said. 'Alex and I between us, we'll find you a part-time job, no problem. What do you . . .'

He broke off in mid-question as Jimmy Buffett sang 'Margaritaville' in his pocket. He retrieved it and saw that Sammy Pye was calling. 'Yes?' he said, impatiently, as he answered.

His son watched him as he listened, saw his mouth drop open in surprise, saw his eyes widen, heard him whisper, 'You're fucking kidding!' and then, 'Who's the SIO?' a question he did not understand. Whatever the answer was it must have pleased him for he nodded and said, 'That's good news. I'd better make contact. Thanks, Sammy.'

'What was that?' Ignacio asked.

'An ex-colleague, a friend; he was letting me know that a man's body was fished out of the River Clyde in Glasgow this morning: live on TV apparently. They don't think he got there by accident.'

'How does it affect you?'

'Because I know him, and given what's passed between us over the last week or so, if I was in charge of the investigation, I'd regard myself as a suspect.'

Forty-Eight

'Can you say for certain that I'm looking at a murder here?' Detective Inspector Lottie Mann asked the pathologist as he knelt beside the body of a man, in a white tent that had been erected on the south bank of the River Clyde, on a patch of grass next to the Scottish Television building, the smaller neighbour of the BBC Scotland headquarters.

'No,' Dr Graeme Bell admitted, 'not until I get him along to the mortuary and open him up to establish the cause of death. All I can say at the moment is that there is a depressed fracture of the skull, above and just behind the left ear, that would probably not have been survivable for more than a few seconds. Even if there's no water in his lungs, I can't go firm on homicide without the forensic people ruling out the possibility of him having jumped into the river and hit his head on something during the fall. How they're going to do that without knowing where he went in, I have no idea.'

'Could he have jumped off the Clyde Arc itself?'

'The what?' Dr Bell grunted as he pushed himself upright, looking up at the woman detective. He was not a short man, but she was the taller of the two by at least three inches.

'The Squinty Bridge,' she said. 'That's its real name, although they might as well change it, 'cos most Weegies don't have a clue that it is.'

'Again, I won't know until I examine him. If he went off the middle of the span, the fall would have been considerable and there would be injuries consistent with that sort of impact, even on water. But,' he murmured, 'I suppose that if you were going to jump you'd want to make a good job of it.'

'This one didnae jump, Graeme,' Detective Sergeant Dan Provan chuckled.

The pathologist turned to him. He knew the veteran from many crime scenes, and tried to remember a time when he had not looked to be in his fifties, and when he had not worn a creased sports jacket and shiny trousers, and when his moustache had not appeared to be stained by nicotine.

'Regale us, Daniel,' he said, managing not to make the mistake of sounding patronising.

'The guy's in a Savile Row suit and a thousand-quid overcoat. He has car keys in his pocket, and he's wearing a diamond-studded Patek Philippe watch that's worth fifty K if it's worth a fiver, and he's got well over a grand in cash in his wallet. He didnae chuck all that into the river in a fit of depression, trust me.'

Mann smiled. 'My colleague has a point, Doctor.' She had worked with Provan almost continuously since her days as a detective constable; he had been a DS throughout that time; he had no ambition to rise higher and had been untroubled when she passed him in rank. In truth he was more than a colleague; he was her best friend, and as a single mother she found herself relying on him more and more in her private life as well as at work.

'As for where he went in,' the dishevelled DS continued, 'yes it is a big river, but the fact that he's got a couple of chips from the Garrick Casino in his trouser pocket along wi' the Lexus key gives us a good place to start looking.'

Graeme Bell nodded. 'Sometimes I wonder what you need me for,' he observed.

'Sometimes I wonder the same. I'll bet you one o' yon casino chips you don't find any water in his lungs. Look at his eyes. They're wide open; you can still see the shock from having the back of his head caved in. He was hit, and he was heaved into the water off the walkway.'

'A mugging, you reckon?'

'Doctor, please,' the DS sighed. 'Our muggers might no' be the brightest, but they're not completely daft. A grand left in his wallet and a diamond-studded wristwatch? No, this was not theft. If you want my opinion, it was calculated, premeditated murder.'

'Mmm. Want to go the whole way, Dan, and give me the time of death?'

'Let me see.' Provan checked his watch. 'Just gone half ten: ye'll find he's been dead for eight or nine hours. It was quiet and dark when he was attacked, around about two in the morning earliest. If it had been the day before, he'd have drifted further or been seen sooner. Any later and he wouldnae have made it this far. Graeme, you and I have been fishin' bodies out of this fuckin' river since it was a stream. You know I'm right.'

'I guess I do,' the pathologist conceded. 'Okay, let me go and prove it.' He was starting to peel off his forensic suit even before he stepped out of the tent.

'What else do his pockets tell us, Dan?' Mann asked as he left.

'There's a phone,' he began, 'but after being in the water it's completely fucked. His wallet, though, that tells us a lot.

According to his credit cards and to a Garrick Casino membership card, his name is Dimitri Rogozin. There's another couple of cards in here, with photographs on them; could be a driving licence, could be an ID card, probably are. But I cannae tell which is which because they're in Russian. There's also what looks like a key card for a hotel room. It doesn't show the name of the hotel, but this guy won't be in a dosshouse, so I'd start looking at the Central, given that it's just up the road from the casino.'

'Dimitri Rogozin,' she repeated when he was finished. 'Why do I know that name?'

'Because your wee Jake supports his football team,' Provan replied, 'on account of his Uncle Dan not allowing him to fall into the trap of supporting either Rangers or Celtic. Didn't I take him there on Saturday, to see them lose to Motherwell, and wasn't he a sad lad when I brought him home? From where we were sitting, we could see this fella in the front row of the directors' box, although I grant you, he looks a bit different now.'

'Of course,' the DI acknowledged. 'There's something else I recall about Merrytown, for all I couldn't care less about the game. Their manager's been charged with killing their star player's wife.'

'Exactly. We'd better get in touch with the SIO in that inquiry. The two might not be linked, but it'll be of interest to him.'

'I suppose it will. It happened in Edinburgh, and Sammy Pye's the DCI there, so he's probably the man. Tell you what, Dan, why don't you head up to the Central Hotel and check the register, while I call him.'

'I'll do that.' He paused in the doorway of the tent. 'By the way, Rogozin wasnae the only guy I recognised in the directors' box on Saturday. Bob Skinner was there too. I wondered why at the time, and then I saw the story in yesterday's papers about the guy Baker and the woman he's supposed tae have murdered actually being half-brother and half-sister. It said that Skinner's daughter's his lawyer. Any bets he's involved?'

'Oh shit,' Mann sighed. 'I wonder if I could persuade Sammy that this death is so closely tied to the Bordeaux murder that he should take this one on too?'

Provan laughed. 'I remember thinking that the lad's ambitious,' he said, 'but I don't recall thinking that he's daft.'

Forty-Nine

'Say that again please, gaffer,' Sauce Haddock murmured. 'I'm not sure I believe my ears.'

'I know,' Pye agreed. 'I felt much the same, but big Lottie doesn't do stand-up. Dimitri Rogozin is dead. What you spotted on the telly news earlier on, that was his body being taken out of the Clyde.'

'Bloody hell! What are they calling it? Natural causes, suicide or the other?'

'A catastrophic skull fracture doesn't sound too natural. Subject to post-mortem, they've got it down as murder. Maybe that minder of his wasn't just for show.'

'Maybe not. Maybe he wouldn't have been any use anyway. Cheeky heard from her grandpa that he spat in big Bob's face on Saturday before he stormed off in a rage.'

'I don't think we'll put him in the list of suspects, not just yet. Mind you,' he added, 'it would be nice if he had an alibi.'

'It must be linked to Russia, surely,' Haddock said. 'There isn't enough money in Scottish football for anybody to get killed over it, and that was all he was involved in here.' He frowned. 'What's Lottie's next move?'

'It's my next move,' Pye told him. 'Her DCI's in the Canary

Islands, so she can't dump it on him, but it does need to go up the line, higher than my rank, though. I've said that given the link I'll take that responsibility on board. If the DCC was here and not in Italy I'd go straight to him. In his absence, and with DCS Marlowe not being there either, I'll have to take it to the chief herself.'

'And the Russians,' Haddock pointed out. 'Somebody will have to tell the consulate.'

'You're right. As it happens, I had a call from the vice-consul fifteen minutes ago,' Pye said. 'Rogozin has no criminal record at home, but there is a file on him. Like we suspected, he was a wannabe, a bullshitter with no links to organised crime.

'However,' he added heavily, 'he was the subject of a police investigation, into a sexual offence. A female journalist accused him of date rape; she said that he drugged her and had sex when she was unable to do anything about it.'

'Was he charged?'

'No. He denied it. There was forensic evidence but he claimed it was consensual and that he'd paid her. He claimed that she'd demanded more money and got stroppy when he refused.'

'Is the file still open?'

'In theory,' the DCI replied, 'but the woman disappeared. He was investigated over that too, but there was nowhere to go really, no evidence of further contact, no evidence of any threat.'

'How about his business?' Haddock suggested. 'Might there be grounds there?'

'Now that is interesting. His travel and leisure company, Rogotron, did okay when it started, but it wasn't a market leader or anything like it, not until around ten years ago when a Geneva registered company called Vachepie acquired a fifty per cent stake, injected capital, and the business took off. Two years after that there was a further share issue to fund the acquisition of a holiday village in Turkey; as a result, Rogozin's share was diluted to forty-five per cent.'

'Who owns what's its name?' the DS asked.

'I don't know, and neither do the Russians. The point is that Rogozin doesn't actually own seventy-five per cent of the football club, only around one-third.'

The DS scratched his chin. 'Suppose whoever owns the Swiss investor wanted rid of Rogozin, and couldn't be bothered to buy him out?'

'Exactly what I was thinking, Sauce, but let's not get ahead of ourselves. I have to call the big boss, Mrs Steele, and someone else, who's going to be as surprised as we are . . . I hope.'

Fifty

'Yes, sir, how can I help you today?'

The receptionist gave him a look of appraisal as he stepped into the foyer. There was a very slight upward movement of her right eyebrow, but as he stepped towards the counter a glossy smile greeted him.

Technically, Dan Provan was not a Glaswegian; he had been born in Cambuslang, a town just outside the city's southern boundary, and had lived there all his life. But he felt like one: he loved Glasgow and knew its heart like the back of his hand, and its outer communities, rough and smooth . . . rarely did the two overlap . . . almost as well.

He knew its icons also, and took most of them for granted. He had commuted by train for most of his life, using his car mainly for off-duty outings, and had walked past the Central Hotel every day, on his way out of the station from which it had taken its name, before the addition of the Grand prefix, but only rarely had he set foot inside, to the police dinners that he was sometimes persuaded or shamed into attending.

The woman's accent was probably Maryhill, he reckoned, but trying hard to be Bearsden. He read the oval badge on her jacket and saw that her name was Krystle; he had met a few of those in his time, even locked one up. An iconic TV series of the eighties had left its mark on a generation of young Scots. *Another* Dynasty *wean*, he thought. *If she's got a brother his name's Blake, for sure.*

He showed her his warrant card. 'Polis, hen,' he said. 'DS Provan, Dan tae you. I'm tryin' to place somebody and I'm wondering if he was a guest here.' He flipped the key card, encased in a plastic slip, from his breast pocket. 'Is this one of yours.'

'Yes, it is. If I can take it out, I can tell yis whose.' Definitely Maryhill.

'I think I know anyway, but go ahead, to confirm it.'

Krystle slipped the card from its envelope and scanned in. 'That belongs to Mr Rogozin,' she announced. She pronounced the name differently from the way Provan had read it, with equal emphasis on each of the three syllables. 'Do you want me to see if he's in?'

'No, Ah know where he is. I am going to need to see the duty manager though.'

The receptionist's eyes showed a mixture of concern and uncertainty. 'I'll see if she's available,' she murmured.

'She'll be available, Krystle,' he said. 'Trust me on that.'

She picked up a phone on the counter, glancing over her shoulder at two people who had come into the hotel since Provan, and were waiting in line behind him. Both were male, half his age, business suited and each was wheeling a small suitcase. The detective saw them reflected in the mirror behind the reception desk, saw that one was frowning and shifting impatiently from one foot to the other. Just off an early train from London, both of them, he guessed.

As Krystle spoke quietly into the phone he glanced over his shoulder. 'Won't be a minute,' he told them.

'I hope not,' the restless one replied. 'We have an important meeting and we don't want to be late.'

Provan glared at him. 'There's worse things,' he growled. 'You could be fuckin' dead, like the guy Ah've just left.'

A gasp from behind the counter told him that Krystle had overheard. He nodded in her direction. 'Sorry, hen,' he murmured.

'That's terrible,' she said. 'Ms Kilmarnock's on her way.'

As she spoke, another woman came into the foyer through an archway on the right of the station concourse entrance, beyond the concierge desk. She wore a pale grey suit; the cut was different from that of the receptionist, but the material was the same; corporate colours, Provan guessed.

They shook hands as she introduced herself: 'Wilma Kilmarnock, deputy general manager.' Provan followed her to a seated area, away from the desk. 'You're enquiring about Mr Rogozin,' she began; her pronunciation was the same as Krystle's.

'He's a regular visitor?' Provan asked.

'Yes,' she replied. 'He stays with us often. Krystle said you've found his key card. Thank you for returning it, but . . . I'm surprised it's a detective sergeant who's handing it in. Should I read anything into that?'

'I'm afraid ye should. You can read the fact that he's dead. His body was found about three hours ago, bobbin' down the river heading for Greenock.'

'How awful,' the manager murmured. 'How did he . . . ? Was he . . . ? Did he . . . ?'

'Did he?' the DS repeated. 'No, he didnae jump. Was he? Yes. He was attacked, almost certainly on the walkway. We have to wait for post-mortem findings to be sure, but we believe he was killed there and dumped into the river.'

'Do you know when?'

'We're looking at the early hours of this morning. Can you tell me when he was last seen here?'

'Yesterday evening,' she replied, at once. 'I saw him myself. He was in the bar, with a woman.'

'Another guest?'

'No, I'm sure she wasn't. I don't always know our guests by sight, but I was in this area when she arrived, just after seven o'clock. I heard her ask reception where the bar was; if she'd been a guest, she'd have known. She was directed to the Tempus Bar. I was there myself a little later and I saw her with Mr Rogozin.'

'What sort of woman was she?' he asked, tentatively.

'What do you mean? Spit it out, Sergeant.'

'Could she have been a . . . an escort girl? I'm sorry to be blunt, but . . .'

'That's okay; I understand. You don't want to imply that the Grand Central Hotel is a knocking shop. It certainly isn't, but we're not blind either. Mr Rogozin has had a few female visitors during his visits to us, exactly the type you suggest. Look,' Kilmarnock said, 'there isn't a lot we can do about it. They never stay for breakfast.'

'I'm not getting at you,' Provan assured her.

'Like I said, understood; however the woman who was here last night wasn't one of those. She was forty-something, small and dumpy; very well dressed, designer clothes, but she did nothing for them.'

'How was the atmosphere between them? Could ye tell?'

'I didn't observe them for long, but I'd say for sure it was tense. She was leaning close to him, and it looked as if she was saying something that he didn't want to hear.'

'I know that Rogozin,' he copied the hotel pronunciation, 'went out later. Do you know, or can you find out, if they left together?'

'No problem; Kerry, our evening receptionist, will know. She misses nothing. Hold on, while I call her.'

Provan waited as she took out her phone; he looked around the formidable space, musing over his casual disinterest over so many years. It had been refurbished expensively and with care since his last visit, in the last year of the last century. He smiled as he entertained a momentary fantasy of surprising Lottie by taking her for a drink in the Tempus Bar. *Probably only the one*, he admitted to himself. *It'll be out of my price range. She deserves it, though; lassie's had no real life since she got wise to that arsehole she married.*

Lottie saw him, he knew, as friend, mentor and confidant. His feelings for her were rather more complicated.

'She left alone,' Wilma Kilmarnock announced, breaking into his thoughts. 'Mr Rogozin left later, with someone else. He had a second visitor, Kerry said, at eight o'clock on the dot. A man; she described him as late fifties, possibly into his sixties, but fit-looking. "Vigorous", was how she put it.'

'Did she say any more about him?' Provan asked.

'Quite a bit: I told you, she misses nothing. She said he was average height, well tanned, and with a full head of silver hair. She remembered his eyes too: blue and intense, she said. He wore an open-necked shirt, white, and a navy-blue blazer with a crest on the pocket.'

'Any chance you've got him on CCTV?'

'It's possible, but I can't guarantee a facial shot. If I don't have, you will, whatever way they went: there are surveillance cameras covering both Hope Street and Gordon Street.'

'Did Kerry say how they were together? Did they look like they were going for a night out or an argument?'

'She said that Mr Rogozin looked a bit agitated; the other man was just, well, normal.'

'Did she have any idea what the badge on his blazer night have been?'

'No, sorry.'

Provan had, though: average height, tan, silver hair. His mind went back to Merrytown Stadium, and the front row of the directors' box, where the Russian had been in prime position, with the Renwick woman, the chief executive, on his left; on his right another female, forties, slim, trim, blonde, and next to her, a man: silver hair, tan, blazer.

The detective sergeant was not a fanatical follower of the South Lanarkshire club, but he knew the basics, that it was wholly owned by Dimitri Rogozin and another man, a bloke from Dundee, whose name was known by CID cops across Scotland.

'What was Grandpa McCullough doin' here on a Sunday?' he whispered, oblivious at that moment to Wilma Kilmarnock's presence.

'Can I see his room?' he asked, dragging himself back to the business at hand.

'Of course, come this way.'

She led him through the arch and into the main body of the hotel, stopping at the lift doors. 'Mr Rogozin has the JFK Suite,' she volunteered. 'He's a great admirer of President Kennedy and asks for it every time he's here.'

'Old Jack's lost a fan,' Provan said, 'no' that he'll be bothered. He never got on wi' the Russians from what I've heard.'

She opened the door with the key that the DS had brought

with him. 'I'm impressed that it still works,' he remarked. 'I wish his phones did.'

'Phones plural?'

'He had two. We've got no idea why, and we're no' going to find out now.'

The suite was plush and comfortable, with a small sitting room, a bedroom with a further sitting area by the window and a bathroom off. 'Has it been cleaned today?' Provan asked, as they stood in the bedroom.

'Yes, it has been.'

'Ye can tell even though it was never slept in?'

'Yes,' Ms Kilmarnock replied. 'The toiletries have been replenished and the towels are fresh.'

'That's a hell of a size of a bed; it's bigger than my garden shed.'

'This is an international hotel, Sergeant,' she reminded him. 'That's what our guests expect, especially the Americans.'

Provan made a face that hinted at his feelings towards Americans and, possibly, foreigners in general. Under the gaze of the late thirty-fifth president, depicted in a mural, he began to inspect the room.

Rogozin's wardrobe was not extensive, he had travelled with a second suit, a pair of dark trousers and the Merrytown FC blazer that he had worn at the match two days before. McCullough's had been blue, but the Russian's was a deep claret shade.

Shirts, socks and underwear were all in a drawer below the hanging garments. 'He had his clothes laundered daily,' the manager volunteered, anticipating a question.

'And his money too, probably,' Provan grunted.

'Not here,' Ms Kilmarnock chuckled. 'Everything went on

his tab and that was settled with a credit card in the name of the football club.'

There was a safe in the wardrobe, sitting above the drawer, with a number pad and a small screen. 'Can you open it?' the detective asked.

'In theory, no. In practice, there's a re-set code.' She leaned past him, blocking his view of the screen and keyed in four numbers: the rectangular door swung open. 'Help yourself.'

There was a document case inside. The sergeant drew it out and unzipped it, then emptied its contents on to the bed: passport, flight documents carrying a Prestwick Airport stamp, a Hertz car rental agreement, a folder of documents, in Russian, and an iPad, the large size Pro model.

Provan picked up the tablet. Jake Mann had the Mini version . . . a tenth birthday present from 'Uncle' Dan . . . and so he knew how to awaken it. He held his finger on the lock button until the Apple logo appeared in the screen then waited until it booted up.

'Probably nae use without a password,' he muttered, but scrolled right nonetheless as the screen instructed. To his surprise, it opened and a list of apps appeared. He studied the icons: some were standard, Settings, Weather, Clock, Newsstand, others were not, but all of them appeared to be games.

He hit the email symbol; there were five messages in the inbox, but they were all in Russian script, undecipherable to him. He closed it and opened the browser; two windows had been opened and left for Rogozin's last session. He clicked in one then, as images appeared, closed it very quickly, realising that his guide was looking over his shoulder.

'Sorry about that,' he said. 'It seems that our man was big on the hardcore porn sites.'

She shrugged. 'You'd be amazed what we find lying about in hotels. There's quite a lot I could tell you about famous people. One or two are on our blacklist; we don't take their bookings any more.'

He moved on, opening the iTunes library. Its late owner's tastes were surprisingly conservative: Il Divo, Alfie Boe and Andre Rieu. Provan, an unreconstructed rocker, winced and closed the window.

The photos that the Russian had stored on his iPad were arranged into named folders, but again the tags were in Cyrillic script. Provan opened the first, and saw a sequence of still images and videos of holiday resorts, all shot in glorious sunshine. He could only guess at the locations, but wherever they were the terrain was green and lush and the beaches were so golden and rock-free that he guessed they might have been artificial.

The second collection had been shot in Las Vegas. All the iconic Strip images were there and several selfies, showing Rogozin in garish tourist clothing and usually with a woman on his arm, but never the same one twice. The detective felt a twinge of jealousy; for years he had wanted to go to Sin City, and had even made a couple of calls to Barrhead Travel, only to pull out at the last minute, imagining Lottie's booming laugh in his ear.

The third folder was football: Merrytown in action, and sometimes inaction, at grounds around Scotland and, once, in Ireland, from a flag that flew on the grandstand. A Europa League qualified that summer, the supporter in Provan recalled.

He clicked on the fourth folder, closed it at once, then opened it again when he realised that Wilma Kilmarnock was no longer standing behind him. It contained thumbnails of a woman and in every one she was naked. She was slim and slender, with skin the colour of coffee. He opened the first to full screen, and went through them one by one. As he did so, the feeling of unease within him grew to revulsion.

In each shot the subject was averting her eyes; it struck him that he had never seen anyone so ill at ease in a photograph. And yet the woman with the desperately sad eyes was, in another context, one of the most alluring faces on the planet.

Even in such bizarre, obscene circumstances, it was impossible not to recognise Annette Bordeaux.

Fifty-One

'Have the media been advised yet?' Skinner asked, without preamble, as he stepped into Sammy Pye's small room, off the CID suite in the main Edinburgh police office. 'I had the radio on as I drove here, but there was nothing beyond a report of a body being recovered from the Clyde.'

'That's all the PR people have been authorised to say so far,' the DCI replied. 'It happens: people get drunk and fall in the river, or they get depressed and jump in. The press have no reason to think this is out of the ordinary, so they haven't been beating the doors down. Rogozin was unmarried but his parents are still alive; they should be advised before any public announcement, even though they're in Russia. Obviously, this is going to spread fast.'

'Tell me about it. In my brief time as chief of the old Strathclyde force, we had a couple of problems involving cops messaging journos on their Twitter accounts. I landed on them very heavily, I can tell you,' he added, with a glacial look in his eye. 'Who's the SIO?' he continued.

'Technically, I am,' Pye said. 'The chief has linked this death with the Bordeaux investigation, until we know different. Mann and Provan will run the Glasgow end, but they'll keep me informed.'

Skinner frowned. 'You've already charged Chaz Baker with Annette's death. Does that mean you fancy him for this one too?'

'I didn't, not until a few minutes ago, when I had an email from Provan with some very disturbing attachments.'

'They've made progress?'

'A hell of a lot in a very short time. Dan Provan searched Rogozin's room in the Central Hotel; he found an iPad, and these were on it.'

He swung his computer screen round so that both could see it. Skinner gasped at the image that was showing. 'That's . . .' he murmured. His expression grew harder and harder as Pye ran through the folder that the Glasgow team had sent to him. By the time the first photograph reappeared, it was one of fury.

'You were right,' the DCI said. 'There was a relationship between Rogozin and Annette.'

'If that's what you can call it. That bastard,' he growled. 'Look at her. That's not a willing participant, no way.'

'Agreed. That's underlined by the info I've had from the consulate, that there was an unresolved complaint of sexual assault made against Rogozin. Now, suppose Annette confessed to Baker that the guy was fucking her: his sister. He loses it, beats and strangles her. Before he can get Rogozin he's arrested and charged, but he's released on bail. He could have chosen his moment.'

'No danger,' Skinner exclaimed. 'If anything this weakens your case against him.'

'Chief,' Pye countered, 'nothing could weaken our case against Baker. When Annette Bordeaux was murdered, there were only two people in her apartment, her and Baker. When he left, she was dead. You and Alex are in denial over this; he killed her and he's a viable suspect for Rogozin.'

'So is Paco Fonter, for fuck's sake, if he'd found out about it!' he protested. 'He's just as likely, more so. Then there's me! That bastard gobbed in my face in a room full of people on Saturday.

'Look,' he said, more calmly, 'for the last week Chaz Baker's been holed up in a cottage on Cameron McCullough's estate in Perthshire. If he'd left, it would have been noticed. Paco's been in the Norton House Hotel, knocking ten bells out of himself in the gym.' He paused. 'Ach,' he growled, 'it's just as well the fucker wound up in the Clyde. A large part of me hopes that Mann and Provan don't make too much progress in finding who put him there.'

Pye winced. 'I feel the same way, but as it happens they have a very strong line of inquiry already. It doesn't involve Baker, it doesn't involve Fonter and it doesn't involve you. It's one I haven't shared with Sauce, and I don't think I will, unless and until I have to. I don't even know if I should share it with you.'

'But you want to,' Skinner said, 'so out with it.'

The detective sighed. 'Rogozin had two visitors yesterday evening, in the hotel. We don't know who the first one was, but it was a female, and the description Provan got from them rang a bell with me. It was a good fit for Sirena Burbujas, Annette's agent. I've sourced an image on the Internet and sent a link to Lottie in Pitt Street; she's going to show it to the hotel manager. She saw the woman with him.'

'And the other?'

'This is the part you're not going to like, the thing I have to keep from Sauce. It was a man, and from the description he was given, Dan Provan is dead certain it was Cameron McCullough . . . Senior,' he added.

'What makes him dead certain? Dan's a Weegie cop, and he barely knows where Dundee is; he's got no reason to be aware of Grandpa.'

'He's a Merrytown supporter. He was at the match on Saturday with Lottie's wee lad and he saw him and Rogozin there; he saw you too.'

He frowned, wrinkles bunched around his eyes. 'He did, did he? Wee Dan's not wrong very often, so let's assume it was Cameron. When did he get there?'

'Just after the woman had left: he went up to Rogozin's suite. They were in there alone for about half an hour and then they left together.'

'Where did they go?' Skinner asked, quietly.

'Don't know yet.' The DCI looked at him frowning. 'Sir, you were with the two of them on Saturday, at the game and afterwards. How were relations between them?'

'By the end of the afternoon, they were non-existent. After Rogozin gobbed in my face and stormed out, McCullough said he'd had enough of him. He may have gone to Glasgow to tell him that to his face.' He frowned. 'The only thing is . . . I wondered at the time how he could make that stick with only a twenty-five per cent stake himself.'

Pye chuckled. 'By resorting to extreme measures?' he suggested.

'Grandpa McCullough doing his own dirty work? I don't see that.'

'Maybe they had a bust-up when he tried to force him out.'

'Come on, you don't sound convinced by that.'

'I can't ignore the facts, sir. McCullough and Rogozin were seen leaving the hotel together, and a few hours later, the Russian was found dead.'

'No,' Skinner conceded, 'you can't. He has to be viewed as a suspect, until he's eliminated.'

'There is a complication,' Pye said. 'Rogozin's share in the business was owned by his Russian company, Rogotron. I have information that he no longer controlled it. He had a partner, a Swiss company called Vachepie, that invested capital in return for a stake that had risen to fifty-five per cent.'

The former chief constable laughed, unexpectedly. 'What do you know about Vachepie?'

'Not a lot. I found the Geneva canton company register on the Internet. Vachepie is listed there, but I didn't see any name I recognised among the shareholders. They're all Swiss.'

'That doesn't prove or disprove anything. They could be nominees, stooges, fronts for the real owners . . . or owner. How's your French, Sammy?'

'Non-existent.'

'I've got a wee bit; Vachepie means literally "cow's foot". But if you leave the last part in English you've got "Cow Pie". You might not know your French, but if you know Dundee and its most famous company, D. C. Thomson, the comic publisher, you'll know that cow pie is their most famous character's favourite dish.' He shook his head, grinning. 'Rogotron's mystery investor is Grandpa McCullough having a laugh. You can bet money on it.'

'If I did and you're right, that means he could pull the plug on Rogozin at the football club,' Pye conceded, 'any time he liked.'

'Yes, without any need for those extreme measures you suggested.'

'But he's still a person of interest, and the last man to have seen Rogozin alive.'

'So what are you going to do about it?'

'Doing it by the book,' the detective replied. 'Mann and Provan should either land on his doorstep, or have him brought in for questioning. But given the sensitivity with Sauce's girl-friend, I'd like to keep it informal for as long as I can. So I'm wondering . . .' His gaze fixed on Skinner.

'You cannot be serious,' he murmured. 'You want me to go up to Perthshire and talk to him? I'm out of it, Sammy. I have no locus.'

'You're also, like it or not, closer to McCullough than anyone outside his family, through his new wife and your son. He might talk to you; with anyone else he'd just take cover behind one of his tame solicitors.' He grinned. 'Come on, Chief. You know you want to. Besides,' he added, 'there's someone else that Sauce and I have to see.'

Fifty-Two

'The Garrick Casino is always willing to help the police, Detective Sergeant, but we're sensitive when it comes to discussing our membership.' Melvyn Holding was a tall man, and he made the most of his height; he smiled as he looked down at Dan Provan with more than a hint of condescension.

The detective smiled back at him, but his had more than a hint of a grimace. 'I'm sensitive too,' he admitted. 'I've got a sensitive stomach; when Ah've to start my day by lookin' at some poor sod that's been howked out of the Clyde, it protests and I have trouble holdin' on to my breakfast. I'm not in the best of moods, so please do not yank my chain.'

The casino manager stiffened, standing even taller. 'I'm sorry,' he said, 'but rules are rules. If you want access to our membership list you'll need a warrant from the sheriff.'

'Let me start again,' Provan rumbled, 'and listen to me this time. I want to discuss one of your members. Ah'm not asking you to say whether he is one or not: I know he is.' He took Rogozin's membership card from a pocket and held it up. 'You can strike him off the list; it was his body that was taken out of the river.'

'I see,' Holding murmured; he seemed to shrink by a couple

of inches as he leaned forward to inspect the plastic rectangle. 'Oh my, Mr Rogozin,' he whispered. He frowned at his visitor. 'You're CID, Criminal Investigation. I take it that means his death wasn't from natural causes.'

'The buzz word is "suspicious",' the DS replied. 'He was hit over the head and tossed in the river off the walkway. I know he was here last night; I can track him on CCTV leaving the Central Hotel and walking down in this direction. There's a gap in the coverage; your entrance is out of shot, but he was heading in this direction and he doesn't come into view of the next camera.'

'I know about the gap in the CCTV,' Holding admitted. 'It's at our request. Garrick Casinos don't like the idea of its members being filmed entering and leaving. We have an understanding with the group that operates the street cameras in all our locations that they won't be.'

'Do you film them when they're inside?'

'There are surveillance cameras, so that we can keep a lookout for any unusual activity . . . people are always out to beat the system, Mr Provan . . . but we don't record them. It's a bit like a TV box; we can pause and rewind, but once the system closes down, nothing is stored.'

'Did you see Rogozin last night?'

'Not personally, but he was a regular customer, so if you tell me he was here, it doesn't surprise me.'

'He wasn't alone,' Provan volunteered.

'Was his companion a member?'

'I have no idea.'

'If he wasn't, Mr Rogozin will have signed him in as a guest. Come with me and we'll see.'

He stepped across the casino's entrance hallway to a desk in the far corner, covering the distance in three strides to Provan's six, and opened a leather-bound book that sat upon it. 'Quiet last night,' he murmured. 'Only half a dozen guests, but . . . yes, here we are. Mr Rogozin introduced a gentleman named, if I can read his writing, Mr McCullough, Cameron McCullough. He gave his address as Black Shield Lodge, Perthshire.' He paused. 'That's interesting; Garrick Casinos' parent company is called Black Shield Leisure. We have sister casinos in Dundee and Aberdeen. Bit of a coincidence.'

'But no' of concern to me,' Provan said. 'If you never saw them last night, is there anybody who would have?'

'It depends what they did. But if they ate here, the restaurant staff would have seen them. Come on.'

Holding led the detective up a broad stairway, then through a double doorway, into a long restaurant, with a bar at the far end. The wall on their left was entirely glass with a view of the river and its south bank, and to the west, the Kingston Bridge across which heavy traffic flowed. Glaswegian folklore had it that several members of the city's criminal underclass had disappeared during its construction, and formed part of its foundations.

It was just after midday and more than half of the tables were occupied by lunching members. 'The restaurant is very popular,' the manager declared. 'Good quality and good value; the gambling tables subsidise the dining tables. Mario,' he called out, possibly a little more loudly than was necessary. 'Mario Valvona, head waiter,' he explained as a man in a red tuxedo and matching bow tie turned to frown in their direction, not best pleased, the detective surmised, at the tone of the summons. Most head waiters he knew saw themselves as masters of their territory.

'This is Detective Sergeant Provan,' Holding announced as

he approached, his voice dropping to discretion level. 'We'd like a word.'

'Right now?' the waiter grumbled.

'I'm afraid so,' Provan replied, trying to sound apologetic. 'One of your members was done in last night, not long after leaving here; I need to ask you about his movements.'

He had captured Mario's attention. 'Which one?' he asked.

'Mr Rogozin,' Holding volunteered.

'No' somebody that'll be missed then,' the waiter retorted, without a trace of Italy in his accent.

'Mario!' the manager protested.

'Don't come it, Melvyn,' Valvona chuckled. 'The man was an arse. You knew it, I knew it, we all knew it. You lookin' for suspects?' he asked Provan. 'If you are, you'll no' go short here. I told you, Melvyn, you should have revoked his membership after that thing with Bernie.'

'Bernie?' the DS repeated.

'Bernadette Crerand, the cocktail waitress. Rogozin offered her two hundred quid to go back to his hotel with him. She told him to fuck off, straight out, and he complained to me, and then to Melvyn when I gave him directions on how to get there.'

'So, not a popular man?'

'As my Italian relatives would say, Sergeant, *una fica assoluta*. Go and look that up if you need to.'

'Ah get the drift. Was he in here last night?'

'Yes, he had a guest, Mr McCullough. Now, he is a gentleman.'

'You know him?'

'Aye, he's been here with Rogozin before, but I knew him from when I did a holiday relief stint up at Dundee. He's a member there, I think.'

Provan made a mental note to find out more about his fellow Merrytown supporter, but moved on. 'How were they?' he asked. 'Were they amicable, or was there tension between them?'

'Well, they werenae smiling when they came in here about half ten: at least Rogozin wasn't. Mr McCullough was okay, but the Russian had a face like fizz. They'd been on the tables; Rogozin tipped young Graham a twenty-quid chip when he seated them. Probably all he had left.'

'Not quite, we found another couple in his pocket. Could you hear what he and McCullough talked about?'

'Very little. Rogozin asked for the table with the most space around it. They each had steak, and didn't say much as they were eating. Afterwards, Mr McCullough did most of the talking and Rogozin did all the arguing. Whatever he was being told, he didn't like it. He shouted something in Russian; I think Mr McCullough must have told him to speak English, for he shouted again, "You not fucking do that to me," loud enough for him to draw a look from Ronnie Argyle, the scrap metal guy. He was at a table with his wife, and Ronnie is a man you don't want to be drawing a look from. Rogozin got the message, for he sort of waved an apology.'

'He was quiet after that?' Provan asked.

'Aye, but . . . Mr McCullough sort of leaned towards him and he said something else. I've got no idea what it was, but the Russian went as white as a sheet. Then Mr McCullough got up, nodded a polite goodnight to Mr and Mrs Argyle, and walked out. He said goodnight to me too on the way past, and slipped me a twenty.'

'And Rogozin just sat there?'

'He did for a while, then he got up and ran after him. Literally, he ran after him.'

'Was that the last you saw of him? Of either of them?'

'Of Mr McCullough, yes, but Rogozin came back. I was having visions of sending somebody up to the Central Hotel with his dinner bill, but he came back in. He had a coffee, finished the rest of the claret . . . he'd had that on his own; Mr McCullough was on the fizzy water . . . and had an Armagnac after that.'

'When did he leave?'

'About one o'clock. He settled up, and was the last diner to leave.'

Provan nodded, happy with what he had heard. 'Was that the last you saw of him?'

'Actually it wasn't,' Valvona replied. 'He was outside when I left, about ten minutes later. I gave him a wide berth; I'd had enough of him for the night. I assumed he was heading back to the Central, but he didn't. It was funny; he seemed to stop in mid-stride, then turned and headed down to the walkway.' He chuckled. 'I remember thinking that maybe Mr McCullough had waited for him outside, wantin' a square go.'

Fifty-Three

'So this is where you work these days.' Cameron McCullough smiled as he gazed out of the smoked-glass office wall. 'Must make a hell of a change from those places with a blue lamp outside.'

'It's quieter up here,' Skinner admitted. 'The view of the city's better; I like that. Mind you, I only spend part of my time here.'

'What do you do with the rest of it?'

'Play golf and hang out with my kids.'

'I wouldn't have thought that's enough for you.'

'My family keeps on expanding,' he said.

'I know; I'm on the edge of it, remember?'

Skinner focused a steady gaze on his visitor. 'Just so we're clear,' he murmured. 'You married a woman with whom I had a one-night stand twenty-odd years ago. That does not make us kin, or even close to it. My former colleagues still have a file on you that would bend my desk in the middle.'

'Incidents and accidents, hints and allegations,' McCullough chuckled, 'as someone once said. Let them show me that file and I'll dismiss or disprove everything in it.'

'You know what,' Skinner sighed, 'I don't care about the past any more. I've been offered serious money for my autobiography. I turned it down flat, but if I hadn't, you wouldn't be in it. You may have been a fucking bogeyman up in Dundee, but that was never my territory, so I don't give a shit. I'm only interested in the present now.'

'So what's this about, this meeting?'

'It's a favour for a friend, who's hoping it can stay informal. I'm glad you could come here, by the way; it saved me a trip up to Perthshire.'

'No worries; I was going to the football club anyway, and this isn't far out of my way. Dimitri can cool his heels for an hour or so. What's the alternative to informal, by the way?'

'A big lady polis from Glasgow; impervious to charm. As for Rogozin, he's cooling more than his fucking heels right now.' He waited, looking for puzzlement to show in McCullough's eyes and finding himself surprisingly relieved when it did. 'He was found in the Clyde this morning, just under the Squinty Bridge. From what I've been told, those big heavy overcoats are surprisingly buoyant.'

'Are you serious?' McCullough exclaimed. Skinner was even more satisfied; he had never seen the man rattled before.

'I don't do funny,' he replied. 'My alibi's good, I'm happy to say, but I'm not so sure about yours.'

'Fuck!' the Dundonian whispered. 'I. . .' He stopped, staring through the glass.

'Why are you going to Merrytown?' Skinner asked, sharply.

'Eh?' McCullough shook his head as if trying to clear it. 'I'm going to meet . . . I was going to meet Rogozin,' he said, 'to have him sign some documents, first and foremost being his resignation. I wasn't kidding on Saturday, Bob. I've had it with the bloke.'

'Is that why you met him in Glasgow last night, to give him that message?'

'Ah,' he murmured, 'that's what this is about. Your big lady polis has been tracing Dimitri's movements.'

'Yes,' Skinner conceded, 'and they have you with him in the Grand Central Hotel, then leaving together.'

'If she's been doing her job properly, she'll have more than that.'

'Take me through it.'

'I went to the hotel initially for a quiet chat. I spent about half an hour in his suite, just talking business mostly. At that point I was still thinking about keeping him onside. We talked about Baker and about how long we could carry on without him: the Motherwell defeat didn't go down well with anyone, I should tell you. Eventually he said we should go out, so we did. Like you said, we left the hotel. Glasgow's like one big film set; there are cameras everywhere, so I'm sure the police will be able to follow us, although not all the way.'

'Where did you go?'

'We walked down to the Garrick Casino. That was Rogozin's idea; he was a member there, and he signed me in.'

Skinner grinned. 'Surely that was unnecessary,' he remarked.

'What do you mean?' McCullough retorted.

'You own the place, Cameron. Garrick Casinos Limited is part of your leisure division.'

'You have been doing your homework. I thought you said you had no interest in me 'cos I wasn't on your patch.'

'When you became my son's stepfather, that changed,' Skinner admitted. 'I made it my business to find out about you, so I read that big thick intelligence file they have on you.'

'Yes, okay, I do own the group, but I'm not the licence holder.

I'm not even on the board of the parent company.'

'No, but the shareholder register tells the story; one hundred per cent ownership. So, go on, Rogozin signed you in. Then what?'

'We spent some time at the tables; he played and I watched him making himself poorer and me richer. He was crap at blackjack, and like most of the punters, he had a roulette system that he thought was foolproof but wasn't. After he'd dropped a couple of grand he started to mutter about there being a footbrake on the wheel. I wasn't having that, so I steered him out of there, with difficulty, and up to the restaurant. That was when it started to get nasty.'

'What triggered it off?'

'Drink, I suppose. We had a steak, and he had a St Émilion decanted. Bloody philistine,' McCullough muttered, 'drinking that after whisky. Once we'd eaten,' he continued, 'I got down to business. I told him that his behaviour in the boardroom on Saturday had been unacceptable, and that he had to apologise to you.'

Skinner smiled, grimly. 'How did he take that?'

'He went berserk, got all Russian on me, started yelling at me. I told him to speak English, and he did. He shouted "I'm not fucking doing that!" or something similar, loud enough to attract the attention of a guy called Ronnie Argyle, who was there with his wife.'

'I've read his file too,' the former chief constable remarked, 'when I was at Strathclyde.'

'Then you'll know why I had to pacify him, then tell Dimitri to shut up. In fact I told him more than that. I said that I had reached the end of the road with him as chairman of Merrytown, and that I'd accept his written resignation next day.

I told him that I didn't want him setting foot in Scotland again, ever.'

'And he took that without protest?'

'It wasn't a negotiation.'

'Did you threaten to freeze him out of Rogotron as well?'

McCullough stared at him, then he whistled. 'You are good, very good. How did you . . . ?'

'I understand French and I used to read the *Dandy*,' Skinner replied tersely. 'Did you? Threaten him?'

'No, because I need him in Russia. His death could create a problem for me.'

'Look on the bright side,' he told him. 'It gives you a motive for keeping him alive, rather than killing him. So, you fired him as chair of Merrytown, you told him to be there to sign off on it this afternoon and then what?'

'Then I walked out. I told him he could pay the bill, said good night to Ronnie Argyle and his wife, tipped Mario, the head waiter, and left.'

He paused, for a second or two. 'It wasn't the last I saw of him though. He came after me, and caught up with me in the foyer. All the bluster was gone by then; he pleaded with me. He said that he'd been planning to leave Moscow because he had big trouble there. Something to do with shagging the wife of a friend of the president; that's why he had Grigor, apparently. I told him to find another one, an ex-Spetsnaz mercenary, someone like that, and put him on the Rogotron payroll. I said we could afford it because I'd be selling the fucking plane. Then I left.'

'What time was this?'

'About quarter past twelve.'

'And you didn't go back? You didn't hang around outside, waiting for him?'

'Of course not. I walked straight up to the Oswald Street car park. My exit will be timed and it'll show up, if your big lady friend wants to check.' He smiled. 'Is that me off the hook, Bob?' he asked.

'You were never on it as far as I was concerned,' Skinner admitted.

'How about you?' McCullough joked. 'Are you off it? You had a motive after Saturday.'

'My alibi is aged five and her name is Seonaid. She woke up to go to the bathroom at half past midnight, just as I was coming up the stairs. I had to read her a story to get her back to sleep.' He frowned. 'I'm trying to get them to lose interest in Baker, though.'

'Why should they want Chaz for this?'

'Because Rogozin was screwing his half-sister.'

'You're fucking joking!'

'No, I'm not, and he took photos to prove it. I've seen them; not nice.'

'In that case I'll regard my problems in Russia as a price worth paying for him being dead. I can put your friends in blue off Baker too. He and his wife had dinner with Mia last night, in my absence, in the hotel restaurant. It went on quite late.'

Skinner beamed. 'That will make my daughter's day,' he said. Then his pleasure evaporated. 'Unfortunately, it'll make them look all the harder at Paco Fonter. I hope he didn't go out for a drive late last night.'

Fifty-Four

'Tell me you're joking,' Dan Provan exclaimed. 'Sammy Pye had Skinner go and interview our suspect?'

'No,' Lottie Mann replied. 'Detective Chief Inspector Pye asked him to have an informal word with Mr McCullough. It did the trick, because he says that the man is no longer a person of interest, and neither is Chaz Baker.'

'I'm confused. Ah never had any interest in Baker.'

'Then you didn't read the Sunday papers yesterday. Annette Bordeaux, the woman whose smutty pictures you found on Rogozin's iPad, was Baker's half-sister.'

The DS frowned at her. 'No, Ah never read the Sundays,' he confessed. 'But there's no evidence to suggest that he would have seen them. Rogozin's sent emails were accessible through his tablet, and he never circulated those photos to anyone. Okay, Baker's out, no' that he was ever in, and we've tae forget McCullough on the say-so of a civilian.'

'No,' she said, patiently, 'on the basis that he was in his car and driving north when Rogozin was killed. Pye verified from the public car park in Oswald Street that he checked out of there at twelve twenty-three.'

'Maybe he parked it then went back down tae the casino and ambushed the guy.'

'And maybe he called in an air strike.'

'Ah still don't like it, Lottie. It's no' proper procedure. It makes me wonder about Pye. I've been checkin' out McCullough with a mate of mine in criminal intelligence. His record is absolutely clean, never had a speedin' ticket, but he was acquitted of murder a few years back. And there was a heroin trafficking charge that disappeared, along with the smack in question, from a secure police store.'

'I never knew that,' Mann admitted.

'I checked him out wi' another source as well. Ah've just been to see Ronnie Argyle, in his yard, just to rule him out. The waiter said that Rogozin had upset him, and Ronnie can be a bit mental, as you know. He and his wife were picked up at twelve thirty in a black taxi, called by the casino staff, and went straight home. He admitted he was upset by Rogozin swearing in front of his wife, but he said that he was with Mr McCullough . . . sick, as they say in the papers, meaning that's exactly what he called him . . . so he let it lie. That tells me plenty.'

'Yes, it does, I'll grant you, but Pye isn't a guy who'd do something like that without a good reason. All he said to me was that things were sensitive with McCullough, and I didn't press him on it.'

'Sensitive as in he's on the guy's payroll?' Provan barked.

'Wash your mouth out, Danny. Are you suggesting that Skinner's on his team as well?'

The sergeant frowned. 'In this brave new policing world of ours, Lottie, I don't know what tae think any more.'

Fifty-Five

'The Amazon couriers must love this place,' Sammy Pye gasped as they reached the third floor of the tenement block in Warrender Park Terrace.

'When's your next physical?' Haddock asked, his breathing normal.

'In a few months; I'd better get back in the gym. Bob Skinner's at least fifteen years older than me, and he could probably run up those steps.'

'Speaking of him, gaffer, shouldn't you have asked me before you sent him off to talk to Grandpa?'

'Probably,' Pye conceded, 'but I wanted to head off Lottie, or to be more accurate, her malevolent hobbit of a sidekick. And I didn't want you involved; it could have gone pear shaped, and that would have been personally awkward for you.'

'But it didn't and now it looks awkward for both of us. Provan's a contrary wee shite. If he goes to the chief . . .' he allowed his warning to tail off.

'If he does, I'll deal with it . . . not that there's anything to deal with. Bob got the job done in an hour and a half, on the quiet. If I had left it to the terrible twosome, they'd have formalised it and Christ knows how it would have gone. Grandpa's clear . . . to your relief, I have no doubt . . . and as a bonus we can forget about Baker.'

'That might bring us under pressure to review the charge against him,' Haddock suggested.

'How many times, Sauce? Rogozin's death does not affect our case. Forget about it for now and let's see what this woman has to say to us.'

He pressed the button on the door on their right. The detectives waited, but not for long; it was opened by a small, plump woman, dressed in green denim jeans, and a baggy white sweatshirt with a bottle of Chanel Number Five depicted on its front. The dark curly perm that both had noticed on their first meeting with Sirena Burbujas was constrained by a wide headband and the brown eyes were hidden behind a large pair of round, frameless, spectacles. She looked up at them, and in those eyes they saw fear.

'Come in,' she said, quietly, then turned on her heel and led them along a corridor and into a large sitting room, with a high corniced ceiling and two large windows with a view of the Meadows, and beyond of the King Robert Village development. In the background, a radio was playing: Haddock recognised the fresh voice of Janice Forsyth.

'Can I get you tea, coffee . . . beer?' The faintly continental accent had disappeared; what was left was bland London. As she spoke, the woman's agitation was apparent.

'We're fine, thanks,' Pye replied. 'Are you okay?'

She shook her head. 'No, I'm not. The news has just been on; they're saying that Dimitri Rogozin's dead, that he was drowned.'

'That's partly true.' The DCI moved towards her. 'Sit down, Ms Burbujas, please.' He took her elbow, gently and steered her to an armchair. 'Can we get you something?'

She nodded. 'There's brandy in the sideboard. Thanks.'

He followed her direction and found a bottle of Martell, with a pair of goblets beside it. He covered the base of one, and gave it to her. She drank, shuddered, then nodded appreciation. 'It's true then?' she murmured.

'Yes and no,' Pye replied. 'Rogozin is dead, but the officers on the scene don't think he drowned. Subject to autopsy, the theory is that he was dead before he went into the river.'

She flinched. 'That's horrible. What's happening to the world? First Annette and now him.' Her face hardened. 'Not that he'll be missed. He was a beast of a man.'

'That's the picture we're getting,' Haddock agreed. 'Look, to get something out of the way, can you tell us where you went after you left Rogozin last night?'

Burbujas looked up at him in surprise. 'How did you know I was there?'

'The Glasgow officers have a description of a woman who was with him in the Grand Central Hotel last night. It's a good fit for you, and now you've confirmed it. So, where did you go?'

'Straight back to Queen Street Station; I caught the first train to Edinburgh. I still have the cancelled ticket if you want me to prove it.'

'Why did you visit him?' Pye asked.

'I wanted to confront him, to give him a message, to let him know he was going to pay. I did that, and I told him I was going to the police. As I am doing,' she added.

'Yes, we were intrigued by your call. You said it was time Rogozin was exposed.'

'For what he did to Annette, that's right. He was . . .'

The DCI held up a hand to stop her. 'Before you continue, Ms Burbujas, I should tell you that when a colleague in Glasgow searched his hotel room this morning he found a number of photographs of Ms Bordeaux on a tablet computer. We've seen them; they're intimate, not pornographic, but they do indicate a relationship between the two of them.'

'Relationship isn't a word I'd use.' She sipped her brandy and peered through her spectacles at Pye. 'What I'm going to tell you, can it be confidential?'

He frowned. 'This is a murder inquiry, madam. You're not a doctor, a lawyer or a priest: nothing you tell us can be privileged.'

'Okay,' she conceded, 'but can you promise me that you'll be sensitive in dealing with this information?'

'We are when we need to be. Come on,' he said, gently. 'Out with it.'

She drew a breath then blurted out, 'He raped her! The son-of-a-bitch raped her.'

The detectives stood, silent, as she composed herself. 'It all started when Paco signed for FC Pugliese, the Italian club,' she continued, more quietly. 'I don't know why he went there. Well, I do,' she corrected herself. 'He went because he trusted that shifty so-and-so Serra, and because he was frustrated. Paco always wanted to play for Real Madrid, but they never came for him. If you ask me, it wasn't because he wasn't good enough, but because he had the wrong agent. Serra's contacts are mostly in central and eastern Europe, not in Spain or England where the money is.

'Rogozin was one of those contacts. When he bought into Pugliese, he had enough money for one big signing, and Paco was it.' She looked up at Pye. 'Do you know Italy?'

'Not really. I've been to Rome and Venice but that's it.'

'Pugliese's a shitty little coastal town, just south of Naples. Paco and Annette lived in the city itself, but neither of them liked it much. She had the same frustrations she experienced here until they settled in Edinburgh. Paco was away a lot too, with the club or with the international side. And when he was away . . . somehow Rogozin was there.'

She shuddered, calmed herself with another sip. 'He was very friendly with them both in the early stages. Dinner in the best restaurants in Naples, that sort of stuff. But soon, whenever Paco was away and she was at home, he'd turn up unannounced. The first time, she thought nothing of it; they went out and it was fine. The second time, she began to feel he was imposing. The third time, she began to realise she was being stalked.'

'And the fourth time?' Haddock asked.

'The fourth time, she tried to tell him to go away, but he said he had business to discuss with her. So she, like an idiot, went to his hotel; they had dinner in his suite. She felt woozy, and passed out. When she came to, she was naked, she was sore,' her free hand fluttered briefly to her lap, 'and he was taking photographs of her with his phone. She was hysterical, and he was laughing. She got dressed and he drove her home.'

'Why didn't she call the police as soon as he was gone, while his DNA was still on her and whatever drug he used was still in her system?'

'Because he threatened her, in every way you could imagine. He said that if she talked, he would deny it all, say that it was her idea and that she had come to his hotel looking for sex. He said he would publish the photos on the Internet. He said that he knew people who would throw acid in her face for a couple of thousand euro. But worst of all he threatened Paco.'

She finished the brandy, slammed the glass down on a side table and sighed. 'This is where discretion comes in, gentlemen,' she said. 'Paco is a clean-living guy save for one thing. He has a small drug habit. Not a problem as such, but a habit; cocaine. He's careful though; he doesn't mess about with the street stuff. His supplier in Pugliese was the team doctor. That's how Rogozin found out about it. Another couple of players were users, there was talk and it reached him.'

'He blackmailed her, through her husband.' Pye's face was grim.

'Exactly. On top of all those other threats, he said that if she breathed a word to anyone, he would end her husband's football career, and that the damage would ripple on to her own. She was terrified, not so much of the physical threat, but of that one. He was a horrible man and she knew he would do what he said.'

'It wasn't just the one time either, was it?'

'No,' she admitted. 'Whenever there was an opportunity, and there were plenty in Italy, he would come back.'

'How did you find out about it?'

'She told me a couple of weeks ago, after the last time. She had thought, hoped, that it was over when they left Italy. She felt more secure in the penthouse; you can't come and go there without being seen. Then, one Friday night when the team was staying over in Aberdeen before a league game there, he called her. He said he was in the flat below, and told her to come down. She did and it was awful, worse than ever. She was desolate.'

Burbujas's eyes moistened; she reached for a tissue from a box on the table. 'That was the last straw for poor Annette. She called me next day, and told me everything. I was appalled; horrified. I insisted that she call the police, but she said no, she'd deal with it herself. She asked me if I knew anyone in London who could get her a gun. I told her not to be crazy, but I was wasting my breath; she had turned. My gentle girl was ready to kill him.'

'The text she sent to Chaz Baker,' Haddock said, 'it mentioned a secret. From what we know now, it's a safe bet that she was talking about her persecution by Rogozin.'

'I suppose,' Burbujas conceded, limply.

'When did Annette tell you about her relationship with Baker?'

'She never did. I learned about it yesterday morning, from the papers. But now I know, certain things make sense. Obviously I knew about Annette's real background, as opposed to the official biography. She did mention once that she'd like to trace her birth parents; I told her it was her business, but please be discreet about it. I didn't want to look like a clown in the press.'

'I suspect you didn't want to risk career damage for her either,' Pye observed.

'One and the same thing,' she admitted. 'To be honest, Annette was my one major client. I have others but none are in the same league; their bookings are run by an assistant out of my London office. I stayed close to Annette all the time; that's why I'm here. This place is rented.'

'Did she tell you when the trace was successful?'

'Yes, she did, but she said not to worry, that it would all stay under wraps. I should have twigged though, after Cisco Serra let slip that Annette had more or less ordered him to recruit Baker as a client, and when Serra made him a part of the move to Scotland.' She sighed. 'But I didn't. I wish I had known; I could have managed the situation. Now it's all gone to hell; she's dead and you're convinced that Baker killed her.'

'Are you suggesting that you're not?' Haddock asked.

'I wouldn't know,' she replied. 'I'm more concerned with who killed Rogozin.'

'Why should that bother you? I imagine you're glad he's dead.'

'I'm very happy about that. I'm worried because he wasn't the only person I saw yesterday. Before I caught the train to Glasgow, I drove out to see Paco at his hotel and I told him the truth about Rogozin as well.'

Fifty-Six

'This isn't proper, you know,' Scotland's Solicitor General said. 'I shouldn't be talking to you.'

'Why the hell not?' Skinner challenged. 'I'm not a lawyer; I'm here as a member of the public.'

'Ask yourself. You said exactly the same thing to me on the same subject when I visited you in the Royal.'

He smiled, recognising the truth of de Matteo's comment, but refused to be thrown off balance. 'I'd had a bang on the head then,' he countered. 'The situation is different too: you were hoping that I'd persuade my daughter to accept a plea deal for her client that was against his interests. I'm here, in your office, as a concerned citizen, trying to save the public purse a large wad of cash . . . even though some of it would come to my kid in fee income.'

'Nothing has changed from where I'm sitting. I'm still happy to prosecute Baker on the basis of the police evidence, circumstantial or not.'

'If you do you'll be risking your reputation,' Skinner warned.

'I do that every time I lead a case in the High Court,' de Matteo countered.

'Which is not very often. This is going to be the biggest trial of your career, Rocco. The whole country will be watching; when you fall over it could be terminal.'

'I am very steady on my feet, thank you. I don't see anything to worry me. The new evidence I'm hearing about from Pye, of sexual profligacy by the victim, strengthens my case against her brother, if anything.'

'I've seen those photographs, but Sammy Pye has just advised Alex of the Burbujas woman's statement. Annette was raped, and subsequently blackmailed, Rocco.'

The lawyer's smile came easily. 'That's all it is, Bob, a statement, by a woman wanting to salvage the reputation of her most valuable property, from whose estate she will presumably continue to draw income, as long as her name remains unsullied. Where's the evidence of rape? Where's the proof of coercion?'

'Have you seen those photographs yet?'

'Of a naked Bordeaux on crumpled bed sheets with come smears on the inside of her thigh? Yes, I've seen them, and so will the jury. When they do they'll find it easy to accept that when she revealed that secret to her brother, he was outraged, they quarrelled violently and in that quarrel he killed her.'

'Man,' Skinner exclaimed, 'you're thinking headlines, you're not thinking logic. If you were prosecuting Chaz for killing Rogozin, Annette's story would offer a strong motive. But you're not and you can't because he was somewhere else when the Russian was murdered. If you ask the jury to agree with your interpretation, then you are inviting them to doubt you.'

De Matteo pursed his lips. 'Thank you for that,' he said. 'You may be right. In that case I won't lead with the relationship with Rogozin at all. His name will never be mentioned. I don't need him, because I have Baker and only Baker at the scene, I have his belt with his fingerprints, and no one else's, around her neck, and I have her blood on his training top. Yes, I'll be conservative, Bob.'

Skinner glowered at him; the man had nothing but face cards and aces in his hand and both of them knew it. 'My ex would make you wash your mouth out if she heard you use that word,' he growled.

'I doubt it. Aileen was very small c conservative. She only backed political certainties. The only risk I remember her taking was with that actor Joey Morrocco, and even that paid off in the long run, as it added a little spice to her CV.' He recoiled slightly as he saw the flash of anger in the other man's eyes. 'Sorry,' he said, 'I shouldn't have mentioned him. You and she were still married at the time, weren't you?'

'You're not sorry at all, Rocco, and you know full well that she was still Mrs Skinner when she was fucking Morrocco. You're trying to wind me up, but it won't work; I'm no paragon either. However, you have just made this personal, and that was a mistake on your part. You lead this case, and I'll make sure you fall flat on your face.'

The Solicitor General's smile was supremely self-assured. 'The only way your daughter will do that,' he said, 'will not be by proving that Baker didn't kill Annette Bordeaux, because she can't, it will be by proving who did.'

Skinner looked down at him as he rose, his mind's eye still picturing him with a hand of cards. 'You know why I had a hundred per cent conviction rate as a cop?' he asked. 'Because I knew when to hold 'em, and I knew when to fold 'em. You're going to learn that knack the hard way.'

Fifty-Seven

'Ah might have reservations about the way this investigation's being handled, but I admit we've made progress,' Dan Provan conceded.

'Of sorts,' Lottie Mann agreed. 'We're no nearer knowing who killed the guy, but we've crossed some people off the list.'

'How about the woman wi' the funny name? She was with Rogozin before he died. Should we give her a closer look, if only tae keep the fiscal happy?'

'No need. Apart from the fact that by every description we have she's too small, she gave Pye a return train ticket to Edinburgh, initialled by the conductor. As for McCullough, his car was picked up on CCTV going on to the motorway at twelve twenty-five. They're out of the picture; now we can focus on Fonter, as Edinburgh suggested.'

'Ordered, ye mean,' the DS grunted.

'No, I meant what I said. Pye's a diplomat; he wants to be liked.'

'He's got some work tae do on that to convince me, but that's by the by. I hope Paco Fonter's no' our man,' he said. 'He's our best player.'

343

He held the heavy door of the Central Hotel ajar for his colleague. 'Ah could get used tae this place,' he remarked. 'I wish our office was this plush.'

'Dan,' she laughed, 'you look like a fish on a bike in here. I know you scrub up well, but you don't do it very often.'

Two desks were positioned just inside the doorway. The first was untended, but a woman, clad in hotel livery, sat at the second. 'You'll be Kerry,' Provan declared as he stepped up to her.

'And you'll be right, sir,' she replied, tapping her lapel badge. Her hair was ginger; she looked and sounded as Irish as her name.

'DS Provan, DI Mann,' he said. 'I was here earlier about the death of one of your guests.'

'It was you that spoke to Ms Kilmarnock, was it? She's gone for the night, I'm afraid.'

'That's okay; you seem to know everything about this place.'

'On my shift, yes. How long will we have to keep the JFK suite closed?' she asked, tangentially. 'We had to move a guest this afternoon, and we have a booking from Thursday through Sunday.'

'As soon as our forensic team is finished,' Mann assured her, 'you can have it back. Tomorrow latest, I should think. For now, though, we have some more questions for you. We know that Mr Rogozin had two visitors here last night, and we've eliminated both of them from our investigation. But did anyone else come here looking for him last night?'

The receptionist nodded. 'As a matter of fact there was,' she replied. 'A young gentleman . . . in his twenties, I mean . . . tall, dark haired, had a Latino look about him. He came in through the station entrance, as if he didn't really know his way around.'

Provan took out his phone and displayed an image on the screen. 'Was this him, Kerry?'

She peered at it, then nodded. 'Yes, yes it was. That's the fellow I spoke to.'

'How did he seem?' Mann asked.

'What do you mean?'

'Can you describe his manner, his attitude?'

'He was perfectly polite. He asked me for Mr Rogozin's room number. I said I couldn't divulge that, and he asked if I could call him. I said there would be no point, as he'd just gone out with another gentleman. I asked if he'd like to leave a message for him, but he said "Thank you, no", then he left.

'How did he seem?' she said, repeating the DI's question. 'Agitated, I would say; wound up, as if he'd an urgent reason for wanting to see Mr Rogozin.' She frowned. 'You don't think he caught up with him, do you?'

'That's what we're trying to find out, Kerry,' the DS replied. 'Thanks for your help; we'll try to free up President Kennedy's suite.' He gave her a smile, that to Mann seemed almost impish. 'I'll bet it's very popular with the ladies.'

The detective stepped away from the reception desk. 'Bugger,' Provan muttered. 'A new name in the frame then, and no' the one I wanted.' He glanced up at the inspector. 'Where do we go now?'

'You know perfectly well,' she retorted. 'We go to the only other place we know that Rogozin visited last night.'

'Have you got the time for that?' he queried. 'What about Jakey?'

'His Uncle Davie's with him, and he'll stay over if need be.

We have that arrangement if there's a panic on at work. It's handy, having a gay self-employed home-working brother.'

'In that case,' Provan ventured, 'do ye fancy a drink while we're here? The Garrick Casino's no' going tae close any time soon, and I'm told the Tempus Bar's quite nice.'

Fifty-Eight

'Why did you do that, Pops?' Alex Skinner demanded, clearly annoyed. 'It wasn't professional.'

'I'm not a professional,' her father pointed out. 'I'm not a lawyer. I'm an amateur helping out.' He beamed. 'Well-meaning amateurs are much in demand these days. Sammy Pye asked me to do him a wee favour earlier on today. Maggie has him overseeing the Rogozin murder investigation.'

'Sammy got you involved in that?'

'He asked me to talk to someone I know; to eliminate him.'

'Why couldn't he do it himself?'

'It was a bit too close to home for him, and he thought the Glasgow approach might be too abrasive.'

'Rogozin was murdered, was he? The police statement struck me as cautious; "suspicious death" was all they said.'

'It's very difficult to cave the back of your own head in, then fly off the walkway into the Clyde. Maggie called me, out of courtesy, twenty minutes ago. The post-mortem showed no water in his lungs.'

'I don't envy them trying to find who did it. There must have been a long queue of people with reason to kill that man.'

'Agreed. All I was able to do for Sammy was determine that

two people couldn't have done it: Cameron McCullough and your client.'

'They suspected Chaz?' Alex exclaimed. 'Why should they? He had nothing to do with Rogozin outside the club.'

'No, but his half-sister did.' He related the story of Provan's photographic discovery in the dead Russian's hotel suite.

'Annette Bordeaux was shagging Rogozin?'

'The other way around; she wasn't a willing participant. The allegation is that it began with a date rape and continued through coercion.'

She shook her head, sending a ripple through her thick hair. 'You really are involved in this investigation, aren't you? On all sides. You can't stay away, can you? How much longer before they draw you back in?'

'To the Scottish police service? Never; my view of it's too well known. The role that Maggie floated before me on behalf of the First Minister? I haven't said an absolute no yet, but I'm not close to saying yes either.'

'If you turn it down he could make you Solicitor General instead,' she suggested with a playful grin.

'There's a big impediment to that,' he pointed out. 'I'm not a lawyer.'

'I don't think you have to be, Pops. It's a government post, Clive Graham could appoint anyone he liked; you wouldn't be able to appear in the Supreme Courts, but very few Sol Gens ever choose to do that. Rocco de Matteo's an exception.'

'Rocco de Matteo's a wanker.'

'That too,' she agreed. 'You still shouldn't have gone to see him, though.'

'Don't worry, I made it clear that you didn't know about it. I did it because I wanted to assess the chances of him dropping the charges against our man, sorry, your man.'

'He won't, I could have told you that. Paula Benedict called me again this morning to offer me that ridiculous plea deal, but she let slip that it was the Lord Advocate's idea, not Rocco's.'

'That doesn't surprise me. Woodrow Butcher's a cautious man. I know that from the golf I play with him.'

'Everybody in Parliament House knows that,' Alex retorted. 'But he won't overrule his deputy. Why should he? It's win-win for him. Either de Matteo gets a conviction that makes the Crown Office look good, or he blows it and has to resign.'

'That makes sense. It also gives us an even bigger incentive to clear Chaz Baker, if we can get rid of Rocco in the process. But,' Skinner continued, 'he was right about one thing. He's sitting with what looks like an unbeatable circumstantial case. There's only one way we can knock it down for sure, and it isn't by demonstrating simple reasonable doubt. We have to show the jury very clearly how she could have been killed by someone other than Baker.'

'Where do we start?'

'With motive,' he declared. 'It's the one thing that the Crown doesn't have; they might suggest one, Chaz's anger over his sister's affair with Rogozin, but they'd be clutching at straws. So why bother? For a viable suspect, we need someone who did have a motive to kill Annette.

'That's where everything changed when Dan Provan found those images this morning, and when Sirena Burbujas came forward with her story of Annette's sexual persecution. Annette spoke of a secret in her text to Chaz. I know from Paco that he'd been off cocaine for three months, long enough for there to be no metabolites left in his system.

'With his career safe, Rogozin's hold over her was loosened.

From Burbujas's statement, it seems that his last visit a couple of weeks ago could have triggered the whole thing. If she told him that she'd had enough, and that she was going to call his bluff, he would have a very clear motive to kill her.'

'I follow that, Pops,' Alex agreed, 'but we still have her body in the penthouse, and Chaz there at the time she was killed.'

'Yes,' he countered, 'but all along, the Crown case has been founded on a basic premise, and we've gone along with it: that she was killed in the penthouse. What if she wasn't? What if she was killed somewhere else, and her body moved there after Chaz had left the building?'

'But is that possible? The place is top security. It's intruder proof.'

'Not if it wasn't an intruder. Rogozin was an insider. We know he used the apartment below, and we believe that he summoned Annette down there, just over a week before she was killed.'

'Hold on a minute, Pops. We know he arrived on the Saturday, and made calls to Annette, but by that time she was already dead.'

'Sure he did, but what if those calls were for show? I suggest that when he arrived in the apartment on that Friday evening, he was actually coming back.'

'Suggest all you like, but how will we ever prove that he did?'

'Maybe we don't need to, after all. All we have to show is a viable alternative to Chaz having killed her.'

'The belt round her neck? The training top with the blood?'

'Rogozin owned the football club, daughter. He had access to the training complex. Chaz told us he kept clothes there. The training top wasn't found in the laundry basket till next day. He had plenty of time to put it there.'

'True,' she conceded. 'What do you do now?'

'I go back to that building and I have a damn good look around. If I have to, I'll insist that Sammy sends the forensic team back in.'

'Will de Matteo allow that?'

'Fuck him. If I have to I'll go over his head to the Lord Advocate. Woodrow will play it safe; he'll agree.' He grinned. 'The lovely thing about this situation is that if we can build a forensic case against Rogozin that's as strong as they have against Chaz, the bastard won't be around to deny it.'

Fifty-Nine

'You're right, Dan,' Lottie Mann mused, as she admired the opulent furnishings of the Tempus Bar. 'This is nice.'

'Compared tae some of the pubs I've been in, it's Buckingham Palace,' Provan chuckled. 'When I think of some of those boozers on the south side, in the old days . . . Those were dangerous places, if you didnae know your way around . . . sometimes even when ye did.'

'So's this, but in a different way,' she observed. 'This smells of power, it smells of money. It's the sort of place where deals are done on a daily basis that affect the lives of thousands of people.'

The bar was quiet; the only other patrons were the two men the DS had encountered in the hotel foyer that morning. Neither looked happy; he guessed that their 'important' meeting had been a failure. Beyond them, in the restaurant, only one table was occupied, by a large man with a transatlantic tan and a heavily bejewelled woman.

His companion cut into his thoughts. 'I miss this, Dan,' she said, quietly, with a wistful expression. 'Being out for a quiet drink in nice surroundings, not being a mum, not being a DI, just being plain Charlotte Mann.'

'You were never plain in your life, kid. You're a good-looking woman and don't you forget it.'

The compliment took her by surprise. To his amazement she blushed. 'Don't go all gallant on me,' she whispered. 'I mean it. Since Scott and I broke up, I've never done this, taken a wee bit of "me time", not once.'

She gazed into her past for a few seconds, then at him, in the present. 'How about you? You're a good friend, away from the office, and you're great with Jakey, but when you're not with us, or we're not at work, I have no idea what you do with your spare time.'

'Same as you, dear,' he confessed. 'Fuck all for the last ten years since Elspeth got fed up wi' me and headed for the hills wi' that electrician that came to put in a new circuit board and wound up rewirin' her.

'Occasionally, when she's havin' a crisis in her life, my Lulu will turn up from London and take her old man out tae the pictures or the like, but mostly my social life consists of the delivery boy turning up wi' the curry Ah've ordered over the phone.'

'What a pair, eh?' Mann sighed. 'Maybe we should register with a dating agency.'

Provan laughed. 'One of those ye see in the telly ads? I'd be a big draw there: Ah'd be the guy that winds up wi' a fuckin' camel.'

She fluttered her eyelashes. 'There are some nice-looking camels around. Me, I'd probably wind up with a deaf mute Icelandic strongman, with BO and a tiny schlong.'

'I could meet two of those specifications,' he observed, 'but Ah talk too much and Ah cannae lift anything heavier than a full pint tumbler.'

She grinned at him, winking. 'Two out of four ain't bad. No, let's give the agency a miss. Tell you what,' she said, 'you got these very expensive drinks in, so in return I'll take you for a very cheap dinner some night. How about that?'

Provan's heart missed a beat, but he kept his expression deadpan. 'You are so lacking in ambition that you're asking a guy who's old enough to be your father out on a date?'

She reached out and cuffed him gently on the back of the head, triggering a small dandruff snowstorm. 'Companionship and friendship, Dan, that's what I need. The size of your schlong is irrelevant . . . or should I say it won't enter into it? How about it?'

He smiled. 'That would be nice; Ah must admit I am getting pissed off with the curry delivery boy.'

Mann finished her drink. 'Settled. Now back to business; let's get down to the casino.'

They exited the hotel and walked down Hope Street, turning left under the Hielan'man's Umbrella, and then right following Jamaica Street until it reached the river, and the Garrick Casino next to the pedestrian suspension bridge that led eventually to the once-notorious Gorbals.

Melvyn Holding works long hours, Provan remarked to himself as they entered. The general manager was standing in reception; he had changed into a white tuxedo, his evening uniform, the DS assumed.

'Sergeant,' he exclaimed. 'Good to see you again. Have you and your lady come to try your luck? I'll be happy to fix you up with a temporary membership.'

'This is no lady,' Provan retorted, 'this is my boss. Detective Inspector Mann, Mr Holding, he's the gaffer here.'

'More questions?' he sighed.

'No,' Mann replied, 'only one. Last night, when Mr Rogozin was here, did he interact with anyone else other than Mr McCullough and your staff?'

'Not to my knowledge, certainly not in the dining room. I'll need to talk to the gaming floor supervisor to be absolutely sure. Give me a minute.'

He bustled off and through a door on the right. 'Funny,' the DI remarked, 'casinos have been part of Glasgow all my life, but I've never been in one.'

'Me neither,' Provan admitted. 'Not as a punter, at any rate. Way back, when I was a plod, we had a call to a slashin' in a place up Buchanan Street. Waste of time; it was gangsters. Nobody would talk to us, so we went away and left them to maim each other. Different now though; casinos are better regulated, and better run. Nobody misbehaves.'

'They have a dining room here, he said?'

'Oh aye; the head waiter's my new best friend. Cheap too,' he added.

'No,' Melvyn Holding exclaimed as he crossed the foyer. 'Mr Rogozin did not speak to anyone else other than staff. He barely spoke to Mr McCullough, when he was down there. I'm sorry not to be of more help.'

'Melvyn, excuse me.'

With a small show of impatience the manager glanced across at a man who was standing beside the sign-in desk. He was big and burly, wearing sharp-creased black trousers and a red jacket with epaulettes, with gleaming patent leather shoes. 'Yes, Derek,' Holding responded, 'what is it?'

'Sorry, I couldn't help overhearing. Mr Rogozin did have a visitor last night . . . or an attempted visitor, I should say. He turned up not long after Mr Rogozin and Mr McCullough arrived, asking if he was here. I said I wasn't allowed to say who was here and who wasn't, but he wouldn't take that. He demanded to know whether Rogozin was in the building, demanded.'

'He was aggressive?' Mann asked.

'Not as such, not towards me, but he was angry all right. I knew quite well that Rogozin was here, but no way was I letting that guy anywhere near him. I told him he had to leave; I said I didn't want to call the police, but we couldn't have a disturbance here. He took that, and he left.' He looked at the DI. 'Given what happened afterwards, I wish I had called you lot.'

'I don't suppose you know who he was?'

'Oh aye, it was Paco Fonter, the Spanish footballer. He's been here before, twice. He's no a member, but he was signed in by Jimmy Pike, the English bloke that plays for Merrytown. He's a member; comes here a lot, sometimes with his bird, sometimes on his own.'

'His bird?' the DI repeated.

'Wrong word maybe,' Derek admitted. 'She's an attractive woman, not a dolly bird. She was all over Jimmy, though.'

'Never mind Pike,' Provan said. 'Fonter. Did he come back at all?'

'No.'

'Did you see if he was hanging about outside?'

'No idea,' the man named Derek replied. 'You could always ask Lucky Louie.'

'Who the hell is Lucky Louie?' Mann exclaimed.

'He's a wino; our resident wino, you might say. He hangs about outside and makes his living by bumming chips off customers when they're leaving. He's a poor sod; he always wears an old jacket with a badge on it. He claims that he went to Glasgow Academy, but I take that with a bucket of salt. He's completely out of his brains most of the time.'

'Ye cannae buy much with casino chips in the Co-op,' Provan observed.

'We buy them back off him,' Melvyn Holding explained. 'They're legal tender in here, so it's no loss to us.' He smiled. 'We could ask the police to move him on, I know, but as Derek said, he's a sad case and I for one don't want to make his life any harder. He's cunning enough to know which clients to approach and which to leave alone, so he doesn't usually upset anyone.'

'Where does he live?'

'God alone knows. I guess he sleeps rough unless he's got the money for a night in a hostel, but most of the time he inhabits the walkway. You might even find him there just now.'

'We'll give it a go,' Mann said.

Thanking the two men, they stepped outside, back into Clyde Street, then turned, following the path that led behind the casino and on to the river walkway. 'I could take this way back tae Cambuslang, you know,' Provan remarked. 'This is an official walking route now. It goes all the way up to the Falls of Clyde and New Lanark.'

'You don't want to try it. You might be mistaken for Lucky Louie.'

'Are you criticising my dress sense?'

'I've never been aware of you having any.' She stopped, pointed ahead of them at a bench, on which a shapeless bundle lay. 'Here, could that be human?'

As they drew closer, they saw that it could. Long, lank, filthy grey hair lay in strands along the bench, and snores resounded from the being on which it grew. The man's knees were drawn up to his chest, but the remnants of a badge could be seen on his jacket, with a line of gold wire peeling away from it.

As they reached him Provan whistled. 'He stinks,' he murmured, a hand to his mouth.

'That's like describing the *Queen Mary II* as a pleasure boat,' the DI countered. 'He takes stinking to a level I've never encountered before. If it wasn't for the snoring, I'd think he'd been dead for a week. No wonder he does well with the casino chips. I'd give him a tenner just to get him to cross the street.'

The DS ventured close enough to shake the sleeper. He woke with a start, swinging instantly into a defensive position, clutching an empty Eldorado bottle tight to his chest, pulling a grey canvas rucksack close to him, and glaring up at them through a grey creeper-like fringe of greasy hair. His eyes were yellow, creased with red and with black dots in the centre.

'Fuck off!' His roar was loud and whining. 'It's mine!'

'You're welcome to it, Louie,' Mann told him, holding up her warrant card, 'and we will leave you alone, I promise, once we've asked you a couple of questions.'

'It wasnae me.'

'I don't imagine it was. We don't think you did anything, Louie, but we're wondering if you saw someone who did.'

The human wreck made an obvious physical effort to focus his eyes on her. 'Wha'?' he muttered.

'Were you outside the casino last night?'

His forehead ridged, as if he was squeezing an answer out of his brain. 'Aye. Always am.'

'How late?'

'Till lights went out.'

'Do you remember a man leaving, just after one o'clock?' *If time means anything to you*, she thought. 'A tall man, dark hair, wearing a heavy blue woollen coat.'

'Bastard!' Louie whined.

'The man?'

He nodded, sending greasy grey locks flying. 'Bastard man! I asked him for chips; tried to kick me, 's if I was a dog.'

'Did you see where he went when he left?'

'Didnae leave. Went wi' the man.'

'What man?'

'Football man.'

'Football man?' Provan repeated.

'Aye. Angry football man. Been there before.'

'Do you know his name?'

'Naw, just football man.'

'Where did they go?'

'Along the walkway; this way.'

'Did you follow?' Mann asked.

'Naw. Went round the back of the casino. They chuck out food after the restaurant shuts; put it in bins.'

'After that, once you'd eaten, where did you go?'

'Then went along the walkway; came here.'

'Did you see anyone then?'

'Naw.' Unexpectedly, he broke into a wide, brown and gap-toothed smile. 'Got lucky though.' He shuffled his feet and for the first time, the detectives noticed that he was wearing odd shoes. One was an ancient brown Hush Puppy; the other was a black, hand-stitched leather brogue. 'Found this,' he chortled, holding it off the ground.

Provan was in no doubt. He had seen its twin earlier that day. He took out his phone, found the image of Paco Fonter and showed it to Lucky Louie as he revelled in having lived up to his nickname.

'Seen him before?' he asked.

The wreck rolled his multicoloured eyes; his befuddled brain had reached the limits of its attention span. 'Fuck would I know?' he mumbled.

Sixty

'We had plans for tonight,' Sauce Haddock said. 'Cheeky wants to see the new *Star Trek* film; she's a fanatic.' It was mid-evening, and the sky was beginning to send happy signals to shepherds.

'There'll be other nights,' Sammy Pye assured him. 'Your consolation is that the overtime clock is running. This can't wait; too much time's elapsed already since the murder. I'd have left it until tomorrow, but given what Lottie turned up in Glasgow, we have to go now.'

'Would you have fancied Paco Fonter for Rogozin?' the DS asked.

'Put yourself in his shoes. If someone did that to Cheeky and you found out about it, would you turn just a wee bit homicidal?'

Haddock glanced across at the DCI, in the passenger seat. 'I hope not, but I can't put my heart on my hand and deny it. DI Mann is sure of her identification, is she?'

'Rock solid apparently, at both the Central Hotel and the casino. The witness for later on is flakier, but Lottie says she has enough for us to detain him, and impound his clothing. There's almost bound to have been a DNA transfer from Rogozin to him in any struggle.'

'How about the other way around?'

'Sure, but after a few hours in the water, forget it.'

'Chances of him still being here if he did it?'

Pye pulled a face as the sergeant drew to a halt outside the Norton House Hotel. 'Let's find out.' He stepped out of the car and headed for the building,

By the time Haddock caught up, at the wood-panelled check-in desk, they had their answer. 'Senor Fonter checked out this morning,' the receptionist told the chief inspector, 'just after eight, when I came on duty. I'm on split shift just now,' he explained. 'Eight till midday, then eight till midnight.'

'Did he give the hotel any advance warning that he was leaving?'

'Not as far as I'm aware,' the man, Carlos, according to his name tag, replied. 'His booking was made by Merrytown Football Club, and it was open ended, one day's notice. I made up his bill and he left. I asked if he'd be returning, and he said that he wouldn't.' He frowned. 'No, not quite. We were speaking Spanish and what he actually said was, *"Después de lo que ha sucedido no quiero estar en Escocia nunca más. Si soy será como un prisionero."* That means, "After what has happened I don't want to be in Scotland ever again. If I am it will be as a prisoner." He laughed when he said it, but it wasn't a funny laugh, if you know what I mean.'

'Yes, we know,' Pye said. 'We know also that he left the hotel last night. Can you tell us when he got back?'

'No, I'm not aware.'

'If he came in after midnight would he have had access to the building or would he have had to call a night porter?'

'There's a keypad by the entrance door; guests have the code.

The porter doesn't sit here, so he wouldn't have seen him on the way in.'

'I did though,' a man remarked. They turned to face him, and saw a tallish middle-aged figure with white hair and a knowing smile on his face. 'Hello, Sauce,' he chuckled. 'You've come a long way from that probationer they gave me to baby-sit.'

'Charlie bloody Johnston,' Haddock exclaimed. 'The man who wrote the book that every time-serving back-watcher goes by to this day. How are you doing, Charlie?'

The former PC spread his arms wide. 'Ye see it all, son. Here, mind that time in the Meadows? You and me in that pea-souper fog, walking smack into that poor bastard hangin' from a tree. Freezin' it was and him wi' no coat either, 'cos wee Moash Glazier had nicked it.'

'I'll never forget it,' Sauce laughed, 'you nearly shit yourself.'

'You too, boy,' Johnston reminded him.

'I thought you got a job in the press office when you retired.'

'Ah did, but then the set-up was reorganised by yon Andy Martin when he got the big chief job, and there was no room for the likes of me. I've been night porter here for nearly a year; I prefer it, truth be told, and so does my wife.' He looked at the DCI. 'It's Sammy Pye, isn't it? Our paths never really crossed.'

'Yes, that's me. They didn't but I've heard all about you, Mr Johnston. Legend has it that you started in the job on the same day as Bob Skinner.'

'Absolutely true. From that day on he never looked back and I never looked forward. There's leaders and there's the rest.

I was always happy being led. Unlike you two, obviously,' he added.

'We're all led, Charlie,' Haddock countered, 'all save the one at the top, and even she's accountable to the Scottish Police Authority. So,' he continued, 'you saw somebody last night.'

'Aye. I guessed you were talking about Paco Fonter the fitba' player. He's the only guest that I saw come in after hours last night. I just happened to be doing my rounds and bumped into him on his way up the stairs.'

'What time would that have been?' Pye asked.

'I started my rounds at two fifteen; that's near the end, so it must have been closin' on two thirty.'

'Did you speak to him?'

'I said "Good morning, sir", then I felt a bit guilty in case he thought I was taking the piss about the hour he was comin' in. He was okay though; he mumbled something about fallin' asleep in his car, and it bein' the first decent sleep he's had for a week. Poor lad; we're all sorry for him, with what happened to his wife.' He looked past the officers. 'He's gone, is he, Carlos?'

'Left this morning,' the receptionist replied.

'Long shot,' Haddock said, 'but did he say where he was going?'

'Not directly, but I know. He asked me if he could use the hotel printer.' He pointed over his shoulder with his thumb to a black box on a table in the corner of the reception area. 'It's wireless, so he was able to access it through the network. I took the document off and handed it to him when it was ready. It was a boarding pass, for a flight from Edinburgh to Madrid; EasyJet, twelve forty.'

'Does that help?' Charlie Johnston asked.

'It tells us where to start looking for him,' Pye volunteered.

The ex-cop's instincts had always been sharper than he had allowed others to see. 'I thought you'd nailed the Merrytown head coach for Fonter's wife's murder,' he observed.

'We have.'

'So this is about something else?'

Haddock grinned. 'Casual enquiry, Charlie.'

'With a DCI and a DS, at this time of the day? Casual, my arse.'

Sixty-One

'I appreciate you letting me see these,' Skinner told Christine Hoy.

'I have no problem with it,' she said. 'The plans to all of the King Robert Village buildings are public documents.'

'I know that, but you could have insisted that I access them like any other member of the public, through the City Council planning department or through the Internet.'

'I have nothing against you, Mr Skinner,' she laughed. 'Why should I send you to the planners? Public document or not, those people all have a class in obfuscation included in their degree course. I made some alterations to my house last year: would you believe that I was refused a completion certificate because one of my steps was one centimetre too high! As for the Internet, it's okay but you can't really see all of the details, and some of them can even be obscured by official stamps.'

She handed him a large folded sheet of coated paper, and pointed him towards a table. It was too small to take all of the plan as he unfolded it, but he was able to find and lay out the east elevation.

'I'm only interested in the top two floors,' he said. 'They describe them as isolated from those below but what does that mean?'

'They have a dedicated lift,' the security manager explained. 'The building has two elevator shafts, but one stops at the sixth floor, while the other goes straight up to the seventh.'

'Yes, I see.' He peered at the drawing, then gave up the struggle and put on his reading spectacles. 'So what about the stairs?'

'It's the same.' She leaned across him and pointed to a detail of the plan. 'See? There's a public stairway but it only goes up to floor six. The seventh, and the penthouse, don't have a stairway as such.'

'What about emergencies? You can't use the lift in a fire situation.'

'No, but look at the west elevation.'

He pulled the plan across the table until he found the section she described. The penthouse and the two apartments below had their own stairway, inaccessible from the lower floors; it led all the way down to a door at the rear of the building on the other side from the main entrance.

'They have a back door?' Skinner murmured.

'Not as such. Each of the three has a self-locking steel fire door; it can only be opened from the inside.'

'What happens if the occupants are out and the lift breaks down? How do they get in?'

'Tough shit,' she chuckled. 'But in practice the lift never breaks down. It's serviced every month, and the tenants are told when it's being done, well in advance.'

'That got through the planners?' he asked.

'The original drawings had conventional locks on the fire

doors, to allow outside access, but they were changed at the request of the purchaser.'

'That's a company, isn't it?'

'Yes, I checked up on the name, by the way. It's Isle of Man registered. It's called Sparkle Holdings.'

'You what?' Skinner exclaimed, wide eyed.

'I think that's how you pronounce it. It sounds Spanish, doesn't it?'

'It is.' *I will never allow myself to be surprised by that man again*, he thought. 'I might know who the owner is. If I'm right, he's very security conscious. I'd like to take a look over there. The penthouse is unoccupied, but it's still a crime scene so no way can I go in, but can you get me access to the unoccupied apartment?'

She frowned. 'It's unoccupied as you say, but it's leased by the football club for occasional use.'

'You have access, don't you, on security grounds?'

'Yes, I do.'

'What about that funny smell that's just been reported?'

Christine Hoy smiled. 'For a retired chief constable, you're not very conventional, are you?'

'Never was,' Skinner admitted. 'Sometimes I think I'm not very retired either.'

Sixty-Two

'He was on the flight, no doubt about it,' Detective Constable Jackie Wright assured her sergeant. 'EasyJet confirmed it; he had a front row extra legroom seat. He booked a car through their website too, a Jeep Renegade.'

'For how long?'

'A week, they said. They gave me the number of the Avis desk at Madrid airport; I checked and a woman there said that he picked it up on time. I've got the vehicle registration.'

'Did they ask him for contact details?'

'Yes, but he gave them the Edinburgh address and a British mobile number. The latter was a waste of time: I had a trace put on his phone; it was found in his car, in the long-stay park at the airport.'

'Bugger,' Haddock moaned. 'That's no help. Thanks, Jackie, I'll take it from here.'

He walked into Pye's small private office; when they had moved to the old Edinburgh police HQ building from the Leith office, they had nicknamed it the 'bollocking room', but only in jest. The DCI had a light touch as a man manager, and a pleasantly even temper; he rarely raised his voice to a junior officer, not least because his famous ambition masked a degree of insecurity. He could never be certain that their roles would never be reversed. With Haddock he was sure that they would, given time.

'Paco's out of reach,' the DS announced. 'Jackie tracked him as far as the car hire desk in Barajas airport, but that's it. We'll need help from the police in Spain from here on.'

'With one of their own nationals, they might need a European arrest warrant for that,' Pye observed.

'Do we want to go that far?'

'That's something I've just discussed with Lottie. Her blood's up; she thinks we should go for one and have him arrested in Spain, but I've got a problem with that.'

Haddock nodded. 'And I can guess what it is,' he said. 'It came up in the inspector's exams. An EAW can only be issued to enable a prosecution; it can't be used just to pick somebody up on suspicion.'

His boss grinned. 'I know you passed your promotion exam, Sauce; you don't need to remind me. You're right, of course. And that's my problem. Lottie feels that she's got enough to go to that stage. I don't. She's got Paco turning up at the casino, demanding to see Rogozin and being turned away. We've got him arriving back at his hotel at an hour that would have allowed him to kill the guy and hightail it back to Edinburgh.

'But before I ask for a warrant,' he continued, 'I'd want to place him for sure on that walkway with Rogozin later on. Lottie reckons that her wino witness is enough to do that. I don't. If I was a Spanish prosecuting judge, I'd be very hesitant about extraditing one of my own people on the basis of somebody who only identified him as "Angry football man". If I was the Glasgow procurator fiscal, considering whether that's enough to charge Fonter, with no other supporting evidence, I'd be doubtful. On the other hand, if the police insist, he'll have a tough time turning us down. I just don't know.'

'Is it your decision, gaffer?' the DS asked. 'Mann and Provan are the investigating officers; they've been told to keep us in the loop, that's all. Could Lottie not go and bully the fiscal herself?'

'Yes,' he agreed, 'and the fact that she hasn't tells me that she has her doubts too. She doesn't want the buck stopping with her.'

'And neither do you. So?'

Pye gave a great sigh, puffing out his cheeks. 'I'm probably going to bottle it and move said buck on.'

'When's DCC McGuire back?'

'Not till Friday; it'll need to go to the chief again, and I don't want her thinking that I'm being indecisive.'

'Which is what you are, chum; ducking out of taking a decision.'

The DCI scowled. 'What would you do, Braveheart?' he retorted.

'Me?' Haddock laughed. 'I'd pass the buck, too; but in the other direction. I'd be telling Lottie it was her call. What does Provan want to do?'

'I'm not sure, but the way she was talking, his inclination is the same, go for it.'

'Then that's what'll happen. She never overrules him. He might be wee and wizened but he's a bloody brilliant detective. She might be his DI, but he's her role model.' He grinned again. 'Just like you're mine. Know what?' he added. 'I reckon all key decisions should be taken at DS level. We'd probably get them all right and if we did screw up, well, we're less in the spotlight than the senior ranks.'

'I could bring myself to agree with that,' Pye conceded. 'I'll take your advice and kick the ball back to Glasgow, but . . . I'd like to make a positive contribution. See if you can raise Cisco Serra on his mobile and ask him if he knows where Paco might head in Spain. If we can pin him down to a location without actually asking the Policia Nacional to arrest him . . .'

The DS nodded. 'I get it,' he said. 'We'll be ready to go if we do get a warrant.' He rose and stepped back into the CID suite.

Personal details of everyone interviewed had been retained in the case file, 'The Murder Book', as the media were fond of describing it. He found Serra's number at the top of the very brief statement that Jackie Wright had taken from him on the day after the crime had been discovered. It had an international prefix that he recognised as Spanish, but when the call connected he heard a British ring tone.

'Cisco,' the agent answered. 'Frank, you no' waste my time. Your offer for my client's story is laughable. I tell you you got to double it, then we think about it.'

'I won't be doing that.'

'Who is this?'

'DS Haddock, CID Edinburgh. I need a word.'

'Sorry; I think you guy from *Daily Star*.'

'That's a bit downmarket, isn't it?'

Serra laughed. 'I no' do business with them, Detective. I just use them ramp up the price.'

'Which client were you talking about?'

'Paco of course; I can't sell Chaz's story. He's going to jail.'

It was Haddock's turn to chuckle. 'You may be in a unique position. My colleagues in Glasgow are very keen to talk to Mr Fonter, in connection with the murder of Dimitri Rogozin.'

He waited, listening to the agent's heavy breathing as he absorbed the news. 'This another joke, yes?'

'For Paco's sake I wish it was, but they can place him at or near the scene of the crime.'

'It should not be a crime to kill that man. But what you say? I saw on TV, he was in the river.'

'When he was found, yes, but he was killed on dry land.'

'How could they tell?'

Haddock could see no reason not to explain. 'He died from a massive head injury, not drowning. Plus, one of his shoes was missing when they recovered the body. It was found on the Clyde Walkway.'

'I see. So why you call me?' Serra challenged.

'Your client has left the country. He flew to Madrid yesterday afternoon and hired a car. We'd like to contact him and ask him to come back voluntarily, and to do that obviously we need to know where he might have gone. Believe me, it's in his best interests, and by extension, yours too.'

'You say,' the agent sneered. 'You're telling me it's best for me to help put another client in jail? How can that be?'

'It's better he comes back of his own accord,' the DS replied, 'than he's hauled back in handcuffs, and through a forest of cameras as he's driven away from the airport.

'Let me put it another way that you might understand better,' he continued. 'If you know where he might have gone and you don't tell me, that would be unhelpful. If I found out somewhere down the road that you'd contacted him to warn him of our interest, that would be criminal. I'm a very suspicious guy by nature so, for your own protection, I suggest that you give me all the help you can.'

Serra sighed, and surrendered. 'Okay. You say he flies to Madrid and has a car. Then I say you that he most likely go to his parents' place. They live in a little town called Zamora. It is north of Madrid and north of Salamanca. They have a café bar, it's called Los Primos, that would be The Cousins in English.'

'Thanks. Is that all you can think of? Does he have friends somewhere else that he might visit?'

'He has some, but you ask me what he most likely do and I tell you it would be go to his mamma. Also he has a place there himself.'

'He does?'

'Yes. When he went to Pugliese, he bought the building where the café is; it's on Plaza Major, the main square of the town. His parents live on the two floors above. Paco and Annette kept the top floor for themselves when they visit. Is that okay?' the agent asked. 'You happy now?'

'If it helps locate him, I will be,' Haddock answered. 'Anything else?'

'No. Paco has no life outside his folks and Annette.'

'Did you know about his drug use?'

Serra's intake of breath was sharp enough to register on the line. 'How you know about that?'

'We found traces of cocaine in the penthouse; Paco admitted it was his.'

'Then yes, I know. But he stop; he kick it about three months ago. Hey,' he protested, 'he was not the only one in that team who took a line. Don't hit on him for that too.'

'I wasn't planning to, but it's hard for a police officer to ignore misuse of class A drugs. Listen, I'm thinking that if you're close enough to a player to know his bad habits, he must be your client. As far as I know you only have three on the Merrytown payroll, including Baker, so you might want to pass a quiet word to Jimmy Pike that we'll be sharing the information we have with colleagues in our drugs unit.'

Haddock ended the call and went back to Pye's sanctuary. 'I got Cisco,' he said, 'and I have a lead. Can you boot up Google Earth on your computer?'

The DCI did as he asked, then turned the mouse and keyboard over to the sergeant. Haddock keyed in the word 'Zamora', then waited as the application found its target.

'Okay,' he murmured, 'let's see.' He zoomed in on the town until he was close enough to read street names. 'Plaza Major, Plaza Major,' he repeated as his eyes scanned across the screen. 'Yes,' he exclaimed as he found it, and as he selected the Street View icon from the top right corner of the monitor. He pulled it down, clicked and a height image appeared of an open square, a photograph shot on a bright sunny day, probably around noon, in the summer months, as the shadows cast by parked vehicles, most of them police cars, were very small.

He rotated the image until he found what he was after then leaned back. 'There you are, gaffer,' he exclaimed. 'See that bar in the photo? Los Primos? That's where we start looking.'

Sixty-Three

'How often has this place been used?' Skinner asked, as they stepped into the apartment.

'To my knowledge very rarely,' Christine Hoy told him. 'I'm always advised for security reasons, but if the club wants to put someone in here they advise Paul Cope, the concierge. He receives the guest and hands over the keys; also he puts the cleaner in there before to give it a dusting over and, afterwards, to change and launder the bedding and towels. He'll stock the fridge as well, with whatever shopping list he's given.'

'That happens every time? Rogozin used it and he was a maverick.'

'Mr Rogozin played by the rules. He didn't have his own key.'

Skinner frowned. 'Are you sure about that? I checked with Mr Cope before I went to your office, and he told me that he didn't hand over the key on the day Annette died, yet we know from CCTV that he was there, and that he let himself in. He must have had one made.'

'It's possible,' Hoy conceded. 'They're not high tech; it's one area where the builder skimped a bit.'

'So,' he continued, 'it follows that if Cope didn't know that Rogozin was here, he didn't put cleaners in after his visit. Any forensic traces that were left on that visit will still be there, and are unlikely to be confused with holdover from his visit nine days earlier, as the place would have been serviced then. I take it the cleaner's thorough?'

'Elsie? She's not the best, but she's okay and she's cheap. She's also Paul Cope's mother-in-law,' she added, with a smile.

'Do you review the security recordings before you wipe the tapes?'

'Not always personally,' she replied, 'but yes, they are checked, either by me or by my assistant.'

'Who would check the footage of this floor and the one above?'

'That is always me.'

'Right. Let's go back to Rogozin's previous visit, on the Thursday of the week before the murder. Can you recall that?'

'Sure. I saw him arrive and I saw him leave next morning.'

'Between those times was there any movement on the penthouse floor or in and out of this apartment?'

'No, none at all.'

Skinner smiled. 'That's interesting, for the police have information that Rogozin and Annette Bordeaux were together on that Thursday night, in one apartment or the other. That can only mean one thing.'

'That they used the fire escape!' the security manager exclaimed.

'Exactly. Show me where it is, please, Christine.'

'Through here; follow me.' She led him through a door that led from the entrance hallway into a second corridor, and from there into a large, lavishly equipped kitchen with a dining area, beneath a west-facing window. 'In here,' she said, opening another door. 'This is a utility room, and there's the fire door.'

He looked at it. Like the rest of the room it was painted cream, apart from a thick brown handle, and a notice at eye level, in large red letters. He looked at the door frame and smiled. 'Abso-fucking-lutely,' he whispered, forgetting his companion for a second.

Various cleaning products, among them sprays, kitchen rolls, and a pack of disposable latex gloves were stacked on a work surface on his right. He plucked a pair of gloves from the box, put them on, then turned the handle. The door opened, inwards.

A fire extinguisher hung on the wall beside it. He glanced at Hoy over his shoulder. 'It never ceases to amaze me,' he remarked as he lifted it from its bracket, 'that designers put these things beside emergency doors with big red signs on them like this one, saying "Fire exit: keep closed", so they can be used to do this.'

He swung the heavy steel door wider and used the extinguisher to hold it open.

His smile grew even wider as he looked out and down, at the concrete landing. He took out his phone and selected camera mode. 'Christine, do you have yours?' he asked.

She nodded.

'Good. I need you to video me doing this, and be ready to swear under oath that neither you nor I had opened this door before this moment.'

He waited until she was ready, then knelt and shot several images of a metre-square area at the top of the fire escape steps. 'Very good,' he said as he stood. 'Now, follow me, please. Try to step across the landing, not on it.'

The stairway led up a dozen steps then turned on itself; twelve more and they had reached the top.

The stairwell was well lit by narrow windows and by LED lights on the wall of each landing.

'Oh yes,' Skinner murmured as he leaned down to peer at the concrete square, focusing on the foot of the closed door. 'Once again, please.' He reached for his phone again, shooting more images, as his escort filmed him.

'That's excellent,' he exclaimed. 'Now for the hard part.'

'What's that?'

'Going all the way down and back up again.'

She shrugged. 'I need the exercise.'

They jogged down the fire escape stair, counting off the floors one by one until they arrived at the foot. There he opened the exit door, slowly, and looked down at his feet, and beyond. He frowned, then stepped outside as Hoy held the door ajar.

He saw that he was standing in a public cycleway, leading from the roadway that ran past the apartment block, down to the Meadows. It was neat and tidy, with hardly a leaf to be seen, even in mid-September, and with absolutely no confectionery wrappers or other detritus.

'That's a bugger,' he murmured, 'but I've got enough. Okay,' he said as he stepped back into the escape stairway, 'time for the climb.'

The ascent took twice as long as the descent, even though they kept up a brisk pace. As they reached the open door, Skinner was pleased to note that his companion was breathing as heavily as he was, for all that she was twenty years younger.

'What now?' she asked, as he hung the fire extinguisher back in position and closed the door firmly.

'Now we get out of here, exactly the way we came in and we lock the door behind us.'

As soon as they were back in the corridor, he produced his phone again, but this time for its original purpose, scrolling to a number and making a call.

'What can I do for you, Chief?' a familiar voice said in his ear.

'Get yourself fitted for sackcloth, Sammy, my friend, and warm up the ashes. If I'm right, this is more than reasonable doubt. You need to get Arthur Dorward and his forensic team back into King Robert Village, seventh floor this time. I'll stand guard until they get here.'

Sixty-Four

'How do we go about this?' Sauce Haddock pondered, frowning as he spoke. 'Cisco Serra's best guess is that Paco would head for home, but that's all it is. We don't know for sure.'

Pye nodded. 'True, but thanks to the ingenious people at Google we know what home looks like. We know also that there appears to be a police station on the same square.'

'We can't just ask them to go and lift him, not without a warrant.'

'I'm not suggesting that, but we could ask them to verify whether he's there or not.'

'Then what?'

'We could ask them to give us the number and then we could phone him. Or we could ask them to ask him to phone us.'

'Thereby alerting him that we're on to him,' the DS pointed out.

'Not necessarily; we could say it's about Annette's murder.'

'We could, but if we involve the Policia Nacional, or the Guardia Civil, whichever it is, or even the Zamora local cops, that starts to formalise it.'

'Yes,' Pye conceded, 'but we still need a number.'

'Fuck's sake,' his junior muttered. 'It's a long time since you sat your inspector's exams. Let me see your terminal.'

He leaned in again, keyed 'Directory enquiries Spain' into the search bar, clicked and waited as a number of links appeared. He chose the first, Telefonica, and entered 'Los Primos'.

'*Et voilà,*' he declared.

'Wrong language, you smug bastard,' the DCI growled, 'which brings up another problem.'

'Not necessarily,' Haddock countered.

He stepped across to the doorway of the small office and called across the CID suite, 'Does anyone here speak Spanish?'

Jackie Wright raised a hand. 'I do,' she volunteered, if a little tentatively. He waved to her to join them.

'We want you to call this number,' Pye said, showing her the computer screen. 'It's Paco Fonter's parents' bar. First and foremost, we need to find out if he's there. If he is, will he speak to us?'

'If they ask me why?'

'Tell them it's to do with the investigation, that's all; that way you won't be lying.'

'I'll try.'

She picked up the DCI's phone and keyed in the number, listening as the call connected, then to the single-beep ringtone. It sounded three times before it was picked up and a strong, mature female voice said, '*Café Los Primos. Cómo puedo ayudarle?*'

The DC took a deep breath and began, '*Esta es la policía de Edimburgo, el detective Wright. ¿Me puede decir, es Paco Fonter allí?*'

'*Padre o hijo? Hay dos.*'

'*El hijo, por favor. ¿Está él ahí?*'

'*Sí, y ¿por qué estamos hablando Español?*'

'You speak English?' Wright exclaimed.

'Yes. I am Paco's mother, Helena Rovegno. I was born and raised in Gibraltar. My son is here. Why do you want to speak to him? Does it have to do with our Annette's murder?'

'It's related. It's something that's come up.'

'Paco is upstairs in his apartment. If you give me a number, I'll make sure he calls.'

'Does he have a computer there?' the DC asked.

'Yes, he does.'

'Can he use Skype?'

'Yes,' his mother said, 'that's how we speak.'

Wright gave her Pye's force email address. 'Ask him to use that, please.'

She handed the phone back to the chief inspector. 'Well done,' he said. 'Good thinking, asking him to use Skype. What was the rest about?'

'Nothing really; his dad's name's Paco too. She wanted to know which one I was after.'

'I see. Thanks, Jackie, that was a big help. We'll take it from here . . . assuming he does call. Three people on a computer screen might be a bit overpowering.'

The two men waited, for five minutes, then ten, until Haddock broke the silence. 'I have this vision,' he murmured, 'of a Jeep Renegade heading for the mountains with a tent and a month's worth of provisions.'

'Is that what you'd do if the police were after you? Become a mountain man?'

The sergeant laughed. 'Hell no. I'd call Cheeky's grandpa and ask for his advice. He's a world expert when it comes to slipping out of the clutches of the polis.'

They were still smiling when a tone from the computer and a flashing icon on the monitor told them that an incoming Skype call was awaiting connection. Pye clicked 'Accept' and Haddock moved round the desk so that both were in line with the inbuilt camera, as Paco Fonter's image filled the screen.

'Gentlemen.' The voice sounded metallic, but it was clear. 'I must apologise for leaving Scotland without telling you. Things became too much for me, and I felt a very strong need to see my mother and father. I did tell Alice, the club physio, that I was going, since she is in charge of my hamstring recovery, but I should have called you too.' As he spoke, the detectives studied his expression very closely, looking for signs of nervousness or fear; all either of them saw was the face of a tired man.

'My mother told me there has been a development,' he said.

'There has,' Pye confirmed, 'but not directly into the Annette inquiry. Yesterday morning the body of Dimitri Rogozin was taken out of the River Clyde in Glasgow. The autopsy confirmed that he was dead when he went in, and the investigators in Glasgow have determined where he was attacked and killed.'

He paused, looking at the screen; Fonter was frowning and his eyes had narrowed.

'It was on the walkway that runs along the north side of the river,' the DCI continued, 'just behind the Garrick Casino. Thing is, Mr Fonter, the Glasgow people have reliable witnesses who put you in the Grand Central Hotel earlier that evening, looking for Rogozin, and later, at the casino, demanding to see him. And there's another, who saw a confrontation between the victim and a man answering your description.'

The footballer leaned forward, and for a moment the Scots

were sure he was going to break the connection. If that had been in his mind, he decided against it; instead he clasped his hands together on the table at which he sat, his gaze fixed upon them.

'Yes,' he declared. 'I went looking for Dimitri. My intention was to beat the living shit out of him and then go to the police with the story that Sirena had told me. She came to see me in the hotel on Sunday; she said that the guy had forced himself on Annie, starting from when we were in Italy.' His face twisted in pain. 'She said that he drugged her . . .'

'It's all right,' Pye said, 'you don't need to go on. We know about it; Sirena spoke to us too.'

'Damn her,' Fonter snapped. 'I told her not to, to let me deal with it first.'

'We knew about it anyway,' Haddock volunteered. 'The team in Glasgow found Rogozin's iPad in the hotel.'

'They saw the pictures? I was hoping nobody would have to.'

'After you killed him?' the DS suggested.

'I didn't kill him. I assure you, I didn't. Yes, I went after him, to the hotel where I knew he stayed when he comes to Scotland. Yes, I knew most likely he would go to the casino. But they wouldn't let me in; they wouldn't even say for sure that he was there. I waited for a while, and as I did, I began to realise that I must not see Rogozin that night, or yes, I might have killed him. So I went to my car and I drove back to the hotel.'

'You didn't get there until after two,' Pye said, unsmiling. 'The night porter remembers seeing you come in.'

'I didn't go straight back; I sat in my car, playing music to calm me down. I left Glasgow after eleven, and then I stopped at the service area on the motorway. I bought a coffee there, some food . . . a baguette with salmon, another with egg and salad and a Snickers: I was hungry for I hadn't eaten . . . and I sat there and ate for a while, thinking what I would do. That was when I decided that before I did anything, I had to see Mamma and Papa. There and then I went online on my phone and I booked a flight next day to Madrid and hired a car.'

'What time would that have been?'

'I get to the service area after midnight; I leave after one thirty. I get back to the hotel when you say. I guess you can check with EasyJet when I book the flight.'

'That probably wouldn't tell us where you were,' Haddock countered. 'How did you pay for your food?'

Fonter's eyes widened very slightly. 'Credit card: Mastercard. That would tell you.' He breathed an audible sigh of relief. 'Gentlemen, what you want me to do? Should I come back to Scotland now?'

'What you must do is speak to the detectives investigating the Rogozin murder and tell them what you told me. If they're content to take a statement from you, and assuming Mastercard verifies the time of that transaction . . .' He paused, considering the situation. 'Your car is hired for a week, I understand.'

'Yes. I still have to book a return flight, but Alice said it would be okay for me to stay that long.'

'Then as long as you speak to Detective Inspector Mann in Glasgow and eliminate yourself as a suspect, it should be okay. I need you to give me your mobile number, and your email address. She may want to speak to you on video as well. And of course I'll need your credit card number.'

'Sure.' He dictated all the requested information to Haddock, who scribbled furiously to keep up.

'Thank you, Mr Fonter,' Pye said, when he had finished.

'What about Annie?' he asked. 'Are things still the same? Is Chaz still accused?'

'That is the situation. Obviously, if there are any developments you'll be advised.'

'I still can't believe it, you know,' Paco Fonter sighed, 'any of it; that Annie's dead, that Chaz killed her, or that she gave in to that animal Rogozin to protect me. When you find *el servidor público*, the public servant, who did kill him, please be sure to thank him for me. I congratulate him for having the courage to do what I could not. Good day, gentlemen.'

'Well,' Haddock exclaimed as the screen went dark, 'what did you think of that?'

'I think it's as well we didn't go for that European warrant. We'd be looking very silly now.'

'Come on now, gaffer. Before we had that conversation he was odds on favourite as the Russian's killer.'

'Granted, but his name can be wiped off the board now. Who does that leave, I wonder,' he mused. 'Sauce,' he continued, briskly, 'see to that Mastercard please. I'll phone Lottie and tell her what's happened here.'

'You'll let her down gently, won't you? She'll probably still want to charge him with leaving the scene of a threat, or any other offence she can dream up.'

Pye smiled. 'Kid gloves, I promise.' He rose from his chair. 'I need a stimulant after that let-down.'

He followed his sergeant into the CID suite, and made himself an instant coffee. 'I don't know why I drink this stuff,' he said, as he stirred in the milk. 'It's pish. Did you ever sample the chief's coffee, that he made in his old filter machine?'

'I never had that pleasure,' Haddock admitted.

'I'm not sure that pleasure is the right word: more of a challenge, I'd say, to see how long it took you to stop trembling afterwards.'

He went back to his office, and to his desk; through the glass wall, Haddock saw him wince as he tasted the coffee. In the same moment he heard the DCI's phone ring, and saw him as he picked up the call. As he watched, he saw his expression change, from casual, to astonished. He was halfway to the office when Pye beckoned to him as he replaced the handset.

'Fucking de Matteo,' he exclaimed, as Haddock reached the doorway. 'He should never have pissed off Bob Skinner. I don't know what he's got, but it's making him very happy. He wants forensic back into King Robert Village, and that means he wants us too. One call to Lottie and we're on our way.'

Sixty-Five

'This investigation's got an extra bloody wheel,' Dan Provan complained, slouched in a chair in the Pitt Street police office.

'Maybe so,' Lottie Mann acknowledged, 'but somehow it's managed to steer the car in the right direction. Pye's DC just called me to confirm that while Rogozin was being killed, Paco Fonter was buying coffee and rolls in Harthill services.'

'But it was him bangin' on the door of the Garrick Casino earlier on?'

'It was him, but he thought better of it. Lucky Louie's let us down.'

'Looks like it,' the DS agreed, mournfully. 'That lands us firmly back at square one. The man McCullough and now Fonter both eliminated as suspects . . . without the investigating officers speaking to either of them, by the way. I fuckin' hate this new force, Lottie; that would never have happened in Strathclyde.'

She shook her head. 'The outcome's what matters, Dan; you know that. Christ, you taught me that. But we're not quite back at the starting gate. We know for sure that Rogozin was killed on the walkway behind the casino, because the CSIs found his blood, hair and skin on a concrete fence post. We've still got Louie's botched identification . . . "Angry football man. Been there before." So we go back to the Garrick and we ask which of their footballing members were in the place on Sunday.'

'Lottie, that's no' going to be as easy as you think,' Provan warned. 'Half the footballers in the west of Scotland are members of the Garrick, and I suspect a few from the east as well. Pike lives in Edinburgh, for example; so do quite a few of the Merrytown guys.'

'But we can focus on Merrytown,' Mann countered. 'It's Rogozin's club.'

'Fair enough, but how many of them actually had anything to do with him? Angela Renwick runs the club; it's her that deals wi' the players and most of the time she's talking to their agents, no' them.

'There's another problem,' he added. 'There'll be no record of who was there on Sunday night. Members aren't asked to sign in unless they're introducing a guest, and there are no video recordings of the gaming rooms. The gaming staff are watching the wheel and the cards rather than the punters, and it's possible for a member to stand in front of a slot machine all night and never be noticed. So anything we get there's no' going to be guaranteed comprehensive.'

'Still, it's all we've got and we have to do it,' the DI insisted.

'Yes, and we will, I will, no argument.' He paused. 'But it's no' all we've got. We still have Lucky Louie: his real name is Brandon Shandley, by the way, but he never went to Glasgow Academy. He must have found the blazer, or stolen it. When I dropped him at the Royal Infirmary last night, after you went home, I spoke to one of the A and E medics, Dr Khan. He reckoned it'll take a week to stabilise him, and to get him over his malnutrition, and to get the Eldorado, the meths and everything else even partially out of his system.'

'He couldn't just walk out, could he? Sign himself out?'

'No, I took care of that. Mr Shandley's going to be unable to walk unaided for a few days, but if he does try to escape, or if he's awkward in any way, Dr Khan's going to section him, for his own safety. The guy's mental, Lottie, but somewhere in there is a memory. With a bit of Louie luck and a bit of time, they might be able to unlock it and get us an identification that's a wee bit more reliable than "Angry football man" or "Fuck would I know?", his last two efforts.'

'True,' she agreed. 'How do we progress this, do you think? Together in sequence or . . .'

'I'll go back to the Garrick,' Provan volunteered. 'I know them there already.'

'Thanks, Dan. You do that and I'll try to contact Mr Fonter on Skype, if he doesn't call me. I can take a statement from him, send it to Spain, then he can scan the signed document and send it back to me to go on the file.'

The little sergeant shook his head. 'I barely understand any of that shite, lass. I'm the last of the Tippex and typewriter generation.'

'Then it's lucky for Fonter that I do,' Mann laughed, 'otherwise he'd be on the first plane back to Scotland.'

Sixty-Six

'Y ou know Ms Hoy, don't you?' Skinner asked.

'Yes, we've met,' Pye said. 'How are you?'

'Overwhelmed by all this police interest,' the security manager laughed, lightly, as they shook hands.

'We didn't start this ball rolling,' the DCI pointed out. 'This one is a private initiative.' He looked at his former chief constable, almost severely. 'Dorward's team are on the way, sir. I hope it's going to be worth their while, or God help us all. What do you expect them to find?'

'I expect them to find the DNA of Annette Bordeaux, Sammy,' he declared. 'This is where she was killed; I'm absolutely certain of it.'

Behind him, the younger detective chuckled, shaking his head. 'I should have bloody known you'd do this,' he murmured.

'I told you Chaz was innocent, Sauce.'

'And you think you've proved it?'

Skinner smiled: no 'sir', no 'chief' this time; the young man was growing in confidence and maturity, challenging him in a manner that drew a reproving glance from Pye. He felt strangely proud.

'The way I'd put it, Detective Sergeant Haddock,' he replied,

'I think I've made him the less likely of two suspects; in the context of the case you've built, that will have the same effect. The charges will be dropped. Do you have overshoes with you, and a couple spare?' he asked the DCI. Pye nodded. 'Good, since this is about to become a crime scene. Let's get booted up and I'll show you what I've found.'

'Shouldn't we wait for Dorward?' the DCI suggested.

The former chief gazed at him. 'You know Dorward,' he chuckled. 'When he gets here he'll seal the place off and raise merry hell if anyone other than his people venture in there. Come on.'

'You don't need me, do you?' Christine Hoy said.

'No, not any more, but thanks for your help and take good care of that video you shot.'

He led the two detectives into the apartment, showing them the layout before taking them through to the utility room. 'Okay,' he began, briskly. 'On Thursday, eight days before Annette Bordeaux was murdered, Dimitri Rogozin checked into this apartment. On that same day, Merrytown FC were away in Finland playing a Europa League tie.

'Telephone records show that a call was made from the landline in this apartment to the landline in the penthouse, directly above. I believe that call was Rogozin summoning Annie, telling her to get down here. And I believe she came.'

'You believe, boss,' Pye said, 'but can you prove it?'

'That's why I need forensics in here. There's no existing security footage of that evening; it was wiped after a week, as is normal, but Christine Hoy is certain that Annette didn't come in here through the front door. That leaves only one alternative: she came in through that fire exit. When they dust it for prints they'll find Rogozin's on it, for sure. When they dust the handle on the equivalent door above, they'll find Annette's.'

Skinner smiled again, in a special way; as a serving detective, it had become known to close colleagues as his 'Gotcha grin'.

'I believe they'll find something else too,' he continued, 'Rogozin's palm print on the outside of the penthouse door. That's how he did it.'

'Did what?' Haddock asked.

'Killed her, and set up Baker.' He waited, letting them absorb his allegation.

'On that Thursday evening, I believe that Annette told him that it was all over; she said that he had lost his hold over her, as Paco had kicked his drug habit three months before and was completely clean. She told him to lay off or else.'

'Or else what? She wouldn't have told Paco, surely. Or gone to the police.'

'No, she wouldn't, I agree. I think she threatened to tell her brother, Chaz Baker.'

The detectives looked at each other; their growing unease was evident.

'We know some of that,' Pye conceded. 'Sirena Burbujas told us as much, but how does that tie in with him killing her?'

'I'll show you,' he replied. 'I believe that when she confronted him, Rogozin decided that Annette had to go. Maybe they argued, maybe he was conciliatory, but either way, he's thinking, "She dies". And he came up with a plan to get rid of her, while diverting the blame on to someone else, Baker.

'She'd come down the fire stair,' he opened the door, carefully using the edge of the handle, and blocked it with the extinguisher, 'and she went back up the same way. Either he accompanied her or he chased her, but whatever, he was last through that door, for on the way out,' he pointed to the work surface, 'he ripped off a piece of that kitchen roll.'

He knelt in the doorway and pointed to a small object on the floor, a wedge no more than one inch square, formed from a piece of paper, folded into itself several times.

Behind him, Haddock whistled softly. 'I'm getting there,' he murmured.

'Follow,' Skinner ordered, crossing the landing in one long stride and jogging up the stair to the top floor. 'Look again.' As the detectives caught up with him, he pointed to an identical impromptu plug, compacted by the weight of the door.

'That Thursday evening,' he told them, 'the bastard Russian followed Annette up here, and was inside with her. I'm sure the original forensic trawl of the penthouse will have revealed quite a few unattributed fingerprints and DNA traces. You need to compare them against his.'

'We will,' Pye promised.

'You'll find matches, I'm sure. He couldn't have been wearing gloves. So,' he continued, 'having gained access and spent however long he did here, Rogozin left by the same doorway, putting that wee wedge in place to stop it closing properly. You'd never have known by looking at it from the inside that it wasn't secure. The door is very heavy and the frame overlaps it by at least the width of the paper square.'

He led them back down to the seventh-floor apartment. 'Before he went back inside, I believe that he went down the escape and wedged open the door that leads to the outside.

'Why? So that he could access the building later, without being seen. I believe that he did that on the Friday of the following week, on a day when he knew Paco was away. He came in through the fire escape exit, and climbed the stairs. First he went into the untenanted apartment, and left the things he had brought with him, Chaz Baker's belt and training top, taken without difficulty from the Merrytown training centre.

'Preparations made, he went up to the penthouse. He entered through the booby-trapped door, and overpowered Annette in her bedroom. He hit her, breaking her nose and leaving the blood spray that Dorward's team found later, then he took her downstairs, where he strangled her with the belt.'

'And then he sent the text to Baker,' Haddock said, 'using her phone.'

'Absolutely. He sent a message that would be bound to bring him running. And then he waited.' He paused. 'He waited until he heard the lift going up to the top floor. He waited until he heard it go down again. Then, once Chaz had gone, he took Annette's body back up to the penthouse and left her there, with the incriminating belt that killed her around her neck. He left by the way he'd entered, then drove to the training complex where he dumped the blooded training top.'

'For us to find,' Pye sighed, 'and draw the conclusion we were meant to.'

'Why did he come back next morning and make that call from the landline, if he knew she was dead?' Haddock asked.

Skinner frowned at him. 'Come on, Sauce,' he said with a touch of impatience. 'He did it because he knew she was dead . . . to throw up a smokescreen in case the investigation uncovered their relationship. He was being very clever, or rather he thought he was; too clever as it's turned out. If he hadn't done that, we might never have discovered that he'd been there a week before.'

He beamed. 'There you are, lads. That's how she was killed and that's who killed her.'

'Subject to forensic confirmation,' the young DS pointed out.

'You find a single trace of her in this apartment, that's all you'll need. Even without it, the circumstantial case against Rogozin is now just as good, no, better than the one you had against Chaz. No way will de Matteo take it to trial.' He paused. 'The only thing I couldn't find was the wedge he used on the outside door, but that pathway is swept regularly, at least a couple of times a week, so it's long gone.'

'Okay,' Pye conceded, grudgingly, 'I'll buy it, Chief, at least for as long as it takes to prove it, or otherwise. Now please, can we get out of here before Dorward arrives and gives us all detention?'

Sixty-Seven

'How much is a membership here?' Dan Provan asked.

Melvyn Holding stared at him, astonishment in his eyes. 'You must be kidding. Detective Sergeant,' he murmured. 'Do you really believe you have to pay to come in here and lose money? Membership is free; you can join in person or online. Either way all you have to do is fill in a form. Why do you ask anyway?'

'I seem to be here so often, Ah thought I might as well join.'

'I might be able to make you a better offer than that,' the manager observed. 'You must be pretty near retirement age. If you'd like to supplement your pension, I could use a guy like you to supervise my security staff.'

The little man's glare told him that he had made a mistake. 'Fuck you very much,' he growled. 'I've got another ten years in this job.'

Holding rushed to repair the damage. 'Sorry, sorry; I was joking of course. How can I help you today, Mr Provan? How's your investigation progressing?'

'We're still focusing on the Garrick,' the DS replied, tersely. 'Specifically on anybody with a football connection who was here on Sunday, at the same time as Rogozin.'

'I couldn't tell you that myself, but let me speak to the gaming room supervisor; in fact, let me bring him up here. Come into my office, please, while I go and get him.'

He led the way into a small room off the entrance lobby; it was furnished minimally, with one desk and two chairs, but its focal point was a window that looked down into a long room where the gaming tables were situated. It was quiet, but some players were in place, a broad racial mix of white, Asian and Chinese. Provan stood looking through it until he saw Holding come into view. He called out to a dark-haired woman in a three-piece suit, an image that reminded him of a snooker referee he had seen on television; they exchanged a few words, and she followed him from the room.

They were with him less than thirty seconds later. 'This is Minah Denis,' the manager said. 'She was supervisor on Sunday.'

'Pleased to meet you,' the woman said, surprising Provan by offering a handshake; he accepted awkwardly.

'You were asking about football people, I'm told,' she began. 'Sunday's a big night for them, players mostly. We do get some coaches in too, and directors, but they tend not to mix socially. Mr Rogozin, though, he was here a lot, not just on Sundays. Speaking ill of the dead, I know, but he was an arrogant man and a terrible loser, and yet . . . I could never help thinking that a lot of the reckless gambling, "Everyzzing on ten black!",' she mimicked in a passable accent, 'and all that sort of stuff, was for show, that he'd created an image for himself and was living up to it.'

'Was he like that on Sunday?' the DS asked.

'He wasn't quite as loud as normal, but he had company. Funny, but thinking back, he seemed a wee bit nervous. The man he was with didn't gamble. In fact he hardly said a word, he just watched Rogozin play, until he, the other man, had had enough. He tapped Mr Rogozin on the shoulder, said something to him, and they left.'

'The other football folk; were there many?'

'We were pretty busy,' Denis replied. 'Let's see. There were a handful from Rangers and Celtic; they all came in together, as they do quite often. The Old Firm guys think they're a race apart. Then there were four lads from Hearts, and two from Motherwell. Mostly it's the foreigner players that tend to come here,' she explained. 'We don't get so many of the Scots lads. Maybe they're family men,' she surmised.

'How about Merrytown? Any from there?'

She nodded. 'Yes, them too. Three of them, Art Mustard . . . he's nice . . . Flowers, the American . . . he's not . . . and Jimmy Pike, the English lad. There was a girl with them; dark haired, Alice, they called her. I hadn't seen her before, at least I don't think I had; Jimmy had been in with a woman before but she wasn't with him on Sunday.'

'I'm no' bothered about their birds,' Provan said. 'I want to know whether any of them spoke to Rogozin, or argued with him.'

'Now you ask me, there was an exchange between them. Big Art Mustard saw him and said hello, but Mr Rogozin more or less ignored him. Then Jimmy said, "Sorry about yesterday," and Mr Rogozin looked at him and said, "You'll be sorrier when your contract is due. You're a crap player," or something like that. For a second it looked like Jimmy was going to have him, but Art held on to his arm and pulled him away. That was when the other man tapped Rogozin on the shoulder and they left.'

'Can you remember when Pike left?

'About an hour later. Flowers and the girl went just after

Rogozin, but the other two stayed later; they were doing well, both of them.'

'Did they leave together or separately?' the DS asked.

'Together,' she replied, 'but whether they split up when they were outside, I have no idea.' She looked at him. 'Does that help you?' she asked.

'Time'll tell,' he told her. 'For now, it gies me another fish to fry.'

Sixty-Eight

'Have you given any more thought to the proposition I floated before you?' Maggie Steele asked.

'When have I had time?' Skinner countered, with a gentle laugh. 'I've spent the last week and a bit undermining the spurious case that my former junior colleagues built against my daughter's client.'

'Don't I just know it,' the chief constable admitted. 'And you've bloody well succeeded,' she added. 'I've just had a call from Sammy; he reported the development directly to me, given that Mario's away on holiday and Marlowe's on a course, and I told him to give me updates as they happen.'

'Who the hell's Marlowe?' he interrupted.

'He's a detective chief super; he was uniform in Grampian before the amalgamation, and before my predecessor saw fit to make him crime coordinator. He's the line manager for Sammy and all the other divisional CID people.'

'Never heard of him; that shows you how detached I am already.'

'So detached you got a result,' she exclaimed, loud enough for him to hold his phone a little away from his ear.

'You were right,' she continued. 'It looks like Annette was

killed in the kitchen of the downstairs apartment,' Steele continued. 'Arthur's team found a blood smear there. It's been sent for analysis and comparison, but they also found a full set of her right-hand fingerprints on a work surface. Arthur reckons she grabbed it while she was being strangled, and pressed hard. There's more work to be done, but that's conclusive as far as Baker's prosecution is concerned. I spoke to Rocco de Matteo just before I called you and told him to advise the court that he won't proceed with the indictment against him. I suggested also that he hold a press conference, but he demurred on that. There will be a briefing, but the woman Benedict will take it.'

'Hah!' Skinner laughed, loudly. 'My daughter is going to love that,' he said. 'She and the advocate depute do not get on. She and her client will of course hold a media event of their own, but I'll ask her to go easy on the Crown. I don't care about de Matteo or Benedict, but I don't want to embarrass the boys.'

'Did they screw up, Bob? Should they have been more thorough?'

'Not at all,' he declared, firmly. 'If you or I had been in their shoes, with what they found, the CCTV of Chaz going in and out, the belt, the bloody training top, the text, her phone dumped along the road, we'd have reacted in exactly the same way. We'd have charged Baker and been confident about going to trial. We wouldn't have gone looking for anyone else. Fuck me,' he chuckled, 'they'd have convicted O. J. Simpson on that evidence.'

'In that case I'm reassured,' she said. 'What should I do with CID, Bob?' she asked. 'Give me some advice, please. How would you make it operate more smoothly?'

'Put Marlowe back in uniform. The very fact that I'd never heard of him means he hasn't been doing his job. Put a criminologist in his place, looking for national crime trends and recommending action areas and priorities, but have the divisional people report to Mario directly, or to an ACC. As for Edinburgh, in practice Sammy's doing a detective super's job, so make him a detective super, and bump Sauce up so he can act as an SIO if necessary. Give him his own space.'

'As it happens, I have a DI vacancy coming up in Edinburgh,' she admitted. 'Becky Stallings wants to be a mum for the next five years, and with Ray Wilding, her other half, having gone across to Fife . . .' She paused. 'Okay, that's the Menu taken care of, but you still haven't answered my question. What about you?'

'I'm not coming back, Maggie,' he replied, quietly, 'not in the way that the First Minister suggests, and not in any way on a full-time basis. If something comes up that you feel calls for my experience, you know where I live, but until it does, I've got a family that's going to become even more demanding over the next couple of months.'

'Fair enough. I'll tell Clive Graham. How is Sarah?' she asked.

'Smashin'. Still working but doing all the right things.'

'And Ignacio?'

'He's going to university next month, courtesy of the Prison Service and the Edinburgh Arts faculty. He wants to be a cop,' he told her, 'believe it or not. When he's ready, I'll be supporting his application. You might not have me back, but the next generation is coming.'

Sixty-Nine

'Hold on, Pops,' Alex said holding up a hand, 'I have to take this call.'

Her father nodded, reaching for another sandwich from the plate that sat between them on her desk, watching as she made a quarter turn in her chair to face the smoked-glass wall.

'Solicitor General,' she said, 'what a pleasant surprise.' She glanced at Skinner, winking. 'Yes, okay, I confess, it isn't a surprise at all. I've heard already.'

She nodded as she listened. 'Of course, of course,' she murmured. 'Yes, I understand. You were bound to act on the basis of the police report; which made your offer of a deal on a culpable homicide plea all the stranger, since that report pointed very clearly at premeditated murder.'

She fell silent, smiling.

'Clearly,' she resumed. 'If you'd known about the Rogozin relationship from the start, that would have made a difference to the investigation.'

She nodded again. 'You'll desert the indictment in court tomorrow? Yes, my client and I will both be there. Wouldn't miss it for the world.

'What's your next step? A formal Sheriff Court inquiry into

Annette Bordeaux's death? Mmm, thank you. Yes, me too.'
Her mouth opened as she stifled a gasp. 'I appreciate the offer,
Rocco, but I don't think so, not at this stage in my career. Maybe
in five years or so, but not now; I'm not ready. Yes, see you
tomorrow.'

She hung up, then drank from a bottle of Lucozade.

'Son of a bitch!' she exclaimed. 'After he'd eaten his humble
pie, he said to me that the incident . . . his description . . . has
made him think that he needs to sharpen up the Crown Office
act . . . his words again. He actually offered me a job as an
advocate depute. Would you bloody believe it!' she said, indignantly. 'I might not like Paula Benedict, but she's more than
capable, and she didn't do anything wrong.'

Skinner shrugged, amused by her anger. 'The guy's a weasel,
love. We both know that. More important, his bosses, the First
Minister and the Lord Advocate, they know it too. He's on his
way out; I hear that your friend Easson Middleton is the likely
replacement.'

'Is there anything you don't hear?' Alex asked.

'Not much,' he conceded.

'Okay, who killed Rogozin?'

'That hasn't reached me yet. I only know who didn't: it wasn't
Paco Fonter, it wasn't Grandpa McCullough and it wasn't me.
Sammy Pye told me that the only relevant witness is a street-
dwelling wino who's facing a week's detox before he can be
interviewed properly, so I don't envy Lottie Mann her task . . . not
that anybody's too bothered, truth be told.'

'It's a murder inquiry, Pops,' she pointed out.

'Into the death of a murderer, rapist and blackmailer. I'm not
saying that Mann and Provan will give less than one hundred
per cent, but they're under a fraction of the media pressure that

Sammy and Sauce were under. Personally, I don't give a fuck who killed the guy.'

'Would you say that if you were still a chief constable?'

'Publicly, no; privately, I'd feel exactly the same way. Some people ask to be murdered, and he was one.'

'You're in no doubt that he killed Annette?' Alex asked.

'None at all,' Skinner declared. 'It's just a matter of joining the forensic dots. This was a lovely, popular woman with not an enemy in the world. If not Rogozin, who?'

Seventy

'You're a supporter, I see.' Jimmy Pike pointed a finger at the small badge that was pinned to Provan's lapel.

'And proud of it,' the DS replied. 'I take the rough with the smooth.' In fact, he possessed identical badges for Celtic, Rangers, and Partick Thistle, that he wore to suit the occasion and his surroundings.

'It was the rough last Saturday, I'm afraid,' the player said. 'Sorry about that.'

'It wasnae your fault. We'd have had a point at least if you'd taken that penalty.'

'I can't argue with that, mate. The truth is, I was supposed to take it, but Orlando wanted to show off to his girlfriend, so I let him have it. I should have known better.'

'You don't rate him then?'

'Not as highly as he rates himself. The only thing I will say for him is that he practises hard.' He nodded towards the training pitch, where the American had lined up half a dozen balls around the penalty spot and was firing them at the youth team goalkeeper. In the time that they had been watching, four of the shots had been saved.

Pike turned towards Mann. Did she read tension beneath his

confident bearing, or was it simply curiosity? 'What can I do for you, Inspector?" he asked. 'Is this about Annie? 'Cos I already told that big fella everything I know about it.'

The DI peered at him. 'Which big fella was that?'

'Skinner, his name was. He came here to talk to me and Art and Orlando.'

Did he, by God? she thought. 'No,' she replied, 'it isn't about the Bordeaux case. What made you think it should be?'

'I just got word that the boss is off the hook,' he told her. 'They're thinking Rogozin did it, apparently.'

The two detective looked at each other, sharing their surprise. 'Fuckin' Pye,' Provan growled. 'He might have told us.'

The DI said nothing; instead she turned back to the footballer. 'This is about Rogozin,' she continued. 'About his murder. He was last seen alive in the Garrick Casino. I believe you were there too on Sunday evening.'

'Yes, I was,' Pike acknowledged, cautiously. 'He was always in the Garrick on a Sunday night when he was here,' he added.

'I'm told also that you had a confrontation with Mr Rogozin, in the gaming room.'

'I wouldn't say that,' he protested. 'We had a conversation, that was all.'

'During which, Jimmy,' Provan countered, 'Rogozin called you a shite player, or words to that effect, and sort of hinted that you'd have contract problems in the summer. You were going to go for him, only Art Mustard pulled you away. That's what we were told. Is that what happened? No nonsense now; we'll be speaking to Art.'

The footballer grimaced. 'Yeah, okay, that's more or less how it was.'

'You were angry,' Mann said.

'Too bloody right I was angry. Bastard was well out of order talking to me like that in front of the rest of them, in front of Alice too.'

'Alice McDade?'

'Yeah. Orlando was there, so she was too. That's the way it is these days.' Unexpectedly, he grinned. 'It all started on the treatment table; that's what we say.'

'Did you cool down after he left?'

'Not right away; I don't forget things like that in a hurry.'

She nodded. 'No, you don't, and sometimes your reaction can be extreme. I did some research on you before we came along here, Mr Pike. You've had eight red cards for violent conduct during your playing career, seven in England and one here, in Scotland. You missed the Cup Final in May, because you were suspended for head-butting an opponent the week before. That suggests that when the red mist comes down on you, you don't think about consequences.'

'Come on,' he protested. 'That's football. Lots of us are different people on the pitch and off it.'

'You're not, though. Your career was held up by a six-month club suspension when you were eighteen, for an assault on a teammate in training that might have got to court but never did.'

'Yeah, when I was eighteen!' he protested. 'I haven't been in trouble since.'

'Eight red cards is most folks' idea of trouble, Jimmy,' Provan pointed out. 'Come on, son, this is serious. We know what time you and big Art left the Garrick. Where did you go after that? I hope you're goin' to say straight back to Edinburgh, but if ye didnae, we'll find out, one way or another.'

'Art did,' Pike said. 'We'd come through together on the train, but I was still fired up by the Rogozin thing; I wasn't ready to go back. He got a lift from the Hearts boys, and I hung around.'

'And waited for Rogozin?' Mann challenged him.

'No! I didn't know he was still there. I'd had a good night and I was feeling lucky, so I went along to the other casino, the Riverboat.'

'Did you go in?'

'No. By the time I got there I'd changed my mind. Instead I got a kebab off a stall, walked up to the Central Station and got a Joe Baksi home.'

'A taxi?' Provan exclaimed. 'Tae Edinburgh?'

'Sure. I was two and a half grand up on the night.'

'What time did you get in the taxi?'

'Quarter past one on the station clock.'

Mann pressed on. 'You didn't go back to the Garrick, lie in wait for Rogozin, crack his head open on a bollard and chuck him in the Clyde?'

'No fucking way, excuse my French. You try and prove that I did.'

'There's one way that we can,' she said, 'or eliminate you if you're telling the truth. Mr Rogozin lost a shoe during the attack, and we've recovered it. There are three sets of prints on it, including his and the dosser who was wearing it when we found him. We're thinking that the third set might belong to the person who heaved him into the Clyde after killing him. If you're innocent, I assume you'll have no objection to our taking your fingerprints for comparison.'

'None at all. Where do we do it?'

'Right here. Wonders of the digital age; we've brought a portable scanner with us. It's wireless too; we'll know the result straightaway.'

Pike laughed. 'I can tell you now, a home win.'

Seventy-One

'If I could invent one piece of kit,' Arthur Dorward grumbled, standing in the hallway of the seventh floor apartment, 'it would be a reliable handheld scanner that would lift fingerprints and palm prints straight off the surfaces where they've been left. Until someone does come up with one that I can trust, we still have to do it the old-fashioned way.'

'You'd still find something to moan about,' Sauce Haddock observed.

The scientist glared at him. 'Cheeky young bastard,' he growled. 'If I was still a ranking police officer, and not a civilian scientist, I'd have you on points duty.'

'If you were still a ranking police officer,' the DS countered, 'I'd be a fireman or a paramedic.'

'God help either service. Anyway,' he continued, setting the banter aside, 'to summarise what we've got here. Your revised theory, that the victim was assaulted in the penthouse then brought here and killed here, you can mark up as correct. Gold stars both, clever boys.

'Your suspect Rogozin's prints are all over the place too. So are the cleaner's, liberally; she doesn't do a very good job. She left us a bonus,' he laughed. 'There's a big skidmark on the toilet bowl that'll give us identifiable DNA.

'The concierge, Cope, whose prints we also have for elimin-ation, there are some of his too, and various others, as yet unidentified. Everything we've lifted from here has been scanned, and comparisons run on the database.'

'What about the distribution?' Haddock asked.

'They're all over the flat, apart from Cope's; his are only on the front door and in the hall.'

'How about the fire door handle?'

'Loads there,' Dorward confirmed, 'most notably, the victim's.'

'That fits the theory,' Pye said, stepping into the discussion, having taken a phone call in the corridor outside, 'that she came down here to see Rogozin, about a week before her death.'

'Good for you; what might not fit it is the lack of any identifiable prints of his on the handle. That said, there's quite a few there, the cleaner's and a couple of the unverified ones: I suppose it's possible that his were there and have been smudged. Good luck offering that in a criminal court, by the way,' he added.

'We won't need to, Arthur. The perpetrator's dead; this isn't going to trial. How about upstairs, that fire escape door?' he continued.

'Shirley did those,' the scientist said. 'I left her in the kitchen scanning the results. Come on and we'll see if she's finished.'

He led the way through from the hall, taking care to touch nothing, even though he was in a sterile suit and gloves. His colleague was identically dressed, but looked slightly comical. She was no more than five feet tall and her paper clothing hung on her like a bin liner.

'What have you got, Shirl?' Dorward asked.

Shirley Hart looked up at him, a pert little face with a teasing smile. 'I've got a surprise,' she replied. 'As you guys expected, I lifted prints from the outside of the door upstairs, right hand, all five fingers and a partial palm. I've just run them and here's the bad news: it's not Rogozin,'

'Bugger!' Pye and Haddock shouted, in duet.

'Ah but,' she continued, 'now the good. I have got a match. It was the weirdest thing; when I'd scanned the thumb print, I ran it through the system and got nothing. When I'd done them all, I ran them again, just for luck and bloody bingo; I got a result on all five digits. Either I did something wrong the first time, or the guy's prints had just been entered into the system.'

'Then put us out of our misery,' the DCI exclaimed. 'Tell us whose they are.'

Seventy-Two

'Don't look so disappointed, Lottie,' Dan Provan said, 'we've still got Lucky Louie to fall back on.'

'That doesn't fill me with confidence,' Mann replied, mournfully, as she prepared to exit the motorway. 'The reality is that Lucky Louie's brain's so fried with cheap wine and fuck knows what else that suppose Yogi fucking Bear killed Rogozin, he still couldn't pick him out in an OD parade.'

'Ye mean an ID parade.'

She laughed softly, shaking her head. 'I did, but given the state of our star witness it's a pretty Freudian slip. Sorry, Dan, I can't help looking disappointed, because I am. I really thought we'd cracked it with Jimmy Pike. At the beginning, there was something about him. Just for a minute he was uncertain beneath all the bullshit; my instinct said we had him. But it was wrong; I'm losing it, Dan.'

'Bollocks,' he exclaimed, 'you're losing nothing, Inspector. You're still the second best detective in Glasgow, after me. We are the polis, Lottie; when we turn up at somebody's work and start askin' him questions about a murder, then I don't care who he is, he is goin' to be nervous until he understands what we're after. Once Pike got there and worked out that he had a black cab as an alibi, he was fine.'

'Louie would have liked it to be him: remember, he said that Pike kicked him, when he asked him for spare chips. "Angry football man", he said, and Pike's red card record fits that description. Do you like the man, or does the fact that he's a footballer cloud your judgement?'

Provan frowned. 'No, he's a shit; I was prepared to believe it was him as well . . . but it wasnae, so that's that. But we're not done; we take a step back, like we agreed, and we look at CCTV around the time of the murder. Okay, we know that the Garrick's a dead zone, but the cameras pick up pretty close on either side. Let's see what that footage shows us.'

'Okay,' she conceded, 'let's do it.' She sighed. 'Of course it's always possible the killer never left the walkway. It starts down at the Transport Museum and goes all the way out of the city.'

'Lottie!' the DS exclaimed. 'Positive, okay?'

'Yes, I know,' she said. 'It's just that I've got a niggle, something Pike said. It struck me as odd at the time, but it's gone right out of my head.'

She focused on the road ahead as they approached the monitoring centre, and was about to turn into the building's car park when she exclaimed, 'And now it's come right back in!' She pulled up in an empty bay. 'Dan, before it goes again I must make a phone call.'

'Phone who? Pye?'

'No. The way their investigation seems to be going it'll wind up with Bob Skinner anyway; I'll speed things up and go straight there.'

Seventy-Three

'If not Rogozin, who?' Skinner asked himself.

The question he had put to his daughter had been rhetorical, and yet it had stayed with him as he returned to his own room. He had always been aware of his analytical powers, and of his ability to piece together a solution from all the available facts. He had known self-doubt only rarely; usually, his conclusions, once reached, acquired a biblical authority, carved in stone.

As a serving police officer, he had spent the last twenty years of his career at a level where his findings were never questioned until they were put to the test in court, and even there they had always been confirmed by juries. He had never been on the wrong side of a trial. Nobody took issue with him other than himself, and that happened very rarely.

And yet . . .

He leaned back in his chair and closed his eyes, visualising the murder of Annette Bordeaux, and the framing of her half-brother, Chaz Baker, by Dimitri Rogozin, in every tiny brutal detail, from its conception to its execution and to its completion.

He played it, and he replayed it, and he replayed it again, his unease growing on each occasion. He ran the mental video through for a fourth time, conception, execution, comple . . .

'Fuck!' Bob Skinner whispered, to his empty office, as he opened his eyes.

He lurched forward in his chair, snatched his phone from his pocket and called Pye. 'Sammy,' he barked, 'I'm wrong. It couldn't have been Rogozin. He'd . . .'

'No, it wasn't,' the DCI agreed. 'Your scenario stands, but it looks as if it was Jimmy Pike. He put the wedge in the penthouse door.'

'But not alone: he must have had an accomplice.'

'One thing at a time, Chief, please. We've got Pike, let us deal with that.'

'Look, I'm telling you . . .'

'Please!' Pye snapped, losing patience. 'Let us get on with our investigation; we're the police, not you.'

The line went dead; Skinner took his phone away from his ear and stared at it, experiencing a unique rush of astonishment and fury, intermingled.

'He had a fucking accomplice!' he shouted, as if the detective, a mile away as an angry crow would have flown, could hear him.

'Baker's free and clear,' he growled, as his rage began to subside, 'off the fucking hook. Do I give a shit?'

In the very moment he realised that he did, his phone vibrated in his hand and the ringtone began to play. He looked at it and saw that the caller was Detective Inspector Charlotte Mann.

'Lottie,' he said, 'is this a misdial?'

'No,' she replied. 'It's probably out of order, but frankly I've had enough of my supervising officer in Edinburgh for a while, so I thought I'd bounce this off you, since you've been involved. I was listening to the radio in the car, to the news on Radio Scotland, and they had a late item, "news just in", that the charge against Chaz Baker was being dropped.'

'As it has been,' he confirmed.

'Well, it's a funny thing, but three-quarters of an hour before that, I heard that from Jimmy Pike, the footballer. Now I can't help wondering, how the hell did he know?'

In that instant, Skinner's battered self-esteem, which had been the real reason for his fury, repaired itself.

'That, Inspector, is a hell of a good question,' he said, 'to which I do not have an answer. However,' he added, as a revised version of his crime scene video began to play behind his eyes, 'I could be two steps away from finding out.'

He was out of his chair before the call was ended and heading for the lift. When it arrived he went up two floors to his daughter's office suite. She looked up, surprised, as he burst into her room. 'Pops?'

'When you called Baker with the good news,' he began, 'did you make it clear he should say nothing to anyone until the Crown Office had made it public?'

'One hundred per cent,' she confirmed. 'I told him I wouldn't trust de Matteo until it was all official, and he understood.'

'Fine.' He turned on his heel and left. He rode the elevator down to the garage, looking over his shoulder instinctively as he unlocked his car.

As he drove into Morrison Street, he gave a voice command, 'Call Chaz Baker.' It was recognised; he heard a dialling tone, then the manager's voice. 'Sorry, whoever you are,' he said. 'I can't comment other than to say I'm pleased.'

'I'm glad to hear that Chaz,' Skinner told him, 'but have you made any calls since Alex spoke to you? To anyone at the club, for example?'

'Hell no,' he laughed. 'Your daughter puts the fear of God in me; it all stayed in-house.'

'Okay.' He pressed the 'hang up' button and turned right, heading for King Robert Village.

The concierge's office was a small room off the foyer of the luxury block, with the name 'P. Cope' on a plate beside the door, at eye level, and its occupant was in.

'My name's Bob Skinner, Mr Cope,' he began.

The concierge sprang to his feet. 'I know who you are, sir. How can I help?'

'Do you hold spare keys for the apartments?'

'No, they're all kept by the security manager.' Skinner felt a rush of disappointment. 'Apart from one,' Cope continued, dispelling it immediately. 'There's an apartment on the seventh floor. It's leased by Merrytown Football Club, but used only occasionally; I have a key for that in case it's needed at short notice.'

'Where do you keep it?'

'In my desk.' He pulled a drawer halfway open, then closed it again. 'I always lock it at night,' he volunteered, reading Skinner's unspoken reproof.

'Who knows about it?'

'Anyone who's ever come here to collect it. Mr Rogozin, for example, and his minder, who brought it back. Then there's Mr Serra, the agent, a while ago. And Mr Flowers; he entertained his lady friend there one night when they had an extra player staying in their apartment.'

'Did he bring the key back?'

'No; as it happens Mr Pike did.'

Skinner nodded. 'I see. Now, I want to take you back to the Friday before last, the day that Annette Bordeaux was murdered.'

'I've already told the police everything I know about that,' Cope insisted.

'This is different. On that day, did anyone pick up the key at any time?'

'No, definitely not.' He frowned. 'But now that I think of it, a funny thing did happen. I stood on it, on the key, as I was getting up to leave for the night. I'd been in my drawer earlier and I must have pulled it out with something else, by mistake.'

'Is that possible?'

'Unlikely, but it must have happened.'

'Before that,' Skinner continued, 'let's say up to a couple of hours before, did anyone come in here?'

Cope hesitated, considering. 'There was a lady,' he said. 'About seven: mid-thirties, golden blond dye job. She came into the office and she asked me if I knew where the health club was. I gave her directions and she went on her way.'

After dropping the key on the floor, Skinner said to himself.

'Were you ever out of this room during the afternoon?'

'Just once, I had a call . . . actually it was a phone text . . . from Mrs Clydesdale on floor five. She said she feared that she'd left her door open, and asked me to check it. I went up and had a look, but it was okay; I wasn't gone for more than five minutes.'

And when you got back, if you'd looked in your drawer, you'd have seen that the apartment key was gone.

He took his smartphone from his pocket and opened its browser. When he had found the website he was after he opened its 'About us' section, and scrolled down until he found an image. 'The woman who came in.' He showed the screen to the concierge, who nodded vigorously.

'Yes,' he declared, 'that's her.'

'Thanks, Mr Cope,' Skinner said. 'That's everything.'

'I hope it was helpful.'

'Sensationally so,' he replied.

421

He left the building and walked to his car, which was parked fifty yards away. As soon as he was behind the wheel and had switched on the power, he made a call.

'Detective Chief Inspector Pye,' he said, coldly, as soon as it was answered.

'Chief,' Pye exclaimed, 'I'm sorry. I can plead pressure, stress, whatever, but it was unforgiveable.'

'I agree, so you're fucking lucky I forgive you. But listen to this and remember it. Warrant card or not, I will always be police. Now, Pike?'

'He's been arrested at the training complex by uniforms and he's being brought through here.'

'No phone calls allowed, I hope.'

'On pain of death or demotion. I've spoken to Paco; he confirms that the boys did use the back entrance on occasion. If they needed a cup of sugar or whatever, they'd call, then nip up to collect it. Usually it was Pike that came. He did most of the cooking.'

'Good, now; you and your familiar are coming on a wee trip with me. No arguments, no discussion, and I choose the music. I'll be with you in ten minutes.'

As he drove away, he made another call.

'Mia McCullough.' She sounded curious; no caller display, he guessed.

'It's me,' he said, '*el padre de Ignacio*. Are you at home?'

'Yes, why?'

'Because there's something I'd like you to handle for me. Don't worry, it's legal and you'll enjoy it, because it involves strong drink. Listen carefully, this is what I need you to do.'

Seventy-Four

'What did we do before we had this facility?' Lottie Mann asked.

'We worked a bloody sight harder,' Dan Provan replied. 'We wore out a lot more shoe leather . . . shoe rubber really; we couldnae afford leather soles on our wages . . . and we got fewer convictions. Wi' CCTV we'd have nailed Bible John; without it we were relyin' on luck and we never had ony on that investigation.'

'The Bible John Inquiry is still live,' the DI pointed out.

'Ah doubt that he is. It was before even my time, but I've always thought stuff was done wrong. The Identikit they released was a likeness for jist about every dark-haired lad in Glasgow, and the bit about him quotin' the bible should have been kept in-house. All it ever did was gie the papers a label they've stuck on him ever since, and no doubt tip off the man himself tae give Jesus a wide berth. But this,' he said, flatly 'this is no Bible John. This is a stupid bastard who's been lucky so far, but that's goin' tae run out,' he smiled, 'just like Jimmy Pike's did. Fancy,' he chided her, 'yer big pal Skinner never tellin' ye he was bein' lifted.'

'He probably didn't know.'

'You believe that if it makes you feel better.'

'I'm ready for you again.'

The detectives turned their attention back to the speaker, the technician who had been assigned to help them search the CCTV footage they were after. The Glasgow operations centre was state of the art, bringing together traffic management and public space coverage in a new open-plan building. They had looked at footage from the west section of Clyde Street, and had isolated half a dozen individuals as they walked towards the casino or away from it.

'I've followed the people on the other tape,' Davie Doyle, the technician, said. 'They all carried straight on, without stopping. But there's one guy; look at this.' He played them a section of the recording that showed a bulky individual ambling purpose-fully through the camera's field of vision, then passing out of sight.

'That's ten thirty,' Doyle told them. 'He never appears on the other camera. In fact he never appears anywhere again, until here.' He ran more footage, showing the same man walking, at a much brisker pace, in the opposite direction. 'I guess he was in the casino,' he suggested.

'We know he wasn't,' Provan countered. He showed a suggestion of a smile and his eyes sparkled. 'So what were ye doing there, Tank Bridges?' he murmured.

'Yes,' Lottie Mann echoed, 'what indeed?'

Seventy-Five

'Is this penance?' Haddock asked, in a text sent from the back seat of Skinner's car to Pye, in front.

The former chief constable had not spoken a word from the moment he picked them up from the St Leonard's police office, driving silently across the River Forth, then up the motorway towards Perth and beyond. Conversation between the two had been made impossible by a music selection that the Mercedes display showed to be a mix of the Stereophonics, Beth Hart and Joe Bonamassa, played at volume.

'Looks like it,' the reply read a minute later. 'I think I've burned my bridges with the big man.'

'That's you fucked then,' Haddock responded, as they turned into a driveway that led a short way to a gated entrance, with a sign that read 'Black Shield Lodge'. It was manned by a security guard, who peered into the car, then, recognising the driver, threw them a quick salute, and raised the barrier.

Skinner nodded an acknowledgement, then drove on, past a modern villa and round a curving road. As a cottage came into view, he killed the music with a touch of a button on the steering wheel, and drew to a halt outside, gravel crunching beneath the wheels.

'Is this your country club, Chief?' Haddock asked him, cheerfully.

'This is the end of the road,' he replied. 'Now come with me, lads. You're going to need your notebooks, by the way.'

'What would you have done differently?' Pye asked, a little rebelliously, as he unfastened his seat belt.

'I'd like to say that I'd have searched that other fucking apartment on day one,' Skinner retorted, 'rather than swallow the incredibly fortuitous scenario that'd been set out for me.' He grinned. 'I'd like to say that,' he repeated 'but my ego's even bigger than yours, so maybe I'd have been so pleased with myself that I wouldn't have . . . not until day two, or maybe even day three. Come on.'

The front door of the cottage opened as they reached it, framing Mia McCullough. 'Christ,' she exclaimed, 'I'm glad you've arrived, I've been pouring champagne for an hour.'

'They're both here?'

'Yes, and Chaz is a few sheets to the wind. Letitia's in the hotel crèche as you suggested, although she can't stay there for much longer. Should I go and get her?'

'Yes, please; keep her at your place till you hear from me.'

'How long will that be?'

'The blue flashing lights on the driveway will give you a clue.' He smiled. 'You'd better warn your husband, in case he thinks they're for him. Thanks, kid,' he added, 'you've done good.'

'I may remind you of that one day. Good luck.'

'Won't need it,' he told her, cheerfully.

He led his companions inside and through to the living room, where two people sat. Chaz Baker looked up at him in bemused surprise as he entered, his expression changing as he saw the two detectives. Lita Baker sat opposite him, clear eyed and curious.

'Bob,' Baker exclaimed, rising half out of his seat, less than steadily, then thinking better of it and collapsing back down. 'What a surprise! It's good to see you. And 's good of you boys too, to come and join the celebrations, all things considered.'

'They're not here to celebrate, Chaz,' the newcomer replied. 'They've come to arrest your wife for murdering your half-sister, and attempting to pervert the course of justice, by trying to stitch you up for it.'

Lita Baker jumped to her feet. 'You're mad,' she squealed, and turned to her husband. 'Chaz! Tell them to get out of here.'

'Nobody's going anywhere, Dr Baker,' Skinner said, 'least of all you,' as she headed for the door, only to see Haddock step across to block it. 'Now sit back down please, while I tell this poor sucker what happened. There are a couple of blanks you can fill in if you want, but otherwise, my best advice is that you stay silent until you have a lawyer beside you.'

Chaz Baker blinked three times, then squeezed his eyes shut, hard, as if he was trying to regain a semblance of sobriety. 'What the hell are you talking about?' he mumbled. 'Alex said Rogozin killed Annie. Alex knows . . .'

'That's what we all thought at first, that he and he alone was the murderer, to stop her blowing the whistle on his sexual predation and his blackmail. But that didn't fit, couldn't fit, because of one question that couldn't be answered.'

He broke off, gazing at Lita Baker. 'Chaz received a text, supposedly from Annette, summoning him to King Robert Village. It was sent by her killer, after she had been beaten and abducted from the penthouse, taken down the fire stair to the apartment below, and killed, brutally, with Chaz's belt, the first piece of incriminating evidence. The second was the training top, smeared with blood that was to be dumped in the Merrytown laundry basket.'

He stopped and pointed a finger at the befuddled manager. 'Problem,' he said. 'Yes, at that time of day he was bound to have come straight from the training ground, but . . . and here's the crucial question.'

He glanced across at Pye and Haddock. 'How could Rogozin, a lone murderer, have known with certainty that Chaz would be caught on CCTV wearing an identical training top to the one that was smeared with Annette's blood and put in the bin? And that had to be verified,' he emphasised, 'or the whole frame-up would be blown. But Rogozin, if it had been him sitting in the apartment below with Annie's body, he couldn't have left the apartment, so he couldn't have seen him.'

The detective sergeant nodded, signalling acknowledgement. 'So there had to be two people involved,' he murmured.

'Exactly, Sauce; and Jimmy Pike obliged straightaway by identifying himself as one of them, through his carelessness in leaving a print when he wedged the penthouse fire door open, after nipping up to borrow a cup of sugar, or whatever he used as a pretext.'

'Jimmy Pike?' Chaz Baker screeched from his chair. 'Jimmy fucking Pike?'

'That's the boy,' Skinner confirmed. 'As for the other . . . Who? There could only be one person. Why? Sorry, chum, but take those three words you've just used "Jimmy fucking Pike" and rearrange them.'

He took a few steps across the room and eased himself into a spare white leather chair, facing the couple. Lita's eyes blazed back at him, endorsing his belief in his solution.

'Even people who don't like me . . . and there are many of

them, including me sometimes . . . will admit that I'm a pretty good detective.' He nodded towards the Menu. 'So are those guys, even if they haven't caught up with me yet.

'My old mentor, Alf Stein, used to say that the best detectives can look at a jigsaw, with its bits all scattered and spread out, but without the image on the box that shows them what it's supposed to look like, and yet can put the whole picture together in their minds.'

He laughed. 'I've never cracked that myself, but Alf could do it, sometimes even though some of the key pieces were missing. I'm not in his class, so I try to do it the other way around: I look for isolated bits of jigsaw, facts, or pieces of physical evidence, and I work from there. When I do, I'm old fashioned. I begin with motive.'

He reached out and took a champagne bottle from a bucket, picked up a discarded flute, then thought better of it and replaced them both. 'Better not; driving.'

He looked up at the detective duo. 'I know that motive isn't the be all and end all any more, but most times I really do need one, and especially in a case like this, a lurid domestic, which is exactly what it is.'

'Domestic?' Pye frowned, still sceptical.

'Obviously,' Skinner replied, firmly. 'I was wrong about Rogozin, initially, because I overlooked an important piece of the jigsaw, but I'm right about Jimmy Pike. We're agreed on that, yes?'

'Yes,' the DCI conceded.

'Good. So, what possible motive could he have for killing Annette, or for framing his boss? He's got no beef against her, and Chaz gives him a starting slot in the team, week in, week out. Answer, none. Therefore . . .' He looked at Haddock, eyebrows raised.

The sergeant read the question correctly and replied. 'Therefore the motive . . . if there is one; okay, Chief, there must be . . . has to lie with his partner in crime.'

'Precisely. Nice turn of phrase, Sauce, for so does Pike. So, who else might have one? And what links the two victims of this crime? Oh yes, Chaz was a victim, just as much as Annie; the plan was for him to lose his life too, in a different way.

'The link? Annie and Chaz were having a relationship of sorts, meeting regularly, and privately. They thought it was secret. That's a laugh: nine times out of ten when a guy thinks he has a secret from his wife, he's wrong; she's twigged.'

He looked at Lita Baker, sharply. 'And you twigged, Lita, didn't you?' He held her gaze, unblinking, until she looked away.

'Exactly,' he murmured. 'You found out about it: how doesn't matter. A piece of carelessness on Chaz's part, probably, but when you did, you seized on an obvious conclusion, one that was tragically wide of the mark. You assumed that they were lovers. You're a proud and vengeful woman, Dr Baker; you weren't having that. Were you?' He smiled. 'Come on, give me something.'

'Okay,' she hissed. 'No comment, or fuck off; you choose.'

Her husband's face crumpled; he sagged even deeper into his chair.

'I'll stick with "no comment" for now, thanks,' Skinner replied. 'As well as being proud and vengeful, you're also a hypocrite, because you had a secret too. His name was Jimmy Pike.'

He grinned again. 'Going back to domestic intrigue, I've observed over a long career that when a woman thinks she has a secret from her husband, nine out of ten times she's right; he hasn't a clue, maybe because his ego wouldn't allow it.

'Look at me,' he chuckled 'I'm a classic case. My ex-wife was shagging an actor, and the tabloids knew about it before I did; as it transpired, they told me about it. You and Pike? Poor old Chaz had no idea about it, until this very moment. I imagine it started in France; I might even make a wild guess that the idea of bringing Jimmy to Merrytown was planted in Chaz's head by you.'

'You have no proof,' she protested. 'No proof of any of this,' but the way that Baker's eyes turned to his wife, narrowing as they did, told Skinner that his wild guess had been on the mark.

'Sorry, Doctor,' he countered. 'There's proof of all of it; I checked it personally. The manager of the Garrick Casino in Glasgow, and the head waiter in its restaurant, have both identified you as a visitor with Jimmy Pike on at least two occasions. The waiter, Mario, described you as intimate with each other. On each occasion, the doorman remembers Pike asking him to order a taxi to take you both to the Crowne Plaza Hotel.

'And the concierge in King Robert Village, he places you in his office, Lita, just after the time of the murder, dropping off, literally, the apartment key that you had borrowed without him realising it earlier in the day. You needed access, didn't you, so you could jam the fire door open, like I thought Rogozin had done.

'That would have been enough,' he said, 'but you signed off on it earlier on today. Jimmy Pike knew that the charges against Chaz were being dropped before that news was made public, and there was only one person who could have told him, as your phone records will prove. You're cooked, madam, done to a turn.'

'There's even more than that,' Pye said, from across the room, as he caught up with the plot. 'Our people found DNA samples in a bedroom in the apartment, ample evidence of sexual activity. We've been wondering about that, but not any more. Normally it would have been serviced after use, but nobody knew you'd been there.'

'Nice plan,' Skinner continued, with a sigh. 'You and Jimmy, who has no objection to a bit of violence, kill your husband's lover and set him on the road to a thirty-year tariff life sentence.

'Only you actually murdered his sister, overreached yourselves, and underestimated the people who investigated your crime, and took on Chaz's defence. Sammy,' he called out, 'it's time to get the polis.'

Seventy-Six

'Do you know what that man said to me?' Tank Bridges asked the detectives as he faced them across the table in the interview room. 'I spoke to him straight after the Motherwell game, and I told him that since Chaz wasn't likely to come back, the squad was going to need more than a bloke to take the training sessions, it was going to need someone with manager authority. I said that I got all my coaching badges, that I was proper qualified, so there was no need to look outside the club.'

His nostrils flared. 'He looked at me like I was havin' a laugh, then he said that he would look for a proper manager, not someone who came across like an ape on telly. Soon as he'd found him, he said, I was out.'

'That's football, isn't it?' Dan Provan suggested.

'He called me an ape, mate,' Bridges repeated. 'He said I was a bleedin' monkey. That's not football, that's an insult. I've been sacked before, four times, but it's always been done with respect, and given me some dignity to take with me. That's all people like me ask for.'

He drank some water from the glass in front of him, then glanced at Alex Skinner, who was seated on his right, having been summoned from Edinburgh. She nodded, then murmured, 'Go on.'

'I'd have banjoed him there and then,' Bridges continued, 'but the boardroom was full. Mr McCullough was there and I didn't want to embarrass him, so when he turned his back on me I just stood there and took it. It never went away though; what he said stayed with me all night and through the next day, until I decided that it had to be put right.

'It was a no-brainer where he'd be on a Sunday night; I'm a member of the Garrick and I'd seen him there, so that's where I headed. But I didn't go in; I knew some of the lads would be there and didn't want to cause a ruck in front of them, so I waited outside. Must have waited for a couple of hours; I was ready to give up when he walked out.'

'And you confronted him?' Mann asked.

'Not quite like that; I was waiting on the path down to the river, and I called to him. "Dimitri, come down here, we've got something to sort out." And he did. We went right down on to the walkway, and I began to wonder if I'd done the right thing, for he was in a mood like I'd never seen on him before. The moon was bright, shining on his face; it made him look full of hell.'

'Did you speak to him?'

'Yeah,' Bridges replied. 'I told him he owed me an apology for what he'd said in the boardroom, I said that as far as I was concerned he could stick his football club up his arse, but he was going to apologise.'

'How did he react?'

'He came for me, like a nutter, straight for my throat. I grabbed him, and I swung him round and shoved him away, hard. His foot slipped and he smashed the back of his head on this concrete post that's part of the river fence. He made this noise and he went down.'

'Did he move at all?' Provan murmured.

'Nah, not a twitch; that was it. I didn't know he was dead, not right away, but when I shook him I realised from the way he just flopped about that he was, for certain. After that, I didn't think; I just lifted him up and heaved him over the barrier, into the river, splash.' He sighed. 'And that,' he said, 'is the whole story.'

Mann looked at him. 'That was a statement,' she said, 'that you make of your own free will, without any promises or inducements?'

'Acknowledged,' his lawyer replied. 'Now, Detective Inspector, can we cut to the chase? Mr Bridges will plead guilty to a charge of culpable homicide, if the Crown will not contest the mitigating circumstances. Are you up for that?'

The DI glanced at her colleague. 'Dan, this is yours more than mine. What do you say?'

'I say yes,' Provan decreed, 'because I'm tired, I want this done with and you're due me a cheap dinner.'

Seventy-Seven

'It's locked up?' Sarah asked.

'They both are,' Bob replied. 'Jimmy Pike is saying it was all her idea, and she's saying nothing, on the advice of Frances Birtles, her lawyer.'

'What are Sammy and Sauce saying?'

'Nothing to me. DCI Pye insisted that they would both go back to Edinburgh in the car with Lita Baker. Maggie called me, though, to thank me for my help in closing the investigation, although she did mutter something about me exceeding my remit as Alex's investigator.'

'You have to admit,' she said, 'that was a bit of a stunt you pulled, driving them all the way up to Perthshire without telling them why.'

He shrugged, and sank some Corona. 'They're detectives; they probably figured it out. Sauce would have for sure.'

'You rate him above Sammy?'

'Sammy rates him above Sammy, which is part of his problem. Maggie should split them up, let Sauce spread his wings. I've told her as much.'

She squeezed his arm. 'So Pye shouted at you,' she chuckled. 'Don't take it to heart. You did say he apologised.'

'So what?' Bob grumbled. 'If he'd listened to me it would all have been sorted even quicker.'

'When did you begin to suspect her?'

'The first niggle was when Cameron McCullough told me that he didn't just mention Alex to Lita when she asked him to recommend a lawyer for Chaz. When I pressed him on it, he said that he gave her three names, Frances Birtles, Susannah Himes, known as the Barracuda, and Alex, who was really only there as a courtesy. He listed them one to three, in order of preference. Lita chose the third on the list, the least experienced, the one who'd only just joined the criminal bar.

'She didn't do that to give her husband the best chance of an acquittal; she chose Alex because she hoped it would secure his conviction. She's now retained Frankie Bristles for her own defence, which sort of proves my point.'

'And the second?'

'It wasn't really a niggle; I thought there was something not quite right about her, that's all. As soon as Pike came into play, it was all so fucking obvious.'

'And Rogozin?'

'Oh, I was wrong about him, I admit it; until I saw the flaw with the planted training top.'

'I didn't mean that,' Sarah said. 'Did you have an idea who killed him?'

'No, not a clue,' he admitted, 'nor did I care. If it had turned out to be Grandpa McCullough I wouldn't have been surprised, but it wasn't. It's worked out nicely for him, though. He'll take over as chairman, Mia will join the board and together they'll vote through the sale of the training complex.'

'What?'

He grinned. 'Angela Renwick told me last Saturday; South

Lanarkshire Council have granted outline planning consent to a building company for three hundred houses on the site; a hundred-million-pound project. The *Saltire* will run the story this weekend. The builder's called Garrick Construction, plc, and it's wholly owned by Cameron McCullough.'

'You mean he's going to sell the land to his own company?'

'Yes, for three million. He's also going to sell Paco Fonter to a Chinese club that's willing to pay twelve million for him. I imagine that Merrytown will pay a bloody big dividend to its only shareholder this year.'

Her mouth gaped open. 'Does that mean this football thing has been a business deal all along for Grandpa?'

'Yes, and Rogozin was a front all along, although I doubt he realised it.'

'Bloody hellfire,' she whispered as she snuggled against him on the sofa.

'Indeed.'

'And you,' she continued quietly, 'what do you do next? Will you go back, like they want?'

'Possibly,' he conceded, 'but as I said to Alex, in my own time and on my own terms, when I can figure out what they are, although that may depend on something else. Meantime, I have other priorities. First and foremost, I would like you and me to remarry before our new child arrives, because she should be on the same footing as the others . . . and for one other reason, because I love you with all my heart. What say?'

She drew his face down to hers and kissed him. 'I say yes,' she murmured, 'on both counts.'

'Thank you, my darling. Sooner rather than later, then.'

She nodded. 'Your other priorities, what are they?'

'One, to get Ignacio settled in at university; two, to get the garage construction project under way.' He paused, and a mischievous smile crossed his face.

'Three?' she asked.

'This may blow your mind,' he replied. 'I had a call this morning from my former wife, the devious Aileen. Her Majesty's Labour Opposition, of which she is now a high-ranking member, is looking to beef up its representation in the House of Lords, and they're sort of talking about sort of offering me a peerage. She wants me to go down to meet her boss to talk about it.'

Sarah sat bolt upright. 'Are you going to sort of accept?' she exclaimed.

'Me? Baron Skinner of Gullane? I doubt that very much,' he said, 'but I've never been in that building, so I thought I might go down and check it out, just for fun.'

'Then you do that,' she told him, 'but make damn sure you come back.'

Seventy-Eight

'What did the chief say?' Haddock asked as his senior officer replaced the phone.

'She said well done,' Pye replied, 'a brilliant investigation all the way through. She praised in particular our initiative in bombing up to Perthshire to confront Lita Baker before she could find out that Pike had been lifted and have a chance to disappear. Once we've taken her formal statement, she wants to see a transcript.'

'Hold on, are you saying she doesn't know that we were hauled up there by the headmaster like a couple of kids caught smoking in the bike sheds?'

'She doesn't appear to have the faintest idea.'

'You didn't enlighten her?'

'If I had,' the DCI said, 'I'm pretty sure that big Bob would be terminally pissed off with me.'

'Christ!' Haddock laughed. He shook his head. 'Where did we start off in this thing? "In all the gin joints . . ." that was it. All I can follow that with is, "Please don't play it again, Sam."'

'He never said that.'

'What?'

'In *Casablanca*: Bogart never said that.'

Read on for an exclusive extract from

STATE SECRETS

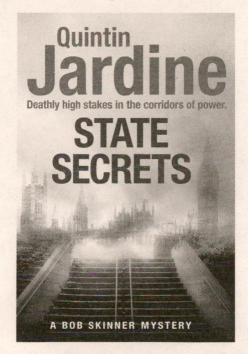

Quintin Jardine's next captivating
Bob Skinner mystery

Available on 19.10.17

www.headline.co.uk

One

Did I really want to be ennobled? Did I see myself as Baron Skinner of Gullane?

No I didn't, when the question had been put. Being Chief Constable Skinner gave me a higher profile than I liked, and I've been happy to be shot of that title. However, I'd been invited to discuss the possibility, in good faith as far as I knew, so it would have been churlish of me to reject it out of hand . . . even though the invitation had come to me via my ex-wife.

And also, as I said to Sarah, the potential Lady Skinner, while I had been a visitor to the Westminster village several times in the later years of my police career, I had never been in their lordships' House; the chance to cross that off my bucket list was too good to pass up.

Not so long ago, I wouldn't have had time to fit it in, not when I was a serving officer, head of Scotland's largest force before it was replaced by one even larger, the controversial and almost universally unloved Scottish Police Service.

My critics, and there were plenty of them, rounded on me when I decided not to pursue my application for the position of chief constable, but it isn't a decision I've ever regretted. The truth of the matter was, I was well past my 'best before' date as a cop when I quit; most of my close colleagues knew that, but none of them ever told me. I like to believe they were too loyal, rather than too fearful, to suggest it.

Any post-career visions or fears I might have entertained of becoming a house parent and scratch golfer were soon blown away, by a couple of private commissions from friends and acquaintances with problems that needed sorting, and another from my older daughter Alex, who is beginning to make a name for herself as a criminal defence lawyer.

They helped me keep my hand in, so to speak, and led me into a couple of situations that got my investigative juices flowing again. One day, chewing the fat with some pals in the golf club, I said I might set up a website and call it 'Skinner Solutions'; they knew I was joking, but a journalist in the bar overheard me and took me seriously. He ran the story; I might have had the devil's own job knocking it down, had I not been well placed to do so.

As a bonus, the first of my private investigations led to me being appointed a part-time executive director of an international media group called, appropriately if unimaginatively, InterMedia. That gives me an office in central Edinburgh, and pays me an almost embarrassing salary, for a theoretical one day's work per week, although in practice I enjoy it so much that I give it much more than that.

Most days you'll find me there, on the executive floor of the building that houses the *Saltire*, the group's Scottish flagship, the only title in the land that maintains its circulation in print form in the face of an all-out assault by digital media.

Not that morning, though, not that fateful morning, as I passed patiently through the detailed but very necessary security process that protects the centre of the British state from the mad, the bad, the fools and the fanatics. It isn't perfect, though; no system ever will be. For example, it didn't find the blue plastic Victorinox SwissCard that I had forgotten was tucked away in a pocket of my Filofax.

There isn't much to it, only a rectangle not much bigger than a credit card, but there are a couple of things in it that should not have evaded the check. I only remembered about it as I was walking into the Central Lobby, but since I had no intention of killing anyone, it didn't matter.

Being Monday, the parliamentary gathering place was less busy than it had been on my previous visits, for security meetings or, once, to appear before a powerless but self-important select committee of grandstanding backbench MPs. There was still some action, though. It was autumn, the party conference season was over, parliament was back from its extended holidays, and political warfare had been resumed.

A Scots voice floated through the rest and caught my ear. I turned towards it, thinking for a moment that it was my one-woman welcoming committee, but saw instead the BBC's political editor recording a piece to camera for the midday news.

In the event, Aileen de Marco was late, ten minutes late. I didn't mind, for I spent the time chatting with a couple of the new breed of Scottish members who recognised me and introduced themselves. Both of them knew all about me, or thought they did. One was my constituency MP, a sharp guy; the other was blunt, and just plain curious. It took him only a couple of minutes to ask me flat out what I was doing there, since I wasn't a cop any longer.

I told him I was down on a lobbying mission. It wasn't a lie; I didn't say who was being lobbied, that's all.

He was trying to frame a supplementary question when

Aileen arrived, calling out her apologies for the delay. 'Sorry, Bob, I was collared by the Chief Whip.'

She was the Opposition as far as my new acquaintances were concerned, more so than the sitting government. The nosy guy turned on his heel and walked away. His companion was rather more polite. 'Ms de Marco,' he murmured, raising an eyebrow.

She smiled at him; there was no malice in it, only amusement. 'It's okay, George,' she said. 'My former husband and I do still speak on occasion.' Then she frowned, switching to business mode. 'How does your leader intend to react to the defence statement this afternoon?' she asked.

'He hasn't told me. It'll depend on what's in it, I suppose. Have you been briefed?'

'No.' Her frown deepened. 'That's becoming typical of the ruling cabal. They see us as severely wounded and hope to finish us off next time around, so the old courtesies are in abeyance. Have you been given any clue?'

'No, but we wouldn't be,' my constituency member replied. 'We're still the hooligans in the eyes of the PM and her hatchet man, the Home Secretary. They think we'd leak it if we were briefed in advance.' He winked. 'We bloody would too.'

'Nobody's being briefed on this one,' Aileen complained, 'not even the political editors. I'm not sure what that means. I called Mickey Satchell . . . the Prime Minister's pumped-up, self-important little PPS,' she added, for my benefit, I assumed, 'and not even she knows . . . or so she assured me.'

'I tried her too,' her colleague said. 'Same result. Yes,' he chuckled, 'Mickey is up herself, isn't she. Boots on the ground in the Middle East was the speculation I heard on Radio Four this morning.'

Aileen shook her head. 'No. I have a friend on the Army General Staff. They'd know if that was happening and they don't.'

'In that case we'll have killed another terrorist with a drone missile. That's my best guess.' He glanced up at me. 'What do you think, Bob?'

'More likely they've killed civilians by mistake,' I suggested, 'but that would probably have been leaked by the victim's side by now. Seems to me it's either something very big or something very small. If you like, I could call the *Saltire* news desk and find out what they're speculating . . . if anything.'

My new friend pointed across the Central Lobby. 'I'll save you a phone call,' he said. 'I'll just walk across and ask its political editor; whatever their reply is, it'd be coming from him.'

'Collared by the Chief Whip, eh?' I murmured as he left us. 'Parliamentary language never ceases to amuse me.'

'You could be a whip yourself if you come on board in the other place,' she countered.

'If,' I repeated. 'I still don't get this, Aileen; this invitation out of the blue. You know I didn't vote for your lot, don't you?'

'I've always assumed you didn't,' she admitted. 'But you fell out with the SNP as well over the national police force. So I figured that you were at best neutral.'

'And at worst, Tory?' I countered, smiling.

'I never thought that for a second. Have that lot offered you a peerage?' she asked.

'I was offered a knighthood,' I replied, 'which I turned down, twice; a peerage, no.'

'The K is routine for your police rank, regardless of politics, and you know it. If you were a Tory you'd have been offered a seat in the Lords by now.'

I had to challenge her assumption, right or wrong. 'Hold on

a minute; you know very well that through all my police career I was politically neutral. A senior cop has to be.'

'Of course I know that, but we were married, Bob. We got drunk together and you let your real self out, more than once.' She tapped her chest. 'In there you're left of centre. Not very far left, I'll admit, but it's there.'

'Privately, yes,' I conceded, 'but I always steered clear of public politics . . .' I stopped myself, just in time, from adding, '. . . until I married you.' That would have taken the encounter in a direction that I wanted to avoid.

Aileen sensed it and nodded. 'But you voted. You said more than once that it's your duty as a citizen.'

'Yes I voted,' I agreed, 'until last time, the last Scottish parliament elections. Then, I gave myself a day off, because none of the parties were saying anything that I wanted to hear.'

'But you're prepared to hear what we've got to say to you today?'

'Out of politeness, yes, and a bit of curiosity too. Who am I meeting? You and who else?'

'Not me,' she said, quickly. 'Not for the business discussion. I'm just the honey trap they used to get you down here. You'll be met in the other place by Baroness Mercer, our leader in the Lords, and by Lord Pilmar, the senior Scottish peer. Do you know either of them?'

'I've heard of her, but that's all. Paddy Pilmar I know quite well from his days as an MP in Edinburgh. What's the lady like?'

'Academic,' Aileen replied, 'with a journalistic background. She was economics editor on one of the broadsheets . . . I can never remember which . . . then had a chair at a red-brick university in the north-west. Intellectually she's top drawer; she's capable on her feet in the chamber, but she's remote from her troops. Her main job is to keep the party on message in the Lords and to keep Merlin's feet on the ground in the shadow Cabinet.'

'That'll be a task,' I observed. Merlin Brady, the leader of the Labour Party, known inevitably as The Magician by the media, had emerged from the drama that had followed his predecessor's incapacitation by a malignant stomach tumour, having been persuaded to stand as a compromise candidate, acceptable to both warring wings of his party. He had been regarded until then as a career back-bench loyalist devoid of personal ambition, but he was rumoured to be settling into the job.

'Whose idea was it to approach me?' I asked her, bluntly.

'It was a joint suggestion really,' Aileen admitted. 'There was a sense coming out of the Lords that we're not being forceful enough. The government pretty much ignore us. Lord Pilmar and I were tasked by Merlin's office with finding a strong man to go in there and exercise a bit of discipline, without undermining Georgia Mercer.

'We kicked some names around, but couldn't find anyone who suited the job description. Paddy suggested Sir Andrew Martin, now that he's no longer head of the Scottish Police Service, but with his tongue in his cheek. We laughed at that, then went quiet, both of us thinking the same thought, until he spoke it.

'I said you'd never do it, but Paddy was fired up by the idea. He persuaded me that there would be no harm in asking, so we took your name back to the leader's office.

'Merlin didn't know anything about you, but when I told him you'd had a big fallout with Clive Graham, that made him sit up. Anyone who's an enemy of the Scottish First Minister is a friend of his.'

'Clive and I aren't enemies,' I protested. 'I like the man, on a personal level. He's okay as a politician too, but when it came to putting pennies before public protection, there we went our separate ways.'

She smiled. Aileen has a very attractive smile when she isn't thinking about running whatever country she happens to be in at the time. Unfortunately, that doesn't happen very often. 'I know that,' she chuckled, 'but I wasn't going to tell Merlin.'

'Do I get to meet him?'

'Depends on how you get on next door,' she replied, then glanced at her wrist. I noticed that her watch was one I'd given her as an anniversary present . . . not that we had many of those. I wondered if she wore it often or had dug it out for the occasion. 'Speaking of which, it's time you were getting along there.'

I stared at her. 'Aren't you coming?'

She shook her head. 'We MPs aren't welcome next door,' she chuckled. 'I'll take you along to meet Lord Pilmar at the Peers' Entrance, then you're on your own.'

We walked out of the great building, past security and past Westminster Hall. I paused and looked at the impressive space, trying to put myself in the midst of the great events that have happened there, and the history that was made, over the centuries. I'm not a romantic by nature, but that place does get to me.

Aileen knows me well enough to understand that; she was smiling as we moved out into the street and turned left, heading for the House of Lords.

'How's Sarah?' she asked, out of the blue . . . or maybe it was the red, given her politics. I searched for anything in her tone beyond a sincere enquiry, but couldn't detect it.

'She's fine, thanks. She's started her maternity leave. How's Joey?'

It was her turn to throw me a sideways look. Joey Morocco is the Scottish film actor with whom Aileen had a relationship before and during our marriage. It became all too public when a paparazzo took a very revealing photograph of her in his house and sold it to the tabloids.

'Joey's fine,' she said, cautiously, 'as far as I know. He and I were never going to be a permanent thing. Why do you ask? Is he still on your hit list?'

I laughed at her question. 'He never was, not really; you can tell him that if you want. If I'd encountered him when it happened, and nobody had been around, I might have clipped him round the ear, but that would have been hypocritical. Joey, you, me: we've all taken a pretty relaxed view of the sanctity of marriage in our time.'

'So why did you and Sarah remarry, after saying you weren't going to?'

'It was the right thing to do for the baby's sake. We're both old fashioned that way. Also, I've changed. I've had a second chance and I'm not going to blow that.' I glanced at her, raising an eyebrow. 'How about you? If not Joey, who? Your friend on the Army General Staff?'

She grinned. 'That would be a she, and I haven't switched sides yet. I'm unattached and not looking around either. I'm number two in the shadow defence team and I hope to be number one after Merlin's next reshuffle. I can't afford any casual relationships.' Then she smiled again, the Aileen smile that I like. 'Besides,' she added, 'Joey passes through London every so often.'

She walked me up to a police box that was guarding an

enclosed forecourt; it was manned by two officers, older cops, the kind whose service had earned them what was probably a nice easy station, most of the time. She spoke to them, quietly, then turned back to me.

'I've told them you're meeting Lord Pilmar,' she said. 'That's the Peers' Entrance over there.' She pointed at a small arched doorway on the other side of the courtyard.

'Not very grand, is it?' I observed.

'We don't have signs over the door in this place. Good luck. I hope it goes well. Please, Bob, give it some serious thought. We're not joking about this.'

'I'll listen,' I promised. I gave her a quick peck on the cheek, then headed for the House of Lords.

Baron Pilmar of Powderhall was indeed waiting for me; he didn't look noble at all, just a cheery wee man with a ruddy complexion. I knew that he was seventy-three years old because I'd done a refresher check on him in preparation for the meeting, but he didn't look it.

'Bob,' he exclaimed, as I came through the double doors, 'good to see you. Come on in and let these lads fit you up with a badge.'

He led me to two more security guards; they were in uniform, but civilians rather than police. There was a security gateway but I couldn't pass through because of my cardiac pacemaker. Instead they gave me a wave down with a hand-held detector, and took my briefcase to put it through an X-ray machine. I told them about the Victorinox card, but they weren't bothered about it.

Once I was official and wearing my badge, Paddy Pilmar returned to take me into his charge. 'Good journey?' he asked, as I hung my overcoat on a vacant peg on one of the racks that filled most of the area. *Search all these for illegal substances,* I thought, *and what would you find?*

'Fine,' I assured him. Rather than risk delay and to avoid the remarkable crowds that can gather in Edinburgh airport departures for early morning flights, I had taken the train down the day before and had booked myself into a hotel. With time on my hands after breakfast I had put yet another tick on my rapidly shrinking bucket list by visiting the Cabinet War Rooms, and making a mental note to take my boys there, on a long-promised visit to London.

'Let's go for a coffee,' my custodian said. 'Georgia's in a committee, but she'll join us as soon as she can get out.'

He led me out of the entrance area and up a wide stone staircase. Halfway up, he paused and pointed at a series of coats of arms that decorated the walls. 'Chiefs of the Defence Staff,' he informed me. 'They all wind up here after they retire and lately they've let them put their heraldic crests on this stair.' He frowned. 'I'm no' really sure why.'

I knew Lord Pilmar pretty well; he had always struck me as one of nature's doubters rather than the full-blooded cynic that a thirty-year police career had made me. He had taken an unusual route to the top. He had been a clerk on the old Edinburgh Corporation, before any of the reforms of local government that led to Scotland's present system, but had switched from servant to master by being elected as councillor for a ward in Leith, combining his public duties with a job as a trade union official, created, I assumed, to give him a salary.

Paddy had made his mark on the council, becoming a committee chairman in his twenties, and was earmarked as a future Labour group leader and political head of the Corporation . . . the Lord Provost having the title and the chain of office, but not the power . . . but he had walked away from that in the mid-seventies to contest and win a Westminster seat.

A popular and active MP, he had spent most of his parliamentary career on the Opposition benches. The highlight had been a brief stint as shadow Secretary of State for Scotland, but when his party's outlook and tone had changed with the creation of New Labour, he had been moved aside and eventually out, with a peerage as a reward.

Our paths had crossed a few times, occasionally at formal social events, the kind where police and politicians had to be seen, but more often professionally, when my work took me into his constituency. We had been useful to each other over the years. I won't say that he was an informant, but he was as firmly on the side of law and order as was I, and there were occasions when he had access to information that my officers and I did not. In other words, people trusted him to keep their names out of it, when they did not trust us.

While he had helped us, he had also been a thorn in my side. If he ever felt that one of his people had been given an undeservedly hard time by the police, I was his 'go to' man when it came to sorting it out. It had led to a couple of confrontations, but mostly I had found it as useful as he had. Paddy had marked my card about quite a few officers who were disasters waiting to happen, letting me correct their attitude or when necessary take them out of the picture altogether, by transfer or, in extreme cases, dismissal.

I hadn't seen him for a couple of years when we met that Monday morning. He hadn't aged at all; if anything he looked younger and his bright little eyes had an added twinkle.

At the top of the stairs we turned into a long corridor. It was busy, but Paddy nodded to everybody we passed and stopped to talk to a couple of them, introducing me as 'a visitor from Scotland'. One had been a member of the 'Gang of Four' back in the eighties; meeting him threw me for a couple of seconds as I had genuinely believed him to be dead.

The little baron must have sensed and understood my confusion. 'I know,' he chuckled quietly. 'This place is like an animated Madame Tussaud's, isn't it?'

Our destination was a large room, a bar, but only coffee and tea were being consumed at that time of day. I hadn't gone there to people-watch, but I recognised several of the faces: a former justice secretary in a rejected government, an ennobled television personality, and a female Conservative Cabinet minister from the nineties. Lord Pilmar greeted each of them with a smile, a word or a nod.

The room in which we sat was opulent. Looking at the wallpaper I remembered the scandal when a lord chancellor was pilloried for the cost of refurbishing his accommodation, and found myself sympathising with him. Opulence was the standard set when the palace was built; faking it with a cheap copy would have been wrong.

'What's your thinking, Bob?' Paddy said, bluntly, after our coffee had been served by a breezy lady who reminded me very much of the queen of the senior officers' dining room in the old Edinburgh police headquarters.

'It starts with a question,' I replied. 'Why me? Have I ever given you any hint that I'm of your political persuasion?'

He shot me a sly grin. 'Apart from setting up house wi' our leader in Scotland, you mean?'

'An alliance which was dissolved,' I countered. 'Come on, answer me.'

'No,' he admitted, 'you haven't. But there have been a few folk joined our party, and others, on the same day they were appointed to this place. We've never discussed politics, you and I, but I know what you are: you're apolitical.'

His forehead twitched, into a small frown. 'You're like me,' he continued. 'First and foremost, we're public servants; my branch of the service called for party membership for me to make progress. As an MP I worked on a short-term contract that was renewed at the pleasure of my masters; they were the party, and ultimately the electors. Your warrant card was your entry to the public service; your progress depended on the quality of the service you gave. Latterly you worked on a fixed-term contract too, that was renewable at the pleasure of your masters, the Police Authority. We're the same animal, you and me.'

'The policeman and politician argument?' I suggested. 'The notion that the two words mean exactly the same thing? Often cited, but not actually true; they have different roots.'

'Never mind that; it's no' what I meant. You're a man who gets things done, and you're a leader; folk like you are needed in this place.'

'Nice of you to say so, Paddy,' I conceded, 'but there must be lots of people like me who are actually members of the Labour Party!'

'Bob, don't be self-deprecating; Christ, there's a big word for a boy from Powderhall . . . by the way, I added that to hint that I actually know what "self-deprecating" means. There are not lots of people like you, period. As for being a Labour Party member, that counts for fuck all now; look at all those Tories that joined for a fiver just so they could vote for Merlin in the leadership election.'

Realising that he might have been overheard, he leaned closer to me. 'I'm going to assume,' he continued, 'that to prepare for this meeting you've read our last manifesto.'

I nodded.

'How much of it do you agree with?'

'Quite a lot, but I could say the same about all the manifestos. But I also read Merlin Brady's policy statement when he ran for leader, and I disagree with practically every line of that.'

'So does eighty per cent of the parliamentary party,' a female voice interjected, 'which is why it won't become official policy.'

I wasn't facing the door, and so I hadn't seen Baroness Mercer arrive. I looked up at her intervention, then I stood. If anything she was even shorter than her colleague, but her perfectly cut, wiry, iron-grey hair gave her an added presence. Paddy did the introductions, and we shook hands.

'We're the Opposition party,' she continued, once we were seated, 'and we're having our backsides kicked in the Commons on a daily basis. This is the place, the Lords, in which we can make a difference and do most to keep a reckless government in check. The problem is, Mr Skinner, as Ms de Marco and Lord Pilmar may have explained, we need to be better organised, and to be honest, better led.'

Self-deprecation seemed to be the order of the day.

Discover the highly acclaimed Bob Skinner series by

Quintin Jardine

Find out more about Edinburgh's toughest cop at
www.quintinjardine.com

Skinner's Rules	Lethal Intent
Skinner's Festival	Dead and Buried
Skinner's Trail	Death's Door
Skinner's Round	Aftershock
Skinner's Ordeal	Fatal Last Words
Skinner's Mission	A Rush of Blood
Skinner's Ghosts	Grievous Angel
Murmuring the Judges	Funeral Note
Gallery Whispers	Pray for the Dying
Thursday Legends	Hour of Darkness
Autographs in the Rain	Last Resort
Head Shot	Private Investigations
Fallen Gods	Game Over
Stay of Execution	State Secrets

HEADLINE